The
English
Girl

Also by Katherine Webb

The English Girl

KATHERINE WEBB

First published in Great Britain in 2016 by Orion Books,
an imprint of The Orion Publishing Group Ltd
Carmelite House, 50 Victoria Embankment
London EC4Y 0DZ

An Hachette UK Company

3 5 7 9 10 8 6 4 2

A CIP catalogue record for this book is
available from the British Library.

ISBN (Hardback) 978 1 4091 4852 4
ISBN (Export Trade Paperback) 978 1 4091 4853 1
ISBN (Ebook) 978 1 4091 4855 5

Typeset at The Spartan Press Ltd,
Lymington, Hants

Printed and bound in Great Britain by Clays Ltd,
St Ives plc

MIX
Paper from
responsible sources
FSC® C104740

www.orionbooks.co.uk

The English Girl

Bedford, England, October 1939

For six days after Uncle Godfrey came to visit, Joan's dad was patchwork. This was a term Joan had come up with herself, because he reminded her of her rag doll at such times – missing some stuffing, and with stitched crosses for eyes. Now Daniel used the term as well, though he was only five and didn't really understand. Joan was seven, and didn't really understand either. Their dad was usually a blur. He was almost always moving, or making noise; singing or proclaiming; juggling apples; tap-dancing on the chipped brown tiles of the kitchen floor. But when he was patchwork he was quiet – all but silent – and moved as though he'd forgotten where he was going. His shoulders slumped, his face went slack; he stopped shaving, and bathing, and wore the same pullover all week. It didn't happen very often, and Joan hated it more than anything. It felt as though the world was ending.

Joan's dad, David, was a small, slight man. He had a long face with clear blue eyes behind wire-framed spectacles, deep creases in his cheeks from his smile, and mousy hair that he combed back with Brylcreem. He smelled of tobacco, shaving soap and menthol for his chest. Godfrey, his older brother, was tall and sharp. He arrived in the biggest car Joan had ever seen, as grey and sleek as wet penguins at the zoo; he wore a dark suit and a hat that he didn't take off, gave their cramped hallway a swift, outraged glance, and smiled at the children in such a way that they were too shy to speak.

'It's your own fault they won't see you, you know that,' Joan overheard Godfrey say to David. She knew she shouldn't eavesdrop, but their house was so small, and the walls so thin, it was hard not to. 'Christ, if they knew I'd come to visit you . . . It's your own fault you're cut off, David.'

'Why do you even come, Godfrey?' David asked, his voice already starting to sound patchwork. Joan had also overheard her mother, another time, telling Mrs Banks from number 12 that David's family were richer than Croesus. She had no idea how rich that might be.

Joan's parents weren't rich – rich people lived in castles, and drove cars like Uncle Godfrey's instead of taking the bus. Joan had only the mildest curiosity about what that might be like. Her dad was the manager of the local cinema, the Rex Theatre, with its musty curtains and red velvet ropes, and regularly took the children to watch films there – sitting on his knee in the projection booth. Afterwards he told them wonderful stories about the places they'd seen – all the different countries and cities and peoples of the world. Joan considered the Rex Theatre a far greater boon than any car or castle might have been. She was the envy of her classmates.

'You can't join up, anyway,' Mum said to her dad, after Godfrey's visit, not looking up from the potatoes she was peeling. The words had clipped edges, and a loaded pause came after them. 'Not with your chest. And your eyesight,' she added. David sat at the kitchen table behind her, cleaning his spectacles with his handkerchief, saying nothing.

Mum's response to Dad being patchwork was to feed him – their meals became as huge and elaborate as the grocer's shelves would allow, and there were gaudy, complicated cakes at teatime – like the strange, saggy one armoured with mandarin slices from a catering-sized tin, that had looked like the fillet of a giant goldfish. But the food had little effect other than to give Dad a pot belly. When Joan and Daniel asked him for a bedtime story, he smiled wanly and shook his head.

'Ask your mother, my loves. Your dad's a bit spent this evening.' But his stories were usually so much better than Mum's. He brought them to life – he had a hundred voices and faces and gestures; he could be an old, old crone, or a wicked thief, or a tiny fairy. Joan wondered if it was the war. War had been declared with Germany just before Godfrey had come to call. Joan knew what a war was, in theory; she had no idea what one looked like or what it meant. She was a bit worried for a few days, because her teacher, Miss Keighley, dissolved into tears as she took the register one morning; but it soon seemed that being at war wasn't going to be very different to normal.

'It'll be all right, Daddy,' she told him, meaning the war, but his smile faded and he didn't reply, and Joan was more confused than ever.

On the sixth day, she knew what she had to do. *The One Thousand and One Nights.* It was her talisman, her secret weapon, because it was her dad's favourite, and hers too. She had the book in her hands when she went to ask him for a story, determined not to take no for an answer. She climbed into his lap so he couldn't ignore her. When he looked down, he seemed to be looking at her from far away; she pressed the book into his hands, tense with the import of the moment. Daniel was at her heels with his blanket clamped under one arm and his thumb in his mouth.

'Please will you read us one? Please?' She stared into her dad's face, at the stubble on his cheeks and the shadows around his eyes. '*Please?*' she said again. David took a deep breath, then reached down and lifted Daniel up beside Joan.

'All right then, urchins,' he said quietly. Joan felt a little dizzy with relief.

Daniel curled up under David's arm, already glassy-eyed

with sleep, listening more to his father's voice than to the story, but Joan hung on every word. It didn't really matter which story he chose, but he chose 'Ali Baba' and, as he began to read, Joan asked him where the places were and what they were like, even though she knew the answers, because with every description he gave, her father got a little better.

'Oh, but don't you know, Joanie? Arabia is overflowing with magic! How else could anyone live in such a desert? Arabia is an ocean of sand, the biggest in the whole world. It stretches for hundreds and hundreds of miles in every direction – can you even imagine such a thing? Rolling hills and valleys, all made of golden sand as dry as bone.'

'And there's nothing in it *at all* except sand?' she asked.

'Well, why do you think the men who live there call it the "Empty Quarter"?'

'But *how* do the men live there? What do they eat?'

'Magic! Like I told you. Genies live there too, and they help the men. Genies can turn sand into gold, or water, or food, or anything else you want – so you'd better make sure you've got one on your side. But they're tricksters, always striking bargains.'

'What kind of bargains, Dad?'

'Well, when I was there I met a genie called Dervish, and . . .'

The more David read and the more Joan asked, the less patchwork he became. Happiness flooded her. She knew that by morning he wouldn't smell of unwashed jumpers or stewed tea any more, he'd smell of shaving soap and menthol again. He'd be himself again – a moving blur, not quiet and lost. Joan knew, with complete conviction, that her dad was a magical man; that *The One Thousand and One Nights* was a magical book, and that Arabia was a magical place. She knew that one day her dad would take her there.

Muscat, November 1958

'Ready?' Rory reached up and straightened Joan's hat, needlessly. 'You look very pretty, very smart,' he said. Preoccupied, Joan forgot to thank him. She took a deep breath and nodded. The air was hot and dry; the taste of the sea on it was unexpected, and oddly not at all refreshing. She was uncomfortable in the long sleeves of her shirt and the trousers she had to wear beneath her skirt, and was trying not to fidget.

'I'm as ready as I'll ever be, I should think. Do go, won't you – she said to come by myself and I don't want her to see that you walked me here.'

'Of course I had to walk you; we're not in Bedford any more. And you're welcome, by the way.'

'Sorry, Rory. Thank you. I'm just . . .' The hand she laid on his arm was slightly shaky. She shrugged one shoulder.

'I know. I know what this means to you. I just hope it's not . . . Well, never mind. I hope it lives up to all your expectations. I hope *she* does.' They spoke in hushed tones because the rest of the little street was empty, and the shadows between the buildings watched like censorious librarians.

The sun shining behind Rory rendered him in partial silhouette; a dark, indistinct version of himself. He had a round face – a teddy-bear face, Joan had always thought of it – with soft cheeks, brown eyes, a slightly pouting mouth and curly dark hair very similar to her own. But the heat and several sleepless nights had given him pouches under his eyes, and a waxy look. He looked hardly like himself at all. Bothered, Joan squinted up at an ancient watchtower on the rocks above them, stout against the dazzling blue. They were standing outside a modest mud-brick house in Harat al-Henna, the district outside of the wall of Muscat, near the main gate. At sunset, an antique canon would fire from one of the ancient forts by the sea, and the gates would close for the night, shutting the district out. After that, nobody could get back into the city without an official permit.

'Of course she'll live up to my expectations,' Joan said, with a smile.

'Yes, but sometimes meeting our heroes can be . . . disappointing. When they turn out to be only human after all, I mean.'

'Nonsense; not somebody this remarkable. Anyway, I've read everything she's ever written; I feel I know her already.'

'Well then. Have you a match for your lamp to come back again?'

'I've everything I need, Rory, really.' She was suddenly impatient for him to leave. She wanted the moment all to herself, and the time and space to absorb it. And she didn't want a witness to her apprehension – it always seemed to make the nerves worse.

'All right. Good luck. Don't get locked out, will you?' He leaned in to kiss her cheek but Joan moved away.

'Tut-tut, Rory – not in front of the Arabs, remember?' she said.

Joan waited until the sound of his footsteps had faded away completely, then she took a breath and turned to the unremarkable door beside her. It was made of ancient acacia wood, like all the others; parched and beaten by the Arabian sun to the texture and hardness of stone. The mud-brick walls had been painted white at some point, but were now patterned with a network of fissures like the veins of a leaf, through which the crumbling render showed. The house was only two storeys high, square and flat-roofed, with its shutters closed against the eastern sky. It nestled back against the feet of the mountains – there could be no back door. Those rusty-brown mountains reared up all around, like jagged hands, cradling the city with incongruous care. Everywhere was stone and rock and hard sun, hard shadows, and no softness anywhere. A minute passed, and Joan berated herself for cowardice – for standing there making observations, delaying a moment she had so longed for. With her heart in her throat, she knocked at the door.

It was opened almost at once by a tall black man, dressed Omani-style in a grey dish-dash – the loose, long tunic men wore – belted, and with the curved dagger, a khanjar, worn at his middle. There were hollows in his cheeks; the whites of his eyes were stained brown, like milky coffee; the irises were entirely black. His beard was white, as were the few tufts of hair visible beneath a knotted turban. Joan couldn't guess his age; his face was ancient but his back was straight, shoulders unbowed; he gazed down at Joan with the silent solemnity of a golem, and struck her dumb. The man's hands hung loosely at his sides and Joan noticed the great size of them – long fingers like spiders' legs. After a moment he spoke.

'You are Joan Seabrook.' His voice was reedy.

'Yes,' said Joan. She blushed, embarrassed by herself. 'I'm Joan Seabrook,' she reiterated pointlessly. 'Is this Maude Vickery's house? I think I'm expected.'

'You are expected, or I would not have opened the door to you,' said the old man. He smiled slightly, twisting his wrinkled lips. His English was almost without accent, each word formed with deliberate care, as perfect as worked stone. 'Go up the stairs. The lady is waiting.' He stood back to admit her, and Joan stepped past.

Inside, the house smelled like a stable. Before she could

stop herself, Joan had put up a hand to cover her nose. It was stifling; no worse than the stables at home but so unexpected. The door closed behind her and she could hardly see in the sudden darkness; behind her she thought she heard the dry wheeze of a chuckle from the old man. She glanced at him but his face was in shadow; he neither moved nor spoke again, but she caught the gleam of his watchful eyes. Flustered, clumsy as a child, Joan carried on across the hallway to the foot of the stone staircase, and went up.

The stairs turned halfway up; light spilled through an open window to reveal a crust of dung pellets like those of a sheep or a goat, and scatterings of hay. Joan frowned in confusion. At the top of the stairs were just two rooms, one to either side of a small landing. Here she paused, but a moment later a voice called from her right.

'Don't dither there, whoever you are. I'm in here. You'll have to forgive me for not getting up, but I can't, you see.' It was a hard voice with a querulous edge, the accent pure Home Counties, and it made Joan's pulse leap up again. She couldn't keep from smiling; for a moment she thought she might laugh. She followed the voice into a square room with white walls and arched windows low down in the front wall, closed off with wooden shutters. Only a single window that faced the steep rocks to the south was open, and the light from it spread softly through the room. There was an antique black bicycle propped against the end of a narrow bed, which was neatly made with faded blankets tucked tight beneath the mattress. To either side of the bed were large potted palms, and an elaborate metal lantern stood on the floor. There was a tidy desk and a long bookcase, the top shelves of which were empty – all the books were at a height of four feet or less, and piled up on the floor when there was no more space. Two wooden chairs faced a red chesterfield sofa on the thready carpet in the middle of the room, and by the sofa a large pile of Arabic and English journals had sagged sideways and slewed across the floor.

Two blonde saluki dogs were asleep in a nest of blankets against the back wall, tangled together so that legs and ears and tails appeared communal. One opened an amber eye to watch Joan, and for a moment their gentle snoring was the only sound in the room; the smell of them was part of the general fug in the air. An inlaid wooden chest was serving as a coffee table, and beside that was a wheelchair – an old-fashioned one made of rattan – in which sat Maude Villette Vickery. Joan tried not to stare. She had the unsettling, almost surreal feeling of being face to face with a person so often imagined it seemed unlikely that they could actually exist in the real world.

The first thing Joan noticed was Maude's diminutive size. She looked almost childlike. Thin knees and elbows made sharp points through an old-fashioned, high-waisted skirt and a pin-tuck blouse with an upright collar; her ankles and feet, resting on the step of the chair, had a doll-like delicacy. She wore thick stockings, in spite of the heat; her hair was straight and iron grey, pulled into a severe knot at the back of her head, and her face, though sunken and lined, had strong bones beneath the skin. After a few seconds her features resolved themselves into the ones Joan knew from photos of her as a young woman – clear eyes, blue-grey, with a keen expression in them; a hooked beak of a nose. Joan kept her distance, not wanting to tower over her. 'Come a bit closer, I shan't bite,' said Maude. Joan stepped forward obediently. Her feet lifted little clouds of dust from the carpet. Maude examined her, squinting up. 'My, aren't you tall? Or perhaps you aren't. Everyone seems tall to me. Abdullah!' she shouted suddenly, leaning towards the doorway and making Joan jump. 'Tea, Abdullah!' she added, though there'd been no answering shout.

She turned back to Joan with a sketchy shrug. 'I know he can hear me. He has the ears of a bat, that old man,' she said. Then there was a pause.

'It's so wonderful to meet you, Miss Vickery,' said Joan. 'It really is a tremendous thrill. I've been such a follower of yours for . . .' She trailed off as a gazelle pottered into the room from across the hall. Joan stared. The animal paused to regard her with liquid eyes surrounded by bold black and white stripes like overdone make-up; then it huffed gently and pottered over to Maude, sniffing at her fingers. Maude smiled.

'You greedy beast. You shall have dates when we do – when Abdullah brings them, and not before,' she said.

'You have a gazelle,' Joan pointed out stupidly.

'Indeed I do. I found him in the souk, ready for the chop. Abdullah wanted to cook him but look at that divine face. Who could resist? And such ridiculously big ears. He seemed such a pathetic thing, I couldn't quite bear to eat him.' She glanced up at Joan ruefully. 'Feeble, I know.'

'I didn't think women were allowed in the souk?' said Joan, at a loss.

'They aren't,' Maude agreed, rubbing the whorl of hair between the gazelle's eyes and offering no further explanation. The animal's golden hide looked as supple as silk.

'Well, at least that explains the—' Joan pulled herself up short, on the verge of speaking far too freely. Maude looked up quickly.

'The muck? Yes. And I suppose it smells bad, does it? Well, my apologies. I'm so used to it, I don't even notice it. I manage to rule in this room, but I've very little control over what happens to the rest of the house. I'll have a word with Abdullah.'

'I'm sorry, Miss Vickery, I really didn't mean to be rude,' said Joan. Maude waved one tiny hand at her.

'You and I will get along far better if you speak your mind. I always have; it saves so much time.'

'Don't the dogs chase him?' Joan nodded at the sleeping salukis.

'Don't be ridiculous. Look at them! They haven't chased a thing in years; they were already past their prime when they were given to me by that wily old man, bin Himyar. The Lord of The Green Mountain. How's that for a left-handed compliment? I used to have an oryx as well, you know. A personal gift from Sultan Taimur bin Faisal, after I regretted to him that I'd never managed to shoot one on my travels. I think he meant for me to shoot it, but it seemed jolly unsporting to do so, with it tied to a post. But it was a wild thing, really, and had to stay outside. Those horns they have! Potentially quite lethal. He soon escaped, my oryx. Never saw him again, and I had to lie and tell the sultan I'd shot it and eaten it and how delicious it had been. I even got those to prove my story.' She pointed to a pair of dark, ridged oryx horns, mounted on the wall. 'Waste of time. I doubt the man even remembered giving me the creature in the first place.'

'I've read that you had a close relationship with Sultan Taimur, unlike that of any other western woman.'

'His father, too. Well, you know,' said Maude vaguely. 'Back then, maybe – I was a novelty at the time, you understand. And he always did like new toys. Just like all men.'

In silence, the tall, elderly servant who'd opened the door to Joan brought in a tray holding a pewter teapot and little glasses, a bowl of dates and another of sugar. He bent down slowly, put the tray on the chest without a clatter, and poured the tea without being asked.

'Do you remember that oryx Sultan Taimur gave me, Abdullah?' Maude asked him.

'Yes, lady. I remember it.'

'What did I call it? Do you recall?'

'You called it Snowy, lady.' Abdullah placed a glass of tea within her reach.

'Snowy! That was it. How imaginative of me.' Maude sighed. 'His coat was the purest white you ever saw. We ought to have coffee with dates, I know, but I'm afraid I can no longer stomach the stuff. What was your name again, young woman?'

'I'm . . . Joan Seabrook, Miss Vickery.'

'So you are. The one who wrote all those letters. Quite a blizzard of them. Thank you, Abdullah. I wonder what happened to Snowy? Perhaps he made it back to the desert, but I rather doubt it. I'm sure he'd have wanted to, as I do. Better off in the desert, the pair of us. But what is it that you *want*, Miss Seabrook?' Suddenly Maude seemed agitated, almost cross. She brushed at her skirt, then clasped her hands together. 'I'm at a loss to fathom it, in spite of all the letters.' As he withdrew from the room, Joan felt Abdullah's eyes sweep over her. She couldn't help but turn to watch him leave. He moved with incredible grace.

'Well, I . . .' she said, distracted.

'Draws the eye, doesn't he?' Maude interjected, fixing Joan with a beady gaze.

'Your servant is indeed a . . . striking man.'

'Oh, he's not my servant, Miss Seabrook. He's my *slave*. I own him. I bought him at an auction, in a cave in the hills near Nizwa. Now, what do you make of *that*?'

'I'd heard that the practice still continues here,' Joan said carefully. She was thrown by this elderly version of her idol, unable to read her mood or her temperament. Maude sat back, looking disappointed.

'Well. I see I shall have to try harder if I want to shock *you*, Miss Seabrook.'

'I'm sure that once I've had a chance to reflect, I shall be very shocked, Miss Vickery. Only, I haven't quite finished being shocked about the gazelle just yet.' There was a pause; Maude's eyes narrowed, and then she smiled a quick, impish smile.

'Ha,' she said, in place of laughter. 'Good girl. You're not too polite; I approve of that.'

Joan took a seat at one end of the red sofa, near the desk; they drank the tea, which was sweet with sugar and bitter with mint, and ate the dates. From outside came the clatter of donkey hooves and the slap of feet in leather sandals; the light began to mellow and a handful of flies buzzed in lazy circles around the room. The gap since Maude had asked Joan what she wanted had grown too wide for her to answer, and she let her eyes roam the room as she waited to be asked again. Maude chewed a date slowly; her eyes were far away but she seemed calm again, almost distant. There was a rosewood pencil tray on the desk, empty except for a ring – small but heavily made, with a twisted pewter band and a coarse lump of bright blue stone.

'That's an interesting ring,' said Joan, leaning closer towards it. 'What stone—'

'Don't touch it!' Maude snapped, interrupting her loudly.

'No, no I . . .' Joan shook her head; she hadn't been reaching for it.

'Do not touch that thing,' the old woman reiterated. Her glare was ferocious, and Joan realised that it was fixed on the ring, not on herself.

She laced her hands in her lap and searched for a way to change the subject; she didn't dare ask anything else about the ring.

'Was this house also a gift from Sultan Taimur, Miss Vickery? After he gave you the oryx?' she said. Maude blinked several times, and then answered as though nothing had happened.

'Certainly not. I bought it – and dearly. Taimur's father, Faisal, gave me permission to live in Oman the rest of my days, and that was generous enough – I think I may be the only one, you know. The only European living here simply because it pleases me to, and not for any official or commercial reason. This current sultan, Said, is Faisal's grandson – every time one of them dies I wonder if I'll be turned out by the successor, but so far, so good. He's as conservative as they come, Said, but he has his quirks – like those American missionaries for example; I have no idea why he lets them stay. Sweet people; silly as geese. They actually seem to think they might be able to convert the Arabs to Christianity. But theirs is the only hospital in the whole country.' She pointed a finger at Joan. 'Don't get typhoid while you're out here, Miss Seabrook – or tuberculosis. The milk is riddled with tuberculosis. Be sure it's boiled before you have any in your coffee. Once I had permission to remain in Muscat, this old house was all I could find to buy. The better houses were refused to me. I think the Governor of Muscat wanted to make sure I was kept in my place, you understand? Have you met him yet? Sayid Shahab? Fearsome chap, all but autonomous with Sultan Said away in Salalah. He made sure I was honoured, but not too much so.' She smiled slightly.

'The government here certainly seems very strict.'

'Indeed. Which begs the question, how on earth did you manage to get permission to come, Miss Seabrook? Oman is not a place that welcomes foreign visitors, or the idly curious. Never has been.' Maude fed a date to the gazelle, which took it delicately from her fingertips.

'No,' said Joan uncomfortably. 'My father was at school with the current wazir – the sultan's foreign minister – which

helped things along. We're staying with him at the Residency
– my fiancé, Rory, and I.'

'Do they still call the post wazir? Vizier? How quaint. But
then, I suppose, Oman is still a British protectorate, isn't it?
Even if they don't exactly call it that any more – not now
everyone's so embarrassed about appearing colonial.'

'And also, for the past six months, my brother Daniel has
been over here. He's a soldier, you see, seconded to the Sultan's Armed Forces – the SAF. I was granted permission to
come out and visit him.'

'But that's not why you've actually come.'

'No. Well, yes, it is in part . . . I just . . .' Joan paused, and
for a second she felt the rise of something like desperation; she
felt like she was grasping at something that was determined
to slip away.

The truth was, she didn't know quite how to put her need
to see Arabia into words. It had been rooted deep inside her
for so long, she'd stopped questioning it; and when Daniel
was posted to Oman, and Robert Gibson became wazir, and
Joan got a little money in her father's will, it had seemed as
though everything was lining up to finally bring her here. To
Oman – a small, far corner of Arabia, but Arabia nonetheless.
And somehow, since his death, it felt as though something of
her father might be here, too. It had taken almost a year for the
paralysing shock of losing him to lessen, and then for the idea
to form, but once it had she knew that nothing would shake it.

It had been difficult telling her mother, Olive, how she
intended to spend her small inheritance. She'd waited until
Olive was cooking – which was when she was happiest –
before mentioning it.

'Isn't it enough I've one child out there in that godforsaken
place?' said Olive, pausing with cubes of bacon fat stuck to
the blade of her big knife and that quaver in her voice that

was becoming a permanent impediment. 'You're not up to it, Joanie. And how could you leave me all by myself?' She'd pulled a rumpled hanky from the pocket of her apron to scrub at her eyes, and Joan had felt the stifling guilt that was becoming all too familiar, welling up, making her question her decision. Olive looked wretched, vulnerable, easy to wound. 'Your father never even *went* there – you know that.' Joan did know. She'd been incredulous to learn, once she was old enough to understand, that her father had never been further than France. In spite of all his tales; in spite of all his dreams and enthusiasm and plans. But he'd wanted Joan to travel, that much she knew; he'd wanted her to live out some of *her* dreams. And Joan had always dreamed of Arabia. She heard her father's voice in her head; pictured his wide, exaggerated eyes. *Land of Sinbad the Sailor and the Queen of Sheba, and frankincense and genies and wishes!* Always over the top – deliberately so; always ready to bring magic and wonder into her world.

Joan tried to swallow the desperate feeling down, but her audience with Maude Vickery was not going at all as she'd hoped or imagined. 'You've been my heroine since I was only a girl, Miss Vickery. I want to go into the desert, just as you did. Into the Rub el Khali – the Empty Quarter. The largest sand desert in the world . . . I know a lot of people have crossed it now, but so much of it is still untouched. I want to go to Fort Jabrin, and do a survey; perhaps draw some elevations. I'm an archaeologist – perhaps you remember from my letters? Well – almost. I haven't actually *done* any archaeology yet, but I have my degree. I've actually just applied for a post at a local museum – a very junior post, of course. It starts in the new year, that's if I get it, which I ought to if I can show them some study I've made while I'm out here; and I really want to . . .' She paused for a breath but Maude was looking at her in an unfriendly way, so she held her tongue.

'A goodly long list of wants, Miss Seabrook.' Maude jabbed a finger at Joan, the nail ridged and stained. 'And may I point out that you are *still* only a girl?'

'I'm almost as old as you were when you first crossed the desert. I'm twenty-six.

Maude made a grudging sound.

'You seem younger. But be that as it may, I fear you're chasing a dream. You want to follow in my footsteps but what good would it do you? That's not exploration. That's not *adventure*. And it is adventure you want, I think? You must find your own path – you must carve it out, all by yourself. Sultan Said himself crossed the Empty Quarter a few years ago – by *motor car*. There's no mystery left there.' She sounded bitter; she leaned forwards slowly, intently, shaking with the effort. 'You must be the *first*. Or it means nothing.'

'But that can't be true! You weren't the first to cross the Empty Quarter – not the *very* first, but it still matters that you did it. The desert is vast ... and no European has ever explored Fort Jabrin, let alone an archaeologist. The maps don't even show clearly where it is. But you went there, didn't you? You've seen it.'

'A ruin, infested with snakes.' Maude waved a hand. She patted her clothes as if in search of something. Frowning, agitated. 'It's not even that old, only a few hundred years; and there's no mystery as to where it is. Go down to Bahla and then turn left.'

'But it's rumoured to hold great treasures ...'

'Don't be foolish. No Arab ever left abandoned treasure behind. You're as bad as a Bedouin – they're *obsessed* with the idea of buried treasure, you know. All that rubbish you read about desert people only valuing water, not gold. They value water, hospitality, grazing, guns and gold, that's what they value.' She counted them off on her fingers. 'There is no buried treasure, Miss Seabrook.'

'But . . . the place itself is a treasure, don't you see?'

'And how do you propose to travel there, in any case? Foreigners are not allowed east of the Residency in Muscat, or west of the army headquarters at Muttrah. Or outside the limits of the city into the mountains, let alone into the desert . . . That has always been the case. Sultan Said is a very private man, and he extends that privacy to his entire country. And, correct me if I'm wrong, but isn't there something of a *war* going on?' Maude's voice had risen; she was almost shouting, though Joan couldn't tell what had angered her.

She took a nervous sip of her tea. 'Not much of a war, really . . .' she said. 'Not compared to the real war; the World War. Mr Gibson calls it "an insurgency". And it's only in the mountains now, isn't it?' Maude glared at her for a moment and then sat forwards with that gnarled finger outstretched again.

'You, Miss Seabrook, are a *tourist*. Nothing more.'

They sat together for a while, uneasily, and then Maude's chin dropped onto her chest; she was silent, and Joan was stiff with embarrassment. When Abdullah came in to clear the tea tray he nodded to Joan.

'Come,' he said quietly, as he returned to the top of the stairs. 'The lady is not used to visitors. She must rest now.' Gratefully, Joan followed him. Abdullah let her out without a word, but his watchfulness was hard to ignore. Somehow, Joan felt judged; she felt as though she'd fallen short. The sun had sunk towards the horizon but the sky was still light and the canons had not yet fired – the *dum dum* ceremony that marked the start of the nightly curfew.

Joan put on her hat and walked the short distance back

through the main gate, smiling shyly at the guards as they bobbed their heads and tried out a few words of mangled English on her.

She stopped a short way into the city. She'd received no invitation to return to Maude Vickery's home. The disappointment Rory had warned her about washed through her, but she was more disappointed with herself than with Maude. The old explorer was known to be difficult – even in her youth she'd been accused of being hard-headed, tactless and sometimes spectacularly rude; it was all there in her writings, her biographies and collected letters. Joan had been prepared for it, but she'd still been sure she would win her over; she'd been sure that Maude would recognise a kindred spirit. But Joan hadn't said the right things. She hadn't impressed her sincerity upon Maude – had not, in fact, impressed her at all. The scorn with which Maude had labelled her *tourist* had stung by being too close to the mark. Sad and agitated, Joan sat down on a step in the gathering twilight, and watched the passers-by as they hurried to be inside or outside the gate before it was locked. Omani women in their black robes and veils; Baluchi women from the sultan's territory in northern Pakistan, unveiled, dressed as brightly as flowers; Indians and Persians and the black faces of slaves, like Abdullah. It seemed, in fact, as though there were more foreigners in Muscat than Omanis.

Evening came early to Oman, just before six o'clock. Even late, the sun was strong, and the temperature, in the high nineties, felt roasting after the cool, wet year they'd had in England. Rory, in particular, had been suffering. His cheeks were constantly ruddy, and he yawned a lot. He was far better suited to winter – a crisp, blowy British winter, when the blush in his cheeks looked healthy rather than infectious. They'd only been in Muscat for three days, after a flight to Cairo with

BOAC – Joan's first ever – a connecting flight to Salalah and a slow chug up the coast by ship.

'I wasn't sure we'd make it,' said Rory, as they disembarked. 'You know what they say about BOAC? You'd be Better On A Camel.' Joan did know, but she also knew he'd been dying to say it. As far as she was concerned, the flight had been magical. She'd glimpsed the pyramids from the tiny window as they'd come in to land at Cairo, and the thrill had sent a shiver through her.

They hadn't yet been able to see Joan's brother, Daniel, at the army base at Bait al Falaj in Muttrah, just around the headland from Muscat. They could either take a boat to get there, or the dirt road that picked a path up the rocky hillside, but either way they had to wait until Daniel was back at base. They'd had word from his commanding officer that he was currently at a post inland, leading mountain reconnaissance patrols. Daniel had explained the insurgency to Joan in a letter, after she'd written to say she was planning to come to Muscat. It had been the main, but not the only, way in which he'd tried to dissuade her.

Even though Britain has recognised the sultan as the ruler of both Muscat and Oman for a long time, traditionally the sultan ruled Muscat and the coast, and let the imam govern 'Oman', the interior – the desert and the mountains. They got along fine like that for generations, but then there was talk of oil in the desert and Sultan Said started to enforce his sovereignty there. There was some serious trouble, but with a bit of help from us, in '55 Imam Ghalib was forced to abdicate. But he was soon back, with his brother Talib egging him on. Now they've fallen back and holed up in the mountains with all their men, and the sultan won't be happy until we've routed every last one of them. So it's a prickly time, Joanie — and not a good time for you to come out here on holiday. I might not even be able to see you at all — it's possible I won't be back at base. There must be somewhere else you'd rather go? Or come next year, if you must, once it's all over.

The thought of war scared Joan; his letter had almost caused her to abandon her plan. War meant the feelings she remembered from childhood, of abject fear and constant dread; of a horrible jittering inside that she couldn't control. But when she'd written to Robert Gibson, her father's old friend, he'd assured her that the situation barely warranted the term *war* any more, and that Muscat itself was certainly in no danger. And, besides, Daniel would doubtless be posted elsewhere once the military action was over. Lastly, crucially, there *was* nowhere else Joan would rather go. Rory had been just as keen to come, and when they'd finally got official permission she hadn't wanted to wait another day. Life at home had settled into a depressing trudge since her father's death; the sudden pain of losing him had mellowed to a persistent listlessness, a sadness that made everything an effort. Coming here had been the only way she could think of to reignite life, and she was desperate to see her brother.

Just then, the drums rolled and the canon sounded; a sudden, booming report that echoed back from the rocks, rumbling on like thunder. Joan picked up her paraffin lamp — it was the law that anyone out after *dum dum* had to carry one — opened the hatch and fumbled in her satchel for a match. She ought to hurry back; it wasn't good for a woman to be out after dark, even with the requisite lamp. But she took a moment longer, with the lantern flame hissing faintly in the hush and the gates of Muscat looming up beside her, to remember where she was, and feel the wonder of it again. It was incredible that she was so far from home, in so strange a place; it was incredible that she had already gone farther than either of her parents ever had. Joan was in the place of her dreams, and she would make the best of it, even if that meant adjusting her expectations. Her father had often warned her against having pre-formed ideas of people, of places. *Wait and see what you find; don't go in with a yardstick ready to measure things against.* She rose and breathed in the warm air, and a pair of gulls, near luminous white, sailed silently above her head as she set off across the city.

The British Residency occupied one of the largest buildings in Muscat, right at the water's edge in the far eastern corner of the city, along from the customs building and the sultan's empty palace. Sultan Said preferred to remain in Salalah, hundreds of miles to the south-west; he hadn't visited Muscat in years. Vast, pale and square, the Residency was two tall storeys high with a crenellated roof and covered verandas all around. From the separate guest rooms Joan and Rory had been allocated, the view was of the horseshoe-shaped harbour – its glittering green water jostling with boats, its steep rock walls inscribed with ships' names, daubed there by their crews over the centuries in what the sultan called his *visitors' book*.

Two seventeenth-century forts, built by the Portuguese when they invaded, guarded the harbour entrance – Merani, from which the *dum dum* canons sounded, and Jalali, the prison fort. Huge and impregnable, gripping its rocky outcrop like a massive barnacle and accessed by a single set of steps carved into the stone, Jalali seemed to loom, overshadowing the Residency. On the first night of their visit Joan had stood at the window and seen a few lights burning inside the fort, re-iterating the blackness of the rest. She'd thought she'd caught the stench of human suffering, carried across from it on the wind. One of the servants had said you could sometimes hear the prisoners rattling their chains.

The Union Jack was hanging limply from the top of the towering flagpole outside the Residency as Joan approached, but when the sea breeze blew, it, and the other flags strung along the guy lines, made a guttering sound like flames. Joan went to the main door and one of the servants let her in with a sketchy bow. Joan blew out her lantern and handed it to him as she pulled off her hat and ran her fingers through her hair. The young man stared at her, and Joan gave him a stilted smile. She wasn't used to servants, or certain how to speak to them.

'Good evening, Amit,' she said, having made a point of remembering his name. 'Would it be possible to send up some lemonade, please?'

'Lemonade, sahib,' he echoed her, understanding the pertinent word. Joan crossed the hall and trotted up the stairs. The inside of the building was shaded and full of echoes. The clerks and secretaries who occupied the offices during the day, typing and sifting papers, had finished and gone home, and only those few in residence remained. Joan wished there was more noise to fill the space. It was like the house at home since her father's death – quiet in a way that seemed stifling, somehow.

Rory's bedroom was at the top of the building – on an entirely different floor to Joan's, which was next door to their hosts', allowing no chance of illicit visits after lights out. He wasn't in it, so she went along the corridor to the little bathroom at the end, checked that there was nobody around to see her, and knocked.

'Joan?' Rory's voice came through the door, so she let herself in. He was in the bath, eyes shut, lying back with his hair in wet, dark curls and a cigarette burning down between the first two fingers of his left hand. Joan knew that the water would be cool, blood temperature, an attempt to quench the heat. She would have locked the door if she was going to have a bath. Rory had never seen her undressed, but it somehow seemed less improper that she should see him. Perhaps because she'd run his bath for him when he'd first come to stay with them, aged eleven; perhaps because he was so comfortable to be seen, even though they wouldn't sleep together until they were married. Rory was simply comfortable to be naked. They often joked about it, given that he was shy and diffident in other ways. She wished she could be as entirely comfortable with his naked body as he was.

Joan crossed to Rory and took the cigarette, knocking the ash out of the window before taking a long pull on it. Through the smoke in her eyes her fiancé turned hazy and grey. Her mother hated her smoking, and she hardly ever did; usually only when she needed to feel stronger, or more capable.

'Don't nod off and drown will you, darling? Or set the place on fire,' she said, smiling as Rory opened one eye.

'I wasn't sleeping, only resting my eyes, and enjoying not feeling as though I'm about to combust. So, how did it go?' He rolled his head towards her and took back the cigarette when she proffered it. She kissed his damp forehead; he tasted of soap and the hard spring water of Muscat. She dried her mouth on the back of her hand rather than licking her lips. They were being careful only to drink water which had been boiled, but it felt like wiping the kiss away.

'It was ... difficult.' She went back to the window and leaned against the sill, with the mauve sky behind her and the sea hoarding the last fragments of light.

'Difficult? Oh, bother – not what you'd hoped?'

'No, I suppose it wasn't.' Joan sighed, feeling her disappointment, her sense of failure. *Tourist*. She didn't feel quite up to repeating Maude's withering assessment of her to Rory.

century. Known as wazir, his job was to guide the sultan in all matters of foreign relations and trade; to advise and to counsel, but never to command. And, of course, to keep the British government appraised of it all. Dinner was served at eight o'clock sharp at the Residency, but they gathered at a quarter past seven on the first-floor terrace, where the current wazir, Robert Gibson, poured generous gins topped off with tonic. The terrace was a huge space with potted oleanders six feet high, laden with pink blossom, and a purple bougainvillea cascading from the sloping roof. From it, the view was of a forbidden land, a line none of them could cross without the sultan's express permission: into the east, beyond the city, past the cape of Ras al Hadd where the coast turned to the south and stretched for hundreds of miles, all the way to Aden by the mouth of the Red Sea. Mountains and desert, dust dry; a salty coastal plain where a brief monsoon touched, every year, and caused flowers to bloom and grass to grow; a land with an ancient heart so foreign and strange that Joan felt hungry staring out at it from the confines of the terrace. Hungry to know it; reluctant to admit that she probably never would.

She looked across at Rory as he chatted to their hosts, dressed in his summer suit with his damp hair combed back and set; she smiled. He'd surprised her by agreeing to come to Arabia with her so readily. *Arabia? Sounds terrific.* He knew how long she'd dreamed of making the trip, and how impossible it had always seemed, until that moment. Then they'd joked that the honeymoon usually came after the wedding, but that they were going to do things differently. Rory worked for his father at the modest auction rooms his family had run for generations – selling off unfashionable furniture and clunky bits of silver from the parlours of people's dead relatives – so it was simple enough for him to ask for time off. And Joan hadn't worked since she'd lost her job as a secretary at a printing works a month before, for repeatedly being caught reading the books instead of typing up invoices. She and her mother had been living off Olive's widow's pension since then, and one of Olive's objections to her spending her inheritance on an overseas trip was the profligacy of it. *That's six months' food and heating for the pair of us, gone on a folly!* Joan felt guilty whenever she pictured the frightened way her mother fingered each bill that arrived, some of them with ominous red lettering: *For Your Urgent Attention.* Her father had always handled the family finances; Olive studied the figures intently, with her pen hovering over her chequebook, as if terrified of failing a test of some kind. But, however imprudent it seemed, Joan knew she'd needed to make this trip.

Rory had asked her before why Arabia – why, of all the many places in the world she hadn't been, she most wanted to go there. It had been six years ago, before they'd become an item; Rory had come into their cramped front room to sit with Joan while Daniel got changed to go out; she'd been reading Freya Stark's *The Southern Gates of Arabia* while some very British rain hit the window in spiteful flurries, with the smell of vinegar and mustard seeds hanging in the air. In the kitchen, where her mother was bottling up the chutney they'd spent all morning making, it was almost too pungent to breathe. When she wasn't at the riding school, helping out in the hope of a free lesson, Joan spent a lot of time reading about Arabia. On her bedroom walls were a portrait of T. E. Lawrence and pictures of desert sheiks she'd found in old books, instead of magazine clippings of Johnnie Ray. But when Rory asked her why, she'd had to think for a while before she could answer.

Her father had started it, of course, by reading her tales from *The One Thousand and One Nights*; but that rainy afternoon, it seemed easier to tell Rory about Aladdin. Aladdin was a horse like none Joan had ever seen before. She and the other muddy stable girls had stood, slack-jawed in awe, as he clattered out of the trailer onto the yard, every muscle fluttering with tension and his tail kinked high over his back as he looked around. His little feet seemed to dance over the concrete. His owner, a neat, haughty girl called Annabelle, made it very clear that Broadbrook Stables was just a stop-gap until she could find more suitable accommodation for her horse – somewhere with less barbed wire and baler twine; fewer puddles; fewer ponies that nipped.

Aladdin's coat was bright chestnut – the colour of fire; he had a long mane, a white stripe down his sculpted face and crescent-shaped ears that nearly touched at the tips when he pricked them up. He was by far the most beautiful creature Joan had ever seen, and when Annabelle told her that he was a pure-bred Arabian, she knew that Arabia had to be every bit as wonderful as she'd ever imagined it. It was a place where you galloped towards a shimmering horizon, rather than trotted in circles in a soggy field with a view of the hairy rump in front of you; a place where you wore silk next to your skin instead of a damp, itchy jumper; where there was no mud, no rain, no slumped grey skies or snoozing suburban streets. Clean, warm, beautiful; entirely wholly *other* than life as she knew it. And Joan was just beginning to realise how very much she wanted life to be other than she knew it.

A loud laugh from Robert Gibson brought her out of the past. At his request Joan had put aside the slacks she preferred and changed into a dress for the evening – a simple linen shift with a green plastic belt. Her leather sandals had a thick strap and buckle that reminded her of school days, and were hardly elegant, but her mother had chosen them for her as a going-away present and she hadn't had the heart to protest. Here in Oman they seemed more fitting, somehow, and a little less graceless. And she always felt rather like a schoolgirl next to the man she called Uncle Bobby, anyway. Robert Gibson was a huge man, always immaculate; leonine, with light green eyes and a moustache of extravagant blonde bristles going up into the nostrils of a broad nose that barely narrowed at the bridge. His hair was thinning and turning white, and he combed it back close to his scalp. The only reason he wasn't her god-father was because David Seabrook had been a devout atheist, and hadn't wanted either Joan or Daniel christened.

Robert had a habit of standing by Joan's side, putting one huge arm around her shoulders and squeezing until she felt her joints creak in protest. He'd done it just the other night, when they'd first been reunited. Her earliest memory of him was of just such a hug, and how alarming it had been – she'd only been five, and her father had laughed at the shocked expression on her face. If Robert had had three or more drinks he would straighten up to his full height as he did it, so that Joan's feet dangled off the floor. It was a hug better suited to a child than to a woman, but Joan still enjoyed it. She didn't like to think that there was no trace of her father left in the universe, which is what he'd believed happened after death. Perhaps there were a few dusty elements in the ash that her mother kept on the mantelpiece at home, in a maudlin ebony box flanked by candles, but there was nothing of his essence there, nothing of his soul. Somehow, it felt as though something of him remained in his oldest friend, Robert, and the rough hugs he gave.

Robert's wife, Marian, was tall and square-shouldered, with a strong face marred by horsey teeth. She always wore her fair hair back in an Alice band; always wore pink lipstick and shoes every bit as sensible as Joan's sandals. She was so entirely respectable, so very much as expected, that Joan sometimes didn't notice whether she was in the room or not. They each took a brimming glass from Robert, who moved his large form with exaggerated care so as not to slop, and settled themselves into patio chairs.

'Chin-chin,' said Robert, raising his glass. Beyond the weak electric light of the terrace, the night was navy blue, not yet black. The sea was tame and drowsy down in the harbour, and the soft wash of it was a constant sound. The first sip of the gin made Joan shudder slightly, and numbed her tongue. Then it went down very easily. Marian's sip was more of a swig, and there was a visible melting of tension in her shoulders as she swallowed.

'Now, Joan, let's hear it. How was the great Maude Vickery?' said Robert.

'Well . . .' Joan paused, considering what and what not to say. 'She was tiny. Quite the smallest woman I've ever seen. A little testy. Rather . . . eccentric perhaps. But no less great for all that, I'm sure.' She took another sip of her gin during the expectant pause that followed.

'But . . . that can't be it, surely?' Robert sounded incredulous. 'Joan, we've heard nothing but Maude Vickery this and Maude Vickery that since you got here! Now you've finally met her and all you have to say about it is that she's small and bad-tempered?' He laughed.

'What was her house like?' said Marian.

'Not as grand as I'd thought it might be . . . Well, it was filthy, actually.' Joan took another mouthful of gin. It was already cantering through her bloodstream, bringing a feeling of warmth and courage. 'She has a pet gazelle, and two salukis, and . . . well, there was an awful lot of muck everywhere.'

'Oh, good gracious, not really?' said Marian. 'Surely she has people to clean up? And who on *earth* keeps a pet gazelle?'

'And she has a slave,' Joan continued.

'Does she now?' Robert raised his blonde brows. 'Well, slavery here is not quite as we know it – not these days anyway.

※ 30 ※

Those slaves that remain here were generally born into it, and often they're a part of the family. But, next time you go, tell the chap he's only to nip along and touch the flagpole in the courtyard out there, and he's a free man. That's the law.'

'Well, Maude's in a wheelchair, so there'd be nothing stopping him.'

'Oh dear, poor woman,' said Marian vaguely.

'I didn't realise she'd got so frail,' said Robert. 'Perhaps I ought to inform the sultan. I know he was rather interested in her, at one time. Then again, perhaps I oughtn't to interfere; clearly the woman likes her privacy. She's turned down every dinner invite I've ever sent, and every one my predecessor sent, as I understand it.'

'Well, she didn't seem the overly social sort,' said Joan.

When they rose to decamp to the dinner table, Robert fell into step beside Joan, touching her arm lightly to draw her back. In spite of his size, or perhaps because of it, he had a great delicacy about him, though he was ripe with citronella oil to keep the flies away.

'My dear girl,' he said softly. 'I have no wish to upset you, but I've wanted to ask how you are. How you're . . . coping, I mean. You were so close to dear David. The past year must have been a very difficult one.'

'Yes.' Instantly, Joan switched her attention to her sense of loss. It was a bit like a dense lump in her gut that never went away, or shrank; it felt more or less the same size and shape now as it had just a week after his death, when she'd finally accepted he was gone. She thought of it as a kind of handicap that she was learning to function around, and found that if she focused her thoughts on other things, she could ignore it. She was getting so good at it that she sometimes forgot he was gone until, for whatever reason, the knowledge reasserted itself with a sudden shock of pain. She shrugged slightly, feeling ill-equipped to explain all that. 'I'm all right, I suppose. I miss him horribly. We all do. But one must . . .'

'Mosey on?' Robert smiled kindly. It had been one of her father's favourite expressions.

'What choice is there, really?' said Joan. She thought of her mother, who'd cracked when her husband died, and had seemed ready to fly apart ever since. She seemed to be getting progressively fainter in the world, when she'd been at best a tentative presence in the first place. 'I find it helps to try to think what Dad would have wanted us to do.'

'Yes, very good. That's just the ticket. And what about your mother? You've a good dose of your father's resilience in you, which I fear Olive lacks.'

'Yes. She's still not herself,' was all Joan could say. She pictured the watery smile her mother had worn – a poor facsimile of stoicism – as Joan had packed her things to come to Muscat. Try as she might, Joan couldn't help feeling a faint, guilty flare of exasperation. Her mother's pain had begun to feel like chains, marooning her at home and in childhood when the rest of the world was carrying on around her. Robert patted her shoulder with his huge paw.

'Time is a great healer, but such a loss will leave a permanent scar. All you can do is try to help her heal. And to forgive her for it,' he said. Joan glanced at him with the unsettling notion that he'd read her thoughts. His look was steady and knowing, but offered no judgement. Joan felt her face grow hot.

'Yes. Of course,' she said.

'And you're quite right. Onwards. You've a wedding to plan, and we must take comfort in remembering your father as he was. Did I ever tell you about the time he and I sneaked into the master's wine cellar at school?'

'Yes,' Joan said, smiling. 'But tell me again.'

Maude returned as the topic of conversation during dinner, and as they talked about her past glories Joan started to forget how strange and awkward the actual meeting had been, and began to remember how important Maude had always been to her. She'd first heard about her in a short chapter in a book about pioneering women – alongside Gertrude Bell and Amelia Edwards and Alexandra David-Neel. She'd been drawn to the photographs of her – a tiny, plain woman with a hooked nose and a fierce expression, posing for a studio portrait with obvious impatience. From a young age, Maude Vickery had travelled alone in some of the wildest parts of the Middle East, to sites of ancient civilisation. She'd published books of her travels, and become a respected classicist and translator in both Persian and Arabic. She was the first woman ever to cross the Empty Quarter of Arabia, via one the hardest routes imaginable, through the dunes of Uruq al Shaiba; but the achievement had been forgotten about because she'd come in second, by a matter of weeks, to her friend and rival Nathaniel Elliot, who was far more famous – he was male, after all, and his career had spanned a lifetime. After being pipped at the post, Maude Vickery had disappeared into obscurity for a number of years, before emerging in Muscat and publishing some translations of classical Persian poetry again. She never wrote about her crossing of the desert, beyond a short article for the Royal Geographical Society, published years after the event.

Joan had wanted to ask Maude about that – why she hadn't written a book about her greatest journey. She'd wanted to ask her about being a woman in a man's world, in an era when that was even truer than now; she'd wanted to ask how Maude had ever managed to convince the Bedouin to take her into the desert. There was so much she'd wanted to ask but hadn't. She ate a plate of roast lamb chops and leathery roast potatoes, an ersatz English dish that hadn't translated well into Arabic, and decided that she could choose. She could choose to be defeated and disappointed; to eat fake European food, to stay close to the Residency under Uncle Bobby's wing – and until recently that was probably exactly what she would have done – or she could choose to do it differently. *Be brave*, her father would have told her. He's said it on her first day of school; and when she hadn't wanted to go to a birthday party; and when they'd moved her onto a bigger pony for her riding lessons; and when she'd left home for university. *Be brave*; when on each occasion she'd been fearful of the change, afraid of putting herself forward. She would go back to Maude's house, perhaps in a day or two so as not to seem too pushy. She would go back and try again; she felt she had to, if things were going to change. If the way she felt was going to change, if life was. The last shreds of her despondency burned away like early morning mist.

Robert interrupted her thoughts, tapping the tip of his knife on the edge of her plate.

'By the way, little Joan, I had some news today that might interest you.'

'Yes?'

'Yes. It seems that brother of yours is back at the base. We can go along tomorrow, if you'd like.' He smiled, pleased by her sharp intake of breath and dawning smile.

'You've had a message from him? And you waited until dessert to tell me, you wicked man!'

'Well, I didn't want the excitement to ruin your appetite.'

'Uncle Bobby, I'm not twelve any more.'

'So you aren't excited? How disappointing.'

'Oh, stop it; of course I'm excited! It's wonderful news. And we'll go tomorrow – you promise?' She couldn't help smiling, even though a knot of unease appeared in her gut, and sent a strange tingle over her skin.

Under the table, Rory squeezed her hand. He knew how much her brother meant to her, especially now. He knew she feared Daniel's long absences, and the dangers he faced in the line of duty. Daniel had gone straight into Sandhurst at the age of eighteen, and straight from there to Malaya to fight the communists, where he'd remained until he was posted to the Suez War in 1956, and to Oman in '57. Joan and her parents had been delighted to know he was that much closer to home, but still. To Joan, he always seemed horribly far away, and even Rory didn't know about the dreams she had, of Daniel shot, Daniel blown up by a mine, Daniel crushed by a rolling jeep; or that when she woke from these dreams the pain that lingered, just for a minute, was the most frightening thing she'd ever known.

'Promises aren't necessary; we'll go,' said Robert. 'I have meetings in the morning, but then we'll head over for lunch. The food's jolly good in the officers' mess – delicacies unimagined around here.' Robert poked disconsolately at the hard-centred potatoes on his plate. 'Marian, you really must stop trying to turn the kitchens here into the Dog and Duck in Putney. It just won't wash.'

'I just get so sick of those spices all the time . . . all that *flavour*,' said Marian wanly.

'I'd go if they only served bread and water, if Dan will be there,' said Joan.

'Of course you would. As would we all.' Marian patted her hand. Her eyes were a little pink, as were her cheeks; her whole face had coloured to match her lipstick, which made her look a bit blurred. But she was all surface, it seemed to Joan; she had a hard varnish, and it was difficult to imagine scratching that surface to get at what was underneath – at what it was that made her drink. Joan suspected boredom.

'Poor Dan. I'm going to hug him madly in front of all the men, and they'll chaff him for it afterwards. But I'll do it anyway,' she said.

She and Rory sat up later than Robert and Marian, with a servant by the door to chaperone them even though they sat tactfully at either end of a sofa. The room was lit by dim electric bulbs which dipped and flickered now and then, with the vagaries of the generator, and there was an oil lamp on the table in front of them as a precaution. The Residency was of a style typical in Oman, the rooms laid out as a square around a central space that reached all the way up to the roof, into which the heat could rise and dispel so that the lower floors were bearably cool. The decor, however, was pure England. The same kind of Oriental rug Joan was used to seeing at home, dotted with polished mahogany furniture from before the war. There was even a drinks cabinet disguised as a huge globe, and unflattering portraits of Queen Elizabeth and Prince Philip, and of sultans old and new, flanked by rifles on the walls. Ceremonial Omani rifles, perhaps, but the effect was much the same. The sofas were Ercol; the bed and wardrobe in Joan's room were Waring & Gillow. If it weren't for the high white walls, the oil lamps and the taste and feel of the air, they could have been in Bedford. Again, Joan felt the tug of all the places she could not go, out there, almost within reach; she had the nagging feeling that she wasn't trying hard enough.

Rory was happier in the cool of the evening; he lost the waxy sheen of sweat, though there were still deep shadows under his eyes. In an effort to sleep better he hadn't had any of the strong Omani coffee all day, even though he loved it.

'I hope you get some proper rest tonight, Rory,' said Joan.

She wanted to take his hand, and had to keep reminding herself not to. The feel of his wide, solid palm beneath her fingers was instantly reassuring, like holding onto the bannister at the top of steep stairs. They had been together for five years, and engaged for two – long enough for it to have bedded in as a constant state, rather than as a prelude to something further. Now and then Joan fretted about the delay in setting a wedding date, and worried at it, but it had hardened off just like Marian, and it was difficult to get to the root cause of it. Part of her didn't want to dig too deeply, in case she found out, and didn't like the reason.

'I hope *you* sleep at all. You must be desperate for tomorrow to come,' he said.

'Yes.' She smiled. 'I can't wait. Dear Dan. He'll be in army mode, you know, all efficient and proper. And he'll get cross with me when I over-enthuse but I won't be able to help it.'

'He'll expect nothing less from you. But he'll probably be exhausted; he's been on active duty, don't forget.'

'I know,' said Joan, stung to be reminded. 'Of course I know. But we haven't seen each other in five months. Five months! It's far too long.'

'Well, at least it'll be one meeting that can't possibly disappoint,' said Rory, smiling.

'Yes, Daniel never disappoints me,' said Joan, and only in the pause afterwards heard the criticism that could be construed there, though she hadn't intended it. Or she didn't think she had. Rory reached forwards for his teacup, though he'd drained it minutes before, and Joan sat silent, caught between reassuring him and letting the comment pass, paralysed by indecision. In the end Rory took a breath and stood up.

'Well, the sooner to bed the sooner it'll be morning. Just like Christmas,' he said, smiling again, with only the slightest trace of reserve in his eyes. Relieved, Joan stood as well. She

particular guest, the severity of a child's misdemeanour – all of these were measured by whether or not they could induce Antoinette Vickery to put aside her needle and frame. Antoinette's eyes were so often cast down at her work, focused upon it, that their direct gaze was a startling thing. Those eyes were unsettling in a way that made Maude want to study them and hide from them at the same time. They were like polished stones, or something glimpsed at the bottom of a rock pool; there was something beautiful but odd about them. Their gaze was always fleeting, but they gave Maude the worrying feeling that her mother was made of entirely different stuff to her. She sometimes dawdled on the threshold of whatever room Antoinette was in, fidgeting, shifting her weight, tortured by the need to be noticed but too uncertain to make a sound.

At eight years of age Maude remained the size of a child of six, which was useful for hide and seek but far less so for climbing trees or being taken seriously by her brothers, Francis and John, who were four and five years older than her respectively. They called her Scrap, and liked to put things out of her reach, throw things to and fro above her head, and sling her across their shoulders to spin her until she turned green. *You're not going to cry, are you, Scrap?* But their father, if he overheard, would often say: *Nonsense; Maude's tougher than the pair of you*, which made her thrill inside. The boys were coming home from school for the summer that very day, and Maude could hardly keep a lid on her excitement. Their imminent arrival, as much as the quiet and the rain, was what was slowing down time. Maude began to feel nervous. After their long absences from her life she always felt shy and afraid to be reunited with John and Francis. Their faces always changed during term time, and they got taller, so that at first they seemed like a pair of strange boys and not her brothers at all. It didn't usually last for long – within half an hour or so they'd have pulled the ribbons out of her hair and hidden her shoes, and made everything entirely normal again.

At two fifteen, Maude heard Thorpe go out in the trap to collect the boys from their train. Her stomach gave a twist and she ran to the hallway window to watch him disappear beneath the willows by the front gate, which trailed their sodden branches right down to the ground. Maude wondered how long it would take for the gardens to consume Marsh House; for the house to be invaded by trees and vines, and covered, and forgotten about – like she and everyone in it seemed forgotten about. Quite a long time, she decided. It was a very large house. The sound of hooves and cartwheels soon faded. Then, at a loss as to what to do with herself in the forty minutes or so it might take Thorpe to return, Maude quickly rehearsed her starting position – how she would receive the boys. She decided to stand at the foot of the stairs with a book in her hand and her face neatly composed, with the portraits of all their ancestors peering down from the walls behind her. She might wear an absent smile, like a grown-up, as though she'd forgotten they were due and wasn't in the least bit excited or afraid.

Next she went into the library, took her father's copy of the *Fortnightly Review* from his desk and climbed the ladder to the narrow mezzanine that ran around three sides of the room. In one corner was a flattened old cushion where Maude often brought herself to read. She flung herself down inelegantly, sneezing on the rising dust, and blocked out the sound of the clock by humming the tune to 'Greensleeves', which her piano tutor had been doggedly attempting to teach her. She studied her nerves, which her father had taught her was the best way to conquer them, and was honest enough with herself to admit that what she feared most about the boys' arrival was that it meant the countdown had begun to them leaving again – to

Maude being left behind again. She hated it with a kind of futile desperation that made her gouge her fingernails into the heels of her hands.

Chewing one thumbnail, she opened the *Fortnightly Review* and concentrated on reading. Her father approved when she read things that should have been far too difficult for her, so Maude practised diligently in his absence. She sometimes needed the dictionary open next to the book itself, but once she'd learned a word she never forgot it. It was the same with French and German and Latin, and she couldn't understand why her brothers struggled so with the conjugation of verbs. '*Of all the places in the world,*' she read, '*Muscat has the reputation of being the hottest, facing as it does the Indian Ocean, and protected from every cooling breeze by rugged volcanic hills without a blade of cultivation upon them . . .*' The article was full of odd-sounding names, of both people and places, and words she had to look up, like *autocratic*, and *condign*. She read of masked women and thronging bazaars full of strange peoples and things; she read of exotic diseases and wondered what they might look and smell like – guinea worm and Gulf fever, and button boils. Gradually, as she read, the ticking stopped. The rain receded, and she stopped smelling kippers and smelled attar of roses instead, and incense, and the raw stink of blood on a butcher's block in a hot, dusty place. She was so wholly transported that the slamming of the front door caused her heart to flap wildly in her chest. Her brothers were home, and she'd missed her chance to pose at the foot of the stairs as they came in. Disappointment and panic rushed in and tightened her throat.

Maude waited, ears craned as the boys clattered into the parlour and were greeted with a vague noise of pleasure by Antoinette; as they thundered up the stairs, briefly, and then into the kitchens – always hungry, always impatient. They seemed to make more noise than two boys alone ought to have been able to make. Faintly, she heard cook's raucous laugh – she loved the boys' cheek and their greediness, though she pretended not to. Unable to keep reading, Maude stared at the page in front of her, listening and waiting; hoping her brothers would come to find her and not just disappear into the billiards room, or stay and sit with their mother to tell her, one talking over the other, everything they'd seen and heard and done; to make plans for the holidays, pointlessly, since nothing would be decided until their father was home. But whatever it was they were doing, they weren't coming to find their little sister. Maude hated to feel sorry for herself. She refused to, and chewed her lower lip instead, until it started to swell up and she could taste a little blood, and thought she'd better stop. The minutes passed and became a long, torturous half-hour, and she decided she would just have to stay up on the mezzanine *for ever* because she was too hurt and angry to ever go down and remind John and Francis of her existence.

Some time later she heard the parlour maid, Clara, calling her to have tea. Her stomach rumbled in response but she still couldn't go down. Her legs were stiff and tired from sitting on the floor, and she had pins and needles in her left foot, but she huddled back against the shelves in misery, nurturing her wounded pride. She couldn't possibly see her brothers again. She tried to imagine a way: she would have to be as entirely aloof, as wholly indifferent to them as they had proved them-selves to be to her. It wouldn't be so hard – just then, she hated them both. The summer holidays would be long and boring and lonely if she refused to play with them, or if they refused to include her in their adventures. Despair made her start chewing her lip again, and then the library door opened with its faint groan, and hope flooded her. She picked up the journal and buried her face in it. Her cheeks began to burn as she heard the ladder creak, and footsteps on the mezzanine. Someone had finally come to get her, and had known where to look. She was desperate to know if it was Francis, her youngest brother, or John, the eldest, but she couldn't look. Somehow, for reasons that were now too complex for her to unpick, she didn't dare.

The boy sat down beside her with a slight sigh, bashing his knee against hers. From the corner of her eye she saw long black socks smudged with dust; short, grey flannel school trousers and scuffed shoes. Without needing to see more she knew it was neither of her brothers. Nathaniel Elliot, who was twelve, the same as Francis, somehow occupied his space in the world differently to the Vickery boys. He was the son of her father's good friend, Colonel Henry Thomas Elliot, who'd been killed in Africa by naked, spear-wielding savages – a fact that Maude found so wildly interesting she had trouble remembering that it was in fact a tragedy and a terrible crime. Nathaniel's mother was frail and had retired to Nice for her health, and Nathaniel's visits to her seafront apartment there were generally brief. She fed him lobster, oysters and champagne and let him sit up until the early hours with her friends as they drank and smoked and played cards; then, after a handful of days, she told him she was exhausted with him and sent him back to England. He had an aunt in London, but he often came to stay at Marsh House instead of troubling her or haunting the barren corridors of the empty school. Maude never knew he was coming until he arrived. When he came from his mother he was pink-eyed and puffy and restlessly argumentative, as though he was sickening for something. When he came from school he was calmer and looked healthier, but was quieter too – more self-contained.

Maude felt herself relax. Nathaniel owed her nothing, and vice versa. They were regulated by the decorum of being unrelated; he was closer to being a friend to her, albeit a distant one, since their four-year age difference was an almost insurmountable gulf and he was, after all, a boy. He smelled faintly of shoe polish, stale socks and mint. There was a pause, and then Maude said: 'You'd better not be too late for tea, or my brothers will have eaten everything.' She still hadn't looked up from the journal so she snatched a glance now. Nathaniel was smaller than both of her brothers; he was narrow and supple and his feet looked too big for the rest of him because his shins were razor sharp. His face was pale and nondescript, and thin like the rest of him – especially his nose – but his eyes had something keen about them, some quality that seemed to see more, and reveal less, than other people's eyes. They were dark brown like his hair.

'Hello, Maude,' he said.

'Hello.'

'I thought I might find you here, stuck in a book. Or a very serious journal.' He gave the corner of the page a flick. Maude shrugged.

'There wasn't much else to do today,' she said, in an offhand manner.

'Don't you want to say hello to John and Francis?' he asked. Maude shrugged again, not quite trusting herself to speak. 'Besides, you're just as likely to miss out on tea as I am. And there are crumpets.' All the impossibility of her situation dawned on Maude again, and a tremor went through the journal she was holding before she could stop it. She felt Nathaniel's scrutiny and the slight pressure of his puzzlement. 'What are you reading about, anyway?'

'I'm reading about the British Protectorate of Muscat and Oman,' she said, a touch haughtily.

'Gosh.' He grinned. 'Sounds fantastically dull.'

'Well, it's not, actually. It's one of the hottest places on earth, and it's full of medieval kings and wise men, and villains too; and the women all have to wear masks because they're so beautiful nobody is allowed to look at them. And the people are sailors, just like Sinbad, and the sultan can feed you to his pet lion if he feels like it, and you have to be incredibly courageous to travel there and explore, because the men all carry daggers and will gut you for the merest thing, and there are diseases all around, and wolves, and leopards.'

Maude took a deep breath at the end of this fraught tirade, and saw that Nathaniel was smiling.

'All right, I take it back. It doesn't sound dull at all,' he said. Her brothers wouldn't have conceded defeat. They would have told her what a *fabulous* imagination she had, and wasn't it just *sweet* that she liked to make up such stories. His acceptance took all of the wind out of her sails.

'Anyway, I'm going to go there and see for myself. Once I'm old enough. I'm going to go everywhere, far away from here,' she said. Far away from the ticking clock and her mother's gemstone eyes. The thought was seductive, exciting.

'But you're just a girl, Maude. Don't you want to get married like all the other girls?'

'No! I'm never getting married.' Marriage was a ticking clock and needlepoint – at eight years of age, Maude knew that beyond doubt. 'I'm going to see the whole world. Just you watch.' His look was sceptical, though he didn't contradict her. Suddenly she needed him to believe her; she needed to believe herself. 'I will. Just you watch,' she said again, close to tears.

'All right then,' said Nathaniel. 'I'll tell you a secret, shall I?'

'What is it?'

'That's what I want to do, too. I want to be an explorer.' He lowered his voice and leaned down towards her; the opacity disappeared from his eyes and Maude saw his total belief. She saw a kindred spirit. Suddenly she felt light, and ready to set out; it brought a fizz of happiness. 'We just did all about Lewis and Clark in history, and I realised. I'm going to be as famous as them, and go on journeys every bit as long and dangerous. But I don't think we ought to start with empty stomachs, do you? Come on,' he said, standing up and straightening his clothes a bit. Maude struggled to her feet. He didn't offer her his hand. In these small, subtle ways, he treated her as an equal; and somehow, the fact that *he* had come to fetch her for tea made it the simplest thing that she should go. It made it the simplest thing to greet her brothers, and not mind that they hadn't waited for her before starting.

Muscat and Muttrah, November 1958

After a brief discussion, they decided to take the road to
Muttrah and the army base, around the headland to the west
of Muscat, instead of one of the boats that touted for pas-
sengers along the waterfront. Marian swung it by stating that
she would be taking the car, whatever the rest of them did.
In the late morning light she was as crisp and hard as the
lines between light and shade; her hair was pinned away with
absolute rigour but she'd put her Alice band over it anyway,
as though to guard against the possibility of strays. Her smile
seemed strained.

'I'm really not in the mood to scout for a lift to the barracks
at the other end. I fear my camel-riding days are over,' she
said.

'Oh, but I'd love to ride a camel!' said Joan.

'Tosh – the colonel would send a Land Rover for us; of
course he would. But you needn't come at all if you don't want
to, my dear,' said Robert.

'Well,' said Marian, adjusting one white glove. 'It makes a
change. And it'll be a pleasure to see Daniel.' She didn't sound
convinced, but Joan was too impatient to be off to care. The
car, driven by a thin Omani youth with pinprick eyes and a
sallow complexion, pulled up to the steps of the Residency and
the four of them climbed in.

'We can take a boat out another time,' said Robert. 'Even a
dhow, if you'd like; we could sail down the coast a bit. Sometimes the most stupendous giant rays come up to take a look
at you.'

'Oh, that sounds lovely,' said Joan. 'But Rory gets awfully seasick, don't you?'

'Sick as a parrot,' he agreed. There were beads of sweat along his top lip that Joan wished he'd wipe away. She rubbed her own face in borrowed frustration. He sat wedged against the car door with his shoulders bunched up high.

'Are you all right?' she asked him quietly, as the car pulled away. 'You look a bit . . . odd.'

'It's just this heat.' He smiled, but only briefly. 'I can't seem to get used to it.'

'Well, as long as that's all,' she said, uncertainly; using the privacy of the car as an opportunity to take his hand. 'You mustn't be shy of saying, if you're not well. No false pride, or dignity, or whatever it is men feel they must maintain at all times.'

'Really, Joan,' he said lightly. 'I'm not too proud to admit it when I'm weak.'

'You're not weak. You're just . . . sweaty.' She laughed, and Rory took out a handkerchief to blot his face. He seemed preoccupied, and she got the feeling there was something he wasn't saying.

'Ready to be reunited with your brother?' said Robert, grinning across at Joan. She took a deep breath that almost hitched in her chest, and nodded emphatically.

They wound carefully through the small city, past flat-topped houses and mosques. There were no minarets or domes; little adornment but for some crenellated roofs and graceful *shanasheel* windows here and there, with their shutters and latticework. They went out through the main gate, which was painted white and dazzling, yet to be worn soft by the heat and the wind. The guards kept to the shade inside, their rifles in a neat row along the wall. Outside the city the buildings thinned out towards the barren hills. Joan craned her neck to look for Maude Vickery's house, but couldn't pick it out. Laundry had been spread out to dry on the rocks behind the houses and it almost looked as though the people had simply lain down and vanished from inside them. Joan's eyes were never still; she wanted to see everything, know everything. She stared up into the mountains. They looked nothing like the rumpled cloth of the Alps, or other European mountains she'd seen pictures of. They looked impossibly intricate, sharp and hostile, and the deep ravines between the slopes were choked with boulders and scree.

They weren't toweringly high or majestic, these bare mountains, but they still gave Joan a feeling of being cowed, defeated, just for looking at them – perhaps it was something to do with the suddenness with which they reared up from the flat coastal plain. They seemed to glower. And Daniel was fighting in them – was somehow navigating them, hunting enemies in them.

Jebel Akhdar will be a tough nut to crack, he'd written to her in his last letter; *they call it The Green Mountain. It has a flattish central plateau at about six thousand feet, surrounded by great, pointed slabs, some of them to ten thousand feet, which can only be crossed via one of a few narrow ravines. Think of it like a brick that's been thrust up through a piece of fabric – the torn tongues of fabric remain, pointing up all around the central brick. When we manage to pick our way up a ravine between the tongues – which are the perfect place for enemy snipers to lurk – we merely find ourselves at the foot of a monstrous, unclimbable cliff about a mile high. The imam's fighters laugh down at us from on top of the brick.*

Joan suddenly thought of the time he'd climbed the wall of an old quarry in Derbyshire, where they'd been staying with their grandparents for Easter: his damp frown of concentration, his mouth slightly open, eyes focused only on the next handhold.

It had been past the time when he'd be bossed by her; past the time when she'd had the authority to order him down. By the time he was ten and a half and she was twelve, he'd been the taller of the two, and long before that he'd been the more wilful and bold. She'd watched the muscles of his thin arms stretch and knot, and the trickle of blood from a skinned knee creep slowly down to his sock. The only sounds had been the scatter of loose grit and the scuffing of his shoes and fingers on the rock. Joan hadn't dared say anything in case she distracted him and he fell, and as he'd neared the top, impossibly high, impossibly small and distant, she'd had to shut her eyes and pretend she was somewhere else. She felt his danger as a thundering in her ears, her insides swooping queasily; as though the open air and the deadly drop were beneath her as well as him. Daniel didn't understand her fear, and shook off her grasping fingers when she tried to take his hand afterwards. *I knew I could do it*, he said. *So I did it. If I didn't know I could, I wouldn't.*

The car went slowly up the winding road, kicking up dust, swerving past loaded donkeys and a string of camels that were making their steady way along behind a worn-looking man. Joan had her compact camera in her bag and her fingers itched to reach for it; but she heard the accusation *tourist* again, and hesitated. Robert had told her she could only take pictures from inside the car, because the sultan didn't want his people exposed to technology they didn't need, so it'd be a difficult shot anyway. By the time she'd finally got the camera out and taken off the lens cap, they'd turned the corner and the camels were gone.

'We'll stop at the top and wind down the window for a photo if you like, Joan,' said Robert. 'There's an excellent view of the city and the sea. But you've plenty of time to take pictures.' Joan wanted to ask how long, but she also didn't want to prompt the answer. Their visit was currently open-ended – it had taken so much time and planning to be allowed to come in the first place that apparently no consideration had been given to when they would leave again. Joan thought about Fort Jabrin, and the desert, and had that same hungry feeling. But today she was going to see her brother, so none of the rest mattered for a while.

Muttrah, a tangle of souks, shops and houses, was the commercial centre of Oman as Muscat was the political centre, and sat along a curving bay far wider than that of Muscat. Robert pointed out a whole field full of reclining camels just as the stink of their dung and greasy wool crept into the car.

'They're not allowed any further into town,' he explained. 'So the caravans stop here and unload.' There were a few tents amidst the herd; trails of smoke rose from a few cook fires. The driver paused while Joan took a photo.

'I think they're marvellous,' she said. She looked at Rory, but his answering smile was distracted.

'Best to steer clear of them,' said Robert. 'I've seen a camel bite – not a pretty sight. Look over there – you see the wide gap in the mountains? That's Wadi Sumail. Follow the road through there and you're into the wild, empty desert – well, if you can call it a road.'

'But doesn't wadi mean river?' said Joan.

'It means riverbed, yes, but one that's usually dry. Wadis do flood sometimes, but only at certain times of the year. Wadi Sumail is wide enough that there's plenty of room for the road – and several villages – even when the river is in spate,' he told her. Joan stared at the yawning gap in the cliffs, longing to see the desert at its far end.

The headquarters of the Sultan's Armed Forces was at Bait al Falaj – 'the house of the water channel' – about a mile inland. It was a large, stark compound, fenced in with barbed wire and dominated by an ancient whitewashed fort flying the scarlet Omani flag from its tower. Inside the complex were officers' tents; long, low mud-brick barracks for the rank and file; a few separate dwellings for the senior commanders and a huge, dusty marquee, which Robert pointed out as the officers' mess. Through the open windows of the car came the mineral smell of parched earth and a wave of heat – the camp seemed to be several degrees hotter than Muscat. Beyond the wire was a short airstrip where two Pioneer planes sat idle, their windows cloudy with dirt.

Joan fidgeted as the car pulled to a halt inside the compound. She scanned the features and figures of the soldiers she could see, looking for her brother, hoping he would hear the car and come out to meet them. She would recognise him at once, at whatever distance – a skill honed by watching from the window as a child, particularly during the war; waiting for him to be home from school, home from Scouts, home from a friend's house. Just then she picked up phantom aromas from memories associated with those times – her mother cooking liver and bacon, and jam suet pudding; the fustiness of the living room curtains, dusty in their creases; her father's aftershave, lingering in the hallway after he'd gone out. When it was just Olive and Joan the house seemed too empty and too small at the same time; Joan had always watched for Daniel's return with as much eager anticipation as anxiety.

*

The war had dominated her childhood – both of their child-hoods; though unlike many of their classmates they'd had the luxury of keeping their father at home – his poor eyesight and asthma exempted him from National Service, and he joined the Home Guard instead. Joan and Daniel made new friends as Bedford flooded with evacuees from the south-east, and a group of them had been out picking blackberries one day when a German bomber had flown over – just a single plane, which Daniel identified at once. He'd thrown a stone at it; Joan had burst into tears. Later, she heard that it had strafed a group of innocent farm workers as it passed by. In July of 1942, when four high-explosive bombs obliterated a crisp summer morning, Joan, aged ten, had stayed hidden under the kit-chen table with her mother for hours after the all-clear, too terrified to move. Paralysed by the thought of fire, and falling walls, and choking; breathing in the sharp smell of their own fear. When they finally emerged they fetched Daniel home at once, though the bombs had fallen nowhere near his school. He'd wanted to go and see the craters, the ruined houses, the clouding smoke; he and his friends collected pieces of shrapnel and shell casing with all the zeal with which they'd collected cigarette cards before the war. Joan was mute for three days. She burst into tears on VE Day, too; at the street party she heard her mother say to a neighbour *my poor Joanie's nerves are shot*, and after that she'd tried to put on a braver face. But she had many memories of being hugged to sleep by Olive, in the dead of a nameless night afterwards; rocked in her mother's soft, encompassing arms when some black dream had woken her.

Most of the men she could see around Bait al Falaj, as they climbed out of the car and exclaimed at the heat, were clearly not British. Marian fanned her face with one hand, achieving nothing, and even Joan began to sweat. Flies buzzed around their faces, and they went over to the shade beside the fort, where the falaj was running – one of Oman's ancient water channels; stone conduits leading from springs in the mountain to every village and town, carrying precious, clean water. There they were greeted by a mild, amiable-looking man in his forties, dressed in a relaxed version of British tropical uniform: a khaki shirt unbuttoned at the collar, baggy shorts and a kaffia around his neck to keep the sun off. His shirtsleeves were rolled up and his bare feet were slipped into Omani-style leather sandals, open at the heel. He had a broad forehead, a soft jaw with a cleft in the chin, and a steady expression in his light blue eyes.

'Mr Gibson,' he said, shaking Robert's hand. 'I got your message. How do you do?'

'Very well, thank you, Colonel, very well. You've met my wife, of course.'

'A pleasure to see you again, Mrs Gibson. How do you do?'

'Sweltering, Colonel; sweltering,' said Marian, in cut-glass tones.

'Yes, indeed.' Singer squinted up at the sun, at its zenith. There were no shadows at their feet. 'Mad dogs and Englishmen, eh? Welcome to Bait al Falaj, by my reckoning the most airless place in this whole airless country.'

'This is Joan Seabrook, and her fiancé Rory Cole,' Robert introduced them. Joan shook hands absently, trying to sneak glances past the colonel, looking for Daniel.

'Lieutenant Seabrook's sister; you finally made it.'

'Yes, finally,' said Joan. Colonel Singer smiled, and didn't seem to mind her rudeness.

'He's been distracted all morning, waiting for you. That's his tent, over there – third from the right. Perhaps you'd like to fetch him and then come up to my office in the fort? I'll

have some coffee brought up. You'll go with her, of course?'
He addressed this to Rory, who bridled slightly.

'Go on, go ahead. We won't get a jot of your attention until
you've seen him,' said Robert. Gratefully, Joan set off towards
the tent with Rory half a step behind.

Just before they reached it, Rory touched Joan's arm to slow
her. She looked up at him, surprised.

'What is it?'

'Joan . . . I know he's your brother, but I've known him a
long time, too. Just . . . try not to . . .' He trailed off, obviously
unsure, searching for the right word.

'Try not to what?' said Joan, baffled. 'Embarrass him? Is
that what you mean to say?'

'Swamp him.'

'Well, I'll be sure to do my best; but he is my baby brother,
Rory.'

'I know, Joan. Don't be cross. I just mean . . . remember
where we are. He's at work, that's all I'm saying.' Rory looked
down at her, gingerly, and Joan stared back, hurt, trying to
work out what he meant.

'Really, I don't see why you feel you need to—' She was
cut off by the emergence of a lean, black-haired man from
the tent.

'Can't you two stop rabbiting on for five minutes and say
hello to a chap? Or haven't you come to see me at all?'

'Dan!' cried Joan, and in defiance of everything she threw
her arms around him. There were the hard ridges of muscle
over his shoulder blades and ribs, the unmistakable smell of
him almost hidden beneath the army smells of soap, socks,
canvas and machine oil. He was at once familiar and strange
– she always half expected the skin and bones child he'd been;
her mind always harked back to that short while that she'd
been bigger than him, stronger than him. She pressed her

nose into his collar and took a deep breath. Every feeling he'd ever caused her came on in a rush – anger, fear, amusement, wonder; all the nuances of their relationship, and beneath them the perfectly simple way in which she loved him. For a second she was home – the home of years ago, when they were small and their mother had more light in her eyes, and their father was the sun around which they all revolved, and the whole world and everything she needed lay within the four walls of their practical, unremarkable house. Then the moment passed, inevitably, leaving a nagging sadness at what had been lost as they'd both grown up.

After a few seconds she put him at arm's length again, in case the hug was too much, but Daniel was grinning down at her. The hard Arabian sun got into his eyes – she saw flashes of grey-blue behind the black lashes. The light put slanting shadows beneath his cheekbones and the point of his Adam's apple, and made his face look gaunt. It was a man's face, pared down, with no spare flesh, but he was still beautiful. His front teeth crossed each other slightly, which suited the lopsided way he smiled – his right cheek always lifting more, creasing more, than his left.

'God, it's strange seeing the pair of you here! Where you really don't belong,' he said. He and Rory clasped arms firmly, and clapped each other on the shoulder. 'How are you, Taps? Looking after my sister, I hope?'

'Yes, of course. Not that she needs me too. In fact, it's rather more the other way around,' Rory admitted. 'Is it Taps, still? You're the only one who uses that nickname, you know. Everyone else has moved on.' There was a tinge of grievance in the words.

'I gave it to you, and you'll have it as long as I live. So don't get your back up; just accept it,' said Daniel. It was a nickname that dated from their school days together. All Joan knew was that it was short for tapioca; neither one of them would tell her more about its origins than that. 'Are you staying for lunch? Shall we walk a bit first – perhaps find some shade? It's hotter than hell's breath in the tents.'

'Yes, but you must come and say hello to Uncle Bobby and Marian first, they're up in the fort with Colonel Singer.'

'Are you really still calling him Uncle Bobby, Joan?' said Daniel, amused.

'Well, he still calls me "little Joan".'

'I wonder why.'

Colonel Singer's office was in one of the upper rooms of the fort. Ceiling fans beat helplessly against the heat, the concentration of flies seemed greater, and a young coolie brought in a tray of iced coffee and dates.

'Help yourselves. Unless you're sick of dates already,' said Singer.

'I can no longer stomach the things,' said Marian. 'I used to like them, but one can definitely have too much of a good thing. I've sent home for some Rich Tea biscuits.'

Joan realised suddenly how obviously Marian loathed being in Oman. They talked of the war and of the rebels, who continued to defy the sultan's rule in favour of Imam Ghalib's, from their stronghold of Jebel Akhdar, The Green Mountain. The sheik of the mountain tribesmen, a man called Suleiman bin Himyar, was loyal to the imam, and the mountain was riddled with caves in which the fighters could hide, dotted with villages to feed and shelter them, and crisscrossed by mule trails used to smuggle weapons to them.

'Why on earth is it called The Green Mountain? I don't think I've ever seen a place less green,' said Rory.

'Well, perhaps it's only green compared to the desert, but I'm told it's another world on the top,' said Singer. 'I haven't managed to get up and see it yet – no westerner ever has; but up on the high plateau it's cooler, wetter . . . they grow fruit and crops that wouldn't have a hope down here. They even have gardens.'

'With *grass*?' Marian asked wistfully.

'With grass, Mrs Gibson,' the colonel confirmed with a nod.

'Somehow, we've to winkle the perishers out of this paradise,' said Daniel.

'But . . . I read that the mountain hasn't successfully been stormed since the Persians did it, nine hundred years ago,' said Joan.

'Quite so; but we hope to be the next to. We've just found one possible route to the plateau using some of the steps they cut into the rock up the east face,' said Daniel. He said it calmly, but that determined light was in his eyes, and Joan knew it well. *I knew I could do it, so I did it.* 'It's a pretty stiff climb, mind you, and they do insist on bombarding us from above. And there's no water. We have to carry it with us on donkeys, and there's a limit to the places you can take a donkey . . .'

'The Persian steps are still there? Oh, I would so like to see them,' said Joan.

'You're an archaeologist, I hear?' said the colonel. He scrutinised her steadily, but not unkindly. Joan noticed how rarely he blinked. 'Well, Miss Seabrook, I'm sorry to say you couldn't have picked a worse time to explore the archaeology of the interior.'

'But if the rebels are stuck up on the top of Jebel Akhdar, they can't be much of a bother down here, can they?' she said. Daniel laughed incredulously.

'Joan . . . it's not a bother – we're fighting a *war*,' he said, shaking his head. 'Don't be absurd.' Chastened, Joan sat back. The colonel poured her more coffee.

'I'm sure there are plenty of things you *can* see while you're here, to make it an interesting visit,' he said. 'And there's wonderful sea bathing, of course. But you must already know that the sultan keeps everything about his country very close to his chest, Miss Seabrook. Explorers, observers, sightseers and journalists are not wanted.'

'Much like schools, roads and hospitals,' said Daniel.

'But . . . he must know that's partly why we're here? Didn't you mention it when you applied for permission for us to come, Uncle Bobby?' said Joan. Robert shifted the mass of his body on the hard chair he sat upon, and looked sheepish.

'I did say in my letter not to get your hopes up about that part, Joan. If I'd mentioned you wanted to come and excavate, he'd never have allowed it. Your visit is purely as a friend of mine, and as the family member of a serving officer.'

'But . . . there wouldn't be any digging this time, of course – that would take proper planning, and a whole team, and all sorts of kit. But I did hope we might be able to go out and make some preliminary surveys, and drawings . . . Perhaps if I was able to show the sultan exactly what we planned to . . .' She trailed off as Singer shook his head.

'Out of the question. Quite apart from anything else, the only road to the interior is littered with mines. We've posted askari – loyal local soldiers – right the way along it, but every time we clear it the rebels creep down from the mountain in the dark and lay more. It's our biggest challenge at the moment; we're losing far too many men and vehicles to them.'

'Oh,' said Joan.

'Really, you oughtn't to be here at all, Miss Seabrook. We've had to fib to the other officers about it, and imply that visiting your brother is just a happy coincidence to other business, or they'd all want their wives and sweethearts to be allowed to drop in. Any excursion into the interior would not only be illegal, it'd be sheer folly.' In the lengthy pause that followed, Robert cleared his throat but then said nothing, and from the next room came the sound of a tense phone call in Arabic. 'It's Fort Jabrin in particular you're after, is it?' Singer asked. Joan nodded, hope kindling. 'Yes, I suppose it is quite a nice one. The ceilings are very pretty. Very colourful,' he said. Joan stared at him in mute dismay.

They lunched together in the officers' mess tent shortly afterwards. It was stifling inside even though several side panels had been rolled up to allow any breeze to enter. The air didn't move, though; it lay around the place like an exhausted animal. Joan rolled her sleeves up as high as they would go, and tried to resist the urge to scratch at the sweat along her hairline.

'You should have been here back in July,' said Daniel. 'This is positively chilly in comparison. We had about fifty British soldiers out here; forty-five of them went down with heat exhaustion, including me. Two died of it.' While most of the common soldiers were local, many of the officers, particularly the senior ones, were British – volunteer mercenaries or sent on secondment from the regular army to help the sultan through the current crisis. They seemed vastly tall and strangely pale in comparison to the Omanis, despite their tans. A lot of them had sunburn across their noses and foreheads, and gold tints in their hair; the backs of their necks were livid shades of red and brown, and the smell of them was everywhere – the pungency of hot bodies, not unpleasant. Joan waited in silence for the food to arrive, feeling quiet and heavy with defeat. Even though she'd known the rules about staying in Muscat, and had known about the war, somehow she'd still believed they'd manage to sidestep it all, and make it to Jabrin. To the desert. But Colonel Singer had left no room for manoeuvre, either in his words or his demeanour.

She glanced down the table to where the colonel was deep in discussion with Robert and another senior officer. Singer might not cut the most formidable figure, physically, but he was formidable nonetheless. There was no question of disobeying the man.

'He's as tough as teak,' Daniel affirmed, when she mentioned it. 'Exactly the kind of man you want in charge. Don't look so glum, Joan. I thought you'd come to see me? Now I'm starting to think I was just an excuse to go to this fort place,' he said.

'Of course not,' said Joan wanly. Steaming dishes of spiced crayfish stew and grilled king fish arrived at their table, with piles of fragrant rice and flatbreads.

'Oh my word, this looks delicious,' said Rory.

'Yes, we're not short of good food here. Last time I ate with Robert and Marian it was rather a different story, however.'

'Jabrin. That's the fort I – we – wanted to see. Fort Jabrin,' said Joan. 'But I didn't think any other Europeans had been to it. I thought it was abandoned and . . . untouched. Now Colonel Singer talks about it as though he just dropped by to kill time.'

'Well, it's down near Nizwa, isn't it? There's a garrison stationed there, and several others at key positions near the foot of the mountain. Of course he's been there – he's been pretty much everywhere. That's his job, Joan. We're trying to stop the mine layers, and block all the supply routes up the mountain. There's no way to get a vehicle up there; hopefully, there'll soon be no way to get a donkey up either, and they'll have to send the women up.'

'Why the women?' asked Rory.

'We're not allowed to stop them, let alone search them. Neither are the rebels.' He shrugged, and gave a quick grin. 'It's whackers, but there you go. Every war has its own set of rules. Our biggest problem, after the mines, is water – there isn't any. We roast, climbing in those rocks, and the only water to drink is what we carry with us. We end up with a mule train a mile long, but even they're no good once it gets really steep. I heard a rumour that we might try training mountain goats to carry barrels.' He paused and smiled at his sister. 'Buck up, Joanie. There's no point banging your fists against a locked door. Like Singer said, you're lucky to have made it out here at all.'

There was a trace of impatience in Daniel's voice, and Joan knew her childish despondency was the cause of it. He often managed to make her feel like the younger of the two of them. She ate in silence for a while, as the two men talked of old friends and current work. It was odd to hear Rory's talk about his work at the auction rooms set against Daniel's tales of reconnaissance patrols, air support and ambushes. Rory was obviously at once slightly envious of the rugged dangers of Daniel's job, and keen to imply that what *he* did also took knowledge and organisation. They teased each other jovially, continually; Joan listened and felt herself superfluous, and sank deeper into that same quiet sadness that had dogged her since meeting Maude Vickery. She'd already decided that now was not the moment to ask Daniel what she knew she must, at some point. She didn't want to ruin this first visit, and she felt she needed to be in a better frame of mind for it. After a while the boys seemed to notice her silence. Rory bumped her gently with his shoulder, and offered her another flatbread, and Daniel said: 'How was Mum when you left?' The question made Joan's heart clench. She looked up from her plate, trying to read him. Something coloured the question – that same impatience, and something else – it might have been guilt. At leaving for so long, perhaps, or for only then remembering to ask after their mother. She thought hard how best to answer.

'The same. Well, perhaps a little better. She tries to be better.' There was a stifled silence, full of the frustration of people who care but can't help. 'I don't know what to tell you, Dan. She misses you dreadfully.'

'Does she?' he said tonelessly.

'Of course she does!' Joan steeled herself. The words seem to come out of their own accord, having been kept in for so long. 'She doesn't understand why you don't come home to visit her. And . . . neither do I.'

'She said that, did she?'

'Yes! Well, perhaps not in so many words . . . but it's obvious.'

'Well, you always did only see what you wanted to see, Joan.'

'What do you mean?' she said.

'Steady on, old man,' said Rory softly.

Daniel looked away into the distance, dragging a hand across his jaw. For a long time nobody spoke, then Daniel reached out and squeezed one of Joan's hands between both of his.

'I know you think I've . . . left you to deal with it all,' he said. 'But I've got a job to do here.'

'You get leave, I know you do . . . all soldiers get leave. Would it kill you to come back and see her? You don't know what it's like, cooped up at home with her . . . with her con-stant . . . *mourning*.'

'No.' Daniel sighed. 'No, I don't. But I can imagine.'

'Nothing's been the same since Dad died. I . . . want to get away too. I want to get on with life. But how can I?'

'Of course nothing's been the same,' Daniel said softly. 'And it never will be. That's how life is.'

'Will you go to see her? On your next leave? Please, Dan.' She stared into her brother's silvery eyes, so unlike her own, and tried to hold them. He had never been able to lie to her, and she saw his reluctance to answer at all, though she didn't understand it.

'I promise to try,' he said, at last.

Something had happened between Daniel and their mother while he'd been home on compassionate leave. Something had been said, though Joan had no idea what it was. She couldn't even guess, though in the raw early days after their father's death everything had seemed strange and unsafe. For a short while, for a few odd moments each day, the three of them had become strangers to each other. A misunderstood glance, or action; a spoken memory that nobody else remembered, or else remembered differently. They had all wanted to draw comfort from one another – strength and reassurance – but somehow they hadn't managed it, and failure poisoned the air along with all the grief and the fear. Shortly before Daniel had left, Joan had bumped into him coming out of Olive's room with his face set and his jaw tense, and, shockingly, the glint of unshed tears in his eyes. Daniel never cried. At their father's graveside his pain had scored his face, and made him look old beyond his years, but he hadn't cried. He'd pushed past her without a word, and Olive, sitting up in bed in a quilted cardigan, still surrounded by cards of condolence and damp handkerchiefs, had looked pale and shaken. But pale and shaken was how she'd looked every moment since her husband had died with such sudden violence, and when Joan asked what had happened Olive merely shook her head, and kept her silence. Daniel left them before his compassionate leave was over, which reduced Joan to tears. Then he didn't come home on his next leave either, and whatever Joan said, Olive persisted in her silence on the subject.

Before they set off for Muscat again, Daniel showed them the tent he lived in, which was sparse and well ordered: a bed, a trunk, a desk and chair, a wardrobe and some shelving. Everything practical and unlovely. Joan picked up his red beret and fingered its silver SAF badge of two crossed khanjars. His rifle, pistol and ammunition were carefully stowed, and the sight of them gave Joan a shiver. They were all too real; she couldn't get used to the idea of her little brother handling such things; using them against another human being. He'd been on duty in conflict zones for the past six years, but she still couldn't think of him as a killer.

'What if the rebels come down from the mountain? Shouldn't you have a brick-built shelter, or something a bit more robust?' said Rory.

'Yes, probably. The thing is, the sultan doesn't actually have a lot of money, and we need more men and vehicles more than we need good housing,' said Daniel. Joan scanned the inside of the tent for tokens of home, but there were none. Not even a photograph. 'It could be worse. At least I'm inside the compound. Colonel Singer's bungalow is over there, outside the wire on the other side of the wadi. We had some horrendous rain a few weeks ago and the wadi turned into a torrent. The colonel was stuck over there for two days. He'd just brought his wife over, and there wasn't even any plumbing in the bungalow when he arrived – just a thunderbox in the bedroom.'

'Ugh, poor Mrs Singer! Speaking of which, where is the necessary?' Joan asked.

'You need to pay a visit? Don't use the Elsans, they stink – not that the scorpions seem to mind. Go into the fort and turn right. I'll take you over.'

'No, don't trouble, I'll find it. In this heat I can follow my nose.'

Joan walked across to the dazzling white fort with the first touches of a hot wind whisking the dust away from her feet.

It wasn't refreshing but it was better than nothing, and she took a deep breath of it. Behind her, Jebel Akhdar, The Green Mountain, seemed watchful and malevolent. Joan didn't know much about telescopes or binoculars or the distances involved; she found herself wondering if she could be being watched, from so many miles away, by an enemy prepared to kill. The skin between her shoulder blades tightened, but when she turned the mountain's black-shadowed ravines and precipitous slopes seemed impossibly far away, and she knew she was being ridiculous. Perversely, frightening as it was, she found herself wondering what it would be like to go nearer. It felt like a dare. *I knew I could do it, so I did it.* She brushed the thought aside and heard Daniel's voice in her head, telling her not to be so childish. But she waved at the mountain – a big wave, using the whole length of her arm. She couldn't help herself; it was something she'd done since she was little, something their father had done – whenever a big hill was climbed, or a grand view gazed upon. You had to wave to whoever happened to be in that far opalescent distance; you had to make that connection to the world around you and the other people in it. And if the family was apart they would turn to face home, and wave at whoever had stayed behind. *We waved to you from the top of the tor – did you see us?*

Afterwards, she went back over to Daniel's tent. Robert and Marian were standing by the car, and Robert tapped his watch. She nodded and pointed towards the tent, but as she got close to it, she hesitated. She could hear Rory and Daniel's voices coming from inside, but they weren't chatting, or joshing or even talking seriously. They spoke in strained whispers, and every unintelligible word was wrung tight with stress. In the darkness of the tent, after the bright light outside, their faces were as indistinct as their words. She saw Rory run his hands through his hair, and Daniel standing with his arms rigid at his sides, squared up to her fiancé as though ready to fight him. The sight slowed her steps. She'd never witnessed an argument between the two of them before, not in the twelve years or so they'd been friends, and she couldn't imagine what it could be about. Rory started to say something else but Daniel cut him off dead; they both fell silent, and Joan walked the last of the distance as loudly as she could.

'Dan, I'm afraid we've got to go now,' she announced, just before she stepped through the doorway. Rory turned away and studied the items on Daniel's desk as though there was something fascinating there. Daniel blinked, his face otherwise unnaturally still. Then he looked down at her and smiled crookedly.

'Right you are, Joanie.'

'Is . . . everything all right?' she asked. Rory turned with an odd expression – a wan smile, with tension around his eyes. He walked over to the doorway and proffered his arm to Joan.

'Yes, of course. Why not?' said Daniel. Joan took Rory's arm and looked up at him, and he seemed quite relaxed again, and she wondered if she'd mistaken what she'd seen. The three of them went over to the car, and plans were made for Colonel Singer, Daniel and few other officers to come to dinner in Muscat at the end of the week.

As the car disgorged them at the steps of the Residency, Joan saw a striking figure in the courtyard, watching from the shade of the customs building next door. She recognised Maude's slave, Abdullah, at once. He stood as still and straight as a column and made no sign or gesture, though his eyes followed her every move.

'Who's that?' Rory asked, following Joan's gaze.

'That's Maude Vickery's man. Go in without me; I'll see

what he wants.' Joan crossed to where the old man waited. They were underneath the towering flagpole, and the Union Jack was caught in a gentle breeze, rippling like water. 'Hello, Abdullah. *Salaam elykum*,' she greeted him, using two of the three words of Arabic she had.

'*Elykum salaam*, sahib,' Abdullah replied in his reedy voice, before switching to his immaculate English. 'The lady wishes you visit once more, if it is possible,' he said.

'I . . . of course. Of course I will, if she's asked for me,' said Joan.

'She asks.' Abdullah turned as though to walk away.

'Hold on, please – when should I go?'

'When it pleases you, sahib.' He inclined his grizzled head.

'Tomorrow then? I'll come tomorrow.'

'*Inshallah*, it will be so.'

'Abdullah, I wanted to say . . . Miss Vickery told me of your . . . position. Do you know, you've only to touch that flagpole to be free. Any slave may do so. It's . . . legally binding,' she said hesitantly. The old man's eyes traced the length of the white pole to squint at the flag against the incandescent sky. Then he looked at Joan again, and she thought she saw the ghost of a smile on his face as he turned and walked away.

By night the boats jostling in the harbour were all but invisible, pulling silvery snags in the water's surface, flicking in and out of sight as stray fragments of light from the town found and then lost them again. Invisible beyond the harbour walls, a navy frigate was at anchor. Its commander and other officers were inside now, drinking whisky with Robert, smoking cigars and talking about things that didn't concern tourists. Now and then the rumble of male laughter came out faintly through the walls. Joan was down near the water level in front of the Residency, leaning over the low railings and listening to the gentle slap of the sea. Jalali, the prison fort, was a vague, bulky outline against the sky, with no lights lit. She was tired – the heaviness of it dragged at her body – but felt wide awake. At first she thought it was her excitement at being invited back to see Maude Vickery again – and she *was* excited, almost enough to offset her disappointment that Colonel Singer had been to Fort Jabrin, and that she would not be going. But it was the argument she had half-seen, half-heard, between Rory and Daniel that her mind kept turning over. She hadn't misread it; she was sure. She imagined a few possible causes for it as the moon rose, baleful and smudged in the gauzy sky, and the wavelets washed in, over and over, and the boats appeared and disappeared. Finally she went back inside, and up to the top floor.

Even though the corridors were silent and empty, Joan still hesitated, jittery with nerves, as she reached the top step. She should wait until morning; it would be outrageous to be caught, at this hour, going into Rory's room. But she didn't want to wait until morning, and she knew she wouldn't sleep until she'd spoken to him. As quietly as she could, she made her way to his door, knocked softly and then slipped inside before she heard an answer, because giving him a bit of a fright was preferable to being caught outside. She thought at first he was asleep and dreaming – there was movement and soft sounds coming from the bed against the far wall.

'Rory? Are you awake?' she whispered. Lit only by the moonlight she saw the movement stop, and then Rory sat up with a start.

'Who's that?' he barked.

'Shh! For heaven's sake, be quiet! It's only me.'

'Joan! Dear God, my heart nearly stopped,' he whispered.

'What was all that wriggling about?'

'What? I wasn't . . . What's wrong? Why aren't you asleep?'

Joan went over to the shutters, opened them a crack to let in more moonlight, then sat down beside him on the edge of the bed. Rory let the sheet fall to his waist; she knew he preferred to sleep naked, especially in the warmth of Arabia. The thought of it was distracting.

'I couldn't sleep,' she said. 'I've been outside, actually, watching the water. Anyway . . . I wanted to ask you about something.'

'I hope you weren't smoking outside. The last thing we need is you getting arrested.'

'At least if I did I'd get to see inside a fort – even if it's only Jalali. Rory . . . what were you and Daniel arguing about today? Before we left?'

'What? We weren't arguing,' he said, and she knew from his stagy tone, if not from the evidence of her own eyes, that he was fibbing.

'Come on, Rory. Whatever it is, you can tell me. I won't be upset. You know I love you both.'

'Really, it was nothing, Joan. Nothing whatsoever for you to worry about.' Somehow, his false tone, the careful too-lightness of it, made her more anxious.

She scrutinised him in the half-light; he emerged in more detail gradually as her eyes adjusted. His hands were in his lap, fingers laced; his shoulders were a wide span against the wooden headboard of the bed, chest dark with tightly curling hair. His eyes were inscrutable, lost in shadow; his skin had a faint sheen to it. She looked down along the length of him, to his broad feet where they poked out from under the sheet.

'Daniel has always confided in you. I know he tells you things he doesn't tell me,' she said softly. 'And that's fine; and perhaps it's how it should be. I'm only his sister. You're his best friend.'

'He adores you, Joan. You know he does.'

'I know. I do know.' She reached out and took one of Rory's hands, lacing her fingers into his. His palm was clammy. 'Did he . . . did he tell you whatever it was that happened between him and Mum that stops him coming home? I think they fell out over something.'

'No. No, Joan, he didn't.'

Joan stared hard at him. She wished she dared switch on a light to see him better.

'Was it about me, then? I mean, about us? About the wedding?' And immediately, she knew she was right. Rory's jaw tightened and his eyes slid away from hers. He ran the fingers of his free hand along the edge of the sheet, and she sensed he wanted custody of his other hand too. She held it tighter. 'Rory,' she whispered, feeling her pulse jump in her throat; 'do you still want to marry me?'

'Joan . . .' Rory turned back towards her, and swallowed. 'Oh, Joan, of *course* I do! I don't know how you could doubt it – why you felt you needed to ask!'

He pulled her hand, pulled her closer to him. Joan twisted her body, put her legs up on the bed beside him and curled herself against his chest in that comforting and forbidden way. Tentatively, she put her hand flat on his stomach. His was the only body, other than her own, that she had ever touched in this way, and the differences between the two of them never failed to fascinate her. She wanted to know every part of him; she moved her hand to the arch of his ribcage.

'It's just . . . been such a long time. That we've been engaged, I mean; and such a long time since we've even discussed actually setting a date.'

'Well, since your father's death . . . I thought—' Rory's voice broke slightly. He cleared his throat; his tongue clicked against the roof of his mouth and both sounded dry. 'I thought we'd discussed it, and agreed. Your mother needs you at home for the moment, and a wedding will be far more fun when the ... shadow of grief has passed. And we need time to save up. For the wedding we want, and the sort of home we want to buy ... There's no point buying a bedsit only to have to move as soon as the first baby comes along – not if we can get what we need from the start.' As he spoke, his voice gained in conviction.

'Yes, I know all that. I just ... I get so fed up, being at home with Mum. I want the rest of life to start sooner, I think. Sooner than we might have said before.'

'Joan ...'

'Don't you just long to be married? I mean ... to be together as man and wife? I do.' She felt the rise and fall of his ribs beneath her cheek; heard the rush of his breath.

'Of course I do, Joan. I ... I thought you wanted to wait, that's all.'

'So we'll set a date soon?'

'Yes. Soon, I promise. Let's discuss it in front of the calendar as soon as we get home.' He kissed the top of her head; she felt the heat of his mouth and something stirred inside her, deep down.

'Was that what the fight was about? Was Daniel pestering you to make an honest woman out of me?'

'Daniel ... only wants what's best for you,' said Rory, and Joan smiled.

'He's so cross with me so much of the time, I sometimes forget that's true.'

'Well, it is true. It really is.'

'Thank you, Rory. Thank you for coming out here with me. I'm not sure I'd have come if you'd said no, and ... and I'm so glad we're here,' she said. Rory kissed her hair again.

'You're welcome,' he murmured indistinctly.

*

She stayed a little longer, as the low burn of her desire soft-ened, and turned drowsy. Then she kissed his mouth, and felt how all the tension had gone from his body, and noticed how wonderfully familiar the smell of him was, and the taste. His lips were soft, every bit as soft as her own. Eventually he got up and checked that the coast was clear before she slipped out of his room.

'Perhaps,' she whispered, from the threshold, 'perhaps this will be the last ever November fifteenth you'll spend a bachelor.' She smiled at him, but it was too dark to see his expression. Sometimes, her love for him went through her like a wave.

'You can count on it,' he said. 'Now go to bed, wicked temptress.'

Wicked temptress. Joan smiled to herself in her empty room. She didn't think of herself that way; that wasn't how things had gone between her and Rory at all. Instead, their coming together had been as slow and sure as two trees steadily entwining their branches. He had been Daniel's friend to begin with, made in the maelstrom of the first week of big school.

Their father had put aside money since Daniel's birth to send him as a day boarder to his own alma mater, St Joseph's Hall, saying that the five years he'd gone there had been some of the happiest of his life. Joan had to be content with the local girls' grammar; and she was content, being more far more interested in ponies than school. Rory was a day boy too, and he and Daniel had bonded because the full-boarders treated them as outcasts. He'd come to stay with them in the Christmas holidays – a big, clumsy boy of eleven, already a full head taller than Joan's brother. Joan had been not quite thirteen but was feeling very grown up. She'd thought nothing of her brother's curly-haired friend other than that he had a soft smile that kindled the impulse to hug him.

After that he became a fixture in Daniel's life, so he became a part of Joan's too, in the drab aftermath of the war when everything seemed to smell of brick dust, the food was awful and Joan's headmistress routinely wept for her lost sons during the hymns in assembly. Seven years went by, until Rory was eighteen and Joan was almost twenty, before she started see him as more than just Daniel's friend, more than just her friend. Altogether more. On the night of her university graduation they drank too much and walked the streets as a colourless dawn broke and bleached the sky, glancing at one another with the startled pride of people who've been up all night; laughing because it seemed such a wild thing to do, and their tiredness made everything surreal. In the end they found a taxi to take them back to Joan's digs, and in the musty back seat, where everything was grey and dank, Daniel fell asleep between Joan and Rory, slumping slack-jawed against his sister's shoulder. She felt Rory cover her hand on Daniel's arm with his own. He leaned across his friend, reached for her and kissed her, and it was the most natural thing in the world that he should do so. The kiss was soft and lingering. The taxi jolted through a pothole and they bumped their chins on the top of Daniel's head, and as they laughed their hands stayed locked together on his arm.

Joan woke late to find the sun hidden behind thick clouds; the air was warm, still and humid.

'Might it rain?' she asked Robert, as she ate a hasty breakfast on the terrace. He looked slightly green, and was swigging at a bloody Mary with a grim determination.

'It might. Are you going out?'

'Back to Miss Vickery's, remember?' Robert grunted, and

gave a nod. There was no sign of Marian that morning. Rory was facing out to sea in a deckchair, reading a three-day-old newspaper. 'What will you do while I'm out?' Joan asked him.

'What you observe is the sum total of my plans,' he said with a smile. 'It is Sunday, after all. I wish you'd let me go with you, though. You really oughtn't to walk about alone.'

'Nonsense, I'll be fine. Enjoy your newspaper.' She kissed him lightly on the cheek and made her escape.

The walk to Maude Vickery's house had none of the overwhelming portent of the first time she'd made it, and it felt easier to be invited rather than grudgingly granted permission to go. Joan's steps were light, and she greeted Abdullah with a cheery smile that he didn't return. He was as immovable, as unreadable, as ever; so ponderously so that Joan wondered if she'd imagined his slight smile of the previous day.

'Should I go straight up?' she asked him.

'If it pleases you, sahib,' he replied, with a stiff incline of his head, and Joan realised that, subtly, Abdullah was showing her greater respect than before.

'Is that Miss Seabrook? Come up, do,' Maude called from upstairs. A good deal of the filth had been cleared from the ground floor and stairs of the house. The tang of ammonia still hung in the air but now there were traces of incense smoke veiling it. A window or a door, Joan couldn't see which, had been opened towards the back of the house, so that a shaft of daylight lit the gloom, and a column of fresh air moved steadily up the stairs with her as she climbed.

The two salukis were asleep in their bed by the wall, just as they'd been before. Maude was sitting nearer to her desk this time, and there were papers and pens scattered over it as though she'd been working on something. The ring with the blue stone, which Joan had been so forcefully forbidden to touch, was in exactly the same place in the pencil tray. It seemed that Maude wouldn't touch it either. In the colourless light of the cloudy day she looked older, her face and hair taking on a lifeless hue.

'Are you writing another book, Miss Vickery?' said Joan, once they'd exchanged a polite greeting.

'No. Well, perhaps. I was considering writing my memoirs. But there's so much, you see; and so much of it such a long time ago. I hardly know where to start.' She smiled briefly. 'Perhaps it's irrelevant anyway, except as a vanity project. I'm sure nobody would read the thing if I did write it.'

'Of course they would! Especially if you wrote about your crossing of the desert. People . . . a lot of people don't know you did it, you see, since you've never written about it fully.' Maude nodded, but said nothing. Her mouth was a tight, flat line. 'I was wondering . . . why that was?' Joan asked cautiously. 'Why you never wrote about it, I mean.'

'Well,' said Maude. She took a sharp breath through her nose. 'There was hardly any point, having come second to that Elliot man . . . Who cares about the runner-up? History doesn't. Never has,' she said. 'So people don't know who I am any more, back in England?'

'They do. I do, don't I? And please do call me Joan.'

'Very well, Joan. People still mention me? And write about me, when they write about the history of Arabian exploration?'

'Of course,' said Joan, after a moment's hesitation. The lie was a small one, and a kind one. In truth, outside certain very specific circles, Maude Vickery had passed almost wholly into obscurity. 'You were the first woman to cross it, after all . . .'

'And do they write of Nathaniel Elliot?'

'Well . . . of course. He's still very famous. He was one of the greats.'

'Was? Has the man died?' Maude asked abruptly.

'No. But he's retired, of course. He must be over eighty by now . . .'

'He turned eighty this year,' said Maude.

'Of course. I forget how well you knew him. You were friends – childhood friends – weren't you? I read that he was almost a part of your family. Are you still in touch?'

'I have not seen or spoken to that man in nearly half a century.' Maude's tone was clipped. 'He's retired, you say . . . I can't quite imagine that. I can't imagine him ever stopping.'

'Well, perhaps the time comes to all of us when it's wiser to . . . slow down, somewhat.'

'Well, we'll see how keen you are to accept that when the time comes to you, Joan,' said Maude tartly. 'Anyway, I didn't invite you back to talk about Nathaniel Elliot.' Her tone brooked no argument. 'Be a good girl and move me over to the sofa, would you? Then you can sit where I can see you.'

Carefully, Joan manoeuvred Maude's chair away from the desk. She'd expected it to be heavy, but it wasn't. Close to, Joan saw even more clearly that Maude was skin and bone, with the fragility of a bird. She noticed a scar on the back of Maude's neck, near her hairline – a strip of silvery skin about the size of a finger, and puckered like a burn.

'Gosh, how did you get that terrible scar, Miss Vickery?' she said, and straight away knew she'd been rude. There was an awkward pause before Maude answered.

'That?' she said. 'The Bedouin branded me. It hurt like hell.'

'They *branded* you? That's barbaric! Why on earth would they do that?'

'Oh, they were only trying to help. The Bedouin cure all kinds of things with a good branding – from toothache to the evil eye. I think they thought I was possessed, at the time.' Her tone was light but studied; something darker crept in at its edges, making Joan too uneasy to ask anything more about it, however curious she was. Abdullah brought in a tray of mezze to go with their tea, but Maude barely glanced at it. 'So, Joan, have you been to visit your brother?' she asked.

'Yes; yesterday, in fact. It was so wonderful to see him, though it wasn't for long enough.'

'And how did you get on with persuading them to take you out to Jabrin?' Maude sounded amused, but not in an unkind way.

'Entirely as you predicted, Miss Vickery.' Joan couldn't keep the despondency from her voice. Maude chuckled.

'Oh, dear girl, don't look so downcast. Jabrin was never going to give you what you want.'

'Yes, you'd told me as much. I suppose I'd still hoped that there might be a way,' she said. Maude grunted.

'There's always a way. You know what the rules are, now, and what's permitted. The question is, if you've got your heart set on the place, are you going to let any of that stop you?'

Joan waited a moment, trying to read Maude Vickery. The old woman's face had come alive; her eyes were alight with mischief.

'I . . . I have no choice but to let it stop me,' she said at last. 'Even if it weren't for Sultan Said's restrictions, nobody will take me. The only road to the interior is littered with land mines. The army were my one hope, but Colonel Singer says—'

'Yes, yes, I'm sure they've all told you it'll be quite impossible. Plenty of people told me that crossing the Empty Quarter was impossible too. They told me a woman could never dream of doing such a thing. They told me I would die trying.' Maude poked the arm of her chair with one index finger, marking each point with a tap of her fingernail.

'Yes. I do see what you're saying. But, surely, since there's a war going on . . . You yourself told me—'

'Pah! Not much of a war, from what I hear.'

'And . . . you did have some help, after all.' There was a stony kind of silence, which Joan scrambled to fill. 'I mean . . . you had the Bedouin to guide you, and . . . and an idea of the path you ought to take. Nathaniel Elliot had done it before you, and . . .' She trailed into silence, because some violent emotion had filled Maude's face; every muscle beneath the skin had gone rigid apart from a tiny twitch at one corner of her mouth. The silence grew and grew. Joan fidgeted under that terrible glare, until she realised, a few seconds later, that Maude was no longer looking at her at all. Her eyes were fixed on something long ago and far away. After a while her lips moved silently, shaping words that Joan couldn't read.

Eventually, Maude blinked and looked away towards the window. Her hands curled around the arms of her wheelchair, gripping and releasing, gently flexing. She took a few slow breaths.

'What day is this?' she said.

'It's Sunday, Miss Vickery,' said Joan carefully.

'I thought so. It's been nearly fifty years since I went to church, but I can still tell when it's Sunday. It still feels different.' She sighed, and took a sip of her tea. 'I miss going to church. The comforting ritual of it, you understand? There was something so *English* about it all – seeing your neighbours, singing the familiar hymns, having sherry and a roast lunch afterwards. I even miss our freezing little church down in Lyndhurst, and our vicar, who had the face of a cherub and tried to give hellfire sermons to compensate.' She sighed again. 'I sometimes can't believe that it all happened in one lifetime.'

'Well . . . we could say a few prayers together, if you like?' said Joan dubiously. She herself hadn't been to church since the previous Christmas, and then only because she liked to sing carols. Her mother's gentle Anglican faith hadn't stood a chance against her father's staunch atheism. When Joan was little he'd urged her to make up her own mind, but she'd known the conclusion he'd wanted her to reach, and reach it she had.

'Prayers?' Maude shook her head, slumping a little lower in her chair. 'I can't pray. I can't go to church. Never again.'

After that, Joan visited Maude every day. She went early, before whatever activity or outing she and Rory had planned; or at teatime when they got back, to tell Maude all about it. The old woman soaked up Joan's news hungrily – details of Muscat and Muttrah, of the sea traffic and the army base, of the people who came and went from the Residency – and Joan began to wonder how long it had been since Maude had ventured outside.

'We could go out for a walk, if you like?' she suggested one day, Maude smiled and looked longingly out through the window for a moment, but then she sighed.

'I don't think so. Thank you.' She paused, her chin sinking to her chest. 'I can't ever go back, you see – to the mountains, or the desert. Sometimes it's better not to see what you cannot have. It only makes the wanting worse.'

'Yes; I understand,' said Joan, thinking of the forbidden landscapes she saw every day from the Residency; the hungry, desperate feeling they gave her. Maude looked up with a strained smile.

'Your stories are enough. So, speak on.' She nodded at Joan's left hand. 'Tell me about that ring; or rather, the fellow that gave it to you.'

So Joan told Maude all about Rory and how long she had known him; how he had grown into adulthood with her, and into love. She talked about his kindness, his reliability, and how he didn't appear to have a temper to lose. She talked about his work at the auction house, and how one day the firm would belong to him. 'So you'll remain in Bedford, then? Once you're married, I mean?' said Maude, watching Joan closely.

Yes,' she said. 'Yes, I suppose so. After all, where else would we live? It's always been home.'

'Where else, indeed. Two years is a long engagement.' It was a statement rather than a question, but Joan rushed to explain.

'Well, we've been saving up, you see. We were nearly there, but then a year ago we lost . . . my father died. It really put everything on hold. Mum couldn't cope, and . . . well, she still can't, really. And then I lost my job.'

'But you can't stay with her for ever, surely?'

'No. No, I hope not.'

'It isn't a question of hoping, Joan. You must decide, and act,' Maude said firmly. 'It can be hard, I know. Family ties are . . .' She shrugged. 'Tenacious. I had nothing whatsoever in common with my own mother. She had no idea why I wanted to live the life I did, and I had no idea how she didn't simply die of boredom, living the life *she* did. Perhaps she did, in the end. Back then I had no choice but to be dutiful towards her, but I always hated that sense of being held back. I came to resent her terribly. Sounds awful, but there you go.'

'Well, I don't resent Mum, I love her and I do want to be a good daughter, it's just . . .' Joan searched for the words. 'I don't know. I know she'd far rather have me at home, so that's always at the back of my mind. Making my decisions for me. She says she couldn't cope without me, and perhaps she's right. I suppose she'd be very lonely if I left, and that makes me feel rotten.'

'It sounds to me like she ought to get out and make a few

friends. And she'll only know if she can cope without you if you let her try.'

'I know. I do know. Only . . . until Rory and I buy a place, there's really nowhere else for me to live, anyway. He still shares a house with his parents and his sister. Rory says . . .' Joan trailed off, embarrassed. Maude's gaze was shrewd, and even to her own ears it all sounded like flimsy excuses. 'He says it doesn't make sense to waste our money on rent.' For a moment she suffered under Maude's scrutiny, but then the old lady shrugged again.

'Well. He's probably right.' She settled back in her chair; hands in her lap. 'I shall have to meet him, at some point.'

'Oh, yes! I'd love you to. I really can't wait to be married, and to start a family.' She said this with as much conviction as she could, unwilling to let on that the idea of a baby made her nervous. She simply didn't feel competent enough, or old enough, though other girls from her school already had two, or even three. She'd decided it was a result of staying too long with her own mother, and hoped that becoming one herself would make her feel like more of an adult, and more sure of herself. 'It's going to be such an adventure,' she said, when Maude remained quiet. The old woman scrutinised her.

'An adventure? Yes . . . I suppose it will be,' she said eventually. 'Not one I ever undertook.'

Equally, when she was out and about with Rory, Joan told him all about Maude. One day, to her delight, they hired camels and rode along the beach at Muttrah. After all her years of riding, Joan adjusted easily to the exaggerated rocking motion, letting her spine absorb the movement. Rory sat stiffly, swaying, off balance, and found it wildly uncomfortable. Smiling, Joan held the reins in one hand and rested the other on her thigh. She thought about the Arabian horse, Aladdin, who had made her dream of one day riding in this very place.

It had seemed such an unobtainable fantasy. For a while she was silent, letting the wonder of the moment sink in.

'If you think you're uncomfortable,' she said, turning slightly in the saddle, 'you should try kneeling, like the Bedouin do. Even Maude couldn't master it.'

'Well, if even the amazing Maude Vickery couldn't do it, I won't even try,' said Rory, mildly nonplussed. Joan grinned at him. He rubbed at his face and then sneezed convulsively, three times in quick succession. 'I think I'm allergic to camels,' he said, dropping his handkerchief as he tried to blow his nose with one hand.

'Poor Rory. Not too much further,' said Joan, and he smiled fondly at her.

'We'll go on as far as you want, Joan.'

At the end of the week, Joan went along to Maude's house, excited to tell her about Daniel coming for dinner at the Residency the following night. Abdullah let her in with a frown, which Joan didn't understand; she assumed it was aimed at her for some reason, until she got upstairs and found Maude in a frantic state. Books had been pulled from the shelves and were scattered across the floor; the desk was awash with papers, many had sifted onto the floor, and Maude was out of her wheelchair, crumpled amongst the mess, searching impatiently through journals clearly decades old.

'Miss Vickery – whatever's the matter?' said Joan, shocked, crouching down beside her. Maude barely looked at her. Strands of her hair had fallen over her face; she had a scrambled look, and Joan was cautious, remembering her temper.

'I can't find the wretched thing,' Maude muttered. 'I *know* it's here somewhere!' She picked up another journal, flicked impatiently through a few pages and then threw it aside.

'Let me help you up, then you can—'

'Don't paw at me, girl! I know it's here, and I *must* find it! He wrote about purity . . . was it purity? Or truth? He wrote . . . he wrote . . . I can't remember exactly, you see. I can't remember.'

'Who wrote what, Miss Vickery?'

'Nathaniel Elliot! Who do you think? I know it's here somewhere. I read it, I'm sure I did . . .' Steeling herself, Joan took one of Maude's agitated hands and held it still.

'Miss Vickery, *please*. I'll help you look; I promise we'll find it. Let me help you up now, and we'll have some tea.'

Maude was breathing hard, and Joan felt a shudder go through her. Her eyes still darted over the mess she'd made, but she let Joan help her up and edge her, slowly, back to her wheelchair. Joan straightened her skirt for her, then moved the chair a little, turning it away from the mess.

'Offering me tea in my own home now, are we?' said Maude, at length. Joan smiled.

'Sorry,' she said. 'But I'm gasping.'

'Abdullah will bring some. I'm sure he's listening – he always is.'

'He was worried about you.' She looked over her shoulder at the scattered papers and magazines. 'If you tell me what you're after I'll keep looking, if you like.' But Maude sighed, and shook her head. Now that the mania was passing she looked tired; defeated.

'Perhaps it doesn't matter,' she said. 'He once wrote that the desert is the world without men – before them, after them; it gives them no significance, offers no deference. He wrote that one can discover there as pure a truth as man can hope to realise. Or something like that,' said Maude. 'I can't remember the exact wording. But he was right, you see. Right, and outrageously wrong at the same time.'

'I don't understand.' Joan shook her head. Maude was

gazing through her, absently, and didn't reply. 'Was it definitely in a journal? Do you remember which one?'

'He carried on, you see. After we crossed the Empty Quarter he carried on exploring, and travelling; he went everywhere, just as he always said he would.'

'I've always wondered why you stopped, Miss Vickery? Or did you carry on?' She was excited by the thought, and had a sudden vision of helping Maude to write her memoirs after all. 'Did you carry on travelling, and just not write about it any more?'

After a moment in which she gathered up some of the journals, glancing at their faded covers, Joan looked across at Maude. Her expression was intense; hard and haunted. Joan stopped what she was doing.

'Something . . . something happened to me,' said Maude softly. 'Out in the desert. I lost a part of me . . . or perhaps it died. Perhaps a part of me died. Do you see?' she said. Joan shook her head.

'No. I'm sorry; I don't understand. What happened?' She went back to Maude's side.

'Perhaps if I went back I'd find it again. Be whole again. But no; I can't go back, not now. Not ever again. I'll die like this, here in this room.'

'Please don't cry, Miss Vickery, or I will too – I always do. Won't you tell me what happened?' said Joan, hating to see tears shining in Maude's eyes. Maude wiped at them hurriedly, as if she hadn't realised and was ashamed. She took a few breaths; pressed her lips together and patted Joan's hand.

'Tell me, Joan, would you call yourself a steady sort?' she said.

'I . . . well, yes I suppose so.' Joan thought of her mother, saying that her nerves were shot. She thought of her father, telling her to be brave. 'Although I don't know exactly what you mean,' she added. Maude was silent again, for so long that Joan wondered if her attention had strayed. But then she curled her hands over the arms of her chair and cleared her throat.

'I wonder if I might ask you to do a favour for me, Joan?'

'If it's in my power, Miss Vickery, then of—'

'Only it must remain secret. Utterly secret; even from your fiancé, and most definitely from anybody else at the Residency. Can you do that?'

Maude was completely serious, and Joan felt wary at once. She paused in silent indecision for a moment, with no idea what Maude could possibly ask. She hated the idea of lying to anybody, but underneath that her curiosity was alight. Almost everything about her visit to Oman up to that point had felt somehow slightly *less* than she'd hoped for; she'd felt *herself* to be slightly less than she'd hoped for – which was to say, just the same as she'd ever been. Only Maude made it extraordinary, something beyond the mundane and the expected. Hard on the heels of her wariness came the excitement of a secret, which, after all, was not the same as a lie; and the pleasure of being needed, trusted, by Maude Vickery. She thought about what else her visit was likely to hold: seeing Daniel, feeling loved but superfluous to his life; watching Marian drink and the boats come and go in the harbour; dinners here and there, and sea bathing; taking photos of camels, and maybe a trip out in a dhow. Tourism. That was all there would be, if she let it. Her mouth had gone dry, but she knew what she wanted to say.

'All right,' she said, meeting Maude's eye. 'I can do that.'

'Good girl. I need you to do something for me, and it's terribly, terribly important.'

Egypt, April 1895

The hotel in Cairo had a vast central courtyard, open to the sky. Around it, clusters of silk damask divans and armchairs were arranged beneath the colonnades. There were vast potted palms and aspidistras; and red lilies with waxy green leaves so dark they were almost black. There was a fountain in the centre, where water spouted from lions' mouths into a pool full of pale, whiskery fish that idled in circles from dawn till dusk. Every afternoon, at four o'clock, the guests took tea under the colonnades. Servants stirred the sludgy air with long-handled fans made of woven palm fronds. Silent waiters with white gloves brought out silver cake stands laden with finger sandwiches and petit fours, and Maude was disappointed because she didn't want high tea in Egypt to look the same as it did in Hampshire, and she didn't want to dine every night with the other British guests at the hotel. She wanted to sleep out in one of the pyramids and meet the ghosts of ancient pharaohs. She wanted to ride across the desert with the sun setting over golden sand, and wear veils, like Scheherazade.

It was April and Nathaniel was with them for an extended Easter break. Elias Vickery never batted an eyelid about bringing him along on any of the trips he planned for his own children, and the expense was absorbed without mention. The Vickery family had been wealthy for so many generations that no one but Elias knew exactly how much money they had, or where it had come from in the first place. The Vickery children, of course, never questioned it. Nathaniel had come from his mother in France, and had spent the first week in silent distress, refusing to explain or talk about the visit at all. He'd slept a great deal. Maude had watched him closely and seen the gradual way he returned to himself, like seeing the green return to a winter-bare tree. His shoulders relaxed down, his head came up. Colour returned to his face, and that keenness to his eyes, and then he found his voice again. Questions and musings and stupid jokes with the boys. The first time he'd laughed uncontrollably, at some pratfall of Francis's, Elias had patted his shoulder and smiled. Maude knew the smile – it was the one that said silently *well done*. She'd wanted to congratulate Nathaniel, though she couldn't say exactly what for. She'd wanted to hug him, but since she never had before she couldn't find the courage to, in the end.

During the heat of the day, Maude spent a good deal of time reading, or practising her Arabic with the staff. Francis and Nathaniel were seventeen, and allowed to go off and do things with their father. They were full of themselves; brimming with talk of going up, of friends and dances and wagers, always trying to sound like adults when it was the childish things in life that still delighted them. Maude was supposed to stay and keep her mother company, since Antoinette Vickery would be alone in Cairo for the latter part of their tour, when they would cross the desert to the Oasis of Siwa. Maude was in such a fever of excitement and anticipation over the coming adventure that she actually couldn't sit still, and burst up out of her chair at random intervals, making her mother gasp with shock every time.

At thirteen, Maude thought she was more than old enough to determine for herself what she should do, but her father, Elias, had decided, so that was that. Her eldest brother, John, was climbing in the Alps with a group of friends. Antoinette Vickery had brought her needlepoint with her, and several novels; she rested a lot, still blaming the fatigue of the journey eight days after their arrival, and had made friends with a stout lady from Esher called Mary Wilson. Sometimes, Maude found herself watching her father for signs of exasperation towards her mother, because exasperation was what she herself increasingly felt. Her days were defined by Antoinette's need for rest and peace. Maude was supposed to keep her company, but since Antoinette was largely silent Maude experimented with following the servants around and pestering them to speak Arabic to her, and was satisfied that her mother scarcely noticed her absence. But Elias was only ever kind and gently solicitous towards his wife, so Maude felt slightly ashamed of her own occasional urge to tip Antoinette out of her chair.

There was no way Maude would be left behind when they went to see the pyramids though – and the sphinx, peeping coyly out of the sand at Giza. Even Antoinette came, though she didn't once dismount from her sideways perch on her mule, and she didn't seem in the least bit astonished by the ancient monuments. The others all rode horses – Maude protested vociferously when, at first, a donkey was brought out for her to ride. The guide looked at her in surprise when she stated, in halting Arabic, that she would take a horse – a full-sized one. He looked closer at her, and she guessed that he'd taken her for a much younger child. It happened a lot.

'The donkey suited you better, Scrap,' said Francis, grinning.

'The donkey reminded me of you, Frank,' she retorted frostily. They set off before sunrise, under a sky the colour of pigeon feathers, as the last stars died and the muezzin cleared their throats to call the city to prayer.

They rode out from the city in single file. Maude watched the far horizon, and then, as the pyramids came into view, she pretended that she was the first person ever to see them, and was coming upon them across miles and miles of empty sand, all alone and awestruck. In this daydream her companions faded away. They stopped at the top of a gentle slope with a good view of the monuments, and stood with their horses shoulder to shoulder as Antoinette caught up with them, her sleepy mule lead by a servant on foot.

'Well,' said Francis, looking across at Nathaniel and Maude beside him. 'Who's for a race? I bet a shilling I can make it to the base of the great pyramid before either of you.'

'No thanks,' said Nathaniel. He rode uneasily, with his feet too far forward, his weight too far back and his reins too long.

'Must *everything* be a competition, Frank?' said Maude. 'Anyway, it's wrong to gamble.'

'What's up, Mo? Scared you'll lose?'

'You've the better horse,' Nathaniel pointed out. Beyond him, Maude saw her father listening intently. He was always listening, and watching. He liked to let them follow their ideas through to conclusion, and only then would he comment. When Antoinette protested some plan of theirs, he told her that this was how a child learned.

'It's not all about the horse, not on this terrain. It's about the horseman.'

'Or horsewoman,' Maude pointed out. Sometimes, she hated Francis and his stupid grin – usually because she was the butt of it. She'd have quite liked to tip him off his horse, which was dark brown and lively and had a slightly demented look in its eye. One hearty thwack across its behind with her crop would be all it took, she thought.

'You're game then, Midget?'

'Francis, you will not address your sister that way,' Elias interjected. Maude stared at her brother for a heartbeat, then another; she didn't blink, so she saw his hands tighten on the reins, and saw him draw breath. She put her heels to her horse and it startled into life at the exact moment he yelled: '*Go!*'

There was a shriek from behind her; Maude looked back over her shoulder and saw Antoinette's mule trotting sideways, jerkily, unwilling to be left behind. Her mother grabbed wildly at its stubby mane. Nathaniel's horse was also following at a loping canter, gathering speed; Nathaniel hauled at his too-long reins, his expression shocked. She turned her attention to the front. Francis was off to one side, rapidly eroding her early lead. His horse was younger and fitter than Maude's, but Maude weighed almost nothing, and her mare skipped lightly across the sand. The air and the horse's long mane whipped at her face. She crouched low; tears streamed from her eyes and her hat flew off, the pins pulled from her hair. Then, straight ahead, she saw a patch of deeper sand – a soft ridge with no gravel or rocks; she was aware of Francis veering left to go around it, and she heaved on the right rein to go around the other way. Above the thunder of the wind she thought she heard another shout from behind her but she didn't dare turn to look. She caught the edge of the soft sand and her mare staggered slightly, sinking in too deeply, struggling to prevent their forward momentum sending them into a cartwheel. She sat back and hauled on the reins to slow down, to get the mare's weight back, angry at the thought of Francis winning. With a scramble and an explosion of sand they were through it, back on firmer ground, and the mare accelerated with an angry buck, laying back her ears as if as frustrated as Maude at the delay.

Then Nathaniel's horse came past her on her right, galloping flat out. The stirrups flapped against its sides, and the saddle was empty. Maude turned back to look but her hair was in her eyes so she couldn't see clearly, and there was no sign of Nathaniel. Francis had almost drawn level with her, even though he'd obviously lost more time in the soft sand, and Maude felt desperate that he might come past them and win when she was so close. She gritted her teeth and then, unable to keep it in, yelled loudly at her horse. 'Come *on*!' She gave it a thwack behind her leg with her crop and the mare bucked again, grunting crossly, but then stuck out her nose and found even more speed, her feet rattling over the pebbles. The landscape blurred; only the vast pyramid ahead told Maude which way to ride. She lay close to the horse's neck; sweat bloomed through its coat beneath her knuckles. When the ancient stones were blocking out the sky Maude sat up and they wheeled about; she saw Francis coming up fast, not more than thirty feet behind her. But she'd won, by a clear margin. 'Ha!' she shouted to her brother, as he pulled up. 'You owe me a shilling, Francis Henry Vickery!' Their horses were blowing hard, pulling at the reins to stretch out their necks. Francis shook his head.

'That was a blatant a false start, Mo. You were off before I said go. You cheated, so it doesn't count.'

'Oh, you *always* do this, Frank!' She was furious; she wanted to hit him. 'I did *not* cheat, and it *does* count! I went *as* you said go!'

'No, you didn't—'

They were still bickering about it as Elias rode up to them at a steady trot, his face stony.

'Children,' he said, and they were silenced at once by his tone. 'Have either of you stopped to wonder about Nathaniel? Or even tried to catch his horse?'

'Oh no!' said Maude, remembering the empty saddle with a flood of guilt.

'Oh no, indeed,' said Elias.

'Is he all right?' said Francis.

'No, he is not. Perhaps you might have thought to ride to one side, away from the other horses, before taking off like that? Perhaps you should have noted that the ground was uncertain, and dangerous to ride across at speed?' He stared at each of them in turn and they stayed silent, ashamed. Francis's face flamed red. 'We think Nathan has broken his wrist in the fall.'

'Oh, no! Oh, don't say so, Father!' Maude cried.

'But can he still come to Siwa?' said Francis.

'That remains to be seen. But it seems unlikely, wouldn't you say? Now, the pair of you go – calmly – and fetch the loose horse back, and I don't want to hear another word from either of you about who won or lost that little escapade. As far as I am concerned, you both lost.'

They didn't stay to explore the pyramids that day, but rode slowly back with Nathaniel, who was pale and silent and cradled his left arm in his right. Once a British doctor had been to the hotel to splint and bandage his wrist, Maude went in to see him. He was sitting in a wicker chair by the open window of his room, which looked out over the chaos of Cairo's rooftops. He was still pale, and his face looked clammy, but he smiled slightly as Maude sat down opposite him.

'I'm so sorry, Nathan,' she said awkwardly. 'We should never have just charged off like that.'

'Well,' said Nathaniel. He smiled sardonically, but there was anger in his eyes. 'Far be it for me to hold a Vickery back from doing what*ever* they wanted.' Maude blushed. She thought that was unfair, at least on her, but she couldn't bring herself to say so.

'Francis says I cheated, so it doesn't count that I beat him. Whenever I do better, he finds some reason why it shouldn't count, or isn't the same, or something. It's so unfair!'

'Perhaps you shouldn't always rise to it when he challenges you, then. Because you always do.'

'You're right. I just . . . I can't seem to help myself. Just once, I should like to win at something and have him be unable

※ 94 ※

to discredit it in any way!' She shook her head, crossly. 'Will you still come with us to Siwa? Do say you will.'

'I don't know. If it still hurts this much in a few days' time . . . I don't see how I shall be able to ride. Let alone unsaddle or put up a tent.'

'Oh, but the servants can do all that for you! They shall have to do it for me, after all.'

'Yes, but you're a *child*, Maude. You're expected to be useless.'

Maude looked down at her hands in silence for a bit, trying to decide if she was more angry or hurt by his words. When the boys had been thirteen, they'd gone on and on about how grown up they were – how they were nearly men, and needed no help or guidance. Now they were seventeen and she thirteen, she was still a child, expected to be useless. She would never catch up, she realised. She could not win that race, and would always be *Scrap*. Frustration made tears prickle the top of her nose. Being told off by her father was bad enough, but combined with Francis being hateful and Nathaniel being angry with her, it was too much.

'But it won't be the same if you don't come,' she said, and was dismayed to dissolve into sobs. She struggled to stop but couldn't.

'Oh, I'm sure you don't need me,' he said coldly. 'Not now you're fluent in Arabic, and your father's so proud of you, and Francis has his place at Oxford despite barely being able to write in English, let alone in Latin. I don't see why you should need *me* at all.'

'Don't talk like that, Nathan.' Maude looked up at him, shocked enough by the bitterness in his voice to stop crying. 'Don't. You sound as though you hate us.' Nathaniel glared at her for a moment but then his face softened, and he sighed.

'I'm sorry, Maude. Don't listen. It's not your fault, really.'

'Please say you'll come. We *do* need you, really. I do. I won't have any fun if you don't come. Not one bit.' It was only as she said this that Maude realised it was true. She felt better when Nathaniel was around. Better about what, or better in what way, she couldn't quite say; just better. Nathan fiddled with the edges of his bandage for a moment. 'Does it hurt very badly?' Maude asked, looking guiltily at the bound wrist.

'Of course it hurts!' he snapped. His skin was taking on a greyish hue, and his eyes looked too bright in comparison. 'Sorry,' he added.

'Perhaps you ought to lie down?'

Nathaniel nodded, and didn't protest when she offered him her shoulder to lean on as he rose. If he'd put any real weight on her she'd have collapsed, but he didn't. Maude felt the shape and warmth of his good arm through the fabric of her dress. She held his hand and saw smudges of ink on his fingers; the nails were cut very short, and his knuckles had faint red bruises which could have come from the fall, or from something else. The smell of him was so very familiar to her, and somehow soothing and enlivening at the same time.

A week later, with his injured arm in a sling and with the use of a mounting block, Nathaniel was deemed fit to ride. They'd taken coaches along the coast road to the start of the Stable Road, south across the desert to Siwa Oasis. It was the route Alexander the Great had taken to consult the Oracle of Amun – Maude had read all about it, and it was largely due to her repeated suggestions, which Antoinette called *clamouring*, that they had chosen that particular route. It was an established path, and though the road was unmade it involved no deep dunes or soft sand, so they could take horses and pack mules rather than camels. Maude had liked the idea of camels, so was a little disappointed about that, but only a little. Nothing could detract from the thrill of the journey, and the fact that Nathaniel was coming with them after all. She almost forgot to wave to her mother as they left her at the hotel in Cairo, 'alone' with her new friends and around thirty servants on hand. The journey to Siwa from the coast was planned to take them a week. They would rest at the oasis for up to five days, and then ride back again by the same route. However much she clamoured, Maude could not convince her father that they should tackle the longer route, eastwards through the desert, all the way back to Cairo.

During the subsequent days' travel they settled into a steady schedule. They were woken at six in their tents – Maude shared a tent with her father – by the servants, who brought them cups of hot coffee. By seven they had washed and brushed and dressed, and eaten the breakfast that was prepared for them – fresh flatbreads, eggs and cheese, more coffee, and dates. They helped to tack up their horses, and packed their personal items into duffle bags while the servants struck the tents, folded up the camp beds and tables and chairs and blankets, and loaded the pack animals. By eight, their little caravan was ready to set off. Their clothes were soon dusty, as was their hair and skin; Maude was tired because it was cold at night and she struggled to keep her small body warm enough to sleep, but she was deeply, profoundly happy. She felt the vastness of the desert and the heavens, and watched the way the spring sunshine changed the colour of the sand and sky throughout the day. She did not miss home, or her mother, or the comforts of Marsh House. She didn't miss John, and even Francis couldn't spoil her enjoyment. She could not hear the ticking clock, choking time – not at all.

They rode, stopping for lunch and afternoon tea, until about an hour before sunset, at which time they found a sensible place to camp and the servants got to work unloading and assembling everything again. One afternoon, when the others were still finishing lunch, Maude rode on ahead for a while. They'd hired experienced trail horses that knew the drill and did not expect to be asked to deviate from it in the least bit, so she had to kick her horse rudely to get it to leave the others. Eventually, she'd put enough distance between herself and the group that she could no longer hear their voices, or the clatter of the coffee pot. She rode on further, up a shallow slope and through a deep depression littered with rocks, and up another rise, where she halted. At once, she felt a peculiar sense of stillness, of absence from herself. It took her a few moments to identify the source of it.

There was no hint of a breeze. Her horse stood still beneath her, and wasn't winded. Her own breathing was quiet, almost inaudible; behind that was utter, total silence. In that precise moment, Maude realised that she had never heard silence before. There had always been the clock, or the servants moving around, or their voices; the wind outside or the rain, or the house creaking as it warmed or cooled. There had always been *something*, however subtle. This was completely different. Maude sat stunned, and listened. Gradually she became aware of the hugeness of the earth, and its incomprehensible age. She learned, finally, how small she truly was, how fleeting. It was beautiful, and not at all disheartening. Quite the opposite – she finally felt that she knew who she was, and she knew her place, and she felt totally at peace with both. She felt she could go anywhere, and do anything; she felt the world turning, peace-fully, resolutely, unendingly. The silence was like a magic spell; it seemed to promise infinite time in which to do all the things she wanted to do. Maude sat on her horse, and absorbed it, and fell in love. When she heard her family and their entourage approaching, the silence slipped away as softly as ice melting, and she knew at once that she would seek it out again. That she would always seek it out.

They reached Siwa just as they'd planned to, on the eighth day out from the coast. They were stiff from so long in the saddle, gritty under their collars and cuffs, and proclaiming loudly the need for baths and comfortable armchairs.

'I'm just *dying* for a smoke,' Francis declared, with extravagant ennui and carefully out of their father's earshot. Nathaniel caught Maude's eye and she burst out laughing before she could stop herself. 'What?' Francis demanded, suspiciously. 'I'm just glad we've arrived. Even you have to admit, Scrap, that one bit of desert looks much the same as the next. It all gets rather dull, rather rapidly.'

'I think you ought to try opening your eyes, Frank,' Nathaniel told him, and Francis scowled.

'Well, at least we managed to get here without you falling off your horse again, I suppose,' he said.

They spent the next few days exploring the oasis on foot – the ancient city of Aghurmi, now abandoned, and the new city of Siwa that had sprung up to the south of it; the large salty lakes with their mysterious islands; the date palm groves, olive orchards, gardens and goatherds. Maude followed her father around faithfully, making notes and sketches in her notebook, practising drawing simple maps and posing as patiently as she could for the lengthy spells of time it took Elias to set up his camera, adjust it and take photos of her in front of interesting views or monuments. Francis came down with a stomach upset, and spent the whole of the third day scooting to and from the privy. Maude tried, with limited success, to feel any sympathy for him. On their fifth and final morning, she woke early in the house where they were lodging, and dressed herself in silence. She took a handful of dates from the kitchen, drank some water, then slipped out as quietly as she could, into the smeary grey light of pre-dawn.

The air was chill, as still and scentless as stone. Maude left the new town and wound her way through the cluttered streets of ruined Aghurmi. The remains of its walls and towers stood against the sky like the bleached trees of a dead forest; a few paths twisted through the rubble, and it was too early for snakes or scorpions. The city climbed up a slope and stopped at the foot of a striated mesa of rock, growing up from the ground like a bizarre mushroom of some kind. Carefully, Maude climbed up to a narrow ledge that ran around it. The stone felt friable and treacherous. A layer of grit came away at her touch, and she wondered how big it had once been, and how long it would be until the desert winds wore it out of existence. She edged along slowly, with her arms out for balance and a knot in her stomach in case she should slip, round to the north-east side of the rock. There she planned to stop, enjoy the silence and watch the sun rise. As she rounded the bend and came towards the place she'd planned to sit, she stopped with a gasp. There was somebody there already – sitting just as she had planned to, with his back to the rock and his knees pulled up. A second later, she recognised Nathaniel.

Maude smiled, and went to sit next to him. She thought to say: isn't it a strange coincidence that we should both have the same idea, and choose the self-same spot to sit? She thought to say: have you noticed the silence? Isn't it wild, and amazing, and utterly wonderful? She thought to say: I wish we didn't have to leave this place, but at the same time I want to go on, and keep travelling, and see more. She thought to say all of these things, but she said nothing. Nathaniel looked across at her without surprise or rancour. He shuffled along to make more room for her at the ledge's widest point, and in silence they watched the sky change colour. It went from grey to a chilly turquoise green, and then almost to white before it turned gold and red and orange as the sun burst into the sky. As one, they raised their hands, and shielded their eyes. A soft breeze came to hum in their ears, and gentle sounds of life drifted up from Siwa; the silence of the desert could not survive so close to civilisation. But still, the moment was long, and serene, and very nearly perfect. And there was nobody else in the whole world, Maude realised, who could have understood it and shared it with her the way Nathaniel did.

When the sun was a hand span above the horizon, Nathaniel took a deep breath. 'I suppose we ought to go down,' he said. He rested his chin on his good wrist and looked at her, smiling easily. 'This is the way, isn't it, Mo?' he said. 'This is how it ought to be.'

'Yes,' she said at once. She felt some important realisation, some huge truth, hovering just out of her reach, just slightly beyond her understanding. She reached for it for a moment, struggling, but the more she did the more it slipped away. 'Yes,' she said again, simply. He offered her his good hand to help her up; they brushed the dust from their clothes and carefully made their way down without another word. From then on, everything that had made up Maude's world since her birth – the familiarity of it and all its rules and safety and security, seemed childish, and stifled, and bound intolerably by the ticking clock. She knew that the second she left the desert she would begin waiting to return to it.

Muscat and Muttrah, November 1958

Joan sat down for dinner opposite a man with scruffy dark-blonde hair that needed a cut. She'd thought the army had rules about that – Daniel and the other British men she'd seen at Bait al Falaj had very severe haircuts. She liked seeing the vulnerable white skin around their hairlines when it had just been trimmed, behind their ears and at the backs of their necks. It reminded her of when Daniel was small, and she'd washed his hair with a jug over the kitchen sink, both of them standing on stools. The blonde man had combed his hair back, but bits of it kept falling forward. He was tall and solidly built, and had brown eyes that swept up and down the room as if looking for an escape. Then he seemed to come to some conclusion and relaxed, looking across at her with a smile. He held out his hand.

'Hello there, we didn't get introduced at the gin and lime stage. Captain Charlie Elliot.'

'Joan Seabrook. You must be one of the new arrivals,' she said. She'd lost track of what Robert had been saying about the new squadron that had arrived – her mind kept shifting stubbornly back to Maude, and to secrets. It kept returning, as persistently as fingers to a snag in a smooth surface, to the favour she'd agreed to do for the old lady.

'That's right. We got here a few days ago. I thought there was a war on, but instead here we are,' he said, grinning amiably. 'Dining with the upper echelons in this grand palace.' He tipped his glass to her and then took a large swig. Joan smiled uncertainly.

'Oh, we're not so very upper. Not me, anyway, I'm an archaeologist; at least I hope to be. But really I'm here to see my brother, Lieutenant Seabrook.' She looked down the table at Daniel, who was deep in conversation with Marian and a barrel-shaped man she didn't know. Next to him, Daniel looked as lean and hungry and a wolf.

They were in the dining hall at the Residency – a long room with an elaborately tiled floor and tall windows facing the sea. The electric lights overhead made it slightly too bright, and too warm. There were no shadows, and hard reflections flattened everyone's eyes. Behind the blonde man was an open window, through which Joan could see Fort Jalali. There was a single lamp burning above the door that faced the harbour, lighting the narrow stone steps cut into the rock that ran up from the causeway. They looked steep, and daunting. There could be no possible way to go up them without being seen. Joan stared, and thought about what she had agreed to do, and shivered with a feeling that hovered, in near perfect balance, between excitement and panic. It spoiled her appetite so she took a mouthful of wine instead, and tried not to stare too fixedly at the fort. After a while, it began to feel as though the fort was watching her.

'How long have you been over here?' Charlie asked her.

'Oh, only about ten days. Just long enough to get my bearings, really. To visit Daniel, and somebody else here who I'd wanted to meet for a very long time. But not long enough to go outside the city, other than to the army base.'

'Well, isn't that about the size and shape of it, for foreigners over here?' he said.

'Yes. So I'm told.'

'Spoken like a person who doesn't necessarily like or believe what they're told,' he said, smiling.

Joan shrugged one shoulder. 'I may not like it, but I have

little choice other than to believe it. And to be bound by it, sadly. There's an important old fort I was hoping to see, in the desert down near Nizwa, the other side of the mountains. But it will be quite impossible, apparently. Unless you manage to storm the mountain and end the war inside the next two weeks. So there we are. And what about you? Where have you come from? You look very tanned. All of you Air Specials do.'

'Special Air Service. SAS – far easier to remember and to say. We've just come from Malaya.'

'Gosh, this must be quite a change of scenery.'

'Yes, rather less jungle here,' he agreed. 'In fact, it's a bit ruddy bleak, isn't it? Between you and me, I'm hoping we can knock this little insurgency on the head quite quickly. It shouldn't be too difficult – I hear they're rather rustic, armed only with donkeys and antique Martini Henry rifles. I doubt they'll know what's hit them. So don't give up hope of seeing that fort just yet, Miss Seabrook.'

Joan looked at Charlie Elliot. He sat with his forearms resting on the table, slouching, but that couldn't disguise a certain poise that suggested he wasn't half as relaxed as he was pretending to be. He tore off a chunk of flatbread before the rest of the food had arrived and began to eat it with a kind of studied disregard for proper form that Joan thought was fake, too self-conscious. His hands were strong, and scarred; he wore the cuffs of his shirt unfastened, though his collar was buttoned right up and his tie was immaculate. He had the air of a slightly rebellious schoolboy, cocky enough to need to step out of line, to seek attention and raise eyebrows. But then, when he looked right at Joan, she could see the intelligence in his eyes, and the sparkle of amusement, and she wondered if he was merely entertaining himself, perhaps at her expense. The young man to Joan's left grunted at Charlie's words, and shook his head.

'It never does to underestimate an enemy,' he said seriously. 'It can come back to bite you.' This man had a thin face with a dour expression; deep lines ran across his forehead and between his brows, as though he was permanently ready to frown. He didn't look as though he'd ever laughed. Charlie sighed theatrically.

'Joan, have you met Walter Cox?' he said. 'Also known as Smiler.'

'Hello, Walter,' said Joan. The wine felt hot in her empty stomach, and she was starting to enjoy herself more. Walter nodded gravely as he shook her hand. 'So, what's *his* nickname?' she asked, nodding towards Charlie Elliot.

'Oh, he doesn't really need one,' said Walter, giving Charlie an unreadable glance. 'We sometimes call him Daddy.'

Charlie smiled, which creased his cheeks and put a slight dimple in the right one, making him look boyish, though Joan guessed his age at past thirty.

Daniel had told her that this body of men, the newly formed SAS, were a special task force; highly trained, highly lethal, drafted in by Colonel Singer to help break the stalemate on the mountain. He'd thought for a moment, before adding: 'I've never seen anything like them, actually. They're the most calmly efficient professional killers I've ever encountered.'

Joan was having trouble reconciling the grey-faced Walter and the raffish Charlie with that description; but then, she already had enough trouble picturing Daniel as a killer – and he had killed men, she knew it; if not yet in Oman then during earlier postings. Taken aim, fixed them in the sights of a gun, fired. It helped when he called them *targets*, or *the enemy*, but they were men. Men and boys, a lot of them probably younger than Joan was now. The magnitude of that was hard for her to comprehend, so she usually didn't try, putting it out of her mind; but now and then it occurred to her and gave her the unsettling feeling that nothing she knew was quite real. Or rather, that she didn't know anything, particularly men, at all – her brother included.

'Don't mind Smiler,' said Charlie, as their food arrived. 'He takes combat very seriously, like he takes the rest of life. I prefer to laugh at it.'

'So who is the better prepared for the mission?' she asked.

'Oh, we both are, don't worry. It's only a question of personality,' said Charlie.

'So when it comes to the actual fighting, you're as serious as Walter is?'

'Absolutely,' he said, and smiled again. 'Deadly serious.'

For a while, Joan chatted to the lady on her right, the wife of a senior officer in the Muscat Regiment, about the awful effects of the hard Omani water on skin and hair, and whether Joan had seen *Gigi* at the pictures before she'd come over. And all the while she heard Charlie Elliot's voice, just slightly louder than all the others at her end of the table, and just loud enough, when he laughed, to be heard throughout the room, above the general hubbub of conversation. She stole a look at him during one outburst: he had slumped back in his chair with his chin tucked into his chest, and laughed with unguarded abandon and his eyes shut.

She looked past him, and caught Rory's eye down the table, rolling her own eyes fractionally. Rory gave her a quizzical look, and a slight smile.

'So, Miss Seabrook, tell me about this friend of yours in Muscat,' said Charlie, suddenly, and she hoped he hadn't seen her mocking expression.

'My friend?'

'Yes, you said you'd been to see—'

'Oh, yes. Of course. Well, she's not quite a friend. Not yet, anyway. She's more of an idol of mine. You've possibly never even heard of her, but Maude Vickery was one of the first great female explorers, in the early years of the century. Well, she was one of the first great explorers, male or female, really, and—' She broke off, piqued because Charlie was grinning again, his eyes dancing. 'Have I said something funny, Captain Elliot?'

'No. Well, inadvertently, perhaps,' he said. He sat forward, leaning towards her on his elbows. 'You see, my father is Nathaniel Elliot. So yes, I have heard of Maude Vickery.'

'Nathaniel Elliot? Not *the* Nathaniel Elliot?' she said, not hiding her amazement.

'The very one.'

'And *that's* why we call him Daddy,' said Walter, at her side. 'Because he can't get through a single conversation without mentioning him.'

Joan stared for a few seconds, experiencing the exact same feeling of surreality as when she'd first seen Maude. 'Oh, please don't hero-worship him now,' Walter murmured plaintively. 'He'll be unbearable.' Joan shut her mouth, which had dropped open.

'You've heard of him, then?' said Charlie, more soberly.

'Yes, of *course* I have. That's really quite astonishing...' said Joan. 'And what a barmy coincidence that I should meet you here, having just met Miss Vickery. I mean, we were only talking about your father yesterday, she and I. Isn't that just *peculiar*?'

'I can't imagine she had many nice things to say about him. But he's a good old stick, whatever she says, he really is.'

'I had rather wanted her to say more about him, since they were so very close at one time. But she doesn't seem to want to talk about him at all.'

'She's jealous, that's the trouble. She just couldn't get over the fact that he beat her across the desert. They turned it into a bit of a race between them, you see. And he won, simple as that. I doubt she'd have made it out without Dad's tracks to follow. She ought to have been happy just to have done it – it was no mean feat for anyone, let alone a woman.'

'Yes, let alone a woman,' said Joan drily. 'Your father's just turned eighty, is that right?'

'I missed his birthday party.' Charlie nodded. 'He'll forgive me, though. Duty called.'

'Are you his youngest?'

'Yes. There were six of us – five boys, one sister.' He glanced away around the room again, just as he had as they'd taken their seats. Looking for the way out. 'There are just two of us left, now. Jemima and me. My parents have had rotten luck keeping us alive.'

'Oh, I'm so sorry. That's dreadful,' said Joan. She thought at once of the roar of a plane in a summer sky, and her headmistress sobbing during the hymns in assembly. Charlie drummed the fingers of one hand on the table top, and fidgeted in his chair, saying nothing, his eyes roving the room, and Joan turned to Walter and asked him about his family, his upbringing, his hobbies; anything to release Charlie from their scrutiny while he gathered himself.

After dinner, the men retired together to one room, the women to another, just as they might have done a hundred years earlier. There were only three other ladies, and Joan sat on the terrace with them for a little while. They talked of home, and of their children, and Joan contributed little.

'I say, did you meet Captain Elliot?' she tried at one point. 'Do you know who his father is?'

'Yes, that famous explorer chap. I met him at a Foreign Office do in London once, years ago; and very charming he was, too. A touch aloof, but very charming. And isn't his son a *handsome* devil?' said the officer's wife, who'd sat next to Joan at dinner.

'The boy you were sitting opposite, Joan? Yes, very handsome,' said Marian.

'He's hardly a boy,' said Joan.

'My dear, when you get to our age . . .' Marian smiled vaguely. 'He has quite a way with the ladies, I hear. I'd be careful around him if I were you, Joan.'

'I hardly need to be careful with Rory here,' she said. Marian's smile faltered ever so slightly, but then she nodded and looked away.

'Of course. Silly of me to say,' she said. They returned to subjects Joan cared little about, and she sat quietly for a while, sipping her coffee, looking past them at the huddled bulk of Jalali until she could stand it no longer, and excused herself.

Restless, she went down to the room where the men were crowding the air with their cigarette smoke and the rumble of their voices. From the darkness of the corridor, Joan peered through the doorway. Robert, Colonel Singer and the SAS commander, Lieutenant Colonel Burke-Bromley, were struggling to talk through their mirth. Walter was sitting in silence at the end of one sofa, and at the other end Rory and Daniel were side by side, talking quietly. Joan's heart leaped up to see them together; she hadn't seen them talk earlier in the evening, and she'd worried that things were still frosty between them after their argument.

She'd wanted to talk to Daniel about it but hadn't managed to get him by himself. She wished she could go in and sit with them now, and join in their talk, but it just wouldn't do. She felt like a child, forbidden to join the grown-ups. She watched them for a minute or two, hoping to catch Rory's eye, or Daniel's, hoping to coax one of them out to talk to her, and was about to give up and go to her room when a voice behind her made her jump.

'So, who are you spying on?' It was Charlie Elliott. He spoke close to her ear – too close. She stepped back and trod on his foot. 'Ow! Watch where you trample.'

'Sorry! Well, actually, I'm not. You shouldn't have crept up on me like that,' she said. He'd been completely silent on his feet.

'I wasn't creeping, only walking.'

'And where have *you* been, anyway? Nosing about?' She thought of his roaming eyes at dinner.

'To the lavatory, if you must know.' He shrugged, the light from the doorway dividing his face into two.

'Oh. Sorry.' She was glad of the darkness to hide her embarrassment. 'I wasn't spying, not really. I was trying to catch Rory's eye to say goodnight. I was about to give up, actually.'

'Well, why don't you just go in and say it?'

'I can't! Not with all those men . . .' She stopped, feeling foolish. Somehow, she couldn't imagine Charlie Elliot understanding the idea of shyness, and she hated that she still let it dictate to her. Still, the thought of walking across that room, and of all their eyes turning to her, was excruciating. 'It isn't important, anyway. Goodnight,' she said, ruffled, and walked past him.

'Wait, Joan,' he said, catching her arm gently. She looked up at him crossly; his over-familiarity made her feel even more like a child.

'What is it, *Captain* Elliot?' But her pointed tone only made him smile more.

'Rory's the big chap with the curly hair, on the sofa?'

'Yes, that's right.'

'What is he to you? If you don't mind my asking, that is.'

Charlie released her arm, he was blocking the light from the doorway now; a tall, rangy silhouette.

'He's my fiancé. Why do you ask?'

'Your fiancé?' Charlie folded his arms, pausing for a beat. 'What a pity. Hold on here, I'll send him out to you.' With that, he turned and went into the room.

Early the next morning, Joan turned from the mirror and waited as Maude appraised her with a squint.

'Not bad,' said Maude eventually. 'More kohl around your eyes though, and smudge it about. Don't be pretty with it; you're not trying to look like a film star, you're trying to look like an Arab servant who's been up since dawn, cooking and scrubbing.' Joan was dressed in a long black robe – an abaya – that covered everything from her hairline to her heels, fitting tight to her forehead like a nun's habit. Abdullah had brought in the outfit, draped over his long arms, his face entirely expressionless; if he had any opinion of her mission, he gave none of it away. There was a black mask as well, with a pointed nose-piece, so that only her eyes would show in the end. She had seen Omani housewives go about their business in this attire; she'd noticed that their costume allowed her to gaze at them with impunity, there being no way to know whether they noticed her scrutiny, or minded it. She thought it was a curious effect, given that the garb was designed to hide a person. She turned to look at the outfit in the mirror again. 'Preposterous, isn't it?' said Maude. 'How on earth they get anything done in that get up, I've never known. But then, they're not meant to get much done, I suppose. You won't catch a Bedouin girl tangled up in all that fabric. They have too much to be getting on with.'

'Handy in this instance, though,' said Joan. Her voice

sounded too bright, almost brittle. Her hands were shaking and she gripped the fabric in her fists to hide it.

'Now, I've heard you speak a few words of Arabic, and I think the best thing will be for you to say nothing whatsoever,' said Maude baldly.

'Right you are,' said Joan, deflated.

'Now, don't sound so crushed, Joan. I'm only stating facts and thinking of the best way to proceed with this endeavour. One must know one's limitations. Show them the letter, let them search the basket; they'll take the money, and then you carry on. They'll either let you in, or not. Hopefully, they will. Your hands are too pale; keep them tucked away. Do your best, and do *try* not to tremble so. Although, I suppose it's not unreasonable for a person to tremble, going into such a place.'

'Is it very . . . bad?' said Joan.

'Yes. It is very bad.'

'What if they don't believe me? If they don't believe I'm Omani, I mean. I could get into so much trouble.'

'They're not allowed to touch you. Even that low-life gaoler won't. And there are British guards in there too, remember – full of honour and decency, I'm sure. The only way they'll find out who you are or where you're from is if you strip off your veil, or start gabbling in the Queen's English. Do neither of those things and it will all go entirely smoothly.'

'There are British guards too? But . . . I didn't know that! Oh, God, if they realise . . .'

'Nonsense. How will they?' Maude dismissed her with a wave of her tiny hand.

Joan still couldn't believe she'd agreed to Maude's request – to go into Jalali and visit one of the inmates there – Abdullah's son, Salim. Most of the inmates weren't allowed visitors at all, but political prisoners were permitted to have their servants bring them extra food and clothing.

'So he's not a . . . a common criminal then?' Joan had asked.

'Certainly not,' said Maude, affronted. 'He's a political thinker, and that's all it takes to get you into trouble around here.'

'He said something to upset the sultan?'

'Sultan Said is an easy man to upset.' Salim had been arrested and incarcerated over a year before. He'd had no trial, and been given no idea of the length of his sentence. He was to remain entirely at the sultan's pleasure, and wouldn't be the first man to be forgotten about, and left to rot. Family members were certainly not allowed to visit him, so Joan, disguised as a servant, was their only hope. The problem was that with the exception of Colonel Smiley, as chief of staff, foreigners were expressly forbidden to enter Jalali. Joan didn't like to think what would happen to her – or to Robert – if a guest of the wazir was caught breaking that rule. But she'd agreed because she'd been flattered that Maude would even ask her to do something so dangerous, and so important. She hadn't wanted to disappoint her, or herself. If she was to be more of a person; if she was to be more than a tourist and less confounded all the time, she would have to find the courage to break the rules now and then. And the injustice of Salim's incarceration was blatant.

She took a deep breath and let it out slowly, fighting to calm her nerves. Her throat was completely dry, and her body felt so watery-weak with fear that she was on the brink of backing out altogether. She crouched down beside Maude's chair as the old woman put the mask over her eyes, fastening it to the edge of the abaya. 'There. Now look at yourself. Your own mother wouldn't know you.' Joan stood in front of the mirror. With all the kohl around them, her eyes were a dark obscurity behind the mask. Without her hair, without her nose or mouth or the shape of her face, she could have been anybody. She relaxed slightly.

'All right,' she said, taking another deep breath. Her voice was muffled by the fabric; she swept it up with one hand so she could talk. 'All right. By the way – speaking of parents, you'll never guess who I met yesterday.'

'You're right, I shan't guess. Who?'

'Charlie Elliot, the youngest son of your old friend Nathaniel. He's come with some special army squadron that's just arrived to help fight the rebels. Isn't that remarkable? Doesn't it just go to show what a small world it is we live in?'

Joan ran her hands down the front of the black robe, smoothing the slubby fabric. After a moment, she noticed Maude's silence, and turned to her. The old woman was staring into nowhere, as Joan had seen her do before. Her face was immobile but two points of colour had bloomed over her cheekbones, giving her a feverish look. Joan crouched down and laid her hand over Maude's on the arm of her rattan chair. 'Miss Vickery, are you all right?' Maude blinked and glanced at her, and Joan caught a glimpse of something deep and wild in her eyes, something almost feral, before she regained control and her usual sharpness returned.

'I'm quite all right. Why wouldn't I be?' She pulled her hand away. 'That man has so many offspring, it's hardly surprising – one of them was bound to turn up here sooner or later.'

'Yes, Charlie said he was one of six. But there's only him and his sister now. All four of his brothers have died, but I didn't get to the bottom of what happened to them. The war, I suppose.'

'Four dead, you say?' Maude said, very quietly; so quietly it was almost a whisper.

'Yes, all of his older brothers. Such a horrible thought.'

Joan stood again, unsure what to do with herself. Maude ran the fingers of one hand in front of her eyes, closing them momentarily. Her papery eyelids flickered. It was an odd gesture, strangely deferential, as if in surrender, or recognition of something. The moment passed, and when she looked up her expression was as hard as ever.

'Well. Life never was easy. Now, are you ready? Abdullah will go with you as far as the causeway but no further; if he's seen from the fort the whole thing's scuppered before it's begun.'

'I'll . . . I'll do my best, Miss Vickery.'

'Good girl. Try not to get arrested, and when you see him, tell him . . .' Maude broke off with a peculiar little sigh, and it took Joan a moment to realise that the old woman's voice had failed her. She peered into the mirror and pretended not to have noticed. Maude cleared her throat and began again. 'When you see him, tell him he is missed, and that I'm doing everything I can to secure his release.'

'I'll tell him,' she said, wondering that Maude should be so moved about a man she'd described merely as her slave's son; or rather, wondering why she had described him thus, when he clearly meant more to her than that.

The sun was hot on Joan's shoulders through the black fabric; beneath the mask her own breath was damply suffocating. She walked silently beside Abdullah and as they neared the Residency, beyond which the causeway crossed to Jalali, her heartbeat got louder in her ears. She didn't dare look up at the terrace, in case she saw Rory, or anybody else, even though there was no way they could recognise her. As far as they knew, she was spending time with Maude, listening to her stories and drinking tea. She almost laughed – a bubbling over of nervous energy that came out as a strange, suppressed whimper. Abdullah paused in the shadow of the building nearest the causeway.

'Here I will stay,' he said. Joan swallowed, and nodded. Wanting to turn and run, she took the basket of food and money to bribe the guards from him.

'All right,' she said shakily. Abdullah looked down at her, and though his eyes never changed, the corners of his mouth twitched.

'Be calm, Miss Seabrook. This is a good thing you are doing. The men here are made to suffer, and they have no news of their release – they have no help, no means to free themselves, and so they have no hope. They live and die according to the word of the sultan. You will bring some hope to our Salim.'

'Yes,' said Joan. 'Yes, I hope so.' Abdullah paused, motionless.

'He is a good boy,' he said, in the end. 'A good man. Tell him that our prayers are with him. Now, you must go on.' The old man stepped back, deeper into the shadow of the building, and simply stood, watching. Joan had no choice but to turn from him, and carry on alone.

Sunlight glanced up from the water, dazzling her as she crossed the causeway. The breeze was briny and warm; a thin trickle of sweat wound its way down her back. She stopped at the bottom of the stone steps and looked up their straight, steep rise. The door at the top was shut, and two Omani guards sat to either side with their rifles resting on their knees. Both of them were peering down, and watching her curiously. Breathing so hard that the fabric of her mask was drawn in and out with it, Joan climbed. Behind her, she felt the watching presence of the Residency, the Royal Palace, and the whole of Muscat. At any moment, she expected to hear her name called out; expected to be stopped, upbraided. To be discovered breaking the sultan's laws was to become subject to his capricious justice – subject to harsh and arbitrary punishment that might leave her locked up in the very place she was about to break into. One step after another, heart in her mouth; she reached the top all too soon and stood stupidly in front of the two men, the basket clasped in her hands. The guards exchanged a look at each other, and then back at her. They were just boys really, fresh-faced and beardless, but there was a narrow-eyed watchfulness about them. They had the restless look of bored young men the world over. Joan's mind went entirely blank; she couldn't for the life of her remember what she was supposed to do next.

Eventually, one of the guards laughed.

'*Salaam alykum*,' he said, and then spoke rapidly in Arabic. Panic force Joan into action. She scrabbled in the basket for the letter Maude had written out for her, and muttered:

'*Alykum salaam*,' before she remembered that she wasn't supposed to speak. The guard frowned at her accent, but he took the letter and read it. With a nod and a grunt he passed it to his companion, his bored expression returning as he motioned her forwards and reached for the basket. He looked through the items Maude had packed, and took the wad of bank notes that were tucked down one side. The money disappeared into a pocket somewhere on his person so quickly Joan could hardly follow the movement. Then he stood and banged on the door, saying something else that Joan didn't understand as it opened with a rattle and a slam of bolts. Holding her breath, Joan hurried past the two men, into the fort.

Inside she had to stop immediately, blind in the darkness. The door shut behind her and a powerful reek made her recoil. She put a hand over her nose and mouth and was momentarily puzzled by the fabric in the way. Behind her, somebody chuckled, and she turned quickly to see two more guards seated in the vestibule. They were British, wearing the red balmorals of the Muscat Regiment, and Joan almost cried out in alarm.

'Stinks, don' it, pet?' said one of them, a chubby man with a ginger moustache, and they both grinned ruefully. Joan stumbled back and turned away from them, certain that despite her veils and mask, they would know her for what she was. 'Any of them give you any trouble, you just give us a yell,' the guard added. Shakily, Joan walked off along the corridor and up some steps, higher onto the fort's rocky outcrop, and was infinitely relieved when they didn't call her back. It was cooler inside; once she was around a corner and out of sight Joan stopped, leaning back against the wall and waiting for her heart to stop thundering. She was inside Fort Jalali. Relief made her giddy; unseen behind the mask, Joan smiled.

When she stood up from the wall, Joan found herself opposite a doorway, through which was a long chamber like a dormitory. Maude had said there were almost a hundred prisoners in Jalali and all but a couple with special privileges lived in these comfortless, communal rooms. One such privileged inmate was an uncle of Sultan Said's, imprisoned for being a drunk and an embarrassment. Those men weren't chained; they had private rooms with beds and personal chefs, but it was in the second communal room that Joan was most likely to find Salim.

She glanced into the first as she passed it. Perhaps twenty-five men were sitting or lying about, their ankles manacled by a heavy iron bar, their hands joined to it with chains. Their clothes were soiled and torn; they had no mattresses or furniture of any kind. Flies buzzed everywhere; there was light but no view from the windows high up in the wall. There was the constant rattle and scrape of metal on stone. A few of the prisoners had gathered in groups, talking or playing a dice game, but many simply sat in silence with their backs against the wall. There was misery in their languor, and Joan felt ashamed to witness it. She carried on past this doorway and up more stairs. There were other rooms and smaller cells, and steps leading off here and there. She kept walking straight ahead, and didn't turn, and soon came to the second long dormitory room. Steadying herself with a slow breath, she went inside.

The room was much like the first, with another twenty or thirty men inside. Joan glanced around, relieved that there were no guards amongst them. She looked for a man matching Maude's description of Salim: in his late forties and taller than most, dark hair worn long, fine-featured and handsome. A man seated near her was watching her closely; after a few seconds he stood up stiffly, pulled a leather strap to lift the iron bar between his ankles, and shuffled over to her. His face was drawn and hollow, his eyes glazed. When he spoke she couldn't understand him. His teeth were broken and stained; when she didn't answer he spoke again, and this time she understood one word, which he repeated, over and over: *ma*. Water. She shook her head.

'Salim bin Shahin?' she said, hoping she was pronouncing the words correctly. The man deflated in front of her; the light went out of his eyes and was replaced by a sullen anger.

He gestured vaguely towards the far end of the room and then returned to his place by the wall, dropping his iron bar with a clang. Joan walked quickly in the direction he'd sent her, keeping her eyes down. There she found a lean, sinewy man with strands of grey running through his black hair. He had a narrow, angular jaw and a long nose; dark brown eyes beneath black brows, and a sparse beard, untouched by the grey. He'd been weathered by a lifetime outdoors; deep crow's feet scored his temples. He matched Maude's description, and the watchful intelligence in his eyes made Joan go and crouch down in front of him. 'I'm looking for Salim bin Shahin,' she whispered, so that only he would hear. The man's eyes widened at her voice, at her use of English. He leaned towards her eagerly, alight with curiosity.

'You have found him,' he said.

Salim stared at her with an unsettling intensity. 'Who are you?'

'I'm . . . my name is Joan Seabrook. Maude Vickery sent me. She sent this for you.' Joan proffered the basket, which Salim ignored. They spoke in low voices, careful not to be overheard.

'But . . . are you *English*? How is it you're here, inside the fort? If you are discovered—'

'I must not be!' Joan hissed, frightened. Salim looked over her shoulder, towards the door, and then back at her, nodding incredulously.

'Thank you for coming. Thank you for the risk you have taken for me.'

Joan paused; she hadn't thought overly of him, in truth. More of not disappointing Maude, and of getting inside Jalali; of doing *something*.

'But who are you to Maude? Why are you in Muscat?'

'A . . . friend. I'm a friend of hers.' Joan wondered if this was true. She felt she was beginning to understand Maude, but there were still times when she was unreadable, unknowable. 'I'm here in Muscat to visit my brother – he's an army officer.' Salim listened to this with a puzzled expression.

'Sultan Said allows his soldiers to receive casual visitors now?'

'No, not really. I have certain . . . connections. I'm staying at the Residency.'

'Connections indeed.' Salim's brows twitched. 'The risk you take in being here is great, even so. Connections won't necessarily help you, if you are discovered; I wonder if Maude made that quite clear to you.' He spoke softly, thoughtfully.

'Yes, I understand the risks, and—'

'Very well, if you say so.' He watched her for a moment, his eyes flicking over her veiled face, returning to the only part of her that was visible. He smiled. 'You've kohled your eyes like a Bedu – you pass well as an Arab girl. Until you speak, that is. It is lucky you don't have blue eyes.' Salim's English was excellent, though he spoke it with the guttural Omani accent.

'I was to tell you that you're in their prayers. Abdullah's prayers, that is. And that Miss Vickery is doing everything she can to secure your release.' Salim considered this. He rubbed one hand over his chin, and turned his face to the light. His skin was deep bronze beneath a film of sweat and grime. 'Perhaps she means to use her influence with the sultan to help you?' Joan ventured. Salim shook his head, frowning.

'She has none. Not with this sultan; perhaps a little with past ones. I do not see how she can hope to help . . .' The shadow of despair passed over his face. 'And perhaps she should not. A man's fate is his own.'

'So you . . . you own your offence?'

'My offence?' He smiled bitterly. 'My offence was to love my people, and hate how Sultan Said keeps them shackled to the past, subordinate to foreign powers. My offence was to want our children to learn, and our sick to be healed. To want us to join the rest of the world in this century, instead of remaining alone in past times.' His voice had risen, and some of the nearest men looked across at them. Salim's eyes flickered nervously. He reached for the basket and rummaged through it, took out a handful of dates and almonds and threw them to the other men, who snatched at them eagerly, grinning. 'My offence was to speak out when the sultan enforced false sovereignty of the interior just so he could take our oil for himself, and sell it to his British friends. He has never had authority out there – in the desert, in the mountains. He claims oil is an external affair, and so his to oversee; but what could be more internal than the black blood of the desert? He is driven by greed.'

Joan stayed quiet; she didn't know what to say. She'd thought of the imam's rebels as a misguided few; it had never occurred to her that they might see themselves differently — that they might legitimately question the sultan's rule. 'See that man near the far wall?' Salim said quietly. Joan glanced across at the man, heaped against the wall with his huge stomach slouched over his thighs. 'He is a swindler and a drunk, and a violent brute who beat his wife near to death for burning his supper. He will pass three years here, and then be free. And me? For the crime of wanting the best for the people of Oman? Perhaps I will rot here for ever. It is a hard fate to accept.' His voice had dropped to a tense whisper.

'There must be a way! You mustn't lose hope.'

'Easy to say, if you are free.' Salim returned to the basket and pulled out a bottle of water. Glancing furtively at the other men, he drank half of it straight down. 'God is merciful,' he sighed, in Arabic, closing his eyes. 'Sayid Shahab, the Governor of Muscat, likes us to suffer. He says we have done wrong, so we deserve it. It is not enough to have no freedom, no dignity; he makes sure we do not have enough water either. Every man in here is half mad with thirst.'

'That's atrocious!'

'That is how it is.' He took out a packet of flatbreads and began to tear off strips, folding them into his mouth. 'It makes us weak, and stupid.' He continued to look through the basket, frowning, and then looked up at Joan. 'There is no letter? No instructions, no other news?'

'I'm sorry . . . this was all she gave me.' Salim leaned back against the wall in frustration, letting his head thump against the stone. 'Perhaps she does have some plan, Salim . . . my visit was supposed to bring you hope; that's what they both wanted. Maude and Abdullah.'

'Is my father well?'

'Yes,' said Joan. Salim looked so different to the elderly slave that Joan supposed his mother must have been Omani. 'Yes, he seems strong. He scared me at first – so . . . serious. So solemn. But now he seems to have accepted me.' She fell silent, wondering if she'd spoken too freely about a member of Salim's family. It was the mask, she realised. It released her from the normal constraint of good manners. But Salim grinned, pleased.

'As a boy, I feared to displease him merely for the look he would give me. But if Maude has accepted you, he will as well. That is the way of things with them.'

Just then there was the sound of footsteps in the corridor outside, and a fat man with a froggy, ill-tempered face sauntered in beside a uniformed officer and a thin youth in khaki drill. Joan glanced over her shoulder at them, and all the air seemed to vanish from her lungs. She was on her knees but lost her balance, teetered sideways and sat down abruptly. The officer was Colonel Singer.

'What is it?' Salim whispered. He didn't touch her to help her up; it was not permitted. 'You know the colonel? Or rather, he knows you?' Joan nodded minutely. 'Be calm. Be silent. He cannot see you.' Joan fought to breathe. Again, and suddenly, the veil over her face felt suffocating. She couldn't get enough air; the blood thumped deafeningly in her head. 'Joan! Be still!' Salim hissed.

'Really, if the men must be shackled in this way, if they must have no beds or mattresses, then they must at least have water when they want it,' Singer was saying. The youth at his side translated this, and the fat man shrugged, and replied in flat, unfriendly tones.

'He says the men must be punished,' the young soldier reported. 'He says they're not here to be coddled like children.'

Singer shook his head slightly, and grunted.

'I shall have to take this up with Shahab again – don't translate that. It's bloody barbaric.'

The three of them turned to leave the room again, the colonel with his hands clasped behind his back. His gaze swept the room as he went, pausing when they lit upon Joan. Their eyes met and for a second she couldn't look away, and didn't dare to breathe. Then she dropped her chin and turned her head away in what she hoped was a show of modesty, and prayed that he'd carry on out of the room.

'You can relax now, Joan. He has gone,' said Salim. 'And perhaps you should also go. I saw the Toad looking at you, wondering. If you stay too long he will make trouble. Take the basket back with you.' He emptied out the last few items of food, and pieces of clean clothing. 'Please ask her to pack more water next time. It is needed; I have some friends in here I would like to share it with. You must wait a few days at least before you return, however; any sooner and they will notice you, and they may refuse to let you enter.'

'Next time?' said Joan. She was exhausted; the strain of the visit, and her fear, had drained the strength from her. Seeing Colonel Singer there had almost been too much. She'd been *sure*, in the first instant their eyes had met, that he would recognise her. She pressed her hands to her sweaty face, blotting it against the veil.

'Don't do that. An Arab girl would never do that.' Salim leaned towards her again, looked around hurriedly and then caught her hand between his. His palms were hard and calloused, cool and dry; there was something vulnerable in his expression – a fierce desperation, not quite suppressed. 'You will come again? Please?'

'I . . . I don't know if I can.'

Joan couldn't meet his gaze. The stink of the place stung her sinuses; the flies buzzed. She wanted nothing more than to be outside, to be free of the prison and its parched, hopeless inhabitants. She hated her own cowardice, and tried to imagine knowing that she might never leave. She had no right to quail. 'All right, yes. Yes, I'll try to come again,' she said. Salim relaxed; he let go of her hand and nodded.

'You are brave. You will always have my thanks for this – for coming here. I hope one day it will be in my power to repay you.'

'I'm not brave.' Joan swallowed laboriously. She longed for a drink of water. 'Have you a message for them? For Maude, and for your father?' A look of sadness stormed Salim's face.

'Send my love and my thanks. Tell them I strive to accept my fate. My prayers are with them; and I pray to see them soon,' he said softly.

'I'll tell them.'

In the vestibule, Colonel Singer was talking to the gaoler, his disapproval plain. Joan had to walk close behind him towards the main door – close enough to smell his aftershave. Her knuckles were white on the handle of the basket.

'At least the dissidents are allowed to have provisions delivered, I suppose,' the colonel muttered as she passed. 'But what about the other poor blighters?' The man with the ginger moustache unlocked the door for her, and the blaze of light outside made her flinch.

She tottered unsteadily towards the steps. Halfway down she paused, and looked out across the bay – at the riot of blue water and sky, unfeasibly bright and clear, and the mud-brown and whitewashed buildings of Muscat, nestled in the bay. High above, two eagles circled in the updraught. The breeze fluttered Joan's robes and veil, and some air crept underneath to cool her. She took a deep breath, and when she exhaled it was with a laugh, an incredulous laugh; she had done it – she had been where few westerners ever had, against all the rules, in a disguise, and come out again without mishap. It may have been illegal, but, thinking of the way Salim had gulped at the water, Joan decided that it being illegal didn't make it wrong. She felt euphoric, invincible; she felt she could stretch out her arms and soar over the city. She hurried down the remaining steps and across to where Abdullah was waiting, and impulsively threw her arms around him in jubilation.

Maude questioned her eagerly upon her return, until Joan had recounted every word that had been said, and every nuance of Salim's demeanour, and every detail of his condition, as she had witnessed it. Then, finally, Maude sat back in her chair with a sigh.

'Ah, the ruddy Muslim faith in fate and the will of God! We make our own fate – I've always told him that. Well. Thank you, Joan. Abdullah may not look it but he has been deeply distressed by Salim's imprisonment. He was against me asking you to visit, but now he's overjoyed I did.'

'He's overjoyed?' said Joan doubtfully. 'Are you sure?'

'Oh, yes. We've been together long enough for me to be able to spot it, and believe me, Abdullah is positively cock-a-hoop right now.' As she spoke, Abdullah came in with the tea tray, his face as solemn and unreadable as ever, and Joan couldn't help smiling.

'You are very fond of him yourself, I think,' she said. 'What happened to his mother?'

'What happened?' Maude fiddled with some crumbs in her lap and shrugged. 'She died. That's why Abdullah raised him here, in my household.'

'Oh. Well, I told Salim I would go back. If you want me

to, of course. He asked for you to write a letter, telling him the news. I think he was very happy to have a visitor.' Maude looked away towards the window for a while, sighing again.

'There's nobody else I can ask, you understand? Nobody else I trust; and nobody who has the wits to be any use at all. But it's risky for you. I cannot ask you to go again,' she said.

One of the saluki dogs got up and stretched with a faint groan. Joan held out a hand for it to sniff, but it merely turned around and settled again. She thought of Salim, and the dignified way he fought his desperation, and his deprivation; the way despair snapped at his heels like a hungry dog. She thought of the feeling she'd had as she left Jalali – the feeling that she could do anything, even fly. Some of that feeling still remained in her; she wondered if it had been there all along. If she'd been capable of it; if it was merely a case of doing the right thing, regardless of fear or nerves. She couldn't believe it wasn't yet lunchtime; days seemed to have passed since she'd first woken.

'But you're not asking me to,' she said. 'I'm offering.'

The next afternoon, Joan and Rory, with two servants to help and chaperone them, hired a canoe-like houri at the waterfront and were paddled a little way along the coast westwards, to a place on the headland where they found a sandy beach amidst the rocks. There was a thick rind of shells and broken coral at the high-tide line; further around the rocks there were fisher-men's huts along the shore, built of oil drums and palm fronds, mud bricks and chunks of coral. A few small fishing boats were making their way in and gulls crowded them, filling the air with white wings and the squabble of their voices. Their crews worked steadily, ignoring the birds; tendon-like lengths of wire in their arms. At the corner of the bay where their boat dropped them was an outcrop of rocks, which gave enough shade for their folding chairs, and enough privacy for Joan to swim and sunbathe without causing too much of a stir. She wore loose cotton trousers and a shirt over her one-piece, and tied her hair back under a scarf. Rory picked his way out along the rocks to dive in, his body milk-pale against the blue and the brown all around. He was grinning when he surfaced, noisily blowing out air and flicking the wet hair from his face.

Joan swam out a little way and then trod water, squinting up at the distant bulk of Jebel Akhdar. The mountain seemed to shimmer in the haze of the day; it drew her gaze irresistibly. No westerner had ever been to its forbidden, secretive summit; right now men were dying in the attempt. She wondered if Daniel would be one of the first to reach it, or Charlie Elliot – inadvertent pioneers. The thought caused an odd feeling, and it took her a moment to realise that she envied them the chance. It was absurd; she knew the dangers that they faced were real, and deadly serious. But perhaps they would reach the plateau without realising the wonder and privilege of what they were seeing; perhaps they would forget to look around, and marvel.

Beneath Joan the seabed was shifting shapes, midnight and azure; her own paddling feet were bright white against it, rippling with sunlight. Rory swam over to her.

'Robert was saying the other day that the sea is littered with old cannons and bits of boat left over from all the various invasions and expulsions. Perhaps we only need to get you a snorkel for a bit of archaeology to be possible after all,' he said. 'Or an aqualung.' The sun glittered on his wet face.

'Perhaps. Though shipwrecks aren't really my thing,' said Joan. She turned onto her back and floated. 'Isn't it bliss? Do you think there are sharks?'

'It is finally starting to feel like a holiday,' said Rory. 'And yes, there are sharks. But the nasty ones stay further out.'

'You asked Robert, didn't you, you big chicken?'

'Of course. Couldn't risk my betrothed being eaten.' The skin across Rory's shoulders was turning pinkish-brown. 'We could have done this far sooner if you hadn't been so fixed on seeing so much of Maude Vickery.'

'Well,' said Joan defensively. 'We have rather become friends now.'

'No mean feat, from what Robert tells me. But then, you are very lovable.' He swam in a slow circle around her, his voice dipping in and out of clarity as the water lapped at her ears, and she allowed herself a little pride that she had persevered, and won Maude over.

The edge of Muscat harbour was just visible around the headland, and beyond that, the furthest tower of Jalali. Joan thought of Salim in there, plagued by thirst and weighted down with irons, not knowing when, if ever, he would see the sky again. It was on the tip of her tongue to tell Rory where she had been, and what she had done; it had been ever since her return, and she knew that telling him would make it real when it had begun to have the unreal caste of a dream. Nobody would have imagined it of her, she knew; nobody would have expected her to walk into trouble, to break rules, to trespass. Not little Joan, with her shot nerves. She'd hardly expected it herself. The urge to speak was like an itch begging to be scratched, but it wasn't the promise of secrecy she'd made that kept her quiet. It was knowing that as soon as she told Rory he would somehow prevent her going back. He would be frightened for her; he would realise the danger from the prisoners, from the guards, from the authorities if she were discovered. She pictured him berating Maude; talking to Robert, to Daniel, perhaps even to Colonel Singer. She imagined being ushered onto a boat home in disgrace. She didn't know exactly what would happen if she told him about it, but she knew for certain that she wouldn't be able to go again. And she wanted to go again. Her fear remained, but she was sure now that she could go in and come out again undiscovered. She had done it, and could do it again. *I knew I could do it, so I did it.* In her place, she knew, Daniel would do the same. Neither he, nor her father, would have been afraid.

She felt the slide of Rory's wet skin against her own. 'What do the two of you find to talk about, anyway? Is it all her old war stories, and battle scars?' he said. 'You're with her for hours at a time. Dan must be feeling rather forgotten about.'

'Don't say that! Of course he's not forgotten about. And anyway, he has a job to do. I can't pester him all the time – as you were the first to point out to me. Maude and I just talk – what do any two people find to talk about?' Joan turned herself upright and trod water again, realising it was probably Rory who felt neglected, and forgotten about. 'You don't mind my going, do you?'

'No. Well, no. I suppose it's just a bit dull with you gone, that's all. Perhaps if I was allowed to come along once in a while, and get to know her, I wouldn't feel so left behind.'

'You will meet her – of course you will. But you'd be even more bored if you came every time,' she said hurriedly, surprised by how easily the lie came out. 'We really just . . . gossip.'

'Oh. So I'm not missing much, then?' said Rory, and the chance to tell him was right there – to tell him she'd done something astonishing, something forbidden. There was a long pause; she managed to keep the words in, and was relieved.

'Not really. I'll mention it to her again – your meeting her. Perhaps I'll see if she wants to come to dinner with us? Come on, let's swim in and get amongst the picnic. I'm famished.'

'I predict flatbreads,' said Rory, and Joan laughed. But she noticed, as they swam together in the crystalline water, that her silence had put a little distance between them – a barrier where there hadn't been one before.

There were more trips out in houris, as far up and down the coast as they were permitted to go; there was wandering the streets of Muscat and Muttrah, where Joan was not allowed into the souks or the mosques. There were short, breathless climbs up the steep rocks to either side of Muscat, to look at the view and what few birds they could spot – turtle doves and dusty brown steppe eagles; black and yellow mynah birds; sparrows just like the English ones, only smaller and thinner, pared down for the desert climate. Once they saw a black and white Egyptian vulture skirting the shore, startling in its size and grace.

Besides these things, there was precious little to do between visits to Maude or to Bait al Falaj, other than sitting on the terrace at the Residency, writing letters or reading. Joan waited impatiently for each such visit. Sometimes her knocking at Maude's door went unanswered, and she heard voices inside speaking in Arabic – Abdullah and another man. Sometimes a man was just leaving as she arrived, with a cloth bag or a packet in his hands.

She nodded to them politely though they tended to scowl at her, or watch suspiciously as she went to the door. If she was turned away in the morning she returned in the afternoon, and every time she went she asked when she should go to Jalali again. Maude seemed to be waiting for something – some auspicious moment – but she didn't disclose what it might be. Joan learned the exact sherbet-orange shade of the sunset on the mountains as the city's generators began their throb and clatter, but the limits of her travels in Oman remained very clear.

Then, one Friday, Maude finally decided that she wanted to

go outside. There was a lengthy spell of fussing and the finding of jackets and hats, and then, carefully, Joan and Abdullah carried first the wheelchair and then the old lady down the stairs between them. The blonde salukis roused themselves and walked sedately at Abdullah's heels. The hair around their muzzles was almost white; their hip bones and elbows jutted. Up and moving, their age was far more obvious than when they lay sleeping. Maude complained steadily until they were out in the street and she was settled, with her hat pinned on securely. Abdullah made soothing noises, and spoke soft words of Arabic, and never once betrayed any impatience with her. In some ways, Joan realised, they were like an old married couple. She squirmed when she remembered telling Abdullah how to free himself.

They walked through the city gate and down towards the sea, Abdullah pushing Maude's chair, Joan and the salukis walking obediently beside them. Maude was silent at first, looking all around; then she grunted.

'This place has hardly changed since I first came here, you know,' she said.

'I can well imagine,' said Joan. 'It doesn't appear to have changed much in a hundred years.'

'A few more buildings; more electricity wires. And I suppose some of these are telephone wires as well, now.' She waved a disapproving hand at the sky. They drew curious looks from shopkeepers and passers-by; the veiled housewives and servants, the men leading their loaded donkeys or walking together in close conversation. 'I rode up to the gates on my camel, and I almost expected there to be . . . I expected to be spotted, you see, and . . . the wazir informed. But I didn't know then . . . I didn't realise . . .'

'That . . . Nathaniel Elliot had beaten you to it?' said Joan cautiously. Maude was silent for a while.

'Do you know, they were far more interested in my camel? Ha!' she said. 'She was a beauty, mind you. A white camel from the Batinah coast – they've always been the best; taller than most and longer-legged, with those lovely pale coats. To an Arab, a good camel is more beautiful and more valuable than a good horse, you know. She wasn't the animal I'd crossed the desert on, you understand – that was Midget. Poor Midget. Everything about us was in tatters by the time we got here. We'd had no water for two and a half days.'

'Good grief! I hadn't realised it was such a close call.'

When they reached the water's edge they paused, looking out at the far harbour walls with their maritime graffiti. Maude sighed, and glanced up at Joan.

'You don't really realise what it was like at all, Joan; but I mean no criticism in saying so. Nobody who hasn't fully pitted themselves against the desert can know.'

'But you did, and you conquered it. And you didn't even go home afterwards. It sounds terrifying. Wonderful, perhaps, but terrifying; I'd have wanted to rest at home, after such an ordeal.'

'No.' Maude shook her head. 'Some things make home seem . . . too far away. Some things leave you lost. I couldn't go back to England. The desert changed me. It changes every-one.' Maude twisted uncomfortably in her chair. 'I made a new life in the mountains here – in the foothills. The villages there are simple, honest places . . . Timeless, in a way. That was where I chose to recover.'

'Well, I think you're incredibly brave. And remarkable. Most people would have run off home to . . .'

'Lick their wounds?' said Maude sourly.

'Recuperate. And to revel in their achievement! Because it *was* an incredible achievement, Miss Vickery, whether you were first or second across – you were still the first woman, after all. I hope you were proud of yourself. I hope you *are* proud.'

'Proud?' Maude Vickery shook her head minutely, her eyes narrow and fixed on the distance. 'I can't say I remember feeling much pride, at the time.'

Gradually, Jalali dragged their eyes eastwards; huddled on its rocks, with its little windows like mean eyes. Joan drew breath to say something about Salim, or to ask when she should go again, but she held her tongue. She knew she didn't need to remind them.

'How long are you here, Joan?' Maude asked.

'I'm not really sure, actually,' she said. 'I suppose we shall have to go back in time for Christmas. My mother is by herself.'

'Tell me about Charles Elliot.'

'Captain Elliot? I ... really don't know what to tell you. I only met him the once.'

'Is he handsome? Charming? Serious? Louche?' Maude's voice was curiously expressionless.

'Handsome, definitely. Tall, built as a soldier ought to be. And he certainly thinks he's charming – he's very confident about that. About most things, it seemed to me.'

'All swagger, or more to him than that?'

'Plenty of swagger. He called the imam's insurgents rustics armed with sticks and stones, or something like that.'

'Did he now?'

'But there must be more to him. This new SAS squadron he's in ... they're supposed to be the very best. They have special training, and weapons. Covert operations, and all that – although their emblem is Excalibur, surrounded by flames. Not very low key.'

'The sword Excalibur? Goodness, how dramatic. What kind of special training and weapons?'

'Gosh, I wouldn't know – I could ask Daniel, I suppose. I got the impression Captain Elliot was quite bright. Brighter than he was letting on, perhaps.'

'Still a boy then, in some ways.'

'Perhaps. He seemed quite old though. Definitely over thirty,' said Joan.

'Really? *That* old?' said Maude wryly. Joan smiled apologetically.

'Why do you ask?'

'I'm just . . . curious, I suppose – as to what the offspring of Nathaniel's marriage might be like.'

'Did you never wish to marry, Miss Vickery?'

In the long silence after her question Joan knew she shouldn't have asked, but she'd learned by then not to try to retract or undo something said. She could only wait it out. Abdullah caught her eye and held it, and she saw the reprimand in his gaze.

'Marriage is fetters,' Maude said eventually. She looked over at Jalali again. 'If you meet Captain Elliot again, find out what you can.' She looked up at Joan with her lips pursed, as if disapproving of herself. 'I'm being nosy, purely and simply. I would like' – she added a dignified pause – 'to hear some gossip.'

'Then I shall gather you some,' Joan said, smiling. 'You might meet him yourself, you know, if only you'd agree to come and dine at the Residency one night. I'm sure I could arrange it all. My Rory wants to meet you too – he's jealous of me spending so much of my time with you.' She expected the suggestion to be rejected out of hand, as it had reportedly always been before, but Maude seemed to consider.

'All right then, I shall. If you can get it all fixed, I'll come,' she said. 'Now, come along, I need to go to the bank.'

'Wait a second, I'd like to take a picture of us – may I?

Perhaps Abdullah could take it? We'll have to be quick about it; I'm supposed to keep my camera hidden.'

'Carry on, then,' said Maude. Joan showed Abdullah where to look through the viewfinder, and which button to press; then she went to stand behind Maude and rested a hand on the back of her chair, smiling proudly. She would have to wait until the picture was developed to find out what Maude's expression had been as the shutter fell.

That night Joan, Rory, Robert and Marian returned to Bait al Falaj, to dine at the officers' mess on Colonel Singer's invitation. Robert had arranged the passes that would allow them back into Muscat after *dum dum*. They went at seven, when the sky was a deep velvety blue and the first stars in it were bright. Joan had put on the best dress she had with her, cut from a deep, mossy-green silk that came to her knees, went well with her colouring, and skimmed her rather boyish figure in a way that subtly implied femininity. She'd put powder on her face and some colour on her lips, though she felt a little foolish about it, hoping that this was the best way to get Charlie Elliot talking. Rory had smiled and twirled her under his arm when she'd come downstairs. His skin had a hot-climate shine to it, and was finally beginning to tan.

'I've always loved that dress on you,' he said, and she'd felt guilty that she hadn't worn it for him. They had drinks with the colonel and his wife at their bungalow across the wadi, where waxy frangipani flowers loaded the air with perfume, and then went together to the mess tent for dinner. As she sat down, Joan felt the eyes of several men drawn to the sheen of her dress and the shape underneath it, even though she was on Rory's arm. A mixture of pleasure and mortification turned her face pink.

She found it compelling being amongst so many men, with

the bass hubbub of their conversation and the smell of their aftershave and hair oil mixing with the pervasive reek of the canvas walls. It made her want to breathe more deeply than usual; she felt entirely safe, though she couldn't say from what. There was more gin and lime to drink with the meal; beer, but no wine. Joan sat opposite Daniel, who looked relaxed and sun-tanned after a few more days rest at the base. His skin looked smoother and the shadows beneath his eyes and in his cheeks less stark; his features had lost some of their hard edges.

'I'll be going back out soon,' he said, when Joan commented on it. 'We all will. The SAS boys reckon they've found a new route up to the plateau, from one of the ravines we've already penetrated. Intelligence are mulling over the best time to attack, and whether we should misdirect and go in quietly, or send in the RAF Venoms to bomb the welcoming committee. I heard a rumour that Singer might move HQ down to Nizwa, and we'll all operate from there. We'd be far better placed for incursions onto the mountain.'

'When?' said Rory.

'Will we be able to visit you there?' said Joan. Daniel looked back and forth between the two of them, his smile hovering between affection and irritation.

'Soon, Taps. And no, you won't be able to visit me there.' He took a sip of his drink and swatted a mosquito against his forearm with expert disregard. 'It'd be a good time for the two of you to head home.'

'But we only just got here!' Joan protested.

'More than a fortnight ago,' Daniel pointed out.

'Let's not talk about it now. Let's just enjoy dinner,' said Rory, as a skinny, black-eyed waiter brought out a first course of curried lentil soup.

'All right. Tell me what you've been doing with yourselves,' said Daniel.

Joan thought at once of Fort Jalali, and Salim, but instead began to tell her brother about their swimming trip. She was interrupted a short while later by Charlie Elliot.

'Mind if I join you?' he said, pulling out the chair beside Daniel. 'Apologies for lateness. I wanted to shave but I dropped my razor into the falaj and the fish made off with it.' He glanced at each of them. 'It's entirely true,' he added. Joan looked at Daniel, expecting to see a disparaging expression, but he smiled instead, albeit guardedly, and she was taken aback. Her brother normally disliked cocky types, dismissing them as *old school bullies*; instead it was Rory she noticed subtly withdrawing into himself. She sensed his dislike of Charlie.

'I'd disbelieve you if it hadn't happened to me too,' Daniel said to Charlie. 'The little devils swarm like piranhas at anything you drop in.' Charlie unfolded his napkin with a flourish and waved at the waiter to bring more soup for him. He looked at Joan and smiled.

'I must say, Seabrook, your sister looks delightful this evening. Don't you agree?' Daniel looked across at Joan as though he hadn't quite noticed her before, and smiled, and Rory laid his hand over hers on the table – protecting her she guessed, or laying claim. 'Quite the most ravishing girl at the table,' Charlie added, and it took Joan a moment to realise that she was the *only* woman at the long table.

They drank, and ate, and laughed, and talked of the war and of home. Joan questioned Charlie as much as she could to find out about his family, and where he had been in the world, and how often he saw his father.

'Would you like to see a recent picture?' Charlie asked at one point. He took a small photo from a billfold in his shirt pocket and passed it to her. Joan studied the black and white image of Charlie, chest puffed, standing beside a thin, elderly man whose dark eyes had a wary expression in them. He had a narrow, fox-like face with a sharp nose; his remaining hair was fine and white, and though he was tall he stood with a stoop in his back and shoulders. There was something in the shape of his mouth, and something about the drag of skin at the corners of his eyes, that made him look mournful. 'That was taken last year, when I was home on leave,' said Charlie. 'Dad doesn't travel so much these days – much to his disgust. He's forever cursing his old bones for packing up on him.'

'He looks so different from the photos I know – the ones in all the books,' said Joan. She pictured him then – straight and strong, with lots of dark hair and a beard which, when he was in his shirt and sarong with his rifle and his kaffia, made him look like one of the Arabs he'd ridden with. Cracked lips and burnished skin, and a wild, faraway light in his eyes. It seemed somehow tragic that such a romantic figure had become an old man with an air of sadness. With a stab of pity, she thought of his four dead sons. 'He must have been pleased to find out you were coming to Oman. To the place of his greatest achievement,' she said. Charlie took the photo back with a slight frown.

'Yes, you'd have thought so, wouldn't you?' he said.

'Maude Vickery is coming to the Residency for dinner one night.'

'Is she?' said Rory.

'Yes – sorry, I meant to say; I need to talk to Robert and Marian and get it all squared away. Would you like to come and meet her?' she said to Charlie. He smiled as he considered.

'Meet the arch rival, eh?'

'Hardly that any more. She's frail and a bit vague sometimes; bad-tempered but rather sweet, really. What do you say? I think she'd be interested to meet *you*.'

'Well, I suppose it would rather pop Dad's cork if I did.

He doesn't even know she's here. Or if he does, he didn't mention it to me.'

'So you'll come?' she said. Charlie lit a cigarette and leaned forwards with his elbows on the table, smiling at her in a way she hoped Rory couldn't see.

'If you're willing to go to all that trouble to get me to come to dinner with you, Joan, then I'll do it.'

When the remains of the food had been cleared, Joan drew Daniel to one side. The thought of him going back into the mountains gave her a plummeting feeling.

'I've been writing a letter to Mum,' she said. At once, Daniel's face went flat and tense, and Joan fought a rising wave of confused desperation. She pressed on. 'Please will you write a few words at the bottom? Just a line or two? Please?'

'Joan, can't you leave off? You don't know everything. You're not the head of the family now that Dad's gone.' He spoke without anger but the words still stung.

'I'm not trying to be the head of the family; I'm just trying to mend things. Who *is* the head? I really don't think we have one any more. In fact, we barely feel like a family any more. And no, obviously I don't know everything, which is hard enough. But I can't go on with the two of you living in separate worlds! It's starting to feel like . . . like we're falling apart. Like Dad was the only thing that held us together.'

'Well, perhaps he was,' said Daniel, looking away with a frown. Joan thought hard for a moment, trying to put her need into words.

'Dan, what if you don't come back?' she said quietly. The words brought tears to her eyes. 'You're about to go into those horrendous mountains which are full of snipers . . . and land mines . . . What if you don't come back?'

'Joanie—'

'What if your last words to Mum were . . . were whatever you said as you stormed out? Is that what you want?'

'What about *her* last words to *me*?' he whispered furiously. A tremor went through him.

'I don't know what they were, but I know she loves you, and I know you love her. One of you has to speak first. Please, Dan, just . . . just write a few words. Please.'

He said nothing, so she scrabbled in her satchel for the letter and smoothed it onto the table in front of him, then got out her pen and laid it alongside. After a few moments he picked the pen up, and Joan sighed in quiet relief. He wrote a line and signed his name, then excused himself from the table. Joan picked up the letter and read.

I am still your son — it turns out words can't change that, after all. We're fighting a war here, and Joan points out that I might not come back from it. So I wanted to say that I hope you are taking care of yourself, and finding peace with it all. Love, Daniel.

She reread it a couple of times, while Charlie told Rory a tall story about the giant bats in the Malayan jungle, and Rory listened with disbelief written all over his face. *I am still your son.* She folded the letter away, not understanding, but decided to let it rest for the time being, and not push her brother any harder that night.

'Is everything all right, darling?' said Rory, leaning towards her a few minutes later. Joan nodded.

'Just Dan, being prickly,' she said, not managing to smile.

'Where's he gone off to?'

'I don't know. I hope he'll come back to say goodbye before we go.'

'Darling, don't sound so wretched — of course he will. I'll

go and find him.' Rory got up, knocking the table clumsily. He swayed a little and steadied himself on the back of Joan's chair as he passed.

'I fear the gin has got the better of your fiancé,' said Charlie, once Rory was outside, draining his own glass. He'd rolled up his shirtsleeves; the skin of his forearms was deep brown, and mapped with small scars.

'So what? It is Friday night, and we are on holiday.'

'Doesn't it make you feel a hundred years old, calling each other *darling* like that? You sound like two kids playing grown-ups. You can't be much over twenty-one.'

'I'm twenty-six, and Rory's twenty-four.'

'Only twenty-four?' He raised his eyebrows.

'Yes. Why?' she said defensively. Charlie raised his hands innocently. 'Excuse me.' Joan got up from the table and went outside.

The night was still and warm, the sky now flat black. In the camp's light Joan could see the red Omani flag, hanging limply from its pole on top of the fort; from the barracks came rapid Arabic chatter, and laughter. A group of men were huddled around something on the ground, watching it intently. Curious, Joan made her way over and gasped when she saw a huge, pallid spider on the ground, its bristled body the length of her hand, its legs stubby and thick. She folded her arms instinctively, goose bumps rising on her skin. The soldiers were laughing and passing money back and forth; the spider sat stolidly, with light gleaming in its clustered black eyes, ignoring its audience and chewing rhythmically – Joan was glad she couldn't see what.

'It's a camel spider,' said Charlie Elliot, behind her, and Joan spun around. He was smoking another cigarette a short distance away, with his spare hand in his pocket. 'Also called a sun spider.'

'It's vile,' said Joan, rattled. 'Why don't they just kill it?'
Charlie shrugged.

'It is what it is; vile is a matter of opinion. One of the men
found it in his pack when he came in from Nizwa; that fellow
there – Karim, I think he's called. He's keeping it as a pet, and
he's been taking bets that there's nothing it won't eat.'

'What if it bites him?' said Joan. She turned to look at the
moon-pale spider again, still steadily crunching, and felt rather
than heard Charlie come closer behind her.

'It hasn't yet, but they've a numbing substance in their
saliva, so they can make a meal of your foot without you even
realising.' Joan's skin prickled. 'You probably shouldn't walk
around the camp on your own after dark, you know,' he said.
'I'm almost sure nothing would happen, but some of the men
haven't seen their wives in a very long time. And most of them
have never seen a girl in a slinky green dress before.'

'I only came out to find Dan and Rory,' she said, turning to
him. She wanted to tell him she was invincible; that she had
walked into Fort Jalali, as bold as brass, and come out again
intact. But just then she didn't feel invincible at all.

'I'll help you look,' he said.

'There's really no need.'

'You're probably right. But still.'

Rolling her eyes slightly, which only made Charlie smile,
Joan walked past him towards the fort. It was locked and dark,
and she paused pointlessly by the door. 'Daniel was upset.'

'He's a big boy now, Joan.'

'Oh, what would you know about it? What would you
know about any of it?' she snapped, surprising herself. Charlie
looked down at the dusty ground and then up at her from
beneath knotted brows.

'I'm trying to help, Joan,' he said, quite seriously. She
couldn't place the source of his sudden, strange intensity.

'They're probably in his tent,' she said, and set off.

'Perhaps we should just wait for them back at the mess?' said Charlie. Joan ignored him.

A good ten feet from the entrance of Daniel's tent, still hidden in the dark, she stopped. The door flaps had been let down but not fastened; a gap of several inches remained, and there was a lamp on inside – just a single paraffin lamp, spreading a low light. It cast Daniel and Rory into partial silhouette; they stood to one side, almost out of sight. They were close together, talking in low voices; or rather, Rory was talking, in a quietly anxious way. Almost imploring. After a moment, Daniel looked away to the outside, directly at Joan, and she froze. But he didn't see her. They were invisible from inside, she and Charlie.

Joan waited, watching, because this wasn't an argument but it was definitely *something*. It was definitely a secret. She waited, and wondered what to do, because with Charlie at her elbow she felt uncertain of everything – what she should do, how she should do it. Some part of her, some deep-seated instinct, suddenly didn't want to see any more. She had an urge to turn and go back to the mess, as Charlie had suggested, and leave them to sort out whatever it was they needed to sort out. But she didn't move. She was still there when Rory reached out and touched his fingers to Daniel's jaw, and gently turned his face towards him; she was still there when Rory kissed her brother, in a way he'd never kissed her – with his eyes closed and his mouth open. She was still there when Daniel kissed him back, and every muscle in both of their bodies went tight with . . . with what? Absently, Joan struggled to name it, before realising it was passion, and nothing more mysterious than that. Charlie was pulling at her arm.

'Joan, come on,' he said softly. She snatched her arm away, turned on her heel and ran.

Lady Margaret Hall, Oxford, 1901

As usual, Maude lost track of time as she was reading. A shaft of June sunshine warmed her reading-room booth in Old Hall nicely. She was in the midst of her final exams, after two years of study in the school of Ancient History at Oxford; the following morning at ten o'clock sharp she had her viva voce – the spoken part of her examination – at which both her parents would be sitting in. She wasn't nervous, exactly; rather, she had a feeling of near total focus; the calm of knowing exactly what was expected of her, and exactly what she needed to do, and of everything else being of minor importance. Almost everything else, that was. Her parents were staying up for a few days to celebrate her nineteenth birthday with her.

Nathaniel Elliot, on the other hand, was just passing through on his way to London, for that day only. Maude read for hours without losing concentration, occasionally making a note, occasionally pausing and staring into nothing, not seeing the dust motes jostling in the sunshine, as she let some fact or argument take root in her mind.

The chapel bell chiming one startled her. She looked at the clock on the wall in amazement, then scrambled up, hastily patting her hair and cramming her straw boater onto it. She left her books where they were and hurried outside, and the pages flicked themselves backwards, losing her place. Nathaniel was waiting at the gates of the college – male guests were not permitted inside – and Maude's heart gave its usual lurch when she saw him. She tried to ignore it, but it seemed to squeeze itself up into her throat and remain there, thudding along; she dreaded him being able to hear it in her voice. The crumpled look of his cream-coloured suit, and the way he wore the jacket open and flung back, only seemed to add to his peculiar, rakish elegance, and Maude was suddenly very aware of the scuffs on her shoes, the smudges of dust on her shirt cuffs from the library shelves, and the lopsided knot of her cravat. Like the other fifty or so girls studying at Lady Margaret Hall, she never wore any make-up, so at least she didn't have to worry about checking it. She clearly recalled the vicarious embarrassment she'd felt for Alice, the last girl John had introduced to them, who'd spent her whole visit with red grease on her teeth. With her rouged cheeks and strong perfume, she'd reminded Maude of a china doll – pretty and hollow and entirely fake. Elias Vickery had clearly disapproved of Alice, and she'd put Maude off the thought of ever over-doing herself in such a way, even though the sight of her own small, plain face in the looking glass, with its awful nose detracting from any prettiness her mouth and eyes might otherwise have had, sometimes caused her small pangs of distress. She was always quick and rigorous in suppressing those pangs. She had a brain, and a will, and no need of a pretty face.

Nathaniel waited with one hand in his pocket, squinting up at the round cupola of the chapel, rocking back on his heels and smoking a cigarette. Maude slowed her approach, making the most of being able to observe him unnoticed. He was much taller than her – most people were; his hair was as dark and silky-straight as ever, and he wore it combed back with Macassar oil, after the fashion. He was still long and narrow, but his shoulders had spread, just enough, to make his figure manly. His feet looked in proportion to the rest of him now; he was clean-shaven, and had a light tan from time spent outdoors. His face had changed a great deal as he'd matured; the ridges above his eyes, his cheekbones and the strength of his jaw always startled her slightly at first, until he smiled, and his face returned to being the one she'd known nearly all her life. He turned and saw her now, and waved, and Maude couldn't stop her cheeks colouring even though she loathed them for it.

'Hello, Mo,' he said.

'Hello, Nathan,' she said, and then laughed as he shook her hand, though she didn't know why, exactly. Perhaps because his touch caused her joy. Perhaps it was as simple as that.

'You look well. Very well. All this learning suits you.'

'Thank you. I believe it does suit me.'

'On course for a First, I heard.' He finished his cigarette and ground it under the toe of his shoe.

'All being well. Not that they'll award an *actual* degree to a woman.'

'Well, even unofficial first-class honours sounds impressive to me.'

'If you'd only studied, Nathan, you'd have done far better.'

'We must all play to our strengths, Maude. And sticking at books just isn't one of mine.' He tucked his hand into his pocket and proffered her his elbow, which she took happily. 'Let's walk for a while and build up an appetite. I've reserved us a table at the Randolph.' He glanced down at her and grinned, but the edges of it were tight, oddly apologetic and defiant at the same time, because they both knew that she would be paying for their lunch. Nathaniel almost never had any money.

On such a fine day Oxford's streets were busy with students and residents; shoppers idling along in the warm sunshine; boys on bicycles, weaving through the traffic of handcarts and pony traps and big, ponderous drays. There were green and powdery smells of blossom and purple wisteria; young leaves hung from the trees, some of them still soft and limp like new butterfly wings. They walked along the riverbank, where the breeze was strong enough to flutter their clothes and hair, but weak enough to be warm. It was the kind of day that made Maude want to walk for miles. Strolling along in the green light beneath the trees, on Nathaniel's arm, she was, just then, entirely happy.

Nathaniel had graduated from Cambridge with a lowly degree – only just a pass in fact – in Philosophy. When he'd turned twenty-one, Elias Vickery had let it be known, gently but firmly, that the unofficial sponsorship he'd had since his father's death would cease. It had paid for his education; without it he certainly wouldn't have been able to go up to Cambridge. Nathaniel's mother was still in the south of France, vague and tremulous and almost an invalid, living between hotel rooms and lodging houses and relying on the kindness of a succession of gentlemen friends as she had long since frittered away her fortune – and her son's inheritance. Nathaniel's lacklustre degree had caused friction between him and Elias, and had exposed the fragility of a familial relationship when there were in fact no blood ties, and no obligations. Maude was relieved that the ties had been cut and Nathaniel was no longer in the care and keep of her family, even if he would always be bound to them by bonds of love and gratitude. Somehow, it made certain things seem much simpler to her. She hadn't yet identified, properly, what it was that was simpler now; what it was, exactly, that she felt the way had been cleared for. She didn't feel quite ready to acknowledge it yet.

Since graduating, Nathaniel had spent a lot of time over in the African colonies; travelling, hunting big game with various friends; flirting, when back in England, with various career paths. It seemed that only the utmost need would induce him to settle one way or another, and perhaps that time was coming.

'I heard from Father that you've taken a position at last,'

said Maude, as they walked. The path narrowed and Nathaniel released her arm to let some others pass in single file. He didn't offer it back again, and Maude clasped her hands in front of her instead; they suddenly seemed superfluous.

'Yes. I'm sure he was pleased to hear it,' said Nathaniel, a little bitterly.

'Only if you'll be happy, and settled. Only because that's all he wishes for – your security.'

'You still won't hear a word against him, will you? No, no. Don't answer. Neither will I, I suppose. Not from anybody else, anyway. From myself . . . Sometimes he can be a difficult man to live up to. All those expectations, I mean.'

'He expects us to meet our full potential. Each of the four of us. He believes we can, and that's why he gets frustrated when we don't,' said Maude staunchly. She made it her business not only to meet her father's expectations, but to exceed them. She, alone of the four of them, had yet to cause him any disappointment. There were John's repeatedly unfortunate choices of companion, and Francis's decision not to finish his degree, and to settle for a career as a clerk of law.

'Oh, Mo. One day you might see,' said Nathaniel, putting his hands in his pockets and letting their arms brush together. She tried not to let it distract her. 'Perhaps not until the first time you want to do something he doesn't approve of.'

'Are you going to tell me about this position of yours, or am I to guess?' she replied. She put the boys' occasional chafing against Elias down to some male need to fight, and prove themselves through obstinacy.

'I'll tell you. It's not so very exciting, though. What's most interesting about it are the possibilities there are for travel. For exploration.'

They walked back to the Randolph Hotel and took their table, and Nathaniel told her about his junior position with the

Political Service in British and Egyptian Sudan, to where he would be travelling in four days' time. He'd been assigned to a small outpost in Kutum, a long way from the civilisation of Khartoum, and spoke of the unexplored territory to the south of there with that look of complete conviction in his eyes that she had seen so many times before.

'This won't be all high tea and shooting lions, like in Kenya, Maude – or high tea and pyramids like in Egypt. This, finally, is breaking new ground. This is what I'm supposed to do.'

'And leaving so soon,' Maude murmured, as their devilled kidneys arrived. 'I can't believe this is the first I'm hearing about it!' She took a mouthful and the pepper burned her tongue. She was gripped by a peculiar mix of jealousy, pleasure and deflation. She loved nothing more than to see that light in his eyes; she was happy that he was starting to do what he had always longed to. But he would be so far away. She saw him only sporadically as it was, but not knowing when she would next see him was very different from knowing that she would not see him at all.

'Well – it's new ground for white men, anyway. They have tribal headhunters there, did you know? Only, they don't collect heads, I hear. They collect testicles.'

'Nathan! Not at the lunch table.' She laughed, glancing around to see if he'd been heard.

'Well, they do! One must always speak the truth, as dear old Elias would say.'

'But one may choose which truths to speak,' Maude corrected him. She cleared her throat softly. 'How long will you go for?'

'I don't know. How long's a piece of string? Until the fun runs out.' He shrugged. 'I say, you don't look very chuffed for me, Maude.'

'I am – of course I am. I'm rather jealous, that's all. And I shall miss you. We all will.'

'I'll miss you too,' he said casually. Then he seemed to hear his own tone, and his face softened. 'Of course I'll miss you. And I'll write often. But you'll soon be off, having adventures of your own. I know you will. Where is it next?'

'Palestine, and Syria.'

'This autumn, isn't it? Delivered from consulate to regional outpost to consulate by a series of Father's helpful friends.'

'That's hardly fair, Nathaniel. How else should I go?'

'But it's true. Not that I blame you – if I had your connections I'd make the most of them too.'

'A girl has far greater need of them than a man.'

'Perhaps. I do sometimes forget to think of you as a girl, Maude.' To this she could think of no reply. The treacherous blush returned to her cheeks with the stirrings of humiliation.

'Oh.'

'Well, girls are silly creatures, on the whole. They can't seem to keep a single thought in their heads for more than a minute at a time; and they're always obsessed with dresses and their hair, and dances above all else. But that's not you, is it, Maude? You've a lot more about you than . . .' He waved his fork. 'Fashion.'

'Oh.' She couldn't quite tell if she'd been complimented or not. 'Yes,' she said eventually. 'I do think Father despairs of your ever marrying.'

'I've no need to marry,' he said. 'Wives are expensive. And she'd want me to stay at home, or at least in one place. And even if one could be found who didn't mind tagging along, most of the places I intend to travel to are bound to be wholly unsuitable for a lady.' He took a large mouthful and paused to chew it.

'You could marry a rich lady, and spend all her money travelling the world.'

'While she spent the rest of it all alone, on drink and cards?' he said sharply. Too late, Maude thought of his mother – her state of lonely dissolution, her slow decline into ruin.

But Nathaniel had moved on, shaking his head. 'No. Like you once said to me, I wonder now if I shall *ever* want to marry.' When she didn't reply, he looked up. 'You still hold to that, I suppose? Although, presumably, you must marry sooner or later.'

'Must I?'

Maude shrugged, then looked out of the window at the bright and busy street beyond. She took a sip of water and couldn't look at him for a while, though she sensed his scrutiny. His words had tipped something off balance inside her, and she needed a moment to work out what it was, and why it had happened. She had the worrying sensation of something slipping away from her; something she truly needed. Something essential to life. Perhaps it was just that he was going off first, starting his adventure first, and she was being left behind yet again. Being left behind had always made her desperate. She ached to be the first to do something for a change, but it certainly wasn't going to be marriage. She thought of Arabia, which she had still never seen. She thought of endless miles of desert, full of ancient mysteries and ancient peoples, lost cities and uncharted ways, and was suddenly filled with such a powerful longing that she had to hold her breath until it passed.

'I'd far rather travel and explore ancient places, and write books about that, than be a wife,' she said eventually, still feeling herself to be far away. But perhaps it was Nathaniel who was already far away. She looked at him. 'Perhaps we'll look back at this moment as the point where our lives diverged, and never again ran along parallel lines,' she said. Nathan smiled.

'You're always so serious, Maude. It makes perfect sense that you'd go from reading books to writing them.'

'I'm not always serious. Won't you stay for my birthday dinner?' she said suddenly, leaning towards him, hoping. 'Or come back up from London for it. Oh, do! Mother and Father will both be here, and I think John is coming too, and some of my friends from Lady Margaret. We can make it your send-off as well – I don't mind being usurped. Nineteen is a pointless, in-between kind of age to be.'

'I can't. Sorry, Maude. I've a packed schedule until I go. That's why I've come down today.'

Maude sat back again, defeated. She wanted to hold on to him, she realised. It was almost a physical urge – to reach out and take hold of him, and keep him there. She made her hands into fists to keep control of them. She didn't want him to be gone; didn't want this to be the point where their lives diverged. She walked back to the station with him after lunch, and waited on the platform until his train came in with the screech and squeal of hot metal, and clouds of sooty steam. The feeling dogged her steps, and made her quiet, until it was so obvious something was wrong that the atmosphere between them grew strained. This distressed her even further. They had always been so easy with each other – easier than she was with her own brothers. Nathaniel frowned as he stood up from the bench on the platform, clearly puzzled as to what had upset her.

'Well, goodbye for now, Mo,' he said, holding out his hand. Maude shook it, and then, impulsively, she hugged him. She had to pull him down towards her, and reach up for him. The crush of his clothing against her cheek was awkward and uncomfortable, but underneath it was the warmth from his skin; she shut her eyes and concentrated on that.

When she managed to let go, he was looking down at her

with a different expression – one more akin to the intensity he had when he spoke of his plans. But it was only there for a moment, and was soon replaced with something quizzical. Maude struggled back into her own skin, back into the shape she knew she was supposed to be.

'Do try not to get malaria, won't you?' she said lightly, and Nathaniel laughed.

'I'll do my best. And do mind you get that First, won't you? If you don't I shall be blamed, for distracting you from your books the day before the viva.'

'Oh, don't worry. I shall get it,' said Maude, with no false modesty.

And to that end, she ought to have hurried back to the reading room as soon as his train had pulled out of sight and there was no chance of a further glimpse of him. But, instead, she stayed a while in the gathering quiet, and waited to feel quite normal again. She stood near the edge of the platform, her eyes fixed on the bright steel rails. She didn't want to walk, or sit, or speak to anybody. She had no idea, just then, what she did want. Eventually, the stationmaster came to ask if she was all right, and so she walked back to Lady Margaret Hall, and back into the reading room, and returned to the booth she'd left a few hours earlier when everything had been clear and simple, and she had been focused, and had known exactly what she ought to do.

She tried to return to reading, but her thoughts strayed, again and again, like cats. Here and there, to past events and imagined future ones; back, again and again, to Nathaniel Elliot. She thought of him far away in the Sudan, and wondered if his life in England would look small and tidy and pointless from there; if *she* would look small and tidy and pointless.

Without wanting to, she caught herself trying to conjure herself at his side in that place. And then she realised, of course, that she was in love with Nathaniel Elliot. Utterly and hopelessly in love with him, and that the only way she could remain at his side from then on would be to marry him. And then, surely enough, she would be at *his* side. He would not be at hers. All their adventures would be his, and she would go along so as not to be left behind. It was impossible; as intolerable a thought as not being by his side at all.

The next day, she somehow found enough focus for the viva exam; helped by the indignity of being given too tall a chair, so that her feet could not touch the floor. She sat up, ramrod-straight, keeping her feet tight together and immobile, not swinging like a child's, and spoke with a trace of extra authority lent to her by ire. Her parents sat to one side – her father watching closely; her mother gazing gently into one corner of the room or another and occasionally fiddling with her gloves or her skirts. Elias sat with his arms folded, now and then checking his pocket watch against the clock on the wall. His face was closed, but as she answered each question clearly and fully, she could sense his approval; even more so when, at one point, she dismissed an entire school of thought on the decline of Byzantium with a single brusque remark. But still, even during the exam and with her father watching, there was a small, important part of her mind that was elsewhere, searching and bereft. She had the First, she knew; but somehow it was no longer good enough. They celebrated her nineteenth birthday as planned, and nobody seemed to notice that part of her was missing. Soon, she began to fill the empty space with plans.

Muscat, November 1958

Joan felt so distracted and stupid from sleeplessness that she hardly remembered to be scared as she climbed the steps to Jalali. She'd hardly heard Rory and Robert when they made sympathetic sounds at the sight of her red eyes and pale face that morning; her hair flat to her head because she hadn't remembered to wash it. She'd hardly noticed Marian's immobile expression, which looked like something held tightly in check. They'd all suggested that she stay at the Residency and rest, but Joan couldn't bear to be there. It suddenly seemed too confined a space; it seemed to make her smaller, to reduce her to insignificance. In the mirror, her face was slack and her eyes seemed to look back at her from further away than was physically possible; as though she had travelled far during the long hours of darkness she'd spent awake, over three consecutive nights. She felt absent from herself, separated from her own senses. It was frustrating, but at the same time soothing; she had the idea that it was protecting her – that it was somehow keeping her on an even keel. It stopped her thinking about what she should say to Rory, or to Daniel. So far, she had said nothing at all.

There was a letter for Salim tied to her calf with string beneath the trousers she was wearing under the abaya, because correspondence was strictly forbidden. Maude had stressed the gravity of it, reiterating that the letter must not be discovered, frowning at Joan's passive quietude.

'What *is* the matter with you, Joan? Are you quite with it?' she'd said in the end, exasperated, roughly sticking more pins than were necessary into Joan's hair to secure the veil. Joan had nodded, calmly enough. She'd been studying the grittiness of the kohl that had got into her eyes: how it had stung at first but now only felt warm, like mild spice; and spent a while trying to tell if the sensation was unpleasant or not. Now the heat of the robes wasn't bothering her; the stifling veil wasn't bothering her; the risk of discovery wasn't bothering her. All she really wanted was to lie down somewhere quiet, shut her eyes and sleep. But for the past few nights, when she did shut her eyes she was beset by images of home that brought on a feeling of searching desperately for something – she didn't know what. Perhaps the feeling of safety, of security, that home ought to have carried with it; that ought to have come from the familiarity of it. But that feeling had vanished. The images were so vivid that when she opened her eyes and found herself in Oman, it came as a real surprise. She longed to talk to her father; her mother too, but mostly her father. It had never really mattered what he said to reassure her, only the way he'd said it; the way he'd looked at her and squeezed her shoulder, that had told her everything would be all right. That she would be all right, when she had that helpless feeling she'd had, trapped beneath the kitchen table as the bombs fell on Bedford. He had made it fade, and disappear, when somehow her mother seemed to mirror and amplify it.

Joan noted the animal stink of the prison but it didn't disgust her like last time. She noted the suspicious gazes of the Omani guards, and the casual speculation of the British guards, but didn't care. She made her way to the second communal room, where shafts of hard white light cut across from the high windows, and as she went in a thin, elderly man, stripped to the waist, stepped in front of her. She stopped, puzzled. He stood stiffly to attention for a moment and then bowed awkwardly, almost losing his balance.

'Your Highness,' he said. 'Your Highness.' The skin clung loosely to his skinny ribcage. Joan stared at him.

'Excuse me,' she said, stepping past him and carrying on. She looked back and saw the old man watching after her with a pitiful, crestfallen expression. Only then did she realise that he'd spoken to her in English, and that she had replied in English too. A sparkle of shock finally penetrated her stupor, and she took a sharp breath, her steps faltering. How had he known to speak in English? She checked herself, her face and clothes, in a brief moment of panic. Salim stood as she approached, and frowned. He was taller than many Omanis; Joan had to look up to meet his eye.

'Welcome, Joan,' he said, in a low voice. 'You need not fear that old man. Nobody knows his name, we simply call him the wallah; he is quite mad, but I never saw him hurt a thing. He doesn't even kill the cockroaches when they crawl over him at night.' He studied her eyes intently, obviously unsure of her mood, her demeanour. 'He often speaks in English to visitors, but you must not be heard to reply.'

'I know,' said Joan. Her dismay threatened to turn into tears, tightening her throat. 'I wasn't thinking.'

They sat down and Joan began to unpack the basket in silence. She felt Salim watching her every move, and it made her want to hide away. She swallowed laboriously.

'Joan,' he whispered. 'What is it? What has happened? You are different. You are unsettled. Tell me, please. Is it Maude? Abdullah?'

'No, I—' She shook her head. 'I can't say, really. But Maude and Abdullah are well. They're fine. She ... she's sent a letter this time. Shall I give it to you now?'

'No, wait a while.' Salim looked past her; his dark eyes were always moving. 'Wait until certain people have moved further away from us. It would be better.'

'All right. Look – there's extra water here, as you asked. You must be thirsty,' she said, keeping her eyes down, but though Salim took the bottle from her, he did not drink. He kept up his scrutiny until eventually she had to look up. There was slight swelling and a small cut on one of his cheekbones but he seemed calmer than last time; he sat with his knees bent up in front of him, his arms resting across them. Joan wondered how the manacles and the iron bar must feel; she saw raw, red welts at his ankles where the metal cuffs chafed. There was dried blood there, and flies kept trying to land. The silence hung between them like one more veil and Joan could hardly stand it. She had to say something. 'The weather will be turning wintery in England by now. This is the first time I've ever felt hot in November.' It was such an absurd thing to say that she blushed, though he couldn't see it.

'You miss your home. Is that what makes you sad? You wish to go back there?'

'No. At least, I don't think so. In fact, I . . . I can't see how I can ever go back.' This made Salim's frown deeper.

'Then it is not your home.'

'That's true. I suppose that's true, yes,' she said. The silence returned and Joan could only stand it for a few seconds this time. 'It's kind of you to even think of me, given . . . your situation. But please, Salim . . . let's not talk about it.'

Salim tipped his head to one side and looked away.

'As you wish.' He took a long drink of water; opened a packet of roast chicken and began to eat.

'I . . . I don't know what's in the letter, but she made me promise to say that we make our own destiny. She seemed . . . upset to think you might be accepting this as your fate.'

'Yes.' Salim grinned at her. 'That sounds like Maude.'

'Don't you think it's true?' Joan thought of Rory, and of home; of her brother, her mother, the memory of her father.

They'd defined who she was to herself – she had known the boundaries of them, their size and shape and orbit and her own shape and place amidst them. Now she felt everything moving, changing, becoming unknown to her. Including herself. Silently, she struggled not to let it happen. She struggled to hold on to them, and to what she knew.

'No man has ever escaped from this jail, Joan.' Salim's voice called her back. 'Even if you managed to be free of the irons, and climbed out somehow, you would be cut to pieces on the rocks. The front gate is the only way, and you have seen how strong it is. Jalali has only been conquered once, many years ago, and that was because the commander was made a fool over a woman, and lost his mind to love, and was tricked.'

'She tricked him?'

'In a way. She was the wali of Muscat's daughter – do you know what a wali is? He is the sultan's representative, and rules a town or a city – something like a mayor, or a governor. The Portuguese invaders had been forced to retreat into Jalali, but their leader fell in love with this girl, who was as beautiful as the sunrise. The commander sought peace with the wali so that he could marry the girl, but the wali was a cunning man, and a vengeful one, and when the fort was opened for the wedding celebrations, the wali's men stormed it, and slew the inhabitants.'

'I wonder if she knew what was planned. The daughter, I mean. I wonder if she loved the commander in return,' said Joan. 'Perhaps on her wedding day, when she thought herself at the start of life, all was lost to her.'

'Perhaps she should not have fallen in love with a man who was the enemy of her people.'

'But people can't choose who they fall in love with.' As she said it, Joan wondered if it was true. She wondered if it was true of her.

She wondered if she'd chosen to love Rory, or whether it had simply been that they'd become entwined; become, inextricably, part of each other's lives. She thought back to the taxi ride at dawn, and the first time Rory had kissed her – the way they had both held on to Daniel, slumped in between them. She thought of Rory's hand over hers on her brother's arm and then shut her eyes because everything was shifting again, slipping away from her. Now that she looked, it seemed that she'd drifted passively into love.

'I *must* accept my fate. My imprisonment here,' said Salim. 'Only the sultan's word can release me, and he will not give it. And he will not be overthrown. Not when he has the British to help and protect him.' At this, Salim's eyes grew fierce, and his mouth tightened. And Joan couldn't tell if it was anger with the sultan, or the British, or at his fate, that burned in him. 'If I may not ever be free, then dreaming of life being otherwise could drive a man mad. Do you see? Acceptance is the only path.' He thought in silence for a while. 'But then, perhaps it would be better to die trying to free myself than to rot in here for ever.' He grinned wolfishly; his eye teeth were sharply pointed. 'Do not tell Maude I said so. I am not ready to die just yet.'

Salim looked around again and then, without changing his soft intonation or moving his gaze he said, 'It is now safe for you to give me the letter. Keep it low. Keep it behind the basket and our legs, and slide it towards me.' Joan fumbled for the paper as unobtrusively as she could. 'Move a little to your left, so nobody will see past you as I read it,' he said. She shifted her position obediently and waited, quite still, while he read the single page. At one point he paused, and looked up at her. Or rather, not quite at her. He didn't meet her eye, but looked higher than that, to where her veil sat securely at her hairline. He read the letter right through twice, then folded it carefully, quietly, and slid it back to Joan. 'Tell me,' he said, 'if you do not wish to return to your home, where will you go? What will you do?'

'I . . . I will go anyway,' she said, with a sinking feeling. 'I have nowhere else to go, after all.'

'But you live in a country full of wealth and opportunities, do you not? And you will soon be wed – Maude wrote briefly about you in the letter, but I had already noticed the ring on your hand. There is your path, surely?'

'Yes. Perhaps, yes.' Joan swallowed. 'Salim . . . do you really not think it's possible to change your fate? Do you really believe all our lives are already . . . mapped out?'

'Everything that happens is according to the will of God. This much I know.'

'But . . . what if what we'd *thought* was our path turns out to have been the wrong one? Isn't that possible?'

'Of course. God decides our path and we must follow it as best we may. But we are flawed, and can make mistakes. Your eyes are tired, Joan. If you wish to go, you should go, and rest. But if you want, I will tell you a story my father once told to me about trying to change your fate.'

'Yes, please tell me it.' Leaving the prison was returning to Maude, and then, unavoidably, to the Residency. The thought of that was like a weight pressing down on Joan.

'I will tell it briefly; you must not stay too long. Once, long ago, the wali – the governor – of Nizwa overheard his qareen speaking—'

'What's a qareen?'

'It means "companion". It is the djinni that walks through life at our shoulder.'

'Like a guardian angel?'

'I don't know of them. A qareen does not guide . . . they can be mischievous, in fact. Let me tell the story. The wali heard his qareen speak dark words about his newborn son's fate – that the child would grow up to kill his father, marry his mother and then kill himself.

'Of course, the wali was much aggrieved to learn this, and determined it would not happen. He took the child and left him out in the desert to die, thinking that this would be better than him living to fulfil such a destiny. But tribesmen found the boy and raised him as their own, and so, a stranger to his true parents, he returned to Nizwa years later and inadvertently trod the very path that was foreseen – he killed his father, and married his widowed mother. And when he realised what he had done, he killed himself, just as had been prophesied. The wali's attempt to change the child's path only set him upon it, do you see?

'We are not supposed to know the way. If by some chance we discover it, it does us no good; so we should not seek to know, and must only live as well as we may.' Salim drank again, wiping his mouth with the back of his hand. 'Man is not meant to understand such things. Fate is riddle, like a snake eating it's own tail – no beginning, no end.'

Salim's eyes swept around them, then he reached forwards suddenly, too suddenly for Joan to react, and pulled out two of the hairpins that Maude had used to secure the abaya. He folded them quickly, invisibly, into the crease of his palm. 'A poor serving girl would not use so many,' he murmured.

'You have such strength, Salim,' Joan said quietly. 'Here I am talking of home, and feeling so helpless, so ... powerless, when I can come and go as I please. I'm sorry, Salim.' She shook her head.

'We are none of us helpless unless we choose to be, Joan. We must all fight to free ourselves, in whatever form that freedom may come.'

'But, if our paths are mapped out for us ...'

'That does not mean we may walk them blindfolded.' Salim smiled.

'But I do wish someone would tell me what to do.'

'That is cowardice. Another thing we only submit to by choice.' Ashamed, Joan looked down. 'A coward would not have walked in here to bring comfort to a stranger,' Salim pointed out.

'But there's so much I'm unsure about. I wish . . . I wish I could talk to my father about it all.'

'He is dead?' Salim asked, with a bluntness that made her wince. 'Forgive me. But if you try, I am sure you will find you know what he would tell you. You should go now, before you draw too much attention.' Bewildered, Joan rose obediently and left him there. The frail old man Salim had called the wallah tried to rise as she passed, presumably to bow again, but the metal bar between his ankles was too heavy, and he did not manage to stand in time.

Rory looked disappointed when Joan said she wanted to go by herself to see Daniel. She hoped to see things more clearly when it was just the two of them together. She hoped to be able to talk to her brother, and understand. Perhaps to see something about him she'd somehow missed before. The day was hot; sweat bloomed through Rory's shirt. Joan thought of how he'd looked in England – smooth-skinned and glowing, everything soft and welcoming from his eyes to his lips and his hair, to the gentleness of him. Here he seemed to be melting, becoming misshapen, like a fruit turned just too ripe, its sweetness corrupted. She shook the thought away; it was the spite of her tiredness, twisting things. And yet everything that was familiar and reassuring about him seemed to be disappearing with this transformation. His presence no longer made her feel secure. Holding his hand was no longer like having a good grip on a bannister at the top of steep stairs; holding his hand now felt like missing a step on those stairs. Like teetering at the edge of a painful fall.

'Isn't he expecting both of us? But all right. He's your brother, after all,' Rory said, in the end. 'I'm roasting anyway, and it's always hotter at the camp.'

'Why don't you go swimming,' said Joan absently.

'I'll wait for you to get back. Then we'll both go.' He held her eye and wouldn't release it until she nodded. She hoped he wouldn't try to kiss her goodbye. She didn't want to betray her confusion, her fear; how reluctant she was to be kissed by him. They were on the terrace of the Residency, catching what they could of the sea breeze. Joan studied its four corners, the wall enclosing it, the canopy above. They seemed to creep in, ever closer, and she shrank a little more as they did.

At the army camp, Joan climbed out of the car as the driver flipped open a comic book and settled down to read. She went alone across the empty space towards Daniel's tent, no longer caring about the curious looks aimed at her by the other soldiers. She stared into the mountains. The dusty air often threw a veil over them, but not today. They were crisp and clear; they looked almost close enough to touch. She longed to see the desert stretching away on their far side; to look down from the green shade of a pomegranate tree in a garden on the plateau and see Muscat and Muttrah as toy towns, and every-one in them as ants, even smaller than she was. The jagged peaks and black ravines no longer looked threatening – in fact she liked their vastness and their hard edges. She was struck by the feeling that in those brutal mountains she would be rid of the notion of the walls closing in. She needed to find a way to be rid of it, a way to go forwards. One of the small Pioneer aircraft ploughed a dusty trail along the runway and coughed into flight. It turned south-west and flew away into Wadi Sumail, heading towards the interior, and Joan stopped to watch until it was a small, pale fleck against Jebel Akhdar's precipitous slopes, and then vanished.

There was no way to knock at the entrance to Daniel's tent, so she halted for a moment because she just couldn't burst in on him, unannounced. Not any more.

'Knock, knock,' she said in the end, awkwardly.

'Come in, you two,' Daniel called. He was at his desk, where he'd been writing. He smiled a closed-mouthed smile when he saw her, and then looked past her. 'Where's Taps?'

'Back in Muscat.' Daniel's face fell so obviously that Joan had to swallow the pain of it before she spoke again, and she didn't dare say that she'd insisted he stay there. 'I don't think he was feeling super. You know how he is with the heat.'

'He must be getting used to it by now? It's a shame – I'm off to Nizwa with my unit tomorrow.'

'Tomorrow? But . . . you didn't say! How long for?'

'I don't know. And I didn't say because you were both coming, so I could tell you today. And say goodbye.'

'But . . . Maude's coming for dinner at the Residency on Thursday. You were supposed to meet her,' said Joan stupidly. She felt like a child in her disappointment; she knew it was disproportionate, but she knew she needed Daniel too. She needed him to help her understand what was happening, because without him she was alone with Rory, and she didn't know how to do that any more. She studied him and was relieved to see that he hadn't changed, not like Rory had. He was still himself. He was just a little further away, a little further beyond her grasp.

'I'm not on holiday, Joan; you know that. I can hardly cry off because of a dinner. I'd have liked to see Rory again, mind you. In case you've gone home before I'm back.' He looked away from her, moving the pieces of paper on his desk with his fingertips.

'Well. You'll just have to see him when you get back here.' Something in her tone made him look over at her; nothing in his face changed, but perhaps something in his eyes did. A minute adjustment. 'And me as well, of course. I'm not going home. Not yet.'

'Aren't you?' He smiled gently. 'You can't stay with Robert and Marian for ever, you know, you'll outstay your welcome. Mum will be expecting you back soon. You can get the Christ-mas decorations up, and—'

'I don't care about the Christmas decorations, and I don't care if she's expecting me. I'm twenty-six years old – shouldn't I have my own life? Why should it be me that goes home? Why should it *always* be me?' She heard her voice rise, thin-ning with desperation. She felt like a moth in a jam jar, bat-tering itself against the glass.

'Because it has to be. Because I can't, Joan.'

'Well, maybe it'll have to be neither of us then.'

'Joan, what is it? What's going on?' They looked at one another for a hung moment, and Joan tried to see the child he'd been – the one she often saw hiding in the lean man's body in front of her, peeping out now and then like he was only playing. She couldn't see it at all, that day.

'I don't know what's going on,' she said, honestly enough.

They had lunch in the mess tent, and Daniel talked about Christmases past, remembering how much their father had loved it. Joan pictured him swinging their mother across the kitchen floor to 'Jingle Bells' on the radio, with the gold and silver paper chains she'd made at school wrapped around him like a boa and his festive red waistcoat buttoned up below a spotted bow tie, chosen deliberately to clash. She remembered him singing along, and her mother laughing, still holding the potato peeler in one hand. Suddenly, it all seemed an impossibly long time ago. Daniel had giggled wildly at their cavorting. When had she last seen her brother laugh uncontrollably? She couldn't think.

'I don't blame you for not wanting to rush back,' he said, wiping a piece of flatbread around his plate. 'Christmas isn't the same without Dad. And anyway, it all seems a bit odd and distant from out here, doesn't it? But you'll have Taps with you. He'll jolly things up, won't he?'

'Oh, he'll try, I'm sure. But it's not that. Not entirely.'

'Then what is it?' Daniel took her hand, squeezed it hard, and his touch brought tears to her eyes. She couldn't look at him, and she couldn't tell him. She felt too far out on a limb, and not ready to let go.

'Do you know what Mum said when I told her I was going to come out here to see you?' she said.

'No, what?'

'She said I'd give myself the collywobbles; she said I was being silly and my nerves weren't up to it.'

'Well, you do know she was talking about herself, don't you?' said Daniel.

'Was she?'

'Of course. Why do you think she and Dad never went any of the places he used to talk about?'

'I didn't think they had the money to go.'

'Well, it was partly that. But also it was Mum – she's afraid to fly, afraid of boats, afraid of foreign food and diseases, and being sold into white slavery.' He smiled, but then fell serious again. 'Think about it – it was always Mum who'd come up with a reason not to go anywhere. And Dad always used to hate it when she fussed around you. I once heard him say she made you more nervous, not less.'

'Oh.' Joan thought about that for a moment. She thought of being trapped under the kitchen table; of how her mother's grip on her hands had been violent, and her breathing had been fast and shallow, more like a dog panting than a person. 'Well, I'm tired of being like that. I'm tired of being *poor Joanie* – of being treated like a . . . a stupid child!'

'What are you talking about? Who treats you like that? Nobody thinks you're stupid.'

'Don't they?' she said, but Daniel didn't reply. 'Are you happy, Dan?' she asked then impulsively.

'Of course.' He let go of her hand and fiddled with his empty plate.

'No, I mean, really. Are you *really* happy?'

'Oh, who is, Joan?' he said, and sighed. 'I don't know anybody who *really* is.'

'I thought *I* was,' said Joan. The words had a broken sound, but Daniel didn't take her hand again.

He walked her back to the car after lunch, and hugged her tight.

'I'll see you soon, Dan,' Joan said, stubbornly reiterating that she wouldn't be leaving Muscat yet. Daniel sighed through his nose.

'Maybe,' he said. 'Maybe so. Give my regards to your affianced. Tell him from me to man up.'

'What do you mean by that?' But Daniel only smiled absently. He held the car door open as she climbed into the back seat, then shut it behind her and slapped the palm of his hand against the roof. Joan felt his desire to pack her off; to have her away from there. He waved once and then strode away, back towards the mess, not looking back. As the car moved towards the gate, Charlie Elliot jogged towards it. The sun put gold into his untidy hair and crow's feet around his eyes. His shirt was unbuttoned at the top, and he'd shoved his feet into his boots without lacing them up. He waved, smiled, drew alongside the car and slowed to a walk, obviously expecting the car to stop.

'Hello, Joan,' he said. Her cheeks blazed and she didn't dare look at him.

'Drive on,' she said, as the car braked. The driver looked at her in the mirror, then shrugged one shoulder.

'Hey, Joan – hang on!' said Charlie, but Joan ignored him, keeping her eyes to the front. She didn't know how to look at Charlie Elliot, let alone how to talk to him. He'd been right beside her outside the tent, and had witnessed Daniel and Rory together. He made it impossible for her to deny what she'd seen. Just then, she wished Charlie Elliot didn't exist. The car pulled away, churning up a cloud of dust. When they were a hundred feet away, Joan dared to look back, and saw Charlie watching them go with his arms folded. She looked away again, ashamed but relieved, and ignored the driver's curious glance in the mirror.

Joan tried not to think too much as she got dressed for Maude's dinner at the Residency. The night before, she'd staggered up from drinks on the terrace with her eyes blurring, certain she would fall asleep right there in her chair if she didn't go up immediately. She'd lain down on the bed fully clothed and slept like the dead, to wake eleven hours later feeling anxious but resolved. She would carry on as if she hadn't seen Daniel and Rory kiss, as if the implications of it hadn't been instantly clear. Ignoring it was by far the best and easiest thing to do, besides which she had no idea what the alternative might be. She'd spent days trying to fathom it, and had come up with nothing. She smudged some colour onto her lips, not meeting her own eye in the mirror because when she did she had that notion again, of being a moth in a jar. Helpless, stupid, frightened. She'd caught one once – powdery silver and brown – when it had been battering itself against her lampshade, distracting her. She'd taken it outside to release it, but even when the lid of the jar was off, the moth had stayed inside, fluttering at the glass.

She put on her green silk dress, twisted her curls into an acceptable shape and pinched her cheeks a few times. Despite the light tan she'd acquired, her face looked pale, even a little drawn. The men had all got into black tie; there were some extra guests from the oil company and the British Bank of the Middle East, and other senior officials at the Residency. Joan was introduced and handed around, feeling peculiarly nervous about Maude's arrival, and the whole evening. She felt like the hostess, even though she wasn't: anxious for things to go well. She drank her first glass of champagne too quickly, and reached for a second as the waiter passed her with the tray. But even with the buoyancy of it in her bloodstream, and the wonderful way it added to her detachment, her heart still sank when Colonel Singer arrived, along with the commander of the SAS and a handful of other officers, including Charlie Elliot. Instinctively, she drifted back to Rory's side, which she'd been avoiding without really thinking about it, and hoped to go unnoticed. From across the room Charlie met her eye briefly, and didn't smile. Joan wrenched her eyes away. He caused her an unpleasant mixture of anger, guilt and embarrassment.

Maude arrived with all the solemnity of a visiting queen. A ripple went round the room as Abdullah wheeled in her chair. They were an odd couple – the tiny, elderly woman in her outdated clothes and thick stockings, towered over by the dark, dignified figure of her slave. Maude greeted Robert and Marian politely, but without smiling, and allowed herself to be the subject of something like a reception line, since everybody wanted to save her the trouble of manoeuvring her chair. Joan went over with a smile, and put her hand on Maude's shoulder. Maude grabbed at it and held it there, so Joan remained, standing just behind her.

'Don't tell me which one is Charles Elliot,' Maude whispered hoarsely. 'I want to see if I can guess from the look of him.'

'All right,' said Joan. She tried to remove her hand and drift away, having no wish to have to talk to Charlie, but Maude held it fast.

'Stay put, won't you,' she said, with some asperity, and Joan paused to think how many years it might have been since Maude had been faced with a room full of so many people, in so formal a setting. Her eyes darted from face to face, and though her expression was calm – even aloof – there was something anxious in the way she held Joan's fingers.

'All right. Will you have a glass of champagne? You look very grand, I must say. I love that brooch,' said Joan, chattering as she might have to her mother when the silence got too much. Maude looked up at her almost fondly.

'Don't panic, girl. I shan't have an episode and show you up,' she said. Joan thought about protesting, but in the end she only smiled wryly.

Charlie Elliot presented himself to Maude, and had the good manners to step back once he'd shaken her hand, to make it easier for her to look up at him. But before he'd even opened his mouth to say his name, Maude made a small, high sound in her throat, and Joan knew she'd recognised him. She couldn't tell exactly what the sound signified – surprise, interest, distress.

'I must say, it's extremely odd to meet you, Miss Vickery. I hope you won't mind me saying so. You belong in articles I've read in journals, and very old photographs of my father's, not here in front of me. It's odd but it's a pleasure, of course.'

'Is it? I'm surprised your father kept any photos from the time before he was world famous. And I can't imagine he's had anything good to say about me, over the years.' There was a slight wobble to Maude's voice, which she tried to hide by speaking sternly. Charlie hesitated for a moment, and Joan saw him shift gear subtly.

'Nothing much at all a lot of the time, in truth,' he said, smiling easily. 'I've no idea what he'll say when I tell him I've met you. I'm rather looking forward to finding out, mind you.'

'Nothing much at all,' Maude echoed. There was an awkward pause.

'Well,' said Charlie. 'He's not said much to me, anyway. A lot of years have gone by, of course – by the time I was old enough to pay attention, all that was already in the dim and distant.'

'All that?'

'Yes. The pioneering days... the race across the Empty Quarter.'

'It was never a race, young man,' said Maude firmly. 'Not for me. I always saw us as a team – we few who wanted to come here and see the desert, experience it. We were kindred spirits, after all. Or so I thought. It was your father who turned it into a race.'

'Well... I suppose if the choice is between being first and being second, I don't know many men who'd choose to come second.' Charlie grinned affably; Joan shifted her weight from foot to foot, wishing he'd shut up and move on, hoping Maude wouldn't get angry. Instead she was quiet for a long moment.

'Yes,' she said eventually. 'As it turned out, winning was far more important to him than anything else. I only wish I'd realised it sooner.' Charlie looked down at her thoughtfully. Joan expected him to be put out by this slur on his father, but he didn't seem to be. He took a sip of his champagne.

'He's a good old stick, is Dad,' he said lightly. 'He was always very kind to us children. Never raised his voice or gave out cross words that weren't deserved . . . He might seem something of a towering figure to live up to, but it never felt that way. He always encouraged us in whatever we wanted to do, whether that was heroic or distinctly not. One of my brothers was trying to become an artist when he . . . when he was lost. Art! We used to barrack him dreadfully, but not Dad. As long as it was honourable, then any calling was acceptable to him.'

'Honourable?' Maude barked sharply. Charlie tipped his head to one side and waited.

Maude's hands clenched around the arms of her chair and she pulled herself forwards, glaring up at him. 'Now you listen to me, young man, because you're old enough to hear this, and I know it to be true: that *towering figure* you think you know . . . that man is a liar and a *thief*!'

The words were brittle with anger, full of conviction. Charlie stared at the old woman with her sharp nose and sharper glare with a look of confusion on his face.

'Miss *Vickery*!' said Joan, louder than she'd meant to. A few heads turned towards them.

'Don't you hush me, Joan! I'm not your mother, nor your charge. And I'm not wrong either. He's every right and need to hear it.'

'I've the right, perhaps, but I'm not sure I've the need. Won't you excuse me, ladies?' said Charlie coolly, and moved away. Maude watched after him hungrily, as though she wished she'd taken a bigger bite, and Joan swallowed her own wounded pride at being snapped at.

'What on earth was that all about? Why would you say that about Nathaniel Elliot?' she said. Maude clicked her tongue against the roof of her mouth, still staring across the room at Charlie's straight back and combed hair.

'I'll tell you when I'm ready, and when the time is right,' she said. Her voice was tight like her shoulders, like her hands still clasping the arms of her chair.

'Well, if you wanted to get to know him, that possibly wasn't the best way to go about it,' said Joan.

'Get to know him? Why would I want to get to *know* him?' Maude pointed one finger at Charlie. 'And besides, that boy will be back to talk to me before the evening's out, just you wait and see. He won't be able to resist coming to tell me how wrong I am. His sort never can.'

'Well, I don't know. He obviously loves his father very much.'

'Oh, yes,' said Maude. She drew breath to say something else but changed her mind and seemed to sink instead, the fire and fight suddenly ebbing from her. 'Yes, I dare say he does,' was all she said. 'Now, where is this fiancé of yours? How is it I've not met *him* yet?'

'Out there on the terrace. Shall I push?' said Joan.

'Yes, do go and find yourself somewhere to sit down, Abdullah – I doubt you'll be welcome to eat with us. The British still like to think their white skin makes all the blood and mess underneath purer, somehow.'

'Yes, lady,' said Abdullah. He smiled with one side of his mouth, inclined his head and glided from the room. Maude settled her hands in her lap and laced her fingers, but just before she clenched them Joan saw how they shook.

It was Rory who managed at get the first smile out of Maude that evening, sitting near her on the edge of one of the terrace chairs so that they were eye to eye. Joan left to fetch Maude some champagne and when she returned Rory was leaning towards the old lady, listening attentively with his eyebrows tweaked up in that way that made him look younger, sweeter, wholly credulous, and Maude was talking with a flicker of amusement brightening her eyes. Joan stopped at a distance from them, and watched. The terrace was brightly lit against the night; mosquitoes and little white moths jostled the lamps; the party glinted with light and Jalali was an invisible blackness hidden against the sky. She looked over her shoulder at Charlie, across the room inside with his back still turned to her, and then at Rory, who looked soft and kind and himself again. But Joan still didn't want to go over to him. She stayed where she was, like a statue at the edge of the party, until Colonel Singer's wife spotted her and drew her across to join their group. Joan said little; just enough to be polite. She kept glancing back at Rory and Maude, trying to decide how it felt to see them getting on so well.

Maude's chair was placed several seats away from Joan at the dinner table, nearer to Robert, Marian, the colonel and his wife – a nod to her age and status. Joan ate little and tried to eavesdrop what her friend was saying, but it was impossible above the rising din of a group of people with champagne in their empty stomachs. The room was hot and she felt her face flush, and sweat prickling under her arms. Rory was sitting opposite Charlie Elliot at the other end of the table, and the depth of their discussion distracted her. She didn't want Charlie near Rory; she didn't want him to know any more about any of them – herself, Daniel, Rory. She did not want him incorporated into their lives in any way – she had a gut-deep feeling that his very existence made it impossible for everything to hang together, and seeing them talk was almost as unbearable as not knowing what they were saying. A slim, blonde Welsh man was sitting to Joan's left and telling her about the workings of the oil company. He had a slightly boring way of speaking that made it difficult for Joan to pay attention, and she didn't try too hard.

When they rose from the table Joan began to move at once towards Maude, but Charlie stepped in front of her. Joan found it hard to look directly at him; her gaze slid off to one side.

'Well might you look guilty, Joan,' said Charlie, sounding serious. 'What was all that about the other day, back at the camp? Although I suppose I can guess.'

'I really must go and see how—'

'Maude Vickery can look after herself. You needn't follow her about like a servant.'

'I wasn't! I'm not.'

'You are, but far be it for me to contradict you. I should like to speak to her again myself before the evening's out.'

'Yes.' Joan smiled slightly. 'She said you would.'

'Well, wouldn't you, if she'd said that about your old man?' Charlie retorted. Joan didn't reply, because he was right. 'I wasn't in the mood for it. We lost one of our boys on the mountain yesterday – Duke Swindells. Picked off a ridge by a sniper. He was a bloody good man. We might have to change tack, start moving more by night than in daylight.'

Charlie frowned into the distance for a moment, then shook his head and looked at Joan again. 'Anyway. How did you get on with Peter?'

'Who?'

'Peter Sawyer? Don't tell me the pair of you didn't even introduce yourselves? I changed seats with him on purpose, just so you could talk.'

'Oh, him. Yes. He seems nice,' Joan said vaguely. Charlie shook his head.

'I suppose I understand,' he said softly. 'But disappearing inside yourself won't solve a thing, Joan.'

'What?' She frowned. 'There's nothing to solve. I really

must get on . . .' she said, but Charlie stayed in her way. He stared at her for a moment before pressing on.

'Peter Sawyer and I go way back. He works for the PDO – the oil company here in Muscat, and he owes me a favour or two. He's flying down to the camp at Fahud for a meeting the day after tomorrow.'

'That's fascinating, Captain Elliot, but I—'

'The camp's right on the edge of the desert – you can see the Empty Quarter from there; you can smell it. They'll be flying over Nizwa to get there. And over Fort Jabrin – with a kind word to the pilot. Joan, did you hear me? I've spoken to him and he's agreed to take you with him. You'll have to stop the night at the camp, and you'll have to pretend to be his secretary, and of course it all has to be kept on the QT, but he'll take you.' Charlie shrugged. 'You'd get to see the interior, even if you won't be able to explore it this time. That's if you're still interested. That's if you're even listening to me,' he finished, exasperated.

Joan stared dumbly at Charlie as his words sank in. Then she glanced past him at Peter Sawyer, the man who'd droned on at her during dinner; he smiled, tipped his glass and winked almost imperceptibly. She was paralysed by some vast emotion trying to claw its way up, and was scared of what it might turn out to be when it reached the surface. She was worried that she might throw her arms around Charlie, and cry.

'Yes,' she said, and then did sob – a sudden dry clench of her chest that she had no control over. She took a breath when it'd passed, but there seemed less room for air in her chest with the rising wave of elation there; the overwhelming tide of relief. She realised only then how badly she needed to go *some*where. 'Yes, I still want to go,' she said shakily.

'Oh Christ, don't cry, will you? Not here. I won't have the first idea what to do, and everyone will think we're having an affair,' said Charlie, but he couldn't hide his pleasure at her reaction. A smile kept tugging at his mouth, however many times he suppressed it.

'I won't cry.' Joan gripped her hands together, digging her nails into her palms. If she could have gone right then, and got on the plane with Peter Sawyer, she would have.

'You – you really do want to go to the interior, don't you?' said Charlie. Joan nodded. Her desire to see it was changing, intensifying; mixing with the overwhelming need to simply *move*. 'Rather a pity you were born a girl. But then again...' He grinned, but Joan was too happy, too grateful, to mind his flirting.

'When? When can I go?' she said.

'Saturday morning, first thing. You need to get yourself to the oil company offices – do you know where they are? I can draw you a map but it's very easy anyway. The plane will take off from Bait al Falaj, so put a scarf over your hair and some sunglasses on, and keep your head down until you're on board, in case anyone at the base spots you. It should be simple enough, but it wouldn't do to get rumbled. Slapped wrists all round. Your cover story for that chameleonic fiancé of yours is up to you. A stopover with Miss Vickery would be simplest, I suppose. Joan, please tell me you're paying attention to all this.'

'I am.' Joan reached out and grasped Charlie's forearm, and they both looked down in surprise. Joan felt the temperature of his skin and the unfamiliar contours of tendon and bone beneath his sleeve; she stared at her hand, and her engagement ring stared back at her.

Wordlessly, she snatched the hand back and looked away. She looked directly at Rory, who was watching from across the room. *Chameleonic.* Perhaps that was what had changed about

Rory's appearance. Perhaps she could now see his camouflage, when she'd previously thought it was real skin.

Later on, the furniture was pushed back at one end of the long sitting room, and the servants put on some outdated records – big band dance hall numbers, and traditional jazz, music that Joan had heard a lot growing up and didn't want to hear any more.

'We should have brought some records out with us,' said Rory, as the two of them danced sedately at the far end of the room, near an open window that looked out to sea. 'Do you think Maude would like "Jailhouse Rock"? Or "Great Balls of Fire"?' He smiled.

'She might, you know,' said Joan. 'She's not your typical old lady. Then again, she sometimes does seem caught up in the past. But that's how life is out here, isn't it? Like travelling back in time, and we can't be let out in case we infect the place with modernity, and upset the balance of everything. Salim says—' She pulled herself up, her heart giving a lurch.

'Who's Salim?'

'Nobody – one of the servants. Never mind.'

'Isn't that rather its charm, though? The backwardness, I mean,' said Rory. They were dancing like brother and sister, Joan realised – not holding each other too closely.

Rory's hand in the small of her back rested very lightly. Joan wondered if they'd always danced like that, and whether she was only just noticing it now. The army officers took their leave and retired early, and Charlie sought her eye before he left, giving her a nod and the mischievous twist of a smile. Joan waved as covertly as she could, and wondered if he'd spoken to Maude again. In the blur of the evening, and the wild rush of the planned trip to the oil camp, she'd almost forgotten what Maude had said to him about his father, and the bitterness with which she'd loaded the words.

Joan's own steps were clumsy from the wine; her dress was rumpled, and the room had a bewildering shimmer to it. She could feel her pulse in her skin, and her thoughts seemed to float slightly behind her, coming a little late to everything she said and did. She was tired but reluctant to retire, feeling that she hadn't quite done something she'd wanted to do that night; but then she heard her father's voice in her head: *Sweetheart, children never think it's time for bed. That's why grown-ups were invented.* The words brought on a stab of pain and longing for him. He would have known what she should do; no decision would have frightened her, with him right behind her. But she heard another voice as well – Salim's. *None of us is helpless unless we choose to be.* She wished she could have talked to him more. He had begun to give her the same feeling of borrowed strength that her father once had.

'I should probably go up,' she said, but the words were a quiet mumble that Rory didn't seem to hear.

'The rebels are about to get a dose of modernity,' said Rory. 'Charlie Elliot was telling me. I almost feel sorry for them.'

'How can you say that? Dan's out there now, you know – fighting them. Maybe being stalked, or ambushed right now.'

'Hush, Joan! I know – of course I know that. Don't you think I'm worried about him too?'

'I'm sure you're very worried. Perhaps more than you ought to be.' As soon as the words were out, Joan regretted them. She looked up at him with a sparkle of fear but Rory continued without noticing.

'You mean because they're so well prepared, and well armed? Well, you're right. They're the stronger force by far, even though the enemy has the high ground. We just have to keep reminding ourselves that.'

Suddenly full of an ill-defined anger, Joan glared past Rory's shoulder, and they finished the dance without talking. She stepped on his foot once or twice, getting more and more clumsy. 'Perhaps it's bedtime for you, darling girl,' said Rory, as the record ended.

'Yes. Goodnight,' she said abruptly, and turned away from him before his puzzled expression could soften her. She went to say goodnight to Robert and Marian, and to Maude, but when she looked for the old lady she found her speaking to Abdullah. Maude was clearly telling him something important. Their heads were close together, their focus such that Joan hesitated and was reluctant to interrupt. When she did go over, Abdullah stood up and clasped his hands in front of his khanjar, and Maude stared up at her, and for a moment their faces were so closed off, so distant and unwelcoming, it was as though they didn't recognise her.

'I'm ... goodnight. I thought I'd go up,' she said, at which Maude finally managed a small, distracted smile.

'Goodnight, Joan,' she said. 'We shall see you anon, I dare say.' It was a cursory dismissal that Joan retreated from uncertainly.

The day after the dinner Joan went to visit Maude, as much to have a reason to leave the building as anything else. In spite of her hangover, she wanted to tell Maude about the trip to Fahud she would take the next day, since Maude was the only person she felt she *could* tell.

A thin man, all black hair and whiskers, was leaving Maude's house as she arrived, shouldering a grubby canvas bag. He flicked his eyes over Joan but didn't pause, and then Abdullah turned her away at the door, telling her solemnly that the lady needed to rest. Shamelessly wishing her time away, Joan bought a coffee from a street vendor, then followed Robert's innocently given instructions to the oil company's offices in the centre of Muscat, to be certain of finding them the following morning. Her need to leave Muscat, to be somewhere else, was growing all the time.

Charlie had told her to be at the offices at first light, but Joan couldn't sleep anyway, so she was there even earlier, slipping out of the Residency when only the servants were awake, and then only just. She left a message with the bleary-eyed houseman that she would be with Miss Vickery all day, and had been invited to remain for dinner, so she'd miss *dum dum* and be back the following day. She hoped her message would get through and that nobody would go looking for her as the day aged. She hoped but didn't really care. She couldn't think past the flight, and seeing the desert, and almost didn't care what happened after that. She tied a scarf under her chin and took her largest sunglasses, which had white plastic frames and were so conspicuous she hadn't dared to wear them yet. Packed in her satchel was a change of shirt and underwear, her nightdress, toothbrush and comb. Only as much as would be appropriate for an impromptu stopover at Maude's, should anybody look into her room. Clumsily, she spooled a brand-new film into her camera with fingers that shook.

The sky turned the colour of fish scales, and sparrows began to chirp at the same time as sounds of human life returned to Muscat – doors and window shutters creaking and clonking, the muezzin calling to first prayers; there was the splashing of water, the rattle of a bucket dipped. Joan waited in a little street beside the oil company offices until she heard the key turning in the lock, and men's voices on the front steps; one English and one Welsh.

When a Land Rover pulled up outside, Joan walked over to it, as boldly as she could. It was driven by a Baluchi solider wearing the red balmoral of the Muscat Regiment, and she hoped he wasn't someone she'd encountered at the army base. To her shame, she realised she hadn't paid the Baluchi faces much attention at all. Her heart was in her mouth and her legs felt weak, but far less so than the first time she'd gone into Jalali. She was even starting to enjoy the feeling – the fear, and the rush of excitement that came with ignoring it; the elation afterwards when she had done what she'd set out to do, and come through it cleanly. She smiled at Peter Sawyer as convincingly as she could, and held out her hand. He gave it a perfunctory shake.

'Miss Seabrook. In you get,' he said, quite calmly. If the other man standing beside him expected an introduction he didn't linger to wait for it. He handed Sawyer an attaché case stuffed with brown files, and shook his hand.

'Good luck with it,' he said to Sawyer. 'Try to get an answer out of him, if there's one to be had.'

'Will do,' said Sawyer. He got into the back seat beside Joan, and the Land Rover pulled away.

'Well, that was easy enough,' she said to him, as they crept out through the city gate. Sawyer glanced significantly at the driver then back at her, raising his brows, and Joan checked herself.

'Let's not count our chickens,' he said wryly.

At Bait al Falaj, Joan waited in the car for as long as she could. She knew that Daniel and most of his fellow officers were away on operations, but as far as she knew Colonel Singer was still coordinating them from his desk in the fort, and there were plenty of other men who might recognise her, women being so scarce there. The Land Rover stayed outside the wire of the camp, circling around to the far side where the runway was cut into the dusty ground. As well as the SAF's two Pioneers, a third plane was waiting – bigger and better-looking, its silver body undimmed by the desert dust. Only once the pilot had strode over from the base, started the twin engines with a stutter and roar of noise, taxied the plane to the head of the runway and opened the door, did Joan get out of the car and march smartly to the steps. She had that same invincible feeling again – behind the fear and the nerves was the hope that she could do anything.

She was half expecting to be stopped, discovered, sent back to Muscat under Singer's withering eye but, strapped into a seat with the din of the engines all around, she and Sawyer were soon juddering along the runway, gathering speed until, with a stomach-dropping lurch, the plane was airborne. Joan craned to look out of the tiny window as the ground dropped away and the old fort beneath them became a child's building block, abandoned in the dust.

She breathed in the oil and hot, stripped metal smell of the plane, quite unlike the commercial plane she'd travelled in before, and did her best not to laugh – the need to bubbled up in her chest, similar to the sob when Charlie had told her about the trip. Beside her, Sawyer was looking through his paperwork with a bored expression; he noticed her obvious excitement with a bemused expression.

'First time in an aeroplane?' he shouted, above the noise.

Joan shook her head. 'First time beyond the palisades, though.'

'Good job the rebels are still doing such a comprehensive job of mining the road, or we'd be making this trip by truck. A lot less fun. Elliot said you wanted a peek at Jabrin, and Nizwa?'

'Oh yes please. If it's possible.'

'It's possible,' said Peter. 'So, how long have you and him been sweeties?'

'Me and who? Charlie Elliot? Oh, no, we're not. I'm engaged, actually.'

'Oh. Right,' said Peter, with a look of pure scepticism.

'No, really,' said Joan, but Peter had gone back to his papers. A little while later he looked up again, appraisingly, and added, 'He's stuck his neck out for you, you know; to get you on this plane.' Joan was transfixed by the view from the window, and said nothing.

They flew beside the vertical outer slopes of Jebel Ahkdar, until they'd risen to such a height that she could look down and see the plateau in the distance. It all looked so peaceful, so calm and empty, lit by the morning sun; it seemed impossible that men were fighting for their lives there. That Daniel was, and soon Charlie Elliot too. She stared down as though she might be able to see them below, even as dots against the rock. Here and there were the green shocks of date palm forests and terraced fields, betraying villages too well camouflaged to discern. It was like a secret garden, away from the dusty heat of the coastal plain; and far from sating Joan's curiosity, this distant glimpse only made her longing to explore stronger.

And then, incredibly soon, they were past them – in under an hour they'd crossed what had seemed an impossible obstacle from below. The mountains were revealed to be a wall, a jagged scar running away westwards and getting lost in the haze and glare of the sun. They were fierce, and formidable, but they were only a boundary – a line between the sultan's coastal lands and the wild interior, the desert that stretched away for thousands of miles. Suddenly, Joan understood why the sultan might have trouble convincing anyone on the landward side of those mountains that he was their natural ruler. It was another world.

Beyond Jebel Akhtar, the horizon vanished into the far, far distance. The plane banked slightly to the right, and flew lower, and Peter Sawyer touched Joan's arm for her attention.

'There's Nizwa,' he said. Joan looked down at the sprawl of clustered mud houses, the enclosures of goats and cattle, the date palm plantations all around, the massive fort in the centre with its round tower like a vast drum. 'It's the sultan's again now, but until only a couple of years ago this was the imam's HQ. Historically, it was always his. There – that's the army base most of the boys will be operating from soon.'

'Have you been there? On the ground, I mean?'

'No.' Peter shook his head. 'No business to. Sultan Said's very keen on people minding their own business. Lucky for you he stays down in Salalah, eh?'

'His governor in Muscat seems scarcely any less strict.'

'Sayid Shahab? Yes, he's a charming fellow, isn't he? I'd keep my head down if I were you, Miss Seabrook. Why do you want to come out here, anyway? Nothing but sand and flea-bitten locals.'

'That's not how I see it,' she said simply. They were silent for a while, as the city passed beneath them and away, and then Peter pointed again.

'Look there – that's Fort Jabrin.'

Joan held her breath as they flew over the place she'd dreamed of seeing, the place she'd been told she would never see. She felt that sparkle again, that tingling feeling that could be tears or laughter. The plane banked again, sweeping around with its shadow, small and black, keeping pace on the dry earth beneath them. The fort was a series of shapes that looked to have been carved out of the same stuff as the ground – sandy brown, pale, ancient.

Outside it, a massive tree spread a wide shade. Joan couldn't see the carvings, or the old imam's tomb; she couldn't see the painted ceilings, the falaj or any of the tall windows, open to the west wind with the heat and taste of the desert on it. Just then, she would have given her soul to be able to walk its corridors, to discover its secrets. But she was there, nonetheless; she was at Jabrin, and she felt the wonder of it. Her stomach shook as the plane circled, banking sharply again, but she didn't mind. That she had made it there seemed to prove, somehow, that there *was* a way. That she could find a way. As they flew on, Joan craned her neck to keep sight of it for as long as she could, scared that the feeling would go when the fort did.

They travelled for another hour, over shallow undulations in a parched, tawny land dotted here and there with stunted shrubs and outcrops of rock. The oil camp lay in a depression between two flat-topped peaks that looked tame after the harshness of Jebel Akhtar. She saw the mechanical tangle of the derrick, the rectangular huts and offices of the camp clustered together a good distance away, and a lonely runway where one other plane sat waiting.

'Hang on,' said Peter, as they flew in low and slithered down onto the runway with a massive spray of dust and grit. Out of the plane, Joan was at a loss. She followed Peter towards a waiting jeep, unsure whether she was supposed to keep up the pretence of being his secretary. The driver, a young man with a cow's lick of hair and glasses like bottle bottoms, smiled at her.

'Hello, who are you?' he said, and Joan hesitated.

'This is Joan Seabrook. She's just visiting,' Peter introduced her, and Joan relaxed. 'Joan, this is Matthew Jones. He's a geologist, but I've no idea what he actually *does*.'

'Not a journalist, are you? The sultan'll go nuts,' said Matthew.

'No. No, I'm a . . . tourist,' said Joan.

'That's all right then. Cup of tea?'

'You'll be all right, Joan? The Oily Boys'll look after you, and you'll get a good lunch in the mess; I'll most likely see you in there after my meeting,' said Peter, and Joan nodded.

The oil camp buildings were up on stilts, like large seaside huts. Everything was clean – almost sterile, in fact – and had obviously been built at great expense. A short distance away were some flimsier huts with palm-thatched roofs, which Matthew told her were where the locals who worked at the camp lived. He showed her to a room in one of the stilted huts – small and neat with white sheets, a bedside table with a lamp and a small, upright armchair – which would be hers for the night. It had a bathroom attached to it, with a shower.

'The water's hot all the time. Don't drink it – it's the stuff they pipe up from underground here, and it's vile. Plus it'll give you the shits – oh, pardon me! Sorry – we don't see many women out here. Any, in fact. It's easy to forget your manners.' Matthew blushed slightly, and Joan smiled. The room was spotlessly clean, and air conditioned. 'What brings you here? Seems an odd place to holiday.'

'I like to do things differently,' said Joan, enjoying the persona she was creating for herself.

'Well, I can safely say you're the first holidaymaker we've had.'

'Can I go for a walk?' she said. Matthew looked puzzled, but he shrugged.

'Sure, if you like. Don't go far, will you? And don't go near the derrick. I'll get no end of grief if you disappear down a hole. In fact, I'd better find someone to go with you.'

'No, it's fine, really. I promise not to get into any mischief.'

The terrain was hard and gravelly, but since Joan only had her leather sandals from home, it was at least easier to walk on than soft sand would have been. She went in the opposite direction to the one they'd flown in from, away from the derrick and the strange, striated mountains. She walked for half an hour or so in a straight line, until the oil camp had disappeared from view behind a slight rise in the ground. Then she stopped and looked into the south-west, where the sands of the Rub el Khali, the Empty Quarter, began. She couldn't see the dunes, but she fancied she could taste them on the air, and catch the scent of them in her nose. She knew that the heat that day was a fraction of what it could reach in summer, but the sun was still hot on her head and shoulders, and the air was drier than any she'd ever known. She felt it drawing the moisture from her mouth and nose, from her skin and eyes. A faint breeze murmured in her ears but, other than that, there was silence.

Joan stood, and stared at the far horizon, and her heartbeat slowed to keep time with some invisible rhythm of the world around her. A pair of ravens flew to a nearby rock and watched her steadily, but besides them she was alone with the desert all around her, and when she felt the first faint urge to walk further, to carry on walking, to see where her footsteps led her, she began to understand what had driven Maude Vickery, and others, to do exactly that.

She marvelled that Maude had ever stopped. She forgot, for a while, that her brother existed; that her mother did, that Rory did. It felt, for that short time, that she didn't quite exist herself – not as she knew herself anyway; and the notion brought with it a sense of complete freedom.

She made sure she was back at the camp before anyone would have a chance to worry about her. It was lunchtime and the mess hall was busy, and after even such a short time in the quiet of the desert Joan found the noise and bustle intrusive. She looked around tentatively until she saw Peter Sawyer, who waved her over to his table. Matthew Jones was also there, and she was introduced to several others.

'Well, how are you finding this little oasis we've built?' said Matthew, as she sat down.

'It's very impressive. But I'm really more interested in the wilderness all around it, to tell you the truth,' said Joan.

'Uh oh – a desert fanatic. I've met your sort before,' said Peter. 'Beer? There's no shortage of it, but I'm afraid we're not allowed anything stronger here.'

'Thanks. Have you ever been into it? The Empty Quarter, I mean?' said Joan. 'Have any of you? Have you seen the dunes?' There was a general shaking of heads and murmuring of *no*.

'Why would we?' said Matthew. 'There's no oil there.'

'But . . . don't you get the urge to, living here so close to it?' The men exchanged looks of amusement.

'I think we'd better put you back on the plane before you go feral, pet,' said a man with an Australian accent. Joan looked across at Peter in alarm, and he smiled reassuringly.

'Don't worry, not until tomorrow, and if you ask for a dawn knock you can get up for the sunrise; it can be pretty spectacular. Besides, wouldn't want you to miss your visitor this evening,' he said.

'My what?'

'Never mind. What'll you have? The steak is excellent, as are the lobster tails.'

Lunch was incongruously rich and delicious, served as it was in a simple building hundreds of miles from easy supplies of fresh water and groceries. Somehow, the chefs had managed to obtain sirloin steak, fresh vegetables, cream and chocolate.

'Money,' Peter said shortly, when Joan remarked upon the bounty. 'There's lots of it. And we haven't actually found any ruddy oil yet.' Joan thought about the men in Jalali, who didn't even have enough water to drink. The prison and the oil camp seemed to belong in different universes. Guiltily, she ate until she could hardly move, and then had to sleep it off in the afternoon. When she emerged, she found a lounge where off-duty workers were playing table football and reading the papers, but after a quick coffee she went out, and sank herself into the peace and solitude of the landscape again. She walked even further this time, and sat on an unforgiving boulder to watch the sun set in a silent explosion of orange and rose pink. The wind changed direction as it did, whistling across her shoulders from behind, as though the sun were dragging the air away with it; and as soon as the last sliver of the sun had vanished the temperature dropped noticeably. Joan watched all of this, and noticed everything, and let herself think about nothing else. It was a wilful emptiness of mind that revived her like a good night's sleep. When she heard the thump of the camp generator start up behind her, she went back through the gathering dark feeling older and wiser, and not caring if the feeling was an illusion, and no solution.

She passed close to the palm-thatched huts of the Arab workers on her way, and saw a group of four men sitting on their heels around a fledgling fire. They were wearing the faded tunics and sarongs of the desert tribes, with their feet either bare or stuffed into worn leather slippers. Each man had his dagger on his belt, and held the vertical shaft of an old Martini rifle for support. In the flicker of the fire they could have been in a scene from centuries before, brewing coffee in a dented pewter pot with pomegranate seeds in the lid to rattle and ward off the djinn. Then Joan saw that one of the older men was blind in one eye – it was clouded, the lids red and swollen almost shut; a crusted trail of dirty tears ran down to trace the crease of his cheek. Another man had a lantern jaw and a twist in his spine that lifted one shoulder above the other. Their stillness began to have the air of apathy; the image of their peaceful timelessness was spoiled by these signs of suffering and dissolution.

Joan refreshed herself as best she could before dinner, having no idea how formal it would be. All she had was her clean shirt, so once she'd showered she put that on, and her trousers without the cumbersome skirt over the top. In front of an unadorned square mirror designed for a man, she combed the sand from her hair. With a start, she realised she hadn't thought of Rory, or of the Gibsons, all day. She wondered if they'd got her message, and had been satisfied with it, or had been out looking for her and found her gone. It all seemed such a very long way away; it seemed safe to ignore her situation from where she was, but she knew it would be waiting for her, inescapably, when she got back. Her trip to Fahud was bought time, that was all – time Charlie had bought for her. She couldn't wait to tell Maude she'd been to the edge of the desert, and that even a tiny glimpse had made her understand it better. The person who appeared at dinnertime, however – her promised visitor – was Charlie Elliot. It made sense, since nobody else knew she was there, but she hadn't expected to see him.

He grinned at her as she appeared in the mess hall, got up from his seat and came over.

'Well, how was it? Did you get a good view of Jabrin?' he said calmly. Joan nodded, and couldn't help but smile.

'Yes. It was amazing, Charlie . . . thank you. Thank you for arranging this – I think I forgot to say that back in Muscat.'

'Yes, you did,' said Charlie. 'But I forgive you. It was written all over your face, after all. I don't think anyone has ever been as excited about a trip to an oil camp before.'

'It's not the oil camp – you know that. It's . . . being away. Out of Muscat.'

'Yes, I know. It must all feel very like . . . a cage,' he said.

Joan looked away uncomfortably, because it didn't seem that they were talking about Muscat any more.

'I walked out to the edge of the desert. It was wonderful,' she said.

'Really?' Charlie sounded sceptical. 'Not bleak, barren, and bloody dead, then?'

'Not at all.'

'Give me a nice jungle any day. Or a forest, at least.'

'How are you here, Charlie? I mean, how on *earth* did you get down here?'

'We all upped sticks to Nizwa yesterday. I persuaded the CO it'd be a good idea if I came out here to talk to the general manager about the landmining situation. They get a bit stroppy about it, to say the least – they keep losing their trucks on the way to the coast, and they do make a substantial contribution to be able to use the road. I thought a visit in person to update them on the situation might not go amiss. The CO knows there's something a bit fishy going on, but I've accrued a bit of leeway. It's a long, dull drive, I can tell you.'

'All the men have gone to Nizwa? So it's about to start, then? The final assault, I mean?' A small, cold knot formed in Joan's gut when she thought of those massive rocks, and the black ravines between them like traps ready to spring, and the pale strip of skin around Daniel's hairline.

'Well, *an* assault. Who knows if it'll be the final one? But I'll do my best.' He smiled, and she thought again that his bravado was an affectation; his arrogance a mask. 'Come and sit down, Joan. I'm starving.'

The food was just as good as at lunch, and the beer as copious. Joan's voice was all but lost beneath the male chatter all around; she was the only woman in the room, and drew more than a few curious looks, but no apparent resentment. Charlie talked a lot, and joked a lot, and the other men seemed to fall into a kind of orbit around him, as though there was no point trying to outshine him. Since Joan could see this effect, she was able to resist his gravitational drag – the way he drew the others in. She remembered what Marian had said, about his reputation as a womaniser, and wasn't in the least surprised. She teased him gently, and refused to be charmed, but it got harder and harder the more beer she was given.

'How long have you got?' Peter asked him, at one point.

'All British troops to be out of Oman by April at the latest,' said Charlie. 'Her Majesty's government decrees it. The UN summit on the Middle East is coming up, and they're twitchy about appearing too colonial after all the hoo-ha with the Suez Canal. You should hear the way Radio Cairo bangs on about our involvement – you'd think the entire British army was out here, running roughshod over the innocent locals, instead of just a handful of us, getting routinely confounded by them on their ruddy mountain.'

'Ought we to be here at all?' said Joan. 'I've heard that we're only helping the sultan to get at the oil, when it really doesn't belong to the sultan at all. After all, he has no sovereignty over the interior traditionally.'

All eyes turned to her, and there was a startled pause before some laughter and raised eyebrows; a few incredulous whistles.

'Joan Seabrook, who on earth have you been talking to?' said Charlie, and Joan's face flamed.

'Nobody,' she said hastily. 'Just something I . . . overheard.'

'Well, "nobody" might be right,' said Peter, with a shrug. 'But who do you think has convinced the imam that the oil is his? Who do you think arms his fighters, and trains them?'

'I don't know.'

'The Saudis,' Charlie supplied. 'And who do you think encourages the Saudis in their ambitions across the Omani border, and sells them the weapons in the first place?'

'The Americans,' said the Australian man.

'Oh,' said Joan, feeling stupid.

'It's international relations by proxy,' said Charlie. 'Like most wars. The west keeps its hands clean so that its leaders can smile and shake hands for the cameras.'

'Ah, enough bloody politics,' said the Australian man. 'Drink their beer and don't think about it too much, that's my motto.'

'Hear, hear,' said Charlie, raising his glass, and the conversation moved on to less serious subjects.

Joan ate in silence for a while, and wondered if Salim knew about the layers of interest and greed behind the conflict. He had spoken of wanting the Omani people to be free to improve life for themselves, free from outside influences; he'd said nothing about the Saudis, or America. She wondered whether she should ask him about it, since it somehow seemed like bad manners to do so.

'I meant to ask you,' she said to Charlie, later on, leaning in close. 'Why do you think Maude said those things about your father? Did you talk to her again – did you get to the bottom of it?' The smile faded from Charlie's face.

'I tried to ask her but she just stuck to her guns, and wouldn't elaborate. She said there was no point talking to a person who couldn't hear.'

'Oh dear. That does sound the sort of thing she might say.'

'As to why she said it – I've no idea. Sour grapes that she lost? Perhaps it's more than that – some old feud she thinks she came out the worst of. But my father is no liar, and he's certainly no thief. I've never met a more honourable sort – he's *impossible* to corrupt, and God knows I tried, as a boy. He's a far better sort than I am,' said Charlie, his voice getting tighter.

'If that's the case then it doesn't matter what Maude says,' said Joan soothingly.

'True. But I still didn't like hearing it. You'd probably have more luck finding out what she was on about than me. You're her trusted emissary, after all.'

'What? What do you mean?' For a wild moment Joan thought he'd somehow found out about her visits to Salim. Charlie looked up and smiled speculatively.

'I only meant that you're her friend – and you might be her only one. Why, what have you been up to? You look very guilty all of a sudden.'

'Nothing, of course,' she said, bringing her expression back under control. Charlie chuckled, shaking his head.

'I didn't really think you'd come on this trip, you know. I mean, I know you liked the idea of it, but I thought when it came to it you'd be too sensible, and too honest to fib to the establishment. Now I wonder if this is just the tip of the iceberg,' he said. Joan smiled, feeling the beer making her reckless – it made her want to tell him about Jalali, but she checked herself.

'Perhaps it is,' was all she said, and Charlie laughed again. 'My dad always used to tell me to be brave. I suppose that, out here, I'm trying to do as he asked.'

'How did he die? Do you mind my asking?'

'I – no, I don't mind.' Joan's tongue went cottony and dry. 'He crashed his car,' she said. 'Or rather, another car crashed into his. He'd been on his way home from work, a journey he'd made a thousand times before.' It had been the first day of rain after a long dry spell, when the roads were greased with the built-up residue of cars and water. She'd been to the exact spot and seen the long, black streaks on the tarmac where the other car had turned too sharply, and swung out of control. 'It . . . it would have been very quick, the doctor told us.' She swallowed. 'He said Dad was already dead before the fire started.'

Charlie frowned down at his hands for a moment, and she saw him take a deep breath. Talking about the accident still made her heart speed and her fingers twitch, as though it was about to happen again, as though she could stop it.

'That's a mercy, at least,' said Charlie, in the end. 'We're ... not so sure about Thomas.' Joan said nothing, watching Charlie, waiting. He looked up at her, and she could tell he felt the exact same way as she did, talking about it. 'My brother, Tom. He was in the Merchant navy, but he died on shore. In a pub in Hackney, of all the places. The place was hit by an incendiary, and went up like a torch. He ... they ... a lot of people were trapped inside as it burned, and couldn't get out.'

'But smoke knocks people unconscious, long before the flames reach them,' said Joan desperately. Charlie nodded.

'Yes. Far better to think about it happening like that.'

'You had four brothers,' said Joan. He nodded again.

'Kenny, Tom, James and Elias.' Charlie held up four fingers; he had a hard, angry look in his eyes. 'Drowned, bombed, Dunkirk, Dunkirk,' he said, ticking them off.

'Your poor parents,' Joan said softly.

'I think Kenny was the worst. He was only ten years old. We'd all been swimming in the river – he got caught in the current and taken over the weir. There was always the thought that we ought to have done something ... prevented it somehow. Less so for me – I was only seven. But James and Elias took it hard.'

'Awful,' said Joan. It wasn't enough, but she knew that no words could be. 'Awful,' she said again. 'And now you're in the army, too. Your parents must have wanted to put you away, safely wrapped in packing paper, and only got you out on special occasions.'

'Too true. But I've no intention of getting shot, don't you worry,' he said, the bravado returning. Joan saw more than ever that it was a shield, and she wished he wouldn't raise it so readily.

Between the four of them, Olive, Daniel, Rory and Joan had stopped talking about her father's accident. Joan was sure that they still thought about it – that it must still haunt them, as it haunted her, but any mention of it was met with a tense and resentful silence; or worse – her mother's tears, and accusations of reopened wounds. *It'll do you no good to dwell on it*, Rory had told her the last time she'd tried to talk to him about it. So Joan had stopped mentioning it, and people beyond her immediate circle had stopped asking about it long before that. She felt too uncomfortable to bring it up, for fear of seeming morbid, and seeing how uncomfortable it made people; yet it seemed wrong to just ignore something so huge, so life-altering. But it didn't feel morbid, talking about it to Charlie. And he didn't seem resentful, or uncomfortable. The simple way he'd talked about his own losses gave her the soothing sense that he understood the need to. She wanted to say more, though she didn't know what; she had the notion that talking about it, airing it, might help ease it; but the moment had passed and Charlie was waving to the waiter for more drinks.

At the end of the evening Charlie led Joan outside, to some knowing looks and winks from the others. He took her hand and looped it through his arm, and held it there at the crook of his elbow, and Joan liked the gesture though it came with a warning bell. It felt odd – she realised that other than Rory, no man outside her family had ever walked with her that way. They went a short distance off into the darkness behind the residential huts. Uneasy, Joan pulled her hand away and stepped back.

'Don't panic. Look up,' said Charlie. He reached into his pocket for a cigarette, and rummaged for a match while Joan tipped her head back and stared. There were more stars than she'd ever seen; they were a blanket that seemed to light up the sky, nothing like the few faint pinpricks of home. The Milky Way was vast and grey-mauve, smeared from one side of the heavens to the other; she could see all seven of the Pleiades, when she'd only ever seen five before. The hugeness of it, the multitude, was dizzying. 'Quite something, isn't it?' Charlie said quietly. 'That's one thing I have to concede about the desert. It's the best night sky on earth.'

'It's beautiful. I've never seen anything like it.' A shooting star flared and died over their heads, and then another, seconds later. Joan thought about telling Charlie to look, but decided to keep them for herself. The wish she wanted to make refused to be put into words, however. Instead she pictured feeling courageous, and free, and wished for that.

When the stars were wheeling with the drink and the rush of tipping back her head for so long, Joan looked back at Charlie, smiling. Silently, he offered her his cigarette, and she took it.

'My mother hates it when I smoke,' she said. 'She says it's common. And creases the mouth.'

'Well, Joan, you're not a child any more. Look where you are! Look at all the rules you've broken. What would she say about that?' he said. Joan didn't answer. Thinking of her mother gave her a teetering feeling, the fine balance of love and resentment. She felt the pull of home, and the security of it, and for the first time wondered if that too was a trap, ready to spring. She smiled, and shook her head, and then Charlie stepped towards her, and put his hand on her cheek, and kissed her. For a moment she let him – the hardness of his mouth after Rory's was fascinating; the rasp of stubble on his top lip and chin; the way he pressed against her and opened his mouth slightly, which Rory never did. The taste of beer and cigarettes was on his tongue, like it was on hers, and there was something else beneath that as well – the unique taste of *him*, unfamiliar, good; like the smell of him that was in her nose, and the warmth of his hand on her skin. Charlie's kiss got stronger; he wrapped his arms tight around her and Joan tensed against the strength of them as a pang of desire shot through her. Then she turned her face away, and pulled back against his embrace. The idea of home, of ever being able to return to it, was slipping away, ever further. With Charlie, there was no safe place.

'Stop it!' she said.

'What's wrong? Joan – I just want to . . .' He kept his hold for a few more seconds, but when Joan didn't relax, he let go. She stepped back, put both her hands on his chest and shoved him hard.

'I said stop it!'

'All right, all right – I've stopped, haven't I?' he said. 'No need to attack me.'

'What do you think you're doing? I'm engaged – you've met my fiancé!'

'I know, but—'

'I was warned about you, you know. God – is this why you organised this trip for me? I thought you were being kind . . . but you thought you'd *bought* me, is that it? Do you think I owe you something, now?'

'No! It's not like that. I just . . .'

'You just what?'

'I just like you, that's all. And I thought you liked me.' Charlie took a drag from his cigarette, and in the weak light of it she saw his face frowning, his eyes turned away. He looked embarrassed, contrite, and Joan felt her ire abate.

'Well even if I did like you, it wouldn't matter, would it?

I'm engaged. I'm getting married soon, to a man I love,' she said. Charlie looked up at her in disbelief.

'But . . . you can't actually *marry* him, Joan. He's queer. What kind of marriage would that be?'

'What? What are you talking about? He loves me. Rory loves me!' Her voice rose. She hoped that if she said it loudly enough, he would believe it. She needed to believe it.

'Joan . . . maybe he does. Maybe he loves you, but not in the way he should. We both saw what was going on in your brother's tent that night, and—'

'No! Shut up – I won't listen to you!' Joan put her hands over her ears, just for a second, until she felt ridiculous. Her heart was racing so fast she could hardly feel the gaps between beats. She wanted to be angry – she wanted to be angry with *him* – but it felt more like fear.

'Joan, remember what we were just saying about you not being a child any more?'

'It's nothing to do with you. Do you understand? *You* are nothing to do with us!' She turned and left him there, ignoring him when he followed her for a while, saying her name. She went into her room and stood with her back to the door, not even putting on the light. She didn't want to catch sight of herself in the mirror; her mother had always told her she looked ugly when she cried.

In the morning Joan went to breakfast with an aching head and a feeling of stony dread, but Charlie wasn't there. Peter told her he'd left at first light, back to the army camp at Nizwa.

With a stab of sorrow, Joan realised she hadn't got up to see the sunrise – what might have been her only chance to see a desert sunrise. Close to tears, she sat down with a cup of tea and a bread roll still warm from baking, and blamed Charlie Elliot entirely. After breakfast she boarded the plane in desperate silence, because the peace and wholeness she'd felt the day before was ebbing with every moment that passed. Only the taste and feel of Charlie's kiss remained, obscuring everything else. For the two hours of the flight she stared hungrily from the window, soaking up the scenery, trying to forget and to remember. Peter Sawyer, obviously mystified by her change in mood, left her to her thoughts. They landed at Bait al Falaj at around ten in the morning, without mishap, and the camp was unusually quiet – the normal bustle of men absent now that the bulk of them had been moved to Nizwa. The hush gave Joan the melancholy feeling of things being over, and of being left behind, left out. She walked to the waiting car without bothering to conceal herself overly much. She was still having trouble caring about the things she knew she ought to.

Still, she returned to the Residency with some trepidation. Robert had already disappeared into the offices but Marian and Rory were on the terrace, finishing breakfast. Joan paused before stepping into view, gathering herself, summoning a breezy demeanour.

'Ah, there you are. We were just wondering when you'd be back,' said Marian, pulling her sunglasses down her nose and peering over them at Joan. She was immaculate; she had that subtle knowing edge to her, and Joan was suddenly aware of her own dusty clothes and the stinging of her lips where Charlie's kiss had chafed them. She wiped her palms nervously against her seat of her trousers. 'Did you enjoy yourself out there?'

'Out there?' Joan echoed. Her mouth was dry.

'Yes, out there beyond the gates, at Maude Vickery's house?'

'Oh! Yes. We had a lovely evening, thank you. I was sorry to miss breakfast here though – it's a rather simpler affair there.'

'Well, there's plenty left.' Marian reached forward for the pot. 'Tea?'

Marian soon rose and left Joan and Rory together. He was very quiet; Joan realised he hadn't spoken since her return. She realised too late that she didn't want to be left alone with him. Daring a glance at him as she sipped her lukewarm tea, Joan noticed the odd look on his face. He looked well rested – there were no shadows under his eyes, but somehow he looked a little older as well: a lowering of his brows, a small crease between them; a tightness to his mouth that wasn't normally there. She had the unsettling sense that there were two people sitting in his skin – one she knew, one she did not. She cleared her throat and tried to steady herself.

'You're very quiet, Rory,' she said. 'Is everything all right?'

'I'm not sure,' said Rory, looking down at his hands, where his fingers were worrying a piece of bread crust into crumbs on the table. Joan had a sinking feeling, and said nothing. 'I went to Maude's house this morning, when the gates opened. I thought I'd walk you back, or take you for breakfast at that little café on the waterfront – the one where all the boatmen get their coffee.' Rory brushed the crumbs from the table with an agitated sweep of his hand. 'But you weren't there, of course. You weren't there last night either.' He looked up at her but she couldn't meet his eye; her mind had gone entirely blank. 'So, Joan, are you going to tell me where you were – and who you were with?'

Palestine and Syria, April 1905

Dear Nathaniel, Maude wrote, *I met the most astonishing man today — he must have been a hundred years old, if he was a day. He showed me the ruins of the fifth-century basilica he was living in with no small amount of personal pride, and I was left wondering exactly how long he had been there, and whether he remembered its builders of old! A moment of whimsy, but it's easy to succumb to them when one spends so much time in the company of one's own thoughts.*

She paused, rubbing her chilled fingers, which were struggling to grip the pen. *How are you? How is Africa?* Maude stopped and put down her pen. She could write letters to her father that ran to fifteen pages of close script, giving every detail of her progress and what she had learned; she could write endless shorter notes to Frank and John, keeping them up to date and sending good wishes to their wives and various offspring. But when it came to writing to Nathaniel, she struggled to find words that seemed quite adequate.

The wind had risen and was pushing the canvas walls in and out as though the tent were breathing. Maude's little mirror swung from its hook on the central pole, sending light from her oil lamp lancing into the corners. Her general factotum, Haroun, a squat, diffident Palestinian whom she'd hired in Jerusalem, always made up her camp bed with military precision, tucking in the blankets so tightly it was sometimes hard to worm her way beneath them, but that night she'd pulled them off and wrapped them around herself to sit at her folding desk and write. The air had a deadening chill, and a draught nipped at her ankles. Her toes were frozen, her ears ached, and there was a drip at the end of her nose that replenished itself endlessly. *It must be warm there, at least. We had hail today*, she wrote. They'd ridden through it for an hour, stinging their hands and faces, making the horses lay back their ears in misery, until, much to Maude's disgust, they'd admitted defeat and taken shelter beneath a stand of scrawny oak trees that were hardly fit for the purpose. They'd lost three hours' riding time, and so had camped far short of the town of Mheen where they'd hoped to restock their dwindling supplies. Breakfast would be a meagre affair, and the horses would have to make do with whatever grazing they could find overnight. Maude's hair was still slightly damp now, and her scalp felt numb.

She put down her pen and breathed into her cupped hands. They'd camped below a stubby outcrop of rock for shelter, and the wind was curling around it with a low moaning that might just be, Maude reflected, the loneliest sound in the whole world. She listened until she fancied she could hear voices in it, and felt herself to be a million miles from everyone who knew and loved her; a million miles from home. Just for a second she wished her father were there. She wished Nathaniel were there – he'd be shivering worse than she was, since he'd always felt the cold, and she could have jollied him along, and beaten him at backgammon, and felt jollier herself. *Travelling isn't all beer and skittles, is it?* she wrote. *Not all the time.* Then, since that seemed a bit defeatist, she added:

But on the whole, of course, there's nothing else I'd rather be doing. Did Father write to you about my little book on the ruins of the Sassanian palaces? It's been getting a good few favourable reviews since it was published, which is satisfying, having gone to all the trouble of writing the thing. Of course

I now look back at it and see only all the ways in which it could have been more thorough and more insightful, not to mention better written, but – onwards and upwards, as Father would say.

She didn't say that she hoped the reviews would lead to increased sales, and then to royalties. As it was, she was going to have to write to her father very soon and ask for more money. Not that the Vickery fortune would feel any kind of pinch when she did; she was just a little embarrassed to have lost control of her budget. Maude wished she had a mug of hot tea to wrap her hands around, but Haroun and the other servants were already in their beds, and she didn't like to rouse them.

She pictured Nathaniel as she had last seen him nine months ago, at her mother's funeral in Lyndhurst: downcast, wearing a borrowed black suit that was slightly too big for him – one of Frank's, who got a fraction rounder with every year that passed. He'd been one of the pall bearers, along with her father, brothers, Antoinette's brother and a cousin to fill in the gap, and Maude had watched him perform this duty with all due grace and solemnity, as she wondered whether or not she was grieving. Antoinette's final year had been one of ever-greater listlessness. She'd taken to her bed with a head cold in July and hadn't risen again. Her illness was amorphous and difficult to diagnose – five different doctors, one after the other, diagnosed everything from hysteria to dropsy, anaemia to a tumour; they tried everything to cure her from leeches and beef tea to tinctures of laudanum and immersion in volcanic waters, all to no avail. One doctor, the third, took Maude aside shortly before he was dismissed, and said: 'Miss Vickery, I fear your mother will never be well unless she somehow finds the will to be well.' Her father had been furious when she told him; it was his distress over his wife's decline that Maude found most difficult to bear.

Personally, she'd thought the doctor had a point. Antoinette lay bundled in lace and eiderdowns and seemed to simply *deflate* – sinking lower and lower into her pillows with each day that passed; reeking of rose water, smelling salts and stale breath. Maude spent months at home with her, reading aloud, fetching her things, dutifully keeping her company as she'd always done while chafing so badly at the delay to her life and travels that she had to practise a form of wilful disassociation from it not to run mad. To begin with, she read the novels and poetry that she knew her mother liked best. However, Antoinette gave so few signs of enjoyment that Maude eventually switched to histories and classics. Often, she started to read out loud and then realised, some time later, that she was actually only reading to herself, and had no idea when the switch had taken place. But when she looked up, guiltily, she generally found her mother gazing vaguely into space, apparently unaware. Antoinette's skin was becoming translucent, taking on the pale, watery quality her eyes had always had; her hands were limp on the coverlet, the nails as delicately pink as seashells worn thin by the tide. Sometimes, when Maude opened her mouth to ask if there was anything her mother needed, anything she could do for her, the words refused to come out. A lot of the time, they sat together in silence.

It was Maude who discovered that Antoinette had died, since the servant who went in to light the fire and tweak the curtains assumed her mistress was still sleeping. When Maude went in, steeling herself against the stuffy smell of the sick room, she knew at once. There was a subtle change to the feel of the room – she couldn't say if it was the absence of her mother's breathing or heartbeat, noticed subconsciously before, or that everything was simply far too still – but she knew at once that she was the only living thing in that room. Her words of greeting died on her lips, and she halted for a moment, letting the realisation sink in. She felt very calm, and oddly disconnected from herself. Eventually, she crossed to the dark side of the bed. Antoinette's hair was limp across the pillow behind her, with a few curls still in their rags stuck to her forehead. Her eyes were shut. Maude noticed, for the first time, the length and beauty of her eyelashes, deep gold against the purplish lids. She waited a while to collect herself before going out to tell the household, and to telegraph her father in London. She waited until the proper feelings of sadness and grief manifested alongside the relief that shamed her. They did come; they just took a little time.

And again, as she helped her devastated father plan the funeral, she had to concentrate on having the proper feelings, and only those; she had to suppress the excitement and happiness that came with realising it would bring Nathaniel back to England. Frank and John arrived at Marsh House first, with their wives and young children who seemed to adore their Aunt Maude, and crawled all over her in spite of her being mystified as to what exactly she ought to do with them. She loved the feel of their sticky, fat little hands, and the warm bulk of them when they sat in her lap, and the way they always seemed to smell of sugar and mud. Echoes of the ticking clock she'd endured during her own childhood always dogged Maude, so she loved to hear their shrieks and yells and laughter shattering the quiet at Marsh House; their footsteps, running with that particular urgency of children who might fall down at any moment. And then Nathaniel arrived, lean and tired, with sun-tanned skin and dirty fingernails, and Maude's heart went up into her mouth so that greeting him was difficult. He mistook her stammering for grief, and held her tightly. When he left again, just a few days after the funeral, Maude began packing her own bags. She hated to leave her father, though he protested over and over that she must follow her own plans, but she found that being left behind there by Nathaniel was something she simply couldn't bear. Only travelling made it tolerable.

Maude abandoned her letter to him before it was finished, hoping to see things the following day with which she could then fill the pages; she was hampered, she knew well enough, by the hugeness of the things she couldn't say. The sheets and blankets were heavy but didn't seem to warm her. Maude lay awake for hours, too cold to drop off properly. She had passed many nights like this on her current journey, and knew the heaviness of thought and mood it would bring to the following day. She'd got used to dosing the feeling with strong coffee, and walking briskly beside her horse when her shivering grew uncontrollable, until warmth returned to her bloodstream. When she did that, Haroun and the other servants fretted; they didn't like to be higher than her, but they didn't want to walk themselves.

Most places she travelled in the Orient she was greeted with a mixture of polite respect and bewilderment – that this foreign woman was so small, and so young, and yet travelled alone at the head of an entourage that wouldn't shame a visiting dignitary. Some local sheiks were suspicious and didn't welcome her, and thought her an abomination or a spy, but she always managed to talk her way through or around them with a mixture of flattery, fluent Arabic and introductory letters from either the British Consulate or the central government of wherever she happened to be. Delivered from consulate to regional outpost to consulate by a series of Father's helpful friends, as Nathaniel had once accused her. Somehow, she didn't feel he grasped the level of skill required to handle the local leaders and the British ones both: they were all, at some level, either opposed to her journeys or mystified by her wish to make them. At least with her mother gone, the demands that she marry had ceased, so she had one less thing to negotiate.

They reached town by lunchtime the following day, and paused while the servants rummaged the souk for supplies and she had lunch with the governor in his house – a protracted, formal affair in which the ceremony and the pleasantries far outstripped the greasy mutton and bland rice that they ate, but it served to get her permission to continue on to the ruins of ancient Palmyra that were the ultimate goal of the journey, even though it meant one of the governor's men, named Habib, had to accompany her. She resented his presence, but such stipulations were often a necessary evil. When it started to rain again, Habib huddled miserably inside his blanket, and muttered a constant stream of complaint and insults about her that Maude surmised he didn't realise she could understand. She smiled to herself, satisfied. Weeks on the road had toughened her – she felt the cold and the lack of sleep, but she never once let them get the better of her. In that way, it actually helped to have this unwanted companion along – she was damned if she'd let him catch her flagging.

'I think the charming Habib wishes he was at home in bed with his wife,' she remarked to Haroun, who rode at her side.

'I think his wife must be glad he is with us,' Haroun replied, deadpan, and Maude laughed.

At the end of the day, as they dismounted and made camp, she turned to Habib and said sweetly, in perfect Arabic, that she hoped he'd enjoyed the ride. She had the pleasure of seeing him try to lie politely, and then watching his mounting chagrin as he realised she'd understood all the horrible things he'd been saying all day. She went into her tent for the cup of tea and the biscuits Haroun had brought her with the satisfaction of having caught him underestimating her.

When they reached the ruined city, they found it situated at the top of a long, shallow rise, the sides of which were carpeted in tiny yellow and white flowers, like an early echo of the warmth and sunshine that would soon return. It lifted all their spirits immeasurably; even Habib, who rubbed his hands together in satisfaction as if his presence alone had brought them safely to that spot. Maude spent four days there, drawing meticulous plans, maps and elevations of the broken ruins, and their location. Her Lebanese cook made good use of the extra time he had during those days to create some delicious slow-cooked stews and roasts.

Habib ate far more than was polite, and more than was his share, so that the night before they were to leave, Maude had a quick word with Haroun, and they quietly struck camp two hours earlier than advertised and departed in the bitterness before dawn without Habib. He caught up with them by mid-morning, with his horse lathered, his baggage in disarray, and an expression of furious panic on his face.

By afternoon, Maude was shivering, but not from the cold. The shudders seemed to come up from inside her; they made her head throb and her body weak. She rode on without a word but collapsed into bed as soon as her tent was up, and fell straight into an exhausted sleep. Haroun knew the signs – she'd had fevers before, and head colds, and short, violent bouts of dysentery. They left her to sleep and weathered her anger when she finally woke to find the day half gone. She rode through the afternoon – Haroun couldn't stop her. Hunched over in silent misery, taking in none of the scenery, her thoughts scattered by a kind of delirium that only her will to keep moving could penetrate. She slept clean through the second day, and felt far stronger by the third. Her hands still shook as she spooned soup into her mouth, and Haroun hovered near her anxiously. His delight when she'd fully recovered was genuine, and even

Habib seemed relieved — there might have been trouble for him if she'd died under his supervision. So they were late back to the British Consulate in Damascus, and her thinness and pallor were noted and exclaimed upon, and Maude reiterated that a bout of fever was to blame, and not the general rigours of the journey, which she insisted were no trouble to her at all.

The British ambassador, who, it just so happened, was indeed a friend of Elias Vickery's, planned a dinner for various members of the expat community to mark Maude's final few days in Syria. She hadn't been back to England in four months and longed to visit her father, and her nieces and nephews. She longed to sit in an armchair beside a welcoming fire, with a stomach full of roast lamb and potatoes; to have a spell of the peace and seclusion of writing — she had already agreed a modest advance with her publisher for the book she would write about this journey. This longing for home was usually matched equally, upon her return, by the desire to be travelling again. She sometimes thought she had a fixed amount of longing inside her that was never sated and only moved its focus depending on where she was, and who she was with. As though she never quite reached the true source of the longing.

On the night of the dinner, Maude put on the best dress she had with her, looped several strings of her mother's pearls around her neck and got help from one of the maids to pin up her hair — she wore it as high as it could be persuaded to go when the occasion permitted, to give her a crucial few extra inches in stature. Her dainty, heeled shoes, the tight corset and the pins supporting her coiffure all felt infuriatingly restrictive after the loose, practical clothing she wore on the road. She did her best not to fidget, and was glad at least for her silk gloves, which hid her broken fingernails nicely. The ambassador, a tall, scrawny man with moustaches like boot brushes, beamed at Maude as he escorted her into the room.

'What's happened, Sir Arthur?' she said. 'You look rather like the cat that got the cream.' She had developed a tone of voice for talking to men, she realised. It was a tone of immaculate confidence, which she only rarely felt, and it was tinged with a kind of amused irony that she hoped wasn't the beginnings of bitterness. It came from being so constantly spoken down to, as a woman – and a tiny, delicate-looking woman to boot. It dared the man in question to condescend to her, but Sir Arthur Symondsbury, annoyingly, seemed quite oblivious to it, and treated her with the warm indulgence of a kindly godfather. He patted her hand on his arm, and beamed even more.

'Just a little scheme of mine, which has pleasingly come to fruition this evening,' he said smugly.

'And do you plan to share it with me?' said Maude, with some impatience, until she saw Nathaniel at the far side of the room, dressed in immaculate black tie and sipping from a saucer of champagne. Sir Arthur patted her hand again as he detached it from his arm.

'Off you go, my dear,' he said. 'You can tell me later on how clever I was in getting your dear stepbrother here this evening.'

Maude couldn't help but stare. Nathaniel was thinner than she'd ever seen him; his cheeks had sunk in on themselves, and his jacket hung loosely from bony shoulders. Her rush of joy and confusion reddened her cheeks, and fear for him came hard on its heels.

'Gracious, what on *earth* has happened to you, Nathan? You look dreadful!' she said by way of a greeting, and was horrified by how pompous she sounded, how falsely offhand, how unlike the way she was feeling. He grinned lopsidedly at her, and stooped to kiss her cheek.

'Dear Maude, you always make one feel so much better,'

he said. 'I've had malaria – isn't it a bore? I'm told it'll come and go forever now – nothing to be done but weather it, they say. The bouts should get less frequent in time.'

'Oh, Nathan! How careless of you! Couldn't you have caught something simple, like the marsh fever I keep picking up?' said Maude, rattling on to hide her panic at the thought of him sickening, dying.

'What can I say?' said Nathaniel. 'You were ever the tougher one.'

'It's a shock to see you here – a nice one, of course. I thought you were in Africa – in fact, I've just posted a letter to you there. Now I'll tell you everything that's in it and it'll be the dullest letter ever when you get back, when it took me hours to write it.'

'I shall like reading it anyway. I always like reading your letters.'

'Do you?' She looked away across the room, embarrassed by her own stupid question.

'They insisted on sending me somewhere cool to recover this time – they suggested England, I suggested here. I was hoping to sneak out into the desert before I have to go back, and I was hoping I'd catch you, of course. Come on – take a glass and tell me everything. I'm dying to hear it.'

Maude told him all that she'd seen and done and learned, and he listened closely, and told her in turn about the landscapes he'd trekked across in Africa, and the near misses he'd had with the Sudanese tribesmen. His journeys were sponsored by the Political Office, who wanted to know about water sources, soil fertility, crop pests and funguses.

'They're mad about locusts. Desperate to know where the swarms are coming from, and where they're breeding. They just seem to appear, you see, out of nowhere. It's all very biblical,' he said.

'And you haven't managed to find anything out?'

'Not yet. They're talking about sending me to look further afield. In Arabia.' Nathaniel smiled as he told her, and Maude stared at him in astonishment.

'But ... that's where I plan to go next!' There was a hung moment, a heartbeat in which the implications of this were weighed.

'It would be tricky to travel together, given that I'd be on official business, and I'd have to report back about everything,' he said.

'But not impossible,' said Maude. She tried to keep her voice level but her rising excitement made it difficult. She wanted to jump up and throw her arms around him. She wanted to grab him and make him promise that it would happen – that they would travel together again for the first time since Egypt, since they'd chosen to climb the same rock to watch the same sunrise, in the same reverent silence. 'I'd thought about starting in the west, perhaps in Jeddah, and journeying south along the frankincense route to see if I can find any Sabean ruins on the way to Marib. There's a lot to get settled first, of course. I'll need to ingratiate myself with the incumbent bigwig, and hire local servants and guides – it'll be too far for my dear Haroun to come ... although, perhaps not. He always said he'd serve me wherever ...'

'Well, I shall have to wait to hear when and where I shall be allowed to travel,' said Nathaniel, more stiffly. 'It's a bit different when one must earn one's keep.'

Feeling the rebuke, Maude was silent for a while. She'd offered, once, years earlier, to cover the cost of Nathaniel accompanying her on a journey. His curt, white-lipped response that he wasn't one of the staff, and no longer needed the Vickerys to support him, had left her too wary to make the offer a second time. She knew she could pay his way and feel no resentment, proprietorship or superiority as a result – after all, she'd done nothing to earn or deserve the money herself – but it seemed that Nathaniel couldn't, and that was that. He took a long swig of his champagne and smiled, nudging her with his elbow. 'Don't look so glum, Mo. You'll get there, and so shall I, eventually,' he said.

'Yes. But let's try to go together, can't we? Just . . . keep it in mind. Keep me up to date with your plans as you find them out.'

'I thought you were a solo traveller? A lone pioneer who didn't want to travel with anybody, even her beloved father?'

'I don't want to travel with anybody *else*,' she said, before she could stop herself, and coloured up again. Nathaniel smiled.

'Dear Maude, we do go along well together. It just won't be straightforward.' He looked off into the distance for a moment. 'How are you? I mean, since losing Antoinette?'

'Oh . . . well enough. As well as can be expected,' she said, unsettled by the question.

She'd long ago concluded that her mother's predominant feeling towards her was perfect apathy. 'I don't miss her letters at least – the twice-monthly imprecations to return to England and marry, as though that were the only way to live.'

'So you still insist you never will? Marry, I mean.'

Maude took a sip of her drink to buy time, because her heart was flapping like a panicked bird, just hearing the word *marry* on his lips. For a fragile, wonderful moment, she wondered if he was sounding her out; she wondered if he meant, at some future date, to propose to her. Her throat was so dry that the champagne burned it, and she coughed. She didn't dare look up at him, and looked instead at the rim of her glass. She picked some imaginary crumb from it with her fingertips. She wanted it more than life itself, she knew. She wanted to be his; she wanted to meet their children, though she did worry about the restrictions a young family might bring. If he married her, of course, her portion of the Vickery fortune would be his, and all restrictions upon him would vanish. She hoped he'd thought of that, since there was no way she could bring it up.

'Oh, I don't know,' she said and, to her amazement, her voice sounded calm, almost offhand. 'I don't really think about it much. I suppose I can't imagine the kind of man who would want me for a wife.'

'Nonsense. Any man would be privileged to have you,' said Nathaniel. 'You're bold, and clever, and loyal, and always honest.' He frowned down at his own drink for a moment, and Maude noticed that he didn't say *beautiful*.

'You're very kind,' she said, 'but I doubt whether many men would count cleverness, or boldness, as desirable virtues in a wife.'

'Well, more fool them,' he said. Maude looked away again, to cover her confusion.

Unbidden, the words *old maid* sprang to her mind. That had been her mother's worst fear, though Maude had only just turned twenty-three when her mother died. Perhaps Antoinette had guessed the truth – that if her daughter could not have Nathaniel Elliot, she would have nobody at all. Maude pictured an old age as a spinster aunt, visited dutifully but wearily by her nieces and nephews; she pictured an empty house and the ticking of a clock she couldn't be rid of. But better that, she decided, than being trapped at home by some other husband, in some conventional marriage, fettered by respectability. Better a life of travelling alone, than one of not travelling; but best of all a life travelling with Nathaniel. Just then, that evening, in that place so far from home, she let herself hope. He had come a long way to see her, she allowed herself to realise. With her heart still thumping so loudly she could hear it, Maude looked up, and smiled.

'And you, Nathan? Don't you want a wife, and a house full of children?' she said playfully. Nathaniel shrugged.

'Yes, I rather do. In fact . . . Well, I wanted to come and tell you in person. I've got engaged you see – to the loveliest girl. Her name's Faye March; we met in Cairo . . .' His voice trailed into silence and even through her shock Maude realised that he *knew* – he knew about her feelings for him, and how this news might affect her. She couldn't fathom why he'd thought it would be better given in person – at least if he'd written it in a letter she could have screamed at the pain, out in the rocky wilds somewhere, all unobserved. Instead, she had to comport herself through a formal dinner during which a great many questions about Faye March were asked and answered, feeling as though a large, bloody hole had been punched clean through her chest.

That night, when sleep finally came, Maude dreamed of the desert. She dreamed of the silence and the way everything slowed down so that the distant past and the future seemed to come within her reach, and she was set free. She dreamed of that sense of serenity, which nothing – not solitude or love or the ragged hole in her chest – could spoil, and woke up weeping for it because life without it was suddenly intolerable. For the first time in her life, being near Nathaniel was intolerable. She scrambled to be away from him. Hoping that the pain would ease once she was home, she boarded the ship from Haifa to Southampton a week early, kept to her cabin, travelled on to Marsh House and immediately discovered that she'd been wrong. There was no peace to be had in being home, in being far from Nathaniel, and there was nothing to make it easier. *Maude's tougher than the pair of you*, she remembered her father saying to her brothers once, long before. She tried to remember what it felt like to be tough, but all she felt was weak, unwanted, full of pain.

Not even her father's obvious disappointment could keep her at Marsh House, so full of echoes of Nathaniel Elliot, and of the ticking clock, reminding her that she had been left behind again. That she would always be left behind. She stayed a mere week before leaving for a hotel in Constantinople where she would write her book. She felt she had to be in a place where neither she nor Nathaniel had ever been before – a place without memories of him, or them. She was invited repeatedly to dine at the consulate, and then into the homes of other expats there. She made a few friends, although the women generally found her too hard, too forthright. Marcus Whittington, the eldest son of a British shipping magnate, seemed to hang on her every word, dropped his chin diffidently when he spoke to her and had an inexhaustible supply of questions to ask her. She was puzzled by it at first, until his sister made a pointed remark and Marcus's cheeks flamed. In spite of her wealth, Maude had never had a suitor before. She was too short, too plain, too brusque. Marcus was a year younger than her, a scholar of the Byzantine Empire; compiling his first history of it. He wasn't too tall, or too vibrant – he had the kind of constitution that Elias Vickery would deem *watery*; but he was fiercely bright, kind, even-tempered, willing to travel with her or to let her go it alone – essentially willing to agree to whatever might induce her to accept his hand.

Maude tried to countenance doing so. As husbands went, she was unlikely to find a more suitable one; he had plenty of money of his own, and he adored her. Elias wrote to her that her mother would have approved – which was his way of gently encouraging her. In his heart of hearts, Elias Vickery believed a woman ought to be married. But Maude noticed the part of her that sank inside when faced with Marcus's evident feelings for her. She knew that, slowly and surely, she would draw that spark of happiness out of him – it would disappear into the hollow space inside her, and find no echo to amplify itself. She turned him down in terse tones brought on by frustration – with him, with herself. Marcus trembled as he took his leave of her, but he kept his eyes dry and Maude found his self-possession laudable. Her own was steely by then, and she respected it in other people. *Marcus is charming*, she wrote to her father. *But in other pertinent respects, altogether too much like me.*

She left Constantinople soon afterwards, for an apartment in Rome where the mosquitoes ate her alive but she had a view of the Roman Forum. She mourned for home – for the idea of it, and the comfort and delight it had once brought. At some point, unnoticed, Nathaniel had become her home, and since she didn't have him she was stateless, without country, without a destination. There was nowhere she could go, nothing she could do to find peace. She could only keep moving, keep travelling, keep leaving it all behind her, and going on into untouched places; places with no echoes. She started to see that she had been doing exactly that ever since Oxford – neither following him nor fleeing from him; merely moving, constantly, unthinkingly, because it was all she could do.

Muscat, December 1958

After the trip to the oil camp, Joan was plagued by a sense of urgent impatience; as though there were something important she knew she ought to be doing, and was late starting. It was something to do with the feeling of flying – the surge and lift of the aeroplane, the racing ground underneath, dropping away so that everything on it became tiny and insignificant. It was something to do with the memory of the desert, and standing at the edge of it by herself, looking away towards dunes she couldn't see and having the exact same feeling – the rush, the rise, the welcome disconnection from earthbound things. It was something to do with the memory of Charlie's kiss, so wildly different to Rory's. Her stomach swooped when she thought of it, and she couldn't tell why – if it was fear of transgression, fear of the betrayal, or if it was passion. She thought about talking to Peter Sawyer again, to try to persuade him to let her go along on another trip to Fahud, but she knew it had been a one-off – a favour called in by Charlie and not to be repeated. She knew she was putting something off but it hovered, tantalisingly, just out of her reach.

Joan had been forced to tell Rory about the oil camp, although she'd kept the details to a minimum and made him promise not to tell the Gibsons. He'd been frosty with her ever since, and spoke with a subtle edge to every word. He made her feel her wrongdoing with his every move, and Joan felt a slow anger kindle at the injustice of that. He had done worse things, after all; told bigger lies. A note came from Charlie on the second day back. The young servant, Amit, brought it out to where she was sitting, having coffee with Rory, and she saw Rory's curiosity as she opened it. It gave her a guilty feeling that she tried to hide; she told herself it was ridiculous – it had only been a kiss. *Sorry not to say cheerio in the morning. Sorry you ran off into the night like that – although it was very dramatic. Sorry I caused you to. C.E.* She read it twice, then curled it into her hand.

'Who's it from?' asked Rory. Joan hesitated before deciding not to lie.

'Charlie Elliot.'

'Oh? Has he got your next illegal outing lined up?' said Rory petulantly.

'No,' said Joan, as calmly as she could. She still felt afraid, she realised. Afraid of Rory finding out what had happened with Charlie. Afraid of the storm breaking. It was one thing to trespass into Jalali, or even as far as Fahud. It was one thing to find the courage to break *those* rules; finding the courage to break her life apart was something else altogether, and she didn't know how to do it.

'Is he sweet on you or something?' Rory asked, frowning.

'Oh, what would it matter if he was?' Joan replied, to which he had no ready answer.

'You shouldn't have gone without me. And you should at least have told me you were going,' he said stubbornly. 'What if something had happened to you? We're not supposed to keep secrets from each other, Joan.' He sounded so righteous, so high on his horse, that Joan's anger sharpened.

'Really, Rory? No secrets *at all?*' she said. The question, or perhaps the tone of it, silenced him.

The mood between them stifled the conversation at dinner, so much so that even Robert seemed to notice.

'So, tell me about your plans for Christmas?' he asked, at length, which Joan took as a subtle reference to the fact that they would soon be leaving Muscat for home. She didn't answer at once, so Rory answered for them, telling him about Christmas lunch with Olive and her neighbours, the Hibbertses, and New Year with his parents at a rented cottage in Wales. Joan listened to the plans in disbelief because she knew at once that none of it could happen, and at the same time she had no idea how to stop it, or what should happen instead. She sat in silence, dry-mouthed. It was like the moment when, staring at an optical illusion, she'd stopped seeing a vase and seen two faces instead. The unsettling feeling that she'd been tricked – that she'd tricked herself, and had been doing so for years. Doing nothing with what she knew was getting harder and harder; the knowledge felt like it was growing somehow, and getting too big to hold. She'd thrown Charlie's note away, crumpled into a ball. Later she picked it back out of the bin, smoothed it flat and hid it beneath her copy of *Selected Letters of Maude V. Vickery*.

After they'd eaten, Joan came back from the bathroom to hear Rory and Robert talking in low voices.

'I think she's just very worried about Daniel,' Rory was saying. Joan paused outside to listen.

'Yes, yes of course,' said Robert. 'It must be so hard for her, with her father gone as well. She was the apple of his eye, you know.'

'Yes, I know. It has hit her very hard; far harder than she lets on, I think. I hope you'll forgive her if she seems . . . surly, at times.'

At this, outrage bloomed in Joan.

'Really, Rory, I've known Joan since before she was born, and I'd forgive her almost anything – without being prompted.' Robert spoke kindly but the rebuke was clear; Joan wanted to hug him, and then immediately felt sad. She *was* worried about Daniel, and she did miss her father, but just then she missed

Rory too. She missed how he'd always made her feel, and how she'd felt about him — two weeks ago she would never have hovered in a doorway and been pleased to hear him put down. She went up to bed without going back in to them. Rory was so tangled up in her life that she didn't know how to have one without the other; if anything changed between them, every- thing would. It made the ground feel less solid beneath her feet. She remembered a bombed-out house in the war — the way the side of the building had been sheared away, opened up, and what had once seemed a solid, impregnable shelter to its residents proved as flimsy as a doll's house — made of paper, dust, and breakable things.

Joan was keen to talk to Maude, and just as keen to visit Salim again. As Abdullah opened the door to her, he wore a strange expression that could have been relief.

'Sahib,' he said, inclining his head. 'We had missed your visits these last days.'

'Hello, Abdullah. How are you?' she said, but Abdullah didn't bother to answer and Joan no longer minded the select- ive way in which he spoke. The gazelle pottered away to the far end of the room when Joan appeared upstairs; Maude woke from a doze and grunted.

'Oh, good. Where did you get to?' she said gracelessly, blinking owlishly.

'I did try to come and see you but I was turned away. And then I . . . went on a short trip,' said Joan, smiling at the news she had to give. Maude studied her for a moment.

'A trip? What's happened? You seem different.'

'Nothing's *happened*, exactly. I went to the desert, Miss Vickery.' She smiled. 'Just to the edge, you understand; I went down to the oil camp, near Fahud.'

'*You've* been into the interior?' said Maude tersely, and Joan prepared to defend herself until she saw envious tears in the old woman's eyes. Maude took a deep breath. 'How was it?' she asked.

'It was . . . it was *wonder*ful!'

Joan went and knelt beside Maude's chair, and took her hand. Maude nodded; her expression knowing.

'Yes. Good,' she said. 'And now?'

'And now . . . and now I want more than anything to go back again,' said Joan. 'It's like . . . it's like only being told half of a story, and not what happens at the end. I feel I *have* to find out.'

'Yes, I know. And it's a story that never does end, you see. Well, there you go,' said Maude. 'I could tell you seemed different. It's bigger than everything else, isn't it? Bigger than every other thing that could possibly happen.'

'Yes, I think so. Bigger than most things, anyway. I only wish the feeling would last,' Joan said wistfully. Maude grunted again, searching Joan's face.

'Yes, I expect you do, but it doesn't seem to work that way. You can't take your troubles into the desert with you, but sadly they're all still waiting for you when you come back out.' Joan stared at her, wondering how much she knew.

'What . . . what do you know about my troubles, Miss Vickery?' she asked. Maude pressed her lips together for a moment, as if choosing her words carefully for once.

'Well, it seems very clear to me that you're engaged to quite the wrong man,' she said. Joan caught her breath, because it was out there now, it was real and couldn't be ignored. Tears blurred her vision and turned her face hot; she looked down, and couldn't look up again.

'You only met him once, but you could see that?' she said.

'I can see it in *you*, silly girl, not in him. What's the matter – don't you love him? Doesn't he love you?'

'I did love him . . . I still do, I think. And . . . I think he loves me. It's just . . . it's just I think he loves my brother more. I think he loves Daniel more.' Saying it was almost a relief, though it brought it even more sharply into focus, and told her all the more forcefully that something had to change.

Maude cleared her throat, and thought for a while.

'I see,' she said. 'Well, you know, I have known several marriages to go ahead successfully regardless of the chap – and sometimes the girl – being as queer as a nine-bob note, if you'll pardon the expression.' Joan looked up at her in amazement. 'It rather frees up both parties to do exactly as they please, with whomever they please, you see. But then, I suppose, everybody ought to be aware of the facts before committing. And I imagine that hasn't been the case?'

'No,' Joan managed to say, shocked to her core.

'No. And does your brother . . . share Rory's feelings?'

'I . . . I don't know.' Joan thought of the kiss she'd seen – the passion in it, the need. The memory of it chimed confusingly with the way Charlie had grabbed her, kissed her. 'I think so, yes. I think he does.'

'And you love your brother, and wouldn't want to be estranged from him?'

'Estranged? No! Never.' This was a consequence Joan hadn't even considered – she'd thought only of what was between her and Rory, not of what was between her and Daniel. She began to cry harder; her head throbbed. She had no idea where Daniel was right then, or when she would see him again.

'Then I see you are in something of a fix,' said Maude calmly. 'But do stop snivelling. That won't solve a thing, you know; if you start feeling sorry for yourself, you're done for. The question is what you can stand, and what you're going to do about the things you can't.'

Joan didn't know the answer to either question, so she said nothing. It took her a few minutes to get hold of herself, and in the end Maude gripped her hand and stared hard at her. Her gaze was hawkish, sharp and unforgiving, and Joan felt something like prey, pinned by it. 'Think about the desert. Think about the size of it, the stillness and the—' Maude broke off, looking right through Joan, right past her, all the way to the dunes. Joan understood then where Maude's mind went when she was troubled, and needed to slip away. She tried it herself and, though she couldn't quite manage it, her tears did stop. 'Tell me how you managed to get there. Tell me everything,' said Maude, so Joan took a deep breath and told her about the early morning flight and the oil camp with its sterile huts and glut of food; about the stars, and the way the wind was sucked towards the sunset. Maude listened intently.

'The sultan visited that oil camp three years ago, you know,' she said. 'On his way to Nizwa to gloat over the imam's supposedly defeated followers. A string of trucks, roaring across the desert – can you imagine such a thing? If they find oil it will never be the same again – there'll be roads, and new towns, and aeroplanes crossing, and cars everywhere, and foreigners. The desert will be settled – it will be destroyed,' she finished quietly. Joan shook her head.

'They haven't found anything yet, for all their drilling. And . . . the desert is vast. They could never encroach on all of it.'

'Even the biggest thing may be gradually eroded away. Where do you think all that sand comes from?'

'I know, but . . . when I was there it all seemed so *small*. The oil camp . . . the army, the rebels, all of it.'

'And will you go again? Will this oil man take you again?'

'I doubt it. He only did it at all because he owed Captain

Elliot a favour. It was Charlie who arranged it all. For me,' she said, blowing her nose.

Maude was quiet again for a while, and her hands curved over the arms of her chair as though she might surge up out of it. 'Miss Vickery, what is it?' Joan asked. Maude frowned.

'Charles Elliot isn't the answer to any of your problems, Joan. I hope you can see that.'

'Why isn't he? I know he's a womaniser, I've found that out myself. But he doesn't seem that bad—'

'They never do, that sort.'

'I know he comes across as terribly full of himself, and as though he needs everybody's attention all of the time, but I rather think it's partly an act. Perhaps being the youngest of so many siblings ... But there's more to him than that, I'm sure of it. I've caught glimpses of it, in spite of all his ... showmanship.'

'Joan, don't be so stupid,' said Maude. Joan sat back on her heels, affronted. 'Those glimpses of his heart you think you've seen? Those ... flashes of a deeper spirit? Those are *part of the act*. I know. They're what he's seen it'll take to reel you in. That type of man ... they adapt. They'll find out the way to attach you to them, and once it's done, they'll do just as they please with you. You mark my words.'

'I'm sure that can't be right ... he doesn't seem—'

'Of course he *doesn't seem*! Well, you're a big girl, you go ahead and make your own mistakes. There's no reason you should listen to me, who's seen it all before,' Maude said flatly. Joan thought of the way Charlie had just grabbed her, the way he'd held her; it had been a stolen kiss, an ambush. She began to wonder if he had simply taken what he wanted; she began to feel foolish for keeping his note, like a schoolgirl.

'Miss Vickery, why do you hate his father so? Why did you fall out – what did Nathaniel Elliot do to you?'

'You'll find out when the time is right – they all will.' Maude folded her hands in her lap; her fingers turned white where she gripped them.

'What do you mean?' said Joan, but Maude was silent, and kept her seamed lips tight together.

Abdullah brought them tea and Joan stood up, her legs gone stiff from kneeling. The tall man's robes swung with his stride; he shooed the gazelle away and looked across at Maude, just once. Maude gave an exasperated sigh.

'Yes, all *right*, Abdullah! I hadn't forgotten,' she snapped. He inclined his head gracefully and left the room. 'Pour the tea, Joan dear,' said Maude. Joan did as she was told, and passed a cup to the old woman. She was weary from thinking, and her head still ached from crying. She patted her hair into place, straightened her blouse and found a handkerchief to blow her nose.

'What hadn't you forgotten, Miss Vickery?' she asked.

'To ask you to go and see Salim today,' said Maude, slurping her tea quietly. 'Will you?' Joan took her own tea over to the window and knelt down, looking out across the roofs of Muscat to its girdle of brutal rocks, and the sun flaring on the surface of the sea. Jalali was almost handsome at that distance, with seagulls gliding above it. But then Joan imagined the birds as vultures circling above dying men, above dead men, and the illusion of beauty dissolved.

'Of course I will,' she said. Maude nodded, and gave her a quick smile.

Joan turned back to the view. 'Marriage was meant to be my big adventure,' she said softly, almost to herself. 'Being a wife; being a mother. It was meant to be the next step – a giant leap into the future. Now I feel as though there's nowhere to put my feet.'

'*Marriage* was meant to be your big adventure?' Maude

sounded sceptical. Joan looked back at her and the old lady put down her teacup.

'You needn't only ever play the cards you've been dealt, you know, Joan; you can choose your own. You could have spent your inheritance on that maisonette you're supposed to be saving up for – or on the wedding. But did you? No. You chose to spend it on a trip to a country most people have never even heard of. Doesn't that tell you something?'

'Well, I don't know. Something like what?'

'Like perhaps, in your heart of hearts, you knew that you wanted something different. Something *more*.' Maude cocked an eyebrow at her. 'Perhaps this is your chance to have a *real* adventure, hmm? I had my share of heartbreak. I had . . . I let somebody . . . take my old home from me. Did I mope? No. I travelled. I stepped off the path people expected me to take, and went places nobody had ever been before. I built myself a new home.' She picked up her tea and dipped a biscuit into it. 'So all you need to ask yourself is this: if you don't want to marry young Rory, what do you want to do instead?'

Joan stood up and turned to Maude. She'd been trying to answer the same question herself for days and days, but just then it seemed very clear.

'I want to go up the mountain,' she said. 'Jebel Akhdar. I want to stand on the plateau, and know that I'm the first foreigner to stand there since the Persians.'

'Now, Joan—'

'You told me when we first met that I had to carve a way for myself. You said I had to be the *first* to do something, or it meant nothing. Well, I want to be first up the mountain. The first white person, anyway.'

'Well then,' said Maude, giving her an appraising look. 'At this precise moment I think you might as well have decided you'd like to walk on the moon. But who I am to judge? Let's see what you can do.'

Joan smiled at her, but it soon faltered. The satisfaction, the resolve of realising what she wanted to do began to fracture at once under the knowledge of how impossible it was. She took a deep breath but there was nothing else to say about it, and certainly nothing to do.

'Perhaps you might fit in a visit to Salim, before you depart?' said Maude, and her mockery, though it was gentle, stung nonetheless.

The package taped to her leg made Joan walk peculiarly. It had an unfamiliar weight and solidity; she was worried about it coming untied, falling off and giving her away. The guards outside Jalali stared hard at her and seemed more suspicious than before, less keen to take the bribe from the basket and let her in. But they could not search her, and in the end they took the money. Joan wondered what had made them more alert, but she waited patiently, and betrayed no tension in her posture or manner. She gave them no cause to refuse her, and was amazed by her own sangfroid.

Salim was asleep when she found him, curled on his side with his face cradled on his hands, the metal bar splaying his legs awkwardly. Joan crouched beside him quietly, hating to rouse him when she could imagine how hard it must have been to rest in that place.

She studied the slant of his cheekbone, the bruise on it almost healed, and the darkness of his hair against the skin of his forehead; she studied his short, black eyelashes, the flicker of his eyes beneath the lids, the hard lines of the skull beneath the skin. She couldn't decide if it was sleep that made him beautiful, or if she just hadn't seen it before. There was something familiar in his face, now; she felt she knew him

– had known him a long time. It was almost like seeing Daniel snooze, boyish and peaceful, with his feet up on a garden chair.

'Salim?' she said softly. Behind her there was a snigger, and she looked round to find a man with an oily face watching her and grinning lasciviously, one hand resting in his groin. Repulsed, Joan reached out and shook Salim's shoulder gently. She knew she shouldn't touch him – a Muslim woman would never touch a man outside of her family, but she was afraid to be in that place without him.

Salim didn't wake at once, but when she shook him a second time he grabbed her hand, lightning quick, his grip bruising the bones of her wrist as he fought for consciousness. 'It's me – it's Joan!' she whispered urgently. He blinked at her, as if he'd never heard the name before.

'Joan?'

'Yes! I'm sorry to wake you, but I . . . I thought I ought to.'

'Of course.' Stiffly, Salim sat up; the metal bar shifted and he winced. He rubbed one hand across his face and looked around and, as if remembering where he was and what his life had become, he seemed to age; the loveliness of his sleeping face disappearing into lines of worry and despair. He coughed once and then couldn't stop for a while.

'Are you all right?' she asked. 'Are you ill?'

'I am well. It is only this place.'

'I've brought something for you, something from Miss Vickery. I don't know what it is – medicines, perhaps? But it's a package, so it might be harder to hide than a letter.'

'A package? Wait – leave it for now. Let me think.' Salim drank from one of the water bottles she'd brought, and ate ravenously – soft cheese pastry parcels, dried fruit and bread.

'I went to the desert, Salim. I know it's forbidden, but I managed to go. I . . . I understand now, I think, a bit about . . . what it's like. About how it might be to belong there. And

I'm . . . so sorry. I'm so sorry you're stuck in here,' she said. Salim studied her intently for a while, and then smiled.

'Beautiful, isn't it? I'm glad you went. I'm glad. I hope it helped you.'

'I wish I could help *you*, though.'

'You do,' he said, frowning.

'I might not be able to come again,' she said. 'My brother, Daniel, has gone into the mountains to fight, with the rest of the SAF. Nobody seems to know when he'll be back – it could be weeks and weeks. Robert's dropping all these hints about when we might set off home . . . and I know Rory wants to go. At least, he does now that Dan's gone. I suppose, sooner or later, I shall have to go. I'll have no reason to give them, you see. No reason to stay.'

'You do not wish to leave. Perhaps that is reason enough,' he said, but Joan shook her head.

'No, that won't be enough. They'll want more.'

'But you need not give it to them – it's up to you. One thing I know from being inside these walls is that *only* walls can hold a person. Only walls and irons can truly hold you. Your will alone should be enough for everything else, Joan. Is it?'

They were quiet for a while, after which Salim stood and shuffled over to where a small drainage hole in the floor was covered by a metal grate. He sat down near it and motioned for her to do the same. Joan loosened the package from her leg and passed it to him, and he slid it quickly into the drain, replacing the cover. They did not speak of it.

'I went to the oil camp at Fahud. Miss Vickery worries that they'll find oil in the desert and it'll be . . . destroyed. Built over.'

'The rape of the wild.' Salim grinned. 'I've heard her say that before. But this country needs wealth; it *needs* progress.

To me the crime is that, when it's discovered, that wealth will go to a puppet ruler and his foreign sponsors, not to the people of that country.'

'*That* country? But it's all *one* country now – Muscat and Oman. The sultan rules it all.'

'It remains to be seen whether he rules it or not,' Salim replied.

'But wouldn't it be awful if the emptiness of the desert were to be ruined? People's lives seem purer here. Uncorrupted by ideas of money and power, I suppose I mean – and all the trappings and silliness of modern life.'

'Believe me, the minds of men here are as bent to money and power as they are anywhere else. As for the simplicity of life . . . it is simple indeed. The people here lead lives of poverty and ignorance, and many die young. Trachoma blinds them. Diseases that could easily be cured consume them,' Salim spoke in a hard, angry whisper. 'The sultan cools his heels by the sea in Salalah, a thousand miles away. He has not come here, to the seat of his kingdom, in years – and do you know why? He says he would be inundated with supplicants, and he has nothing to give them. He builds no hospitals because he says there is no point in children surviving into adulthood only to starve or die of some disease. He builds no schools because he doesn't dare to educate his people – he doesn't dare let them learn how backward he has kept them.' Salim sat back, his eyes afire. 'There are half a million people living in Oman, and less than half would claim Sultan Said as their leader. He is a parasite, but the British tell him he is a potentate so that they may prospect for oil, and play power games with the Americans and their Saudi puppets.'

As Joan listened to him, she felt childlike and unsure, just the way Daniel sometimes made her feel. She knew absolutely that she no more belonged in Oman than Marian did.

'You sound like you hate us. The British, I mean,' she said.

'I can hate a nation when it tries to control my people. Many foreign powers have come here, throughout history, and tried to do by force what the British would do by flattery. None have succeeded for long, and neither will this latest invasion. But I do not hate you, Joan,' he said, more gently. 'I owe you a great debt.'

'I'm glad to have been of use. I'm glad to have helped somebody while I was here.'

'You already speak of your time here in the past tense?' said Salim, smiling. 'Perhaps you are ready to leave after all.'

'No. No, I'm really not. I feel terrible at the thought of going back to England, and leaving you in here. And it feels dreadful to go back and leave my brother here. I know he's a soldier, and this is his job, but still.'

'You would prefer to take him with you?'

'Yes,' she said simply. 'Always. But I'd rather go to where he is.'

'Jebel Akhdar?'

'Yes. I . . . can't really explain why.' She thought for a moment in silence, knowing that there was no way she could put her confusion about Rory and her brother, or about Charlie, into words. 'I so desperately want to see it,' she said. 'The plateau at the mountain's heart. I want to be the first white person to stand up there.'

'You would put yourself in grave danger.'

'I know. I know it's impossible, but that doesn't stop me wanting to.' She looked at him, studying him in the way that only the veil made possible. As if reading her thoughts, Salim stared hard at her.

'I would have liked to see your face, Joan,' he said. For a wild moment, Joan's fingers went to the edge of the mask. She wanted to remove that barrier between them. Salim put out his fingers to stop her, shaking his head, and with a shiver she remembered where she was, and the danger. Flies buzzed around the food she'd brought him, and the smell of it mixed nauseatingly with the sweat and ammonia stink of the place. Salim smiled. 'You've done all you can do for me, Joan. And that is more than most would have done.'

'I won't ever forget you,' she said, then got up and left in a hurry, without another word, feeling that it was the only way she would be able to leave at all.

When she got to her room, Joan took Charlie's creased note out from under the book and read it again. Three apologies, and a gently teasing tone that didn't make them seem any less sincere. She thought of their kiss, then remembered what Maude had said and dangled the note over the bin again. But she didn't drop it. Joan knew she needed a plan, but try as she might she couldn't begin to formulate one. *Walk a different path*, Maude had told her. *Find a new home*. Reluctantly, she began to think about what she would say to Rory. She struggled; she didn't seem to have the right vocabulary for it. He was still right there, at her side, and would remain so until she said otherwise; and while Daniel would always be her brother, she did not yet know what Rory would end up being. He'd been part of her life for so long she could hardly remember the time before him – certainly, she didn't know what adult life looked or felt like without him. When she thought about that she felt fear stealing her resolve.

The more she dwelt on it, the more questions occurred to her. She thought about why Rory might have courted her in the first place; she thought about the arguments she'd seen him and Daniel having. She thought about the wedding, and how Rory had been putting it off for months and months. Suddenly, there were new reasons for all of it, and she longed for the bliss of her former ignorance.

Now, every time she saw Rory, words teetered on Joan's lips. She didn't want to speak in anger, like a child, but without something to force her she questioned whether the time was right, and somehow never quite managed to open her mouth. She went down to the terrace early one evening, mixed herself a gin and leaned on the balustrade, staring across at Jalali, sending her thoughts to Salim. She ought to have wished him courage and strength, but ended up hoping he would send her some instead. A short while later, Rory came to stand beside her. She looked across at him as he stared out to sea – the familiar curve of his cheek and jaw, the soft brown of his eyes beneath thick brows, a rounded forehead and curling hair. He must have been aware of her scrutiny, but for a long time he didn't return it. Eventually, he seemed to have no choice. He looked at her quickly, with a snatch of a smile, his eyes always moving and never quite alighting on hers. He blinked a lot; his mouth was tense.

Startled, Joan saw that he was afraid. He was afraid of her, and what she might say. Something inside her snapped – she wasn't sure if it was her resentment, or her resolve, or what. She laid her hand on his arm and squeezed it gently, and they both seemed to sense that a truce had been called, even if it was a temporary one. They relaxed. Rory rested his elbows on the top of the wall, his shoulders drooping. He looked exhausted, and as she accepted that she would say nothing that night, Joan felt the same fatigue wash through her, a lassitude coming in to fill the spaces where tension had been. It was cowardice, she knew; it was another small defeat, but it was a welcome one.

The night was humid, warm and black; there was no moon in the sky. In the south-west, over the distant bulk of the mountains, sheet lightning flickered in the sky. Joan watched

it for a while, thinking of Daniel out there somewhere, perhaps trying to sleep under that fitful sky. He'd been afraid of
thunderstorms as a child; he would come into her room, crawl
into bed and curl up beside her, rigid and wakeful. Then she
fancied it was artillery she was seeing, or grenades going off;
she wondered if she was witnessing the war playing out, and
went to bed troubled, to dream of chaos and gunfire. She slept
sketchily, and woke while it was still pitch black, certain she
had in fact heard the crack of a gun firing, not too far away.
She sat up, breath held, waiting, but heard nothing more and
eventually slept again.

In the morning, Robert was disturbed at breakfast by a steady
stream of clerks, bringing him whispered reports and pieces of
paper that he frowned at. Eventually, he abandoned his coffee
and stood up.

'Anything the matter?' said Marian.

'Is it Daniel?' Joan asked at once, with a chill.

'No, no. I haven't heard anything about him, Joan. No, it's
something rather closer to home. A prison break.'

'A what?' said Marian incredulously. 'I didn't think that was
possible.'

'Well, if the fellow manages to get away scot-free, he will
indeed be the first,' said Robert, with a nod. Joan found she
couldn't swallow the mouthful of bread she'd been chewing.
Her lungs seemed to have shrunk; she couldn't get air into
them.

'From Jalali? Who?' she said, with an effort. Robert glanced
at her, still frowning.

'A fellow called Salim bin Shahin. Somehow he's slipped his
irons and got hold of a gun. Apparently he shot and killed one
of the guards, then forced the second to unlock the gates. And
now he's simply vanished.' Joan shut her eyes, not knowing

how to feel. Her first impulse was joy – a surge of it, hot and sparkling; but it was brief, and a kind of terror came hard on its heels.

She remembered the gunshot she thought she'd heard in the night; pictured herself sitting up in bed, ears straining, as the blood and life had drained from one of the guards. Cold with dread, she tried not to think about which of the young men it had been; she was shocked to her core that Salim had killed one of them. Remembering the peace and beauty of his sleeping face, she couldn't believe he was a murderer. The realisation that she didn't really know him hit her hard. 'God knows how he's done it,' Robert went on. 'I'm told a serving woman has been visiting him, so perhaps that's how. The blasted Arabs never search women. One witness says he saw the two of them touch, so perhaps this woman was more than a servant.' Skirting the edges of panic, Joan thought back, thought hard; tried to think if there was any way she could be identified. The thought of Robert finding out, of Colonel Singer finding out, was too terrible; their outrage and disappointment would be just as bad, just as frightening, as being arrested as an accessory.

'Good Lord – so there's a criminal at large? What was his crime?' said Marian. She fluttered her hands, but it seemed more for show; she still sounded almost bored.

'It's rather more serious than that, I'm afraid, dear. He's one of bin Himyar's tribe, from the mountain, and one of the imam's fighters – one of his commanders, in fact, and a quite brilliant one. Second only to the imam's brother, Talib; and a wholly lethal sniper, by all accounts. He was arrested during the uprising last year, leading the rebels towards Muscat from the south-east. The sultan will be furious if he gets away; not to mention Colonel Singer. The colonel must be told at once

– bin Shahin will undoubtedly try to reunite with his comrades in the mountains. Do excuse me, won't you all?'

Joan sat in silence with her insides shaking. She was aware of Rory watching her curiously, and Marian as well, with that oddly penetrating air she'd had of late. Then Rory put out his hand and covered hers.

'They'll catch him before he gets to the mountains, I'm sure,' he said. 'Don't worry. Daniel won't be in any danger from him. Well, in any greater danger, anyway.' Joan shook her head.

'It's not that. It's . . .' She looked down at the table, and fell silent. With a stab of guilt, she did think of Daniel then, and next of Charlie Elliot. She simply couldn't imagine Salim as one of the men they were fighting – those were faceless, nameless men; tribal savages dressed in rags and armed with antique guns, as Charlie had made her think of them. And even as she remembered Salim's hard words, and his anger, she was glad he was free of Jalali – she couldn't help it. Perhaps he wouldn't try to get back to the mountain at all, or back to the fighting. Perhaps he knew they would seek him there, and would slip away into exile instead, and pose no threat to Daniel or the others. Joan held on to that hope, and fed it wilfully, because she remembered him taking pins from her hair, and she remembered the heavy package that Maude had secured to her leg, and she knew exactly how he had escaped, and her part in it. Beneath her relief for him was a hard wedge of fear. She couldn't yet see the size of the thing she had done; she didn't know what to set it against to judge its scale. But she knew it was huge. Terrifyingly so. She had helped a prisoner escape; she had allowed a man to be murdered.

She took her fear to Maude Vickery's house – the only place she could take it – and Maude didn't look in the least bit surprised to see her again so soon. She stared up from her wheelchair with defiance and a new *froideur*, and Joan wondered if the old lady had now got what she'd wanted from her, and would end their friendship. The realisation that she had been used came as a shock.

'Did you know?' she asked pointlessly.

'Did I know what?'

'You told me Salim was a political thinker, and that his imprisonment was entirely unjust. Did you know he was one of the imam's fighters – one of his commanders?'

'Of course I did. Don't be foolish. I know everything about him.'

'And you used me to free him, knowing that my brother is out there in the mountains, fighting those men?'

'Oh, you knew what you were doing!' Maude snapped. 'You're not an idiot.'

'I didn't! I didn't know . . .' Joan thought about it. She thought of the way she hadn't paid attention to the hairpins, or the package; the way she'd never asked Maude about them. Had she deliberately looked the other way? Maude pointed a finger at her in triumph.

'Ha! There – you see. I knew it!'

'I didn't know he was a soldier. I didn't know he would kill a man to get out.'

'Guns tend to do that,' Maude said flatly. 'Needs must.'

'I didn't know I might be helping a man who would be a danger to my own brother!'

'Oh, what does it matter?' said Maude sourly. 'None of it matters.'

'How can you say that? Have you forgotten what a human life is worth, Maude? Have you been out of the world for so very long?'

'And what would you know about the value of life? You've barely even started to live – everything you think you know you've merely been told, and have accepted like a child. The world isn't the safe, simple place you think it is, Joan. Salim would have died in there, eventually, and that would have been a worse injustice than anything that might happen as a result of his freedom. You should be proud of yourself. You did something real for a change.'

Joan stared at her, stung.

'I thought we were friends. I thought you were the sultan's friend – aren't you in the least bit loyal to him? He lets you live here, after all, but now you're helping one of the imam's commanders.'

'The last sultan who was a friend to me was a different man, in a different time – he knew where he ruled and where he did not. The year I crossed the desert, 1909, an imam was elected at Tanuf for the first time in years, and Faisal knew he'd lost control. The interior rules itself. The men of the desert and mountain tribes cannot be governed by a man who has lived in luxury by the sea all his life.' She thought for a moment and then grunted. 'Perhaps they cannot be governed at all. It was always about loyalty – personal feuds, family feuds. Salim grew up a part of all that; he understands it better than anyone.'

Maude turned her gaze away across the room, and Joan stood helplessly in front of her with anxiety and a strange kind of outrage tying her thoughts into knots she had no hope of unpicking. Eventually she turned to go. Abdullah stopped her at the front door. He put his vast hands on her shoulders for a moment, and gazed down at her. Joan looked up and saw that the fear, which she hadn't recognised for what it was before, had vanished from his face.

'You have freed him; his fate is his own again. For this, I thank you. We are in your debt,' he said.

'What are you saying to her, Abdullah?' Maude called querulously from upstairs. The old man heard, and smiled.

'The lady is grateful. It makes her angry – she does not know how to be grateful. Salim wishes to thank you. He wishes to see you,' Abdullah said softly, and Joan caught her breath. 'He told me this. Where the road rises, where it turns to Muttrah; he will wait there at moonrise, in the rocks to the east.'

'Tonight? I don't know if I can—'

'He cannot wait.'

'All right,' said Joan. 'All right.'

Rory glowered suspiciously at Joan when she said she would be dining and staying with Maude again that night, but he didn't say anything.

'Well,' said Robert, 'We'll miss your company, Joan, but I suppose opportunities to visit with Miss Vickery are running out, so I do understand. But opportunities for us to see you are also running out,' he said, smiling gently as she left. She drifted through Muscat's narrow streets for a long time, then sat in a doorway to rest. She only needed to be outside the gates when they were shut as night fell. An Indian shopkeeper, whose storefront she had walked past three times, came out to offer her directions, and when she said she needed none he gave her a small bag of nuts instead. She ate them hungrily, as the shopkeeper's wife and daughter grinned at her from inside, bright in their orange dresses, their pink trousers.

Merani's cannon sounded *dum dum* and Joan took out her lantern, but didn't light it. She tucked herself away in a quiet corner in the city's furthest edge and watched as the darkness deepened, until she could hardly see, and felt the comfort of being hidden by it.

Joan heard the creak and slam as the guards closed the gates. She waited a little longer until the darkness was the colour of blue ink, then set off along the dirt road up the hill. She wasn't sure exactly what time the moon rose and didn't want to risk missing Salim. At the bend in the road she turned aside, stumbled a short distance onto rough ground, then found a flattish rock to sit on while she emptied the stones and grit from her sandals. Then she simply sat, listening to the thud of her pulse in her ears with a growing sense of unreality. She remembered her father once saying that the night-time was a different world, and sitting there, with the sparse lights of Muscat scattered below, she finally knew what he meant. Anything could happen. The rock she sat upon was still slightly warm from the day – the same temperature as her skin. The moon rose in the east, a silver semi-circle like a fish scale. Suddenly, Joan knew she was not alone; she stood calmly, though her breath seemed to get caught in her throat, and turned.

Salim was also in darkness. For a second, Joan didn't recognise him from his height or his posture, because she was used to seeing him in shackles, but then there was something in his outline, in the way he moved, that was profoundly familiar. She wondered if she ought to feel endangered; she made herself think of the dead prison guard, and that Salim must have killed many men in the war against the sultan, and to gain his reputation. By the weak light of the moon she saw a pistol tucked into his belt alongside a plain, functional khanjar; there was a rifle slung across his back, and ammunition belts across his chest. He was dressed in a tunic and sarong, and smelled of incense and tobacco; his grin was a gleam of white teeth.

'You wait in the dark, like an outlaw,' he said quietly. 'I didn't know if you would come, now that you know who I am. Now you see what you have done in freeing me.'

'What have I done?' said Joan uneasily.

'Made a friend of your country's enemy; of your brother's enemy,' he said simply.

'Will you return to fighting them?'

'Of course. There would be little point to my freedom if I did not.'

'You could live in peace, somewhere else. You could go into the desert.'

'And do what? Lose myself to it, until I no longer know who I am — like Maude?'

'It's not so bad, not knowing oneself,' Joan said quietly, and Salim grinned again.

'Turn around.' He stepped past her, turning his back to the moon. 'I want to see your face.'

Joan did as he said. The moon glowed over his shoulder so his face was invisible to her. He was one more dark thing, part of the blackness all around, and the moon seemed bright in her eyes. He studied her for a long time. The moment stretched; time marched on around them, and Joan was unperturbed. She felt that they'd stepped aside from it all. At last, Salim put up one hand and touched the dark curls at her temple with his fingertips. 'I'd pictured it fairer,' he murmured, letting his thumb brush along her jaw. His touch lingered, and for a moment Joan thought he was going to kiss her. The idea was unsettling, beguiling. But he let his hand drop and stepped back. 'You are so young. But I see no fear in you. I see a person who does not sit easily in the life she's been given.'

'I was afraid,' said Joan. 'I am afraid.'

'No.' Salim shook his head. 'You've only been taught to be. Taught to think you *should* be.'

'I don't know what I'm going to do.'

'Nor do I. But it will not be nothing.'

'What will you do?'

'That I know, but cannot say. It is safer that way. But I have an offer to make you.' He stepped to the side so that a little light fell on both of their faces, and Joan looked up at him. He was so different in bearing to the man she'd met in Jalali. He was a fighter, a leader of men; she ought to have felt reduced by him, by his assuredness, but instead he seemed to lend her some of it, in just the same way as her father had once lent her some of his.

'There is a great debt between us, Joan. I owe you my freedom. Whether you knew what you were doing or not, you came to me in kindness, and with courage, at a time when I was close to despair, and you brought me hope. You do not wish to return to England, but you cannot remain in Muscat. I must remain hidden for a short time yet – two days, or three. I must allow the sultan's men to lose heart, and grow lazy in their search for me. But then I will go to Jebel Akhdar, and I offer you the thing you want. If you will come, I will take you up the mountain with me.'

Joan said nothing for a long time. She concentrated on breathing in and out; her heartbeat was slow and loud, like the tread of heavy feet, but she felt too light, somehow; she felt disconnected from the earth – that same feeling she'd had before, of the potential for flight, or perhaps for falling. Salim waited patiently.

'I don't know,' she blurted out. She thought of her mother, alone at home with her quilted bed jacket and her listless-ness; she thought of all the things she and Rory hadn't said to each other, and needed to say; she thought of Daniel in the mountains, and Charlie Elliot.

Then she thought simply of the mountains: that vast, ancient presence that had been there every second of her time in Muscat – watching, waiting – and something clicked into place inside her. It was her plan. It was precipitous, too fast, frightening, but it was her plan.

'I don't know,' she said again, even though it wasn't true. Part of her knew that to go would simply be running away, but still she wanted to go at once, and not look back, and guilt came hand in hand with that.

'You must decide,' said Salim gently. 'I cannot come back if you change your mind when I have gone, and you will not be able to find me once I have.'

'I know,' she said, believing it entirely.

'Do you know what you want to do?'

'Yes. I think so.'

'And have you the courage to do it?' The question hung between them, unanswered. Salim gazed up at the moon, now the span of two hands above the horizon. 'Two days,' he said. 'I will be here again, at this time, the day after tomorrow. Then I will go. If you wish me to take you, be here too.' He waited for some sign that she'd heard, and when she nodded he turned, and was gone. She didn't hear him make a sound; he left her with a feeling like the ground was moving gently beneath her, like coming ashore after being at sea.

Joan spent the rest of the night at Maude's house – downstairs with Abdullah, who pressed his finger to his lips as he let her in, and gave up his bed in the back room for her. Before leaving her he gave her a jug of water and a cup, and a soft bundle wrapped in canvas. She opened it by the light of a single candle flame, and saw the black abaya, the mask and veil.

'If you go with him, wear them,' he told her. 'The lady does not know of this plan.'

Joan nodded, and thanked him. She spent a sleepless night, dry-eyed, her thoughts returning irresistibly to the mountains, over and over. Their draw was even stronger now that they were nearly within her reach; it was almost a physical pull. But she hadn't asked Salim if she would ever be able to come back, if she went; she had not asked him where they would go, what they would do. She wondered if any of that mattered.

She wondered if the choice was as simple as living the same life, or living a different one – if the first step towards freedom had to be the biggest one.

Rory knocked at the door in the watery cool of the early morning, and seemed almost disappointed to find Joan where she'd said she would be.

'I thought I might be invited in for breakfast,' said Rory, as they walked away side by side. Scratchy-eyed from lack of sleep, Joan glanced up at him, and missed the moment to answer. The silence had a loaded, strained quality that she was too tired to diffuse. 'Joan, we're going home,' he said. 'There's a boat calling in on the way down to Aden on Friday, and we'll take the Aden Airways flight from there to Cairo – Robert's arranged it all for us.'

Rory waited for her reply, but Joan said nothing. Just as she'd known she wouldn't be spending New Year's Eve at a cottage in Wales with Rory's parents, she knew she wouldn't be on that boat. A tingle went through her at the implications of that. She thought about saying to Rory *I saw you with Daniel. I saw you kiss him.* She thought about turning to him and saying *I know*; she thought about saying, *You have lied to me for years.*

'Well? Aren't you going to say anything? Personally, I can't wait,' he said. 'This place hasn't turned out to be at all what I expected. There's nothing here but dry rock.' He squinted upwards as if even the sky had disappointed him in some way. 'We've done what we came to do – we've seen Dan, and the Gibsons. You've met Maude Vickery – you've practically gone to live with her, in fact. And you've gone off on your own into the desert, against all the rules. You ought to be happy.' He put his hands in his pockets, a show of nonchalance that Joan didn't believe. She knew an opening volley when she saw one, but she let it go by, and they walked the rest of the way to the Residency in silence.

From then on Rory made a show of asking questions about packing, and observed repeatedly that this would be the final time they did this, or that; and here was something they ought to remember to do as soon as they got home. Joan made a non-committal sound in response to each suggestion, and smiled thinly when Marian said how much she would miss having them there, even though she believed Marian completely. She was distracted by the enormity of what she was about to do, and harried by the fear that she wouldn't do it; that she wouldn't have the courage, when it came to it.

'Your mother and I never particularly got on,' said Marian, one night after the gin and the wine. Her voice was rich and soft, with the subtle blurring that alcohol gave it. 'But give her my best wishes. I suppose she must feel very stranded without your father. Cut off, I mean – and I can wholly sympathise with that. He was rather the driving force in her life, was he not? In all your lives.'

'Yes, I suppose so. Although *driving* doesn't sound right, really. Where he led we all wanted to follow.'

'Of course. They were very happy together, weren't they?'

'Yes, very.'

Marian put down her glass and leaned towards Joan, lowering her voice, even though Rory and Robert had gone out onto the terrace. 'We visited them shortly before they were married. I remember your mother having many of the same doubts I suspect you might be having, Joan dear.'

'Oh,' said Joan uncertainly. She'd hoped her doubts had gone unnoticed in the two weeks since the dinner at Bait al Falaj, but then Marian often seemed to see more than she let on. Joan didn't really want to discuss it with her. 'Well, I'm told cold feet are natural,' she said, with a vague shrug. Marian reached out and took her hand for her attention.

'*Many* of the same doubts,' she said intently. Joan stared at her, and when Marian saw she was listening she let go of her hand, and patted it uncomfortably. 'Yes. I remember we went out shopping, Olive and I, and your father had gone off on one of his camping weekends with that friend of his – what was his name? James? Jim?'

'John.'

'Yes. Him. John Denton, was it? Anyway. Your mother fretted the whole time your father was away. But I think what she was most worried about was that *he* would back out of the wedding – your father, I mean. He was always such an honourable chap, you see. But then, you know that. In the end there was so much about him that she loved, she decided she'd rather have him, in whatever shape or form he came, than not at all. Perhaps she told him as much, in the end – I've no idea. But the wedding went ahead, of course.'

Marian sat back and swigged her drink, and Joan stared into her own glass, trying to decipher what she'd just been told. It made little sense. 'Best not to do anything too rash, I always think,' Marian concluded, looking away as though losing interest.

'Yes. I suppose so,' said Joan, puzzled. But Marian couldn't *know*. There was no way she could know, unless it was obvious. Unless only she, Joan, had been blind, but she didn't think so. She went to bed still thinking; her head felt prickly with fatigue but she slept in fitful snatches, and was beset by dreams of walking in darkness, waiting to trip and fall down.

She thought about her father's friend John Denton – she hadn't thought of him in years. He was a travelling salesman, selling spare parts for vacuum cleaners, and every few months during her childhood he'd dropped in on his way somewhere to have dinner with them, and he and David had sat up late into the night, talking and laughing. Her father had had such a sparkle about him when John was there that Joan had been jealous, even though she liked John, and had refused to go to bed for fear of missing out. She tried to remember seeing John at her father's funeral, but the day was too obscure in her memory; she'd been too numb and stupid with grief. *Whatever shape or form he came in.* She puzzled over Marian's words, and every time she thought she was close to understanding, it slipped away again. It was like trying to see something in a steamed-up mirror, but Marian's overall message was clear — that a marriage could work regardless of what you didn't like about a person, so long as there was enough about them that you loved. Joan thought about that a lot, and ended up not at all convinced that it covered all eventualities.

It planted a seed of doubt, however. The day of Salim's departure dawned; Joan invented a farewell dinner with Maude to explain her going out at sunset, and so that she wouldn't be missed until morning. She pictured the long, empty night she'd spend, alone and out of the city, if in the end she didn't leave. If she got on the boat to Aden, and flew back to England, and went back to the house she'd grown up in in Bedford, and married Rory, and moved with him to a maisonette nearer the station. She pictured their children. She pictured Christmas lunch with the Hibbertses. She pictured all the things she'd been looking forward to, before she came to Oman, and marvelled at the feeling they now gave her — a groggy, sinking feeling, like falling asleep when you wanted to stay up. At teatime she wrote a note to them — Rory and Robert and Marian, but mostly to Rory. She left it in her room, in a not-too-prominent place that wouldn't be obvious to a casual glance through the door, but would certainly be found during a proper search. It read: *Sorry to do this. Sorry if you'll worry — try not to. I am in good hands, and I'm sure we'll see each other again.* She wondered if a single word of it was true. She wondered if she'd tear it up later and pack her trunk, choking on her cowardice.

As the sun was blurring in the western sky, Joan went up to Rory's room and dithered outside the closed door. Inside, she heard soft sounds of him moving around. Packing, probably, or dressing for drinks on the terrace. She put up her hand to knock but hesitated, and when her knuckles did connect with the wood it was so tentative, so non-committal a sound that she wasn't sure he'd hear it. But the sounds inside stopped. Joan's heart sank when she thought he might actually answer the door. She didn't think she could see him just then, and still leave. If he was kind to her, if he was conciliatory; if he was sweet and soft and made her feel safe, she might fall irresistibly into that stifling sleep. She shut her eyes. She had no idea if she wanted that to happen or not. But Rory didn't open the door; the soft sounds inside resumed, and Joan didn't knock again. Taking a slow breath, she left him.

She took nothing but her small overnight bag, her camera in it, and the bundle Abdullah had given her, stopping in a deserted alleyway to put on the abaya and masked veil. Her hands were shaking; she thought about the mountain, about being the first to walk its high plateau; about being a pioneer, not *poor Joanie* whose nerves were shot. The gate guards barely seemed to see her dressed the way she was. She could have been anybody. And that was how she felt as she walked up the hill, her resolve growing with every step she took away from her past life — she could be anybody, and she could choose. Not even Maude had ever seen the summit of Jebel Akhdar; Joan was going beyond normal life, so none of the normal rules applied any more.

As she stood in the rocks where she'd last seen Salim and

looked back down at the city and the sea, she felt so distant from that other life that she wondered if there were two of her – if another version of her was down there at the Residency, packing. The boat that would take that Joan to Aden was already at anchor. She watched a small lighter travel out to it, its wake a pale ribbon behind it. The Joan that would board it would say nothing to Rory about what she'd seen at the camp because staying with him, marrying him, depended on that. It would have to be as if it had never happened, she realised; and she knew how difficult that would be. The marriage would be compromised from the very start. *You needn't only ever play the cards you've been dealt*, Maude had said, and Joan was going to change hers.

When she heard the soft sound of Salim's footsteps, and smelled incense and metal, her heart began to speed. The choice was made; there were seconds left to unmake it, and though she knew she wouldn't the fear was still there – like walking along a cliff edge, knowing that she might fall however much she didn't want to. Salim said nothing at first. He looked at her seriously, nodded once, then beckoned her to him and put one hand on her shoulder.

'I knew you had the courage,' he said. 'But be warned – the mountain will change you, and you won't ever be rid of it. Come, follow me. Be silent, if you can.' He turned and set off, further from the road, deeper into the steep, sharp rocks. Joan followed him, breathing hard, and didn't look back.

Salalah and the Empty Quarter, Oman, March 1909

Maude saw Nathaniel just once between Faye's death and her own departure for Arabia. It was at Christmas, at Marsh House, and he'd had that same red-eyed, tightly wired look he'd once had as a boy, arriving from a visit to his mother in Nice. Faye had succumbed to a tumour that had, by all accounts, cruelly robbed her of her alabaster loveliness before it robbed her of her life. Maude had met her just once; doing so – and seeing how Nathaniel loved her – had been so acutely painful that she'd been laid up for a short while afterwards; not physically sick but so weak in spirit that she couldn't go out, or see anyone, or eat. Ashamed of such weakness, she'd hidden her collapse from everyone, especially her father, claiming that she was in the final throes of completing a manuscript. Nathaniel's three-year marriage to Faye had been childless, and marred by bouts of illness for both of them. They'd lived in Tripoli for much of it, and then in Baghdad, and the hard climates and lack of comfort in each place had taken their toll on Faye, who had wilted steadily, by all accounts, though she never complained. Maude tried not to hate the girl, who was blameless, but it was difficult. Her death caused Maude such a ringing absence of feeling that she avoided Nathaniel altogether for a while. It was far too hard to know what to say, and she couldn't stand to see his pain – it brought on a sensation of being steadily, inexorably strangled. She sent a formal, black-edged card of condolence, and hoped he would be too preoccupied to notice how profoundly inadequate it was.

By that Christmas at Marsh House, the Christmas of 1908, Faye had been dead for six months. Nathaniel looked older, more pared down, as though grief had stripped away the last vestiges of boyish insouciance. He no longer stood with his jacket flipped back and his hands in his pockets; he no longer leaned fluidly against the mantelpiece in a room; he stood straight and with his weight slightly forwards, as though poised for some unforeseen attack.

Maude still couldn't talk to him with the ease she'd once had. She loved him as deeply as ever, and she was still grieving herself – for the death of all her hopes, extinguished the moment he'd told her about Faye. Faye's death was no cause for those hopes to be revived; it was clear that Nathaniel was still in love with her memory, and even if he hadn't been he wouldn't have felt any differently about Maude. They talked mostly of travel; of her plans to cross the Rub el Khali – the Empty Quarter of the Arabian desert – never yet crossed from south to north, the longest route. That she would be the first, if she managed it, was almost incidental to Maude. It added a satisfying frisson of excitement, but she was already a reputed traveller, explorer and classicist; her books were given grudgingly favourable reviews from even the craggiest old scholars. Some had even stopped using *for a woman* to qualify their praise. But what really drew her to the Empty Quarter was its emptiness. Pristine desert; untouched; unrivalled in its lonely majesty. She'd had a taste of it during earlier journeys, and each taste fuelled rather than sated her appetite.

Nathaniel listened to her plans as they ate roast goose and redcurrant gravy, and went out riding in the flat, grey drizzle, and had sherry and shortbread with the vicar; and, as he listened, the avid look slowly returned to his eyes. So Maude talked more, because seeing how he absorbed her words caused happiness to gather beneath her ribs.

'Perhaps that's the answer, Mo,' he said late one evening, when it was just the two of them, sitting by the dying embers of the fire. 'I don't know why I didn't think of it before – I've just been so tired and . . . I don't know. It's been so hard to think, since Faye . . . passed away. Hard to think of anything at all. But the desert would change all that – of course it would. Like that first time, in Egypt, when I was so angry with the world and everyone in it. The peace there. It was impossible to be angry. It was impossible to mind anything; it all just . . . fell away. God, that's what I need now, Maude! That's what I need.' He leaned towards her with a hungry look.

'Come with me!' said Maude impulsively. 'Take some time away from the Political Service . . . The cost is no matter. Please let me do that for you.' But as soon as she spoke, she saw a little of the fire go out of his eyes, and a little of the fatigue return, and she knew he needed to go alone; that he could not be her companion, a Vickery hanger-on. She tried not to feel the sting of it. They sat without speaking for a while, as the fire seethed and quietly collapsed, and when she looked at him he was as known to her, as familiar, as every part of herself – and infinitely more precious. Perhaps it was because she'd had too much brandy after the claret at dinner, or because the room was almost dark, but suddenly Maude had to tell him one true thing that she'd meant to say months ago. 'If I could take up your burden for you, I would,' she said, her heart rising up into her throat. 'If I could take away your pain, even if it meant I felt it for ever, I would do it in an instant.'

'I know,' he said softly, after a pause. But she saw at once that the words had pushed him away rather than drawn him nearer. He stood, and let his hand rest on her shoulder for a moment before going. 'I know you would, Maude.'

The following year she wrote to him from Salalah, the southernmost town of Sultan Faisal bin Turki's realm, where the palace in which he spent most of his time opened its big windows seawards to capture the breeze. Maude was sitting in a folding chair on the sandy shore with a curdled grey sky above her, sweating slightly in the muggy, salt air. Her letter to Nathaniel was damp and fragile, the thin paper had become rippled. She wrote on a wooden tray resting on her knees, and the ink pot wobbled dangerously when she shifted her position. The sea and sky were one colour; the sand a pale shade of clay. It was harmonious, restful, strangely lifeless.

> *I have my final audience with His Highness Faisal bin Turki later this afternoon*, she wrote. *I think he will give me leave to travel, though none such has been granted to a foreigner before. He seems to have taken something of a shine to me — or perhaps I am merely a novelty. The women here are kept on a far tighter leash.*

She thought hard and then didn't set down what she'd been about to, since the letter would have to be given into the hands of the sultan's men to be forwarded on, and she was quite sure they would read it first. She had been about to write: *Of course, I shall go anyway, whether I have permission or not. It will only be slightly trickier if not.* Once she was in the desert, not even the sultan could touch her, or protect her. *Then, all will depend on the Bedouin guides, on my judgement, and on luck. I thank God I shall have dear Haroun with me. Somehow I feel nothing truly bad can befall me if he is there, fussing like a maiden aunt.*

Maude was the only person on the beach, which ran for miles in either direction. A few stray dogs picked their way through the fish scraps at the high-tide line; a few gulls did the same. Pale yellow crabs tiptoed across the hard sand nearer the water, running to and from their burrows with startling speed. It was hours yet before the fishermen would come in with the second catch of the day, and hours since they'd landed the first and turned their boats around to go back out. A few were visible opposite the beach – little white skiffs, and smaller, plainer vessels she would not have liked to set out to sea in. Along the coast to the north were the remains of the city of Surmurham, to the south those of Balid, both of which she had been given unprecedented access to explore and map. The maps and drawings were all she needed to complete her book on the cities of the ancient frankincense trade routes of Arabia; the trip into the desert, whatever she told the sultan, was for her alone.

She and Haroun had taken rooms in a merchant's house at the edge of the harbour. It had sandy floors and cracked walls; the colour had been leeched from every surface by years of salt and sun. Haroun found little to like about Oman. He complained about the humidity above all else – then the biting flies, then the flat-tasting water, the shifty eyes of the Omanis and the primitive savagery of the Qara tribesmen, who came down from the hills to wander the markets wearing next to nothing. Just then, Haroun came hurrying along the beach towards Maude.

'Esteemed lady, lunch is prepared for you,' he said, arriving at her side and mopping his brow with a white handkerchief. For the first time, and for no reason, Maude noticed grey whiskers among the black of his moustache.

'Did you manage to find any fresh apples? Or strawberries?' she asked, in Arabic.

'With humblest apologies, I could not. I do not think they grow them here,' he said.

'A pity,' Maude sighed. 'I had such a yen for something fresh before we commit ourselves to travel rations.' She handed him her writing tray as she rose. Her breeches and shirt were sticking to her skin, but though she made few concessions to femininity on her travels she stopped short of yanking at her clothes in public. Several sand flies had got beneath the mesh of her hat and were zigzagging infuriatingly around her eyes. Maude took the hat off and flapped it about in disgust. 'I'm starting to agree with you about the insects here, Haroun,' she said. Her servant nodded.

'They are more populous than the grains of sand in the desert,' he said mournfully.

Maude thought about her father as she got changed after lunch. The sultan preferred to see her dressed as a woman, so she put on a long tea dress cut from soft beige lawn, which hung loosely around her waist and ribs even though she'd long since given up wearing corsets. The dress was rumpled from the trunk but that couldn't be helped, and Salalah's humidity performed at least one useful function in encouraging the creases to drop out. She draped a shawl around her shoulders to make sure she was modest enough. *It doesn't do to scare the horses*, she'd written to her father, having described her odd wardrobe choices. He'd written back: *When travelling afield, far from the creature comforts of home, practicality is of far greater import than convention.* Lately, he'd taken to reiterating lessons he'd given her as a child, and seemed wholly unaware that he was repeating himself. It caused Maude the first stirrings of concern for him, but she hadn't the time to devote to those concerns just yet. Soon she would; when she was home again after this journey. Instead she wrote to her brothers and instructed them both to visit often, and take care of their father. John and Francis had settled early, and comfortably, into middle age. They seemed to find their sister deeply unsettling, and loathed her upbraidings well enough to do whatever she told them, most of the time.

At the appointed hour, and shaky with excitement, Maude

made her way to the palace. It was cool and uncluttered; guarded by skinny Omani soldiers and enormous, muscular negro slaves in matching blue tunics. A fountain splashed musically in the courtyard, murmured Arabic echoed in the corridors, and the chatter of songbirds came in from the garden. Maude wished Nathaniel were there with her. She could picture him easily – swimming in the sea, sleeping in the shade. Catching the sun in the fine hair at his temples. The thoughts were distracting, so she banished them. Sultan Faisal bin Turki was a small, well-built man in his mid-forties, with hard brown eyes beneath straight brows, a full lower lip and a short beard. He wore the royal turban – red silk like his flag, striped with gold. He'd been aloof with her to begin with, almost cold – she knew he'd only agreed to see her at all because he was curious about her appearance, her foreignness, her being female. Her renown in other parts of the world meant nothing to him. But gradually, over their subsequent interviews, she'd noticed him warm towards her. Now he seemed almost poised to smile, though he didn't, quite. Maude curtsied, and then sat down on the simple wooden chair that had been positioned facing him, slightly closer than was comfortable. She had to look up at him, of course, and she was careful not to cross her legs or arms. He smelled strongly of rose water, frankincense and coffee. They exchanged the traditional polite greetings for some length of time, and then Faisal watched her steadily for a while, not blinking.

'You are enjoying your time in Salalah, I hope?' he said.

'Very much so, your highness. Though I do feel you ought to instil a good deal more decorum into some your subjects.' Maude smiled, letting outrage begin to grow on Faisal's face before adding: 'The sand flies, your highness. They are quite unruly.'

'But we are all God's creatures, Miss Vickery,' he said,

smiling briefly. 'I am glad you like Salalah. You are welcome to lengthen your stay here as you see fit.'

'My thanks, your highness. You are most generous.' Maude couldn't tell if he wanted her to show impatience, and ask about the journey, or whether to do so would be disastrous.

There was another long silence, and then the sultan smiled again, more broadly.

'You may go about the realm as you see fit, Miss Vickery. I fear for your safety in such wild places, but you are clearly not the normal sort of woman. And I perceive your love of my country – I am an excellent judge of such things.'

'You have my humblest and deepest thanks, your highness,' said Maude, breathless with triumph. She kept her face and tone subservient.

'I wonder,' said Faisal, leaning forwards slightly, his eyes twinkling. 'I wonder who you think you are fooling with such displays of meekness?'

'I know I could never hope to fool you, your highness.'

Maude insisted on meeting the Bedouin who would guide her. They were of the Bait Kathir tribe – less hostile than some – and she looked each man in the eye to assess his character; she haggled their exorbitant fees down to a more reasonable amount, and refused to pay more than half in advance. She disputed with them over the number of camels she would need to buy, and who she should buy them from, and in the end took them along with her to the dusty market in the hills behind Salalah, to help select the animals. At first disrespectful, even openly derisive of this tiny, foreign woman with her mad plan to cross the desert, Maude soon saw a grudging acceptance of her creep over them – and the harder she argued with them, the more it grew. She argued hard.

She was happy to have procured the services of one man

in particular. Khalid bin Fatimah was strongly built, and had a look of deep intelligence in his eyes. He could have been any age between thirty and sixty, and he watched and listened a great deal. He spoke to her with a reserved kind of respect that neither assumed she deserved it nor assumed that she did not, which Maude thought wholly reasonable. He pointed out which camels were used to the desert, which to the hills; which would go lame as they crossed the vast gravel beds that made up a great deal of the Rub el Khali; which would founder in the dunes and refuse to cross. The herd they finally put together were all female, and all but one seemed docile and cooperative, though Maude already knew from experience that even the kindest camel could have its moments. She'd seen one, near the ancient Nabatean city of Petra, dispatch her bullying owner with one fatal, well-aimed kick of her foreleg. Maude introduced herself to her new, bad-tempered camel – the smallest of the herd – by feeding her a few dates. 'I know about feeling small and cross with the world,' she told the animal. 'Let's call you Midget, as I used to be; and if you ever bite me I shall skin you, and make sandals and water bags from your hide.' Midget thumped Maude's shoulder with her hairy nose, so that Maude was forced to take a step backwards. The camel rumbled deep in her throat, and peered down through her long eyelashes, and Maude swore she saw amusement there.

We leave tomorrow, Maude wrote in another letter to Nathaniel, one that wouldn't be posted until the journey was completed – if it ever was. Khalid and Haroun seemed to hit it off reasonably well, and the other Bedouin seemed to defer to Khalid, as much as they deferred to anyone, and Maude thought with some satisfaction that she could not have designed the group better if she'd tried. There were three younger Bedouin, who all looked rather alike to Maude at first, with their matted black hair, thin whiskers, faded tunics and bare feet. All carried their rifle and ammunition belts as well as their khanjars, and wore knotted kaffias around their heads. One of them had a broken Swiss wristwatch, of which he was inordinately proud. Maude didn't like to think how on earth he'd come to have it. She learned their names at once – Fatih, Ubaid and Kamal – but was not always completely sure, to begin with, whether she was applying the right name to the right man. There was also an older man, who claimed to have crossed the desert in every which way possible. His hair and whiskers were white, and he looked out at the world through a mass of wrinkled skin; his name was Sayyid, and the younger men spoke to him with cheerful disdain, which surprised Maude. Apparently, respect was not automatically conferred upon elders. The focus of most derision, however, was a bony lad called Majid, hired in Salalah by Haroun as a general dogsbody. He spoke little, had the frightened eyes of a deer, and looked no more than thirteen.

To begin with, they rode steadily north and east from the coast, across vast gravel fields dotted with spherical geodes and peculiar rock formations like petrified flowers. The camels browsed at short thorny trees as they went. The air shimmered. They startled up gazelle here and there and the Bedouin took turns shooting at them, laughing and throwing casual insults when the gazelle escaped without injury – as they generally did. They carried supplies of flour, salt, water, dates, coffee, sugar, whiskery onions and dried goat meat. When a gazelle was shot, on the fourth day, the fresh meat made a welcome change, and Maude realised how sick of sandy bread and dates she was likely to be before they reached their destination. Haroun kept a supply of sweet biscuits, black tea, coconut ice and Turkish Delight in a locked strong box, for Maude's exclusive use. He kept the key to the box about his person at all times, guarding it as closely as any chatelaine.

'The tribesmen are like children for sweets, esteemed lady,' he told her seriously. 'And, like children, they will steal them.'

'Haroun, our lives depend on these men,' Maude reminded him, amused. 'Would it hurt to share a little?' Grumbling about how quickly the treats would run out, Haroun offered the box of Turkish Delight around, and the men took as much as they could before he snatched it away again. They grinned as they ate it, with powdered sugar sifting down into their beards. Young Majid, who had never tasted it before, shut his eyes in astonished bliss. After that, Maude gave him a piece every night, when nobody else was looking.

The Bedouin were amused by Maude's tent, her folding camp bed, table, wash-stand and chair. They took no pains to keep their mocking remarks quiet, or hide their laughter, as Haroun and Majid hurried to assemble Maude's lodgings each night – there was Haroun's tent as well, and the small, vertical tent, like that of a Punch and Judy show, which served as Maude's privy. As all this construction went on, Maude sat on her chair by the fire, drinking tea and swapping stories with the Bedouin. They all ate together – the men took turns making flatbreads on a griddle over the fire, in which they rolled shreds of the dried goat meat and, inevitably, a great deal of sand. Then came dates and coffee, which could not disguise the rancid taste of water that had been stored in a goatskin under a hot sun, but did make it a little more palatable. The Bedouin drank little, and ate little. They appeared, to Maude, as self-sufficient as their camels – able to survive on far less than seemed possible. After a week Maude learned that one of the younger men, Fatih, the most garrulous, was Khalid's eldest son. Suddenly she saw it – how the boy's constant talking and singing and tall tales begged for his father's attention and approval. In the day the men sang – sections of the Quran, or prayers, or long-winded folk songs, apparently to any meandering tune that came to mind. When the end of the song was reached, the singer began again. After several hours of this, one day, Maude broke into a loud and rousing rendition of 'Jerusalem the Golden', to which the men listened with bemused attention, before bursting into delighted laughter.

Their route was dictated as much by areas of grazing for the camels as it was by watering holes, so it was convoluted, and Maude tried not to chafe too much at the inefficiency of it. Still, ten days into their journey she was dismayed by how little distance they'd covered. She frequently took bearings from her compass, and kept up a detailed map of the whole route as best she could. She took photographs, and sketched as well – the craggy ridges of rock they passed, and the flora and fauna they saw – of which there was precious little. Large, pale green scorpions; black beetles; crows; bat-eared foxes and occasionally a ferocious-looking lizard with a thick tail like a club, sprinting for its burrow. On the day Khalid shot an oryx, she asked for half an hour before it was butchered in which to draw its beautiful black horns and white coat, pristine but for the splatter of blood across its ribs. Soon it was strips of flesh, tied to a wicker frame to dry in the sun, and gathering a crust of sand and flies. The hide and horns disappeared into the men's luggage. The Bedouin lived hard lives, and had no time to find wild things beautiful. Khalid looked at her drawings of it curiously.

'We will not see many,' he said eventually. 'Such creatures are shy of men, and run fast.'

'A good job, or perhaps none would remain,' said Maude.

'God wills it so,' Khalid agreed. 'Each of us has a means to live, and a means to die.'

'And thanks to your sharp shot, we have a means to eat dinner,' she said, and the sturdy man smiled.

Maude was soon heartily sick of dates, which formed the

bulk of their diet. They caused her guts to cramp, and even on the days there was precious little else to eat, she often went hungry instead. By the end of each day her back ached fiercely from the incessant rocking motion of the camel, and her backside was numb and bruised. She attempted to ride by kneeling behind the hump, as the Bedouin did, but soon decided that this was a posture one must have to adopt from infancy to make it the least bit bearable. She tried walking beside her camel for a while, but the relief of it soon ended when she realised how weak her legs were – how feeble the diet had rendered them. The dry heat was cracking her lips, and she was thirsty from the moment she woke until the moment she slept. The Bedouin seemed to need no more sleep than they needed food or water, and they talked late into the night, keeping her awake. She had to bite her tongue not to rush out and demand silence one night, as an argument over some tracks they had passed entered its second hour: whether the camels had been old or young, fat or starving, loaded or packed lightly, for raiding. She found the only way to tolerate it was to compose it silently, in her mind, into the letter to Nathaniel. *In some ways they are like little boys, arguing over conkers. But then, one of the things they boast about is how many men they have killed.*

Her eyes began to stream constantly from the glare of the empty sky, which was mirrored from below by the low hills of pale sand they were crossing. After two days of dabbing at them – and getting sand into them each time she did – Maude was persuaded to let Khalid kohl her eyelids for her. The Bedouin all carried a small metal tube of the stuff, with a wand set in the lid. Khalid drew the stick sharply along the lower rim of each of her eyes, and she blinked wildly at the sting, and the oddly hot, gritty sensation. But when it had eased and she was used to it she found that it did reduce the glare, and she was far more comfortable. That afternoon they saw another party of Bedouin at the top of a rise ahead of them. Khalid stared as the others drew in around him. He dismounted, crouched and threw a handful of sand into the air to signal their peaceful intent, and there were dark mutterings when the signal was not returned. The strange men simply stared at them, and Maude felt a chill; her Bedouin took their rifles into their hands and stared back, unwavering.

'A raiding party?' she said to Sayyid, beside her. The old man nodded.

'They are not Bait Kathir. Rashid, perhaps. They are out-numbered and will ride on, but we must watch for them in the darkness.'

That night was a nervy, sleepless one, and when one of the camels grumbled, the Bedouin were on their feet in an instant, reaching for their weapons. Other travellers they met were more friendly, and stopped to speak with them for lengthy spells that made Maude chafe, until she realised that they were swapping news of grazing for the camels, and of raiding parties in the area. They lost a whole afternoon's travel one day, when they were forced to shelter from a strong wind. It didn't seem too bad at first. Maude tried unsuccessfully to cajole the men into going on, but the camels were couched, their handlers tucked themselves into the leeward side of them and wrapped their kaffias across their faces. Haroun and Majid struggled to get the tents up in the growing gale, and Maude stood with her back to it, fascinated by the way the sand moved in wisps and billows and strange, finger-like tendrils – just like smoke. It stung any exposed skin, and stuck there. It made talking impossible, and seeing difficult. Maude wished she could draw it – the way the sand lent the wind a physical form. By the time she was forced into her tent, she was coated from head to foot, and her ears were ringing.

By morning there was a profound calm and a sky of flawless blue. The Bedouin cursed the sand cheerfully as they shook it out of everything they owned, pummelled it from the camels, and ground it between their teeth as they ate breakfast. In the next breath they acknowledged stoically that the wind had been God's will. In the cool of dawn, Maude walked a short distance away and climbed onto some rocks. She was hungry, thirsty, exhausted, and deeply, deeply happy. *I wish you were here with me*, she wrote in her head. *You're the only person who could share this feeling without shattering it; who could share this paradise without spoiling it.* She was filled with a sudden rush of optimism. Of course, she'd always been sure that she was up to the journey, and that the journey was possible; but perhaps she'd also been so well aware of all the many things that could go wrong and force them back that she'd been waiting for one of them to happen. Just then, she stopped waiting. She saw the end, though it was still a long way off; she could imagine finishing the journey in triumph, and knowing for the rest of her life that she had been the first to do it – and a woman to boot. She decided on a title for the book she would write about the journey: *Arabia: Travels Amidst the Wind and the Stars*. There was still one star shining that morning, over in the west – a tiny silver freckle, fighting against the light of day.

But just a couple more days' trek caused her optimism to ebb. The journey was the most gruelling she had ever undertaken; the terrain the least forgiving, the least changing. Moving on each day began to feel like digging a hole that never got any deeper; she felt she was treading water in a sea of dust and gravel. When they pitched camp one night, she longed to lie down and sleep, but Haroun seemed to take an age getting everything ready. Waspish with fatigue, Maude snapped at him.

'What in heaven's name is taking so long, man? I could have built myself a castle of sand in the time it's taken you to put up a tent and brew some tea.'

'My most humble apologies, esteemed lady,' said Haroun, bowing, clearly distressed. 'It will be only a few more minutes.' Then Maude noticed the laboured way he was breathing, and the sweat on his brow, and was immediately filled with remorse.

'Haroun! Are you unwell?'

'It is nothing, sahib. A slight ague.' But his hands were limp and restless, and his eyes had a dazed look, and shadows beneath them.

'Majid – get Haroun's tent up as quickly as you can,' she ordered the boy. 'Haroun, sit down. I insist. And as soon as your tent is built, you are to go into it and lie down.'

'But—'

'I will hear no arguments about it. Majid and I can manage.'

'Yes, lady.'

They could manage, but barely. Maude's tent went up crooked, and only with Khalid's help, and there was no time after that for tea. She unfolded her bed and put sheets and blankets on it, and didn't bother with any of the other furniture. The night was stony cold, and she shivered by the fire as she waited for her share of the bread and meat. Majid returned from Haroun's tent with his plate untouched, and said that the servant was asleep.

'Good,' said Maude, deeply uneasy. 'He needs to rest. I should have noticed it sooner; it was selfish of me not to.' Preoccupied as she was, she forgot herself and spoke in English, and Majid looked on uncomprehendingly, eyes wide with consternation. By morning Haroun was up, but he shook all over, and reeled dizzily as he tried to make her breakfast.

Majid helped him away into the rocks, and Maude questioned him as delicately as she could afterwards.

'Is it dysentery, Haroun? Speak freely, you cannot embarrass me with such things.'

'Perhaps it is only the dates, or the water, esteemed lady.'

'Perhaps, and I hope so. But I shall mix you a tonic in any case.'

'You must save your medicines, sahib. You might have need of them.'

'I have need of them now, for I cannot do without you, Haroun,' she said, and had the pleasure of seeing him smile a little.

The Bedouin argued vociferously against stopping where they were – there was no grazing for the camels, they said, and their water supplies were running low. They needed to press on to the well which Sayyid said was still a day's ride away. Maude would not be moved. Haroun could not ride, and there was no way she was going to sling him over his camel, as one of the men suggested, or leave him behind. Some dark looks and muttered words were exchanged, and a discussion was taken aside, which Khalid eventually curtailed with a few well-chosen words.

'Two will ride on to the well and fill the skins,' he told Maude. 'The camels can eat dates for two days, maybe three. Then, we must move or perish.'

'Very well,' said Maude. 'Thank you. I am sure he will be well recovered by then.'

Khalid nodded, and left her; and Maude wondered if the two young men who were sent on to the well would come back, or carry on and try their luck elsewhere. If they did, with the majority of the water skins, those left behind were doomed. Suddenly, she had a very real taste of the danger they were in – she'd known it before, but not felt it. One bad decision, or one botched navigation, could mean death. The fear of it had an actual taste – like copper; just a hint of it, in the back of her throat.

The place where they'd stopped was surrounded by low dunes of hard sand, on which they left only shallow footprints. Maude studied the map she had drawn as though it might reveal the way ahead as well. She showed it to old Sayyid, and tried to pin him down as to how far they had come, how far they still were from the dunes of Uruq al Shaiba, the barrier of vast dunes that made her anxious whenever she thought about them. She'd even suggested to him, when she heard about them, that they go around them instead. The old man had smiled. There was a vast area of quicksand to the east, and waterless desert for many days to the west. There was, in short, no way around them, and only once they were across them could they turn east, and leave the desert for the mountains that then lay between them and the sea, and the end of their journey. The sultan had asked that she send word from Muscat when she arrived there – if she arrived there. Maude studied the terrain, and noted how easy it was to walk on the low, compact dunes. She suggested to Khalid that crossing the Uruq al Shaiba mightn't be that hard. He shook his head.

'Few have crossed successfully. Men have dashed themselves against the dunes like waves dashing themselves on rocks. Sayyid, alone of us, has done it – we must all rely on him to guide us safely through; and he will, God willing.'

'God willing,' Maude echoed heavily.

As the second day dawned, Maude sat with Haroun while he slept on, and they all checked the horizon repeatedly for the return of the others from the well. There was little else she could do. The Bedouin stripped their rifles down, cleaned out the sand and reassembled them; they argued and sang. Fatih walked off and returned, hours later, with a withered sheaf of devil's thorn that the camels ate with a marked lack of enthusiasm. Their listlessness was thirst, Maude knew. Haroun muttered in his sleep for several hours, and then seemed to grow more peaceful. Maude didn't know if that was a good sign or not. She mixed another stomach tonic, and added some powered iron for strength, but could not rouse him to drink it. His face was sunken and shiny; his breath was sulphurous. Maude thought of his wife, alone with their children, so many miles away in Palestine.

'Haroun,' she said, close to his ear. 'Haroun, you must get better. Please. I order you to! I shan't leave you here, but we must move soon. So I need you to get up, and make ready. Do you hear me?' She tried to sound authoritative, but instead her voice came out small, and pleading. She swallowed. *Haroun gave me a bit of a scare*, went her invisible letter to Nathaniel, with desperate optimism. *We had a short delay at just the wrong moment, when water was low, while he recovered from a bout of dysentery. But recover he did, and we are back on our way.*

'We must brand him. It will cure him – I was cured of the exact same illness myself last year, with this brand,' said Fatih, pulling up his sleeve and showing her the scars of three short, parallel burns on his forearm.

'Nonsense,' said Maude. 'I won't hear of it.' Fatih walked away muttering about the stupidity of foreigners, and women, and the godless.

'Sahib,' said Majid tentatively. 'Branding is most effective. It could save him.' The boy looked at her with his wide, frightened eyes, and Maude bit back a sharp retort. She shook her head.

Haroun died with the minimum of fuss, slipping away

without a murmur. His final breath was lost beneath the sudden cries of delight and joyous cracks of rifle fire that went up as the water carriers were spotted on the horizon. Maude sat numb beside him. Suddenly, she had absolutely no idea what to do. She cried for a while, still inside the tent with him, but made sure her face was dry before she eventually went out to tell the others what had happened.

'You should have let me brand him,' said Fatih, as the Bedouin took over, wrapping Haroun in his blanket and carrying him out. Khalid spoke lines of the Quran for him, and he was laid out to wait until, by sunset, enough rocks and stones had been gathered to cover his shallow grave. Maude didn't insult her friend's faith by saying any Christian prayers over his resting place. She searched her luggage for some token she could leave for him, but Khalid warned her that anything she left would be pilfered by the next men to ride that way.

'I thought graveyards were sacred to Muslims? Sacred for eternity?' she said angrily.

'With regret, this is not a graveyard. This is the desert, and though there is faith here there is not always piety. He was with you a long time?'

'Yes. He was . . . he was very dear.'

Maude barely slept, and when she did, she dreamed of cold, running water – brimming glasses of the stuff that she couldn't quite reach. Her mouth, by morning, felt leathery, and as they set off only she and Majid seemed in sombre mood. The desert men were unchanged – if anything, they were cheerful, happy to be riding on towards the well. *The Bedouin have no hearts, and no feelings*, she wrote to Nathaniel; but she knew it wasn't true. Haroun had not been one of them, and they had seen many men founder. If they allowed themselves to be moved by every death, they'd soon be exhausted, overladen with feeling.

Majid wept a bit as they left the cairn behind, for which

Maude was grateful, even if she suspected he feared more for himself than he mourned Haroun. The boy was even thinner than he'd been when he joined them; it was hard to imagine how he could get much thinner without disappearing altogether. They reached the well by the end of the day, but the water was brackish and foul, and the camels refused to drink it. The air filled with the rank whiff of the water, with the rumbled outrage of the camels and the curses of their handlers. Bracing herself, Maude took a cup and drank deeply. It tasted awful and would give her cramps, but it slaked her thirst. She filled another cup and drank again. With a gurgling sigh, the smallest camel, Midget, followed her example. Then, one by one, the other camels stopped struggling and came forward to drink. Khalid, Fatih and the others stared in amazement, and then laughed in delight.

'You are the mistress of the camels, lady,' Ubaid told her, grinning. 'God is good!'

For four days they rode along a shimmering salt flat between large, rolling sand dunes. Other than the singing and arguing, the only sound was the crunch of the crust beneath the camels' spreading feet. Maude searched inside herself for the optimism she'd felt just a short while ago, but could find none of it. Without Haroun, she felt desperately alone. The desert seemed endless; her thirst and hunger were constant. The water gave her diarrhoea, which in turn made her even more thirsty, even more weak. At night she and Majid couldn't erect her big tent securely, so she took to using Haroun's little one instead. Her furniture stayed roped together in a heap on the ground. There were no sweets left, only a little tea, which Haroun had taught Maijd to make. Maude spoke very little. She felt Khalid keeping an eye on her, though – he gave her the subtle feeling of being watched, and she was grateful. She took bearings and kept up her map, but her journal lapsed and there were no more drawings of the things they saw. She noticed her own hands one morning – filthy, wizened, scratched, unsteady.

Then, at around noon one day, a dune appeared on the horizon ahead of them. A vast, undulating golden mass, running right across their path as far as they could see in either direction. Its leeward side faced them – far steeper than the windward side would be; it had a sharp ridge at the top of its precipitously steep flank, poised like a wave about to break.

Maude stared at it in disbelief as they rode on in silence – even the singing stopped as they came closer and closer to this terrifying obstacle. Suddenly, Maude understood: the dunes they had seen up to that point, the ones to either side of the salt flat, had been infants – miniatures compared to this monster, and presumably to the others that lay behind it. She prayed that a way to climb it would become obvious as they neared it, but none did. They stopped in the shadow of the cliff and stared up it. The ridge was two hundred feet above them, perhaps three hundred, it was hard to tell. Maude's heart strained with every beat; the Bedouin seemed restless, and even old Sayyid frowned up at the dune as though he had never seen it before.

'But this is *impossible*,' said Maude, to anyone who could hear. 'Nobody could possibly take a camel up such a slope!'

'Sayyid has done it. He will show us the way,' said Fatih, not sounding in the least bit convinced.

'We are in God's hands now,' said Khalid, his face troubled. 'May He be merciful.' Majid darted him an anxious look with his doe's eyes.

'It's impossible!' Maude said again, and then fell silent, ashamed of the note of panic in her voice. The only other way was back, and that was risky enough – they didn't have quite enough water to get back to the last well; if they missed it, as was always possible, they would perish. And even if they made it back, all hopes of completing the crossing would end. All the hardship – and Haroun's death – would be for nothing. They had to go on.

Maude tried to steady herself; she tried to swallow but her throat was too dry. She thought of her letter to Nathaniel, but her mind was blank – she could think of nothing else to add to it. Nobody was coming to help her, nobody but this handful of men even knew where she was. She wished she could feel defiance towards the dune, but the thought of struggling through all that sand made her want to lie down and sleep, and perhaps, like Haroun, remain that way for ever. They dismounted and couched the camels, and brewed coffee while Sayyid walked first one way and then the other; frowning, muttering prayers to himself. He looked for all the world like a man without the first clue what to do next.

Jebel Ahkdar, December 1958

They walked for hours, through darkness; south-west, away from Muscat and the coast towards Jebel Ahkdar. Joan soon had cuts and bruises on her shins from boulders she couldn't see, and the heaviness of fatigue made her clumsy. When she looked up, the stars seemed to swim across the inky sky. She was breathing hard – air as fresh as water, and with the same mineral taste. Salim was a dark figure, sure-footed, always ahead of her so that she could only just see him, only just follow. He paused regularly so she could catch up, and catch her breath.

'The night will be a long one,' he said, offering her water from his bottle. 'We dare not use the road. But by morning we will be in a safer place, and you can rest.'

'I'm fine,' said Joan; and it was true. She still felt as though she could fly, in spite of the sweat soaking her underarms, and the bruises, and her dry mouth. She felt as though she had left the real world behind and gone into a wholly different one; one in which she was untouchable. If there was any part of her that warned she was breaking every rule, and whispered that she didn't belong there, then she refused to hear it. She didn't think about Rory, or Robert, or Marian, or even Maude. They were already far behind her and she only wanted to go forwards. She was nearer to the mountain with every step.

Some time in the murky light of pre-dawn, a soft voice came from up ahead. Joan gasped, but Salim answered calmly enough; there was a muted conversation, a chuckle, a rough embrace between the two men. Joan hung back in her black mask and robe, just one more shadow. She made out two sturdy mules tethered nearby.

'Come, Joan. We can rest our legs a bit,' Salim said cheerfully. In the darkness, Joan couldn't tell if the man who'd brought the mules was surprised to see her or not. Salim offered to help her up but Joan mounted swiftly, automatically sitting astride. She concentrated as she settled into the hard, unfamiliar shape of the saddle. The reins were stiff, made of knotted cord rather than leather; she took hold of them and the mule lifted its chin in protest. 'All right,' she told it quietly. 'Don't worry. Light hands it is. I've never ridden a mule before,' she said to Salim. 'Are they as stubborn as everyone says? He seems rather dear, with those long ears. What's his name?' There was a startled pause, and then Salim laughed quietly.

'He has no name; he's a mule. And no one will believe you are an Arab woman if you ride like a man,' he said.

'Well, does it really matter if they do? I can't ride sideways; I'm not a sack of grain. Anyway, no one will see me in the dark.' Salim mounted his own mule and turned its head towards the mountains.

'Very well. But there may be times, in the next few days, when I will need you to do as I ask. Until we are in a safe place,' he said seriously.

'Yes. I understand.'

Joan remembered her daydreams, and how she'd fantasised about riding though Arabia, and how, though she'd got her wish, it didn't look anything like she'd imagined it. But then that was true of most imagined things. It was a dream realised nonetheless – and finally. Her eyes felt hot so she shut them for a moment and thought of her father, and all the dreams he'd never fulfilled, telling herself that whatever happened from then on she would never regret leaving Muscat; whatever happened next, it would be worth it for the feeling she had just then. 'Are we in Wadi Sumail?' she asked, and Salim turned to nod.

'We are crossing it – we have no choice; we must be quiet, Joan. There could be askari near – guard pickets. Many are on our side, in secret, but not all.'

'You mean they're double agents?' Joan's first thought was that she ought to tell Colonel Singer, but she checked it. She realised she no longer had any idea which side she was on, and decided to be on no side at all. She decided to see and think as little about the war as possible; she was not a part of it. 'What about the mines? Isn't the road here covered with mines?' she said, alarmed.

'Yes, but I know the safe stretches. Ahmed told me where to cross, back there.'

'But how will we avoid detection if we go this way – if the wadi is full of guards? My brother said there was no way onto the mountain from this side.'

'I am glad they still think so,' said Salim, and she caught the flash of his grin. 'But we must go *along* a good way before we can go *up*. We will keep close to the mountain's feet, once we have crossed. If we need to hide, there are caves, and ravines.'

On the far side of the wadi, they picked their way a short distance into the large boulders at the base of the mountainside, climbing a little until the gradient became too steep before turning south again, to follow the route of the dry riverbed as it cut through the mountains away from the coast. The way was mostly level, and Joan was glad not to have to climb for a while. At times they passed through sleeping forests of date palms; at times through scatterings of crumbled mud buildings that might have been abandoned two months ago, or two centuries. Dawn broke, revealing the black rock to be a deep golden brown, and the silhouetted palm trees to have pewter bark, and green leather leaves. Joan had the same surreal feeling she'd had the only other time she'd stayed out all night long – the night of her graduation, when Rory had first kissed her. The feeling was of breaking a habit so ingrained, so immured, that it seemed as though something momentous must happen as a result. Something momentous had happened last time, she supposed – she and Rory had become an item. But now that memory was bewildering, and muddled in her mind. She remembered Daniel slumped between them, and both of their hands on his arm; both of them supporting him. What had it all meant, really? Where had all their loyalties lain? She no longer knew. Tentatively, she thought about that other first kiss – Charlie's. The only man other than Rory to kiss her that way – not that the two kisses had been at all alike. She wondered what that second kiss meant; if, instead of being the less honest, as Maude had made her think, it had in fact been the more so.

Before long, they stopped opposite the village of Sumail, at a place where a narrow ravine cut deeply into the cliff above them. They dismounted and led the mules a short way up this crack before stopping, tucked into a shallow overhang of rock.

'Stay here. Rest a while,' said Salim. In the light of morning he seemed more human than he had; less commanding, less serene. He wore a look of extreme concentration that made Joan cautious.

'Where are you going?'

'Into the village for news, then I will return. Rest, Joan, and keep out of sight. This is a safe place.' Joan nodded, and sat down against the rock. She peeled off the veil and scratched at her sweaty scalp. Her hair would dry wiry and stiff, with the curls all awry, but that was how it would have to be. The mules looked tired and Joan wished they'd found a place to water them. She tipped her head back against the rock and shut her eyes. Fatigue tugged at her consciousness at once, and she let it. Sketchy dreams flickered to life, of home, and of riding in darkness, and of stumbling. She woke once with a start, to the sound of an army truck making its laboured way along the wadi. From where she was sitting, one short stretch of the road was visible. She saw it pass – a rattling old jalopy; saw the pale skin of the driver and his front passenger, the darker skins of the soldiers in the back. She wondered if they were looking for her yet; if they would look for her in the interior at all. They couldn't possibly guess her destination. Above the rumble of the engine she caught a snatch of laughter, as quickly gone as heard. When her heart had slowed to normal, Joan slept again.

Salim returned some hours later, bringing a bundle of warm flatbreads. There was sweat and dirt on his forehead but he seemed calm, and resolute. He moved over the rocks with the same surefootedness as the mules, Joan realised. He was in his element.

'I had hoped to carry on now, but we must wait until the afternoon,' he said. 'Which means you can rest longer.'

'Where are we going?' she asked. Salim glanced at her and she saw a look of boyish happiness behind the grown man's gravity.

'Home,' he said, smiling. 'We will follow Wadi Sumail to the far side of the mountain, where the way up to the summit is much less steep, and then climb – to Tanuf first, where I grew up. It's destroyed now – your RAF planes and their bombs finished it last year – but there is still shelter to be found there. Then up to another village, Misfat al Abreen. There, you will see the real beauty of this country. There it will be safe for you to remain.'

'But . . . can't I go with you to the plateau?'

'It is not safe.' He shook his head.

'None of this is safe. Please, Salim? Please take me up with you – even if just for a day. I . . . want to go up; I want to be the first. You said—'

'*Why* must you be first?' he said tonelessly. Joan fell silent, stung. He thought for a while, with a frown. 'I will see what I can do, but I can make no promises. But when we have reached Misfat and I have gone on, I cannot stop you. I do not want to. Your life is your own.' He took his rifle from his shoulder and rested it against the rocks beside him, adjusted his belt, then leaned back and shut his eyes. Joan felt uneasy at the thought of that time ahead – the time when she would no longer be in Salim's hands, but on her own, in charge of herself. Not marshalled by her father, or by Rory, or by Salim. It was a state she had never known. If she let it, the unease might turn to fear, so she tried not to dwell on it, and went back to sleep with the warm push of the breeze on her face, and the occasional shifts and sighing of the mules, and the smell of rock and the distant desert.

For three days and three more nights, they travelled like this – sporadically by day, steadily by night. After two days, Joan stopped asking if they were near their destination – she wasn't sure if she wanted to know. She wasn't sure if she wanted to arrive. While they kept moving, she knew exactly what she was doing. What came after that, she wasn't so sure about. She tried to think like Maude; tried to revel in the thrill of not knowing. Food appeared for them, sometimes brought back from a solo foray by Salim, sometimes brought by a veiled woman from a nearby village. Salim exchanged news with them, words Joan couldn't understand. They drank from any open falaj they passed, and refilled Salim's bottles. The terrain was unrelenting. They passed along the foot of one cliff so high, so fierce, that they stopped to stare up at the mountain's pitted, monochrome skin.

'No foreign army has ever successfully stormed The Green Mountain,' said Salim.

'Yes, the sultan's soldiers are well aware of that. But no man had ever escaped from Jalali, either. Until you did,' she said. Salim was quiet, and she glanced at him nervously. 'I am not a part of this,' she said carefully.

'You are not,' he agreed. Joan held her tongue as they carried on.

Wadi Sumail opened out to the vastness of the desert beyond the mountains, where Nizwa stood guard. They reached that point in darkness one night, and Salim turned north, climbing higher onto the more gradual slopes on that side of the mountain. Joan stared back behind them, and fancied she could see the sparkle of Nizwa's lights. The army camp was there; Daniel and Charlie were there, just a few miles away. They would never have believed she was there. For a moment, Joan's stomach dropped, and her chest seemed to squeeze. She couldn't believe she was there either, and it suddenly seemed impossible that she was. So impossible that she wasn't sure, in that instant, if any of it was real. The journey, the broken sleep, the darkness; everything had taken on a flimsy, dream-like quality that she half believed she would wake up from at some point. When she slept, too exhausted to mind the hard, cold ground, she dreamed she was still riding. Sometimes when she was riding, she dreamed that she was asleep. Once she dreamed she was back in Muscat, and had never left, and woke to the confusion of not knowing where she was. When memory returned to her, it came with relief, and amazement.

The mules trudged on stoically. As they climbed, the temperature dropped; Joan shivered in the damp of the early morning. Her whole body ached from riding. Weariness had settled over her like a blanket, but the ruins of Tanuf, when they reached them, still startled her. They halted the mules in silence, and looked out over them for a long time. Broken walls with blind windows like mournful eyes, rubble piled all around, and splintered wooden beams, pottery; sometimes a wall with a beautiful arched doorway remained, leading nowhere.

'Mud buildings stand firm if they are looked after. If they are not, they will wash away, in time. They will rejoin the earth,' Salim said quietly. He pointed to one street, to a wrecked house Joan could not distinguish from the rest. 'We lived there a good many years. I remember running in these streets as a child, to be home before dark.'

'Salim . . . I'm sorry. It must be terrible to see it like this.'

'Things change,' he said bitterly. 'And they will, whether we wish it or not.'

'Were many people . . . killed?'

'No, thanks be to God. They were warned that the bombs were coming. The sultan's army only wanted to give us nowhere to hide, nowhere to live. But that is city thinking – that is British thinking. Mountain men need only the mountain to live upon.'

They made their way around the ruins to the open falaj that still ran beneath a spreading tamarind tree, full of deep, clear water, unaware that the village it had once watered had been destroyed. Salim stripped to the waist then stood with the lip of the trough at his hips and leaned forwards, dunking his whole upper body into the water. Joan stared, trying to work out what was so unexpected about his appearance, so incongruous. He surfaced with a gasp and a shower of droplets; Joan looked away quickly, but not before he'd grinned at her. 'We are coming to safer places, Joan, though we must be wary here still. SAF patrols come this far, regularly; trying to go higher. But if you wish to bathe, you may.' His mood seemed lighter; she felt his relief at reaching Tanuf undiscovered, but for a moment pictured the madness of bumping into Daniel there, on patrol. Joan felt gritty all over; she had never before gone so long between baths. 'I will stand guard, over there, but please don't take all your clothes off. We are probably being watched, and others are due to meet us here.' Salim glanced up at a long ribbon of white water tumbling down a crease in the slope above them. 'Soon you will see why it is called The Green Mountain,' he called, as he walked away.

Joan took off the abaya and veil, and the trousers underneath. Her shirt was long, and reached the middle of her thighs; it was made of lightweight cambric and would dry quickly, so she kept it on and climbed into the falaj, gasping at the chill of the water. She scrubbed her fingers through her hair, raking out the dust and dirt. She drank, and felt awake, fully awake, for the first time in days. There was something about the water – it had made Salim smile even though he was surrounded by the broken ghosts of his home town; it made Joan not care about the future she'd left behind, or the unknowable one ahead. She decided to make no plan, but to see what would happen, that was all. It was liberating. Shoals of little grey fish darted around her, and she thought of Charlie Elliot, and his claim that the fish had stolen his razor. As she felt them butting gently at her fingers and toes, she finally believed him – and caught herself wishing she could tell him about it. She wished she'd replied to his note, at least to accept his apology. Lying back in the water, paddling her hands against the current, she stared up the empty mountainside and thought about Salim's skin – the spare torso she'd glimpsed as he washed himself. Scars across his ribs; jutting shoulder blades with lean muscles running over them, as hard as the bones. And yet something was not quite right, something was not as she'd expected it to be, though she hadn't known until that moment that she had any expectations at all. She could not put her finger on it.

Joan put the abaya and her trousers back on, then took off her shirt and hung it from the lowest branches of the tree to dry. It had turned overcast; the sky was full of bulbous clouds and a few cold drops of rain came in on the breeze. She shivered. Without the sun on it, the mountain looked bleak, as dead as the village.

'Daniel told me about the rains you sometimes get here. A year's rain in an hour or two,' she said, sitting down next to Salim beneath a section of unbroken roof in what had once been somebody's home. She tried using the hem of the veil to dry her hair.

'Yes. A year's rain here is not as much as you are used to, but it is still a lot. It can happen. The water runs from the mountainsides like blood from fresh wounds. The wadis flood with sudden fury; then, just hours later, nothing is left.'

They slept for most of the day. Joan woke once to the sound of Salim praying: his softly murmured words, the quiet shift of gravel beneath his knees. For a while she watched his face as he genuflected – his eyes shut, all his attention inwards, upwards, towards his God. The grey light was fading when she woke again to find him sitting on a broken wall a short distance away, cleaning his rifle. She was hungry, and stiff, and listened again for the sound that had woken her. The scuff of a footstep, the rattle of a loose stone. She sat bolt upright with a gasp but Salim looked up at the same time, and smiled. He called out something in Arabic, and there was an answering shout, and Joan relaxed. She reached for the veil and mask and quickly put them on. A group of six men surrounded

Salim, grinning, patting his shoulders, clasping his arms. Joan watched the reunion cautiously.

'This is my cousin, Bilal,' Salim called across to her. 'I've told him he moves noisily enough to wake an exhausted girl. It is thanks only to God he has not yet been shot.'

'We've been watching you for two days, cousin. I can be quiet when it is needed,' Bilal replied, in heavily accented English. He was short and thin, with catlike cheekbones and a sharply pointed chin.

'When Maude taught me to speak English as a boy, this one lingered outside the door, and listened,' Salim explained. 'You can take off the mask, if you wish. I will have no secrets from these men. They are my brothers.' Joan did as she was told, and the men stared at her. Salim grinned, and she guessed he'd aimed to shock them.

'It's a pleasure to meet you, Bilal,' she said, as calmly as she could. 'And all of you, of course.'

Their rapid exchanges in Arabic did not abate for some time. They moved back into the house with the partial roof and strung a sheet of canvas across the open part. A fire was lit, coffee brewed, dates handed round.

'I have told them how you helped me escape, and how I have rescued you from a marriage you did not want, to repay the debt,' Salim explained to Joan. 'Now they want to know if I will take you as my bride, or if you are already my concubine.'

'And what have you told them?' she asked. Salim looked across the fire at her, with its yellow light in his eyes.

'I have told them your will is your own,' he said. 'They haven't quite grasped it yet. They do not know how things are where you come from. Hassan bin Altaf there says that there is no accounting for the infidel.' He smiled. 'But don't worry;

I have vouched for you, and they will protect you as part of my family now – I am known for my unusual connections.'

'He is known for being unusual,' Bilal corrected him, with a laugh.

The talk reverted to Arabic and Joan sat quietly with her coffee, watching their faces, lively with delight at having Salim back with them. She supposed Salim hadn't mentioned Daniel, and didn't know about Charlie – a friend and a brother in the enemy camp, the enemy that had destroyed the very village in which they sat, and would subjugate these men if they were able. She tried to imagine these jovial, skinny men trying to kill her brother; she tried to imagine Daniel trying to kill them. It made no sense to her. One of the imam's soldiers had the white whiskers and sunken cheeks of a grandfather. His eyes returned to her, over and again. There was no malice in them, only a kind of appraisal, as though he was trying to decide what type of creature she was, with her hair cut like a boy's and her pale face on show. Later, as the fire died and the moon rose, the men slipped away.

'Why don't they stay and sleep here?' said Joan.

'Because you are,' Salim said simply. 'It is not decent.'

'Oh.'

'Rest, if you can. Before dawn we will set off for Misfat.'

'Your friend – Hassan bin Altaf. "Bin" means "son of", doesn't it? But I thought Altaf was a woman's name? One of the servants at the Residency is called Altaf, I'm sure of it.'

'Yes. In some tribes a man takes his mother's name as his family name, rather than his father's. It was the custom of this village, and others in this region.'

'If Bilal is your cousin ... does that mean you have other family here? Aunts? Uncles?'

'He is my cousin because we grew up shoulder to shoulder;

there is no shared blood between us. You ask a good many questions, Joan. Rest instead. It is safe – the men are watching the approach to the village.' Beneath the canvas, beside the glowing embers of the fire, Joan curled up inside her robe with the smoke and water scent of her hair, and slept.

Misfat al Abreen was built into the side of the mountain, and its terraces were lush with plants. Narrow streets and stone steps ran between the houses, and the falaj charted a compli-cated path through it all – a stone gutter furred with green inside, with different branches and sluices, dropping through the village. Glistening frogs jumped away from their feet as they walked, and the warm winter sun turned green as it shone through the leaves of palm trees, fig trees, pomegranates, lemons. There were yellow and white frangipani flowers, and pink bougainvillea flowers, the brightest things Joan had seen since the Indian wives of Muscat. She heard a child laugh, close by but out of sight. Salim turned to see her expression, and smiled.

'See? Is it not paradise?' he said. And it was, though the women were still veiled, and the men she saw were either lame or ancient – the fit and the young were all higher up the mountain, living in caves, fighting for the imam. 'We will go to the house of Bilal's mother. There you can remain, if you wish to.'

'For how long?'

'I have no answers for you, Joan, no more directions. From here I must go on, and fight with my brothers.'

'But ... you'll be back, won't you? You'll come back and take me up to the plateau?'

'I will try. When the war is over, I will come to live here. If the mountain is lost, I pray I fall with it. I cannot go back to Jalali.'

'No,' said Joan. 'I understand.'

'You regret your choice? You wish to return to Muscat?'

'No, it's not that. It's just . . . what if . . . I don't know what to do here, you see. I don't know what I should do.'

'Joan,' he said, watching her with a shake of his head. 'I cannot advise you. I am not your father, nor your brother. That is how you see me, is it not?' He paused, and Joan made no reply. 'I wonder,' he continued softly, 'if you could ever come to see me in a different way?'

His question took her by surprise and she stayed silent, uncertain what to say. Salim looked deep into her eyes for a moment, as if seeking something there. Then he abandoned his search, frowning and looking away. 'You helped me to freedom, and I have done the same for you. I can do no more just now,' he said. Joan nodded. The feeling she had then, of him washing his hands of her, was familiar; Daniel had made her feel it before.

'What if the SAF come here?' she said.

'Put on the mask and veil, if that happens. You will be allowed to leave with the other women.'

'I should . . . I should very much like to see you again, Salim bin Shahin.' She was suddenly fearful, suddenly sensed him gone, and for ever. Salim stopped beside a gnarled wooden door, and smiled as he thumped on it with his fist.

'And I you, Joan Seabrook. We will, if God wills it,' he said.

'Is it not enough that we will it?' she said, but he didn't answer her.

And there it was again, that nagging feeling that she had noticed something about him but yet not defined it. There'd been something when she'd seen him wash at Tanuf, and there was something now in what had just been said. 'But the summit, Salim?' she said. 'You said you would take me up with you.'

'I said I would try. I must go alone first. I must speak to our leaders, and learn all that has happened in my absence. If it is possible for you to see it, I will come back for you.'

Salim delivered her into the hands of her hostess, who did not seem surprised to see them. The mountain, Joan was learning, was a closely woven grapevine – a highly efficient system for the transmission of news. Soon afterwards, Salim took his leave and was gone; without him Joan felt the last thing anchoring her cast off, and knew she was entirely adrift in the world.

Bilal's mother was pot-bellied and wistful, taciturn without being sullen, blind in one eye with trachoma. Her name was Farizah, and her days were shaped by prayers in a cramped, unadorned side room of the tiny mosque, which Joan was not permitted to enter; by preparing food and cooking; by mending, cleaning and tending the fire; by washing clothes and linens at a deep stone pool, around which all the women met to sing and talk and scold each other. More than ever before, Joan realised just how out of time Oman truly was. After dark life was lived by candlelight, and meals were cooked over open coals. Outside the house the women all wore their masks and veils, and yet they seemed to recognise each other at once, before a word was spoken. At first Joan had no idea how they did it, but within a few days she began to spot familiar things about Farizah and her array of daughters, cousins and neighbours – the certain stoop of a shoulder, the size or shade of an iris, the grace or lack of it in a walk. She knew from the way she was watched that her own mask and veil gave her no anonymity there.

The days had a specific, irresistible rhythm to them, and were marked for Joan by silence – her own. Farizah and the other women had no English; beyond a greeting and *thank you*, Joan couldn't seem to pick up any Arabic. Farizah gave her instructions she could not understand, accompanied with gestures she could; Joan watched, and helped however she was able. This was how Maude had lived for decades, contentedly, and Joan tried to be content as well; in a very real way, she was following in her idol's footsteps. But Maude had spoken fluent Arabic, and without the language, without her voice, Joan felt cut off, even from herself. It was lonely. She sat out every night, staring up at the endless expanse of sky; at the fat moon that rose red over the desert and turned silvery pale as it sailed over the mountain. That these were the same heavens that she had looked up at from England seemed a laughable idea. It was so beautiful that some of the wonder she had felt as a child, dreaming of Arabia, returned to her at those times; but she had already accepted that such wonder belonged in childhood, and couldn't be kept. It belonged in the hearts of those who still believed in magic.

Joan learned where the steep steps led, between the terraces; she learned who tended the long-haired brown goats that grazed the shrubs between the rocks. She watched ravens patrolling the broken ramparts of the ancient round tower, and turtle doves courting along the rooftops. She thought all the time – as she fanned the flies away from the meat Farizah was preparing; as she stood at one end of a sodden sheet to wring the water from it. She thought about her mother, and about Daniel, letting her love for them swell and wrap iron bands around her ribs. She thought about Charlie Elliot and the way his reckless attitude masked something deeper, something better. She was sure of it, whatever Maude said. Then she thought about Rory.

It took longer; it was more complicated. She opened herself to every memory of him she possessed, every action and feeling; every irritation; every time he had made her laugh. She thought and thought until his betrayal had a specific shape and size, until she could see it clearly, and had the measure of it. And then she focused on that, and tried to pinpoint her feelings. She thought of how comfortable he had always been to be naked in front of her, more like a brother, and wondered again if she had been willingly blind to where he really loved, and how. She spent an entire day trying to picture life at home without him, but she couldn't. The dreariness of going to work each day, along familiar streets, and coming home either to her mother or to a flat shared with some other girl, was oppressive. Without him to cheer her up, without the wedding and their future to work towards, without their children to distract her, her life would be aimless.

Her thoughts got clearer after her first week in Misfat, sleeping through the nights, working through the days; the pace of it, and the honesty of the labour, was restorative. She couldn't remember ever being so calm, awake, or clear-thinking. And what she realised was that she was waiting. She was still waiting for something or someone to come along and make a decision for her, or tell her what to do; and the forbidden plateau of Jebel Akhdar was still waiting, like an unfinished story. She needed to complete the journey she'd set out on; that was the one thing she knew without doubt. She tried to ask some of the women the way up, but they couldn't understand her questions, and she couldn't understand their answers. Setting off without a route or a guide would be folly.

Life in the village was simple, even if it wasn't easy. Joan got used to the lack of creature comforts, the lack of communication; to knowing nothing about the outside world. She tried to imagine staying for ever, choosing that life as Maude had. She tried to imagine marrying an Omani, and converting to Islam, and spending her days behind her mask with nobody any the wiser that she was British. She tried to imagine marrying

Salim, if he would have her. The idea was an uneasy one, but flattering. He was so much older and wiser than her; so much a complete person. She pictured a scatter of coffee-coloured children at her heels; waking to the sunrise; drinking from the mountain's clear bloodstream. Nobody need hear from Joan Seabrook ever again, if she chose.

It would be straightforward, but she didn't think she could do it. She didn't think it would be right. Now and then the distant thunder of artillery echoed through the village; the rattle of automatic rifles, or the scream of an RAF Venom's engines; and for a few seconds afterwards even the leaves on the trees seemed to still. There was a silence like a massive, communal held breath; a pause before the world began to turn again. The war was near, and to Joan it was a constant reminder of time passing, and that the world she'd stepped out of was hard on her heels. It was a constant reminder of Daniel. She longed to see him, and talk to him; she thought back to the last time she'd visited him and cursed herself for not saying more.

She wasn't counting days or keeping track of time, but she guessed she'd been at the village at least ten days when she decided she had to leave. By that time Olive Seabrook would have been informed of her daughter's disappearance; Daniel too. Robert Gibson was probably blaming himself and wasting time and resources looking for her; Rory had to be desperate. She had finally framed a question for him: she wanted to ask him how he felt about her, and if he had only ever courted her to stay close to Daniel. She felt ready to ask those things. Her life was her own, and it was her right to do as she chose, but the people who cared about her also had rights that she couldn't ignore. Slowly, inexorably, she realised that she was not Maude Vickery, and that this was not the life she wanted. Every day, she watched for Salim's lean, assured figure, striding back into the village, back into her life. He *had* to take her up to the plateau with him — she could not turn back without reaching her goal, or without seeing him again. He had been the means by which she had made her escape; he had given her the route, and fortified her, and she needed him again before she made the return journey for the same reasons. She needed to hear him say that she had the courage to go back and face the people she'd deserted — and, by saying it, make it true.

Soon afterwards, on a cold day with a restless wind that smelled of rain, Salim came back. Joan was helping a tiny, silent girl called Salwa fill water jars when she saw him coming around a higher terrace, close to the foot of the wall, and wondered if her decision had summoned him somehow. She stood suddenly, with a shout, letting the jar splash into the water. Salim turned towards her, searching, and smiled as he waved. He was covered in weaponry, weary in his face but not in his body. With a chuckle, Salwa said something in a know-ing tone that Joan didn't need to speak Arabic to understand. She heaved the full jar up from the bottom of the trough, set it down sloshing, and went to meet him.

'You have not learned to be quite modest enough yet, Joan,' he said. 'An Omani girl would never shout like that.'

'I couldn't help it,' Joan told him breathlessly. 'I haven't spoken since you left.'

'You have been lonely?' He stopped her as she began to lift off the mask. 'You must not, out here in public.'

'No. Yes, a bit,' she said. 'But I've been . . . thinking a great deal.'

'Come to the house, come back and tell me.'

'All right — just let me fetch the water I was meant to be bringing.' They walked back to the trough together. 'Tell me how you are, Salim? What's been happening? We've heard lots of bombing, lots of . . . explosions.'

'I am well. The planes bomb our caves and our sentry posts
– or they try to. The rock shrugs them off; so do we.'

'Why have you come back?' She was impatient to know,
couldn't wait to be told.

'I came to fetch you. And to warn you of the dangers of—'

'You'll take me up?' she interrupted him, and he frowned.

'Yes. But I must tell you things first.' Joan shut her eyes
for a moment, pausing as they walked, because his *yes* was
electrifying.

In the deep shadows of the house, they sat down on the dusty
mat to talk. Salim smelled of smoke and stale sweat; his fingernails were black crescents, and when Farizah gave him food he
ate it with a steady urgency that spoke of deprivation. 'They
are trying to block every route to the plateau; they are trying
to starve us, or drive us into recklessly exposing our positions.
They strive all the time – *all* the time – to beat a clear path to
the plateau. They will never manage it. They seek a way to
reach the summit without us knowing; they do not know that
as soon they make a plan, word comes straight to us from their
guides and muleteers. We know what they will do long before
they do it; we cut off each patrol, we block each advance. They
will *never* gain the summit. Sultan Said will never rule the
mountain.' He spoke with an intensity, a kind of grim certainty
that somehow wasn't wholly convincing. It sounded to Joan as
though, on some level, he needed to convince himself. But the
thought of the treacherous Omani guides betraying Daniel –
the thought of him running into an ambush when he thought
his movements were secret, gave her a chill. As if sensing this,
Salim glanced up at her, and fell silent.

He ate quietly for a while, exchanging a few comments with
Farizah in Arabic. 'She says you are no bother, for a godless

heathen,' he told Joan with a smile. 'She says you are a help to her.'

'Please tell her that these days I have spent with her have been some of the best of my life,' said Joan, meaning it completely. Salim gave her a long, steady look before relaying the remark. Farizah nodded with a shrug, as though she'd guessed as much.

'So you will not stay here then?' he said to her at length, and Joan shook her head.

'I don't know what my life will be, but it can't be this. Not for ever.'

'You do not think it can be with me, in the fighting? You know it cannot be.'

'I know. I don't have a plan. It's frightening, but . . . at the same time, not at all.' The truth of this surprised her. Somehow, being immersed in the foreignness, the complete *otherness*, of life in Misfat al Abreen had shown her that her fear of change was only a habit — and one that could be broken. 'Once I've seen the summit, I can go back. I said I would be the first, and I will. For the first time in my life, I'll . . . lead. I have to do it, before I can do whatever comes next.'

'I will take you. At first light. For one day only. Yesterday we sent the SAF back down the mountain to Nizwa; it will be some days, perhaps weeks before they will try again. This is the way of it. But the planes pass when they pass, and bomb where they bomb. The danger is real, and I cannot protect you from it. And we must keep hidden — from my people as well as yours. Those men you met, who are loyal to me, know of this plan, but nobody else would countenance it. Do you understand? This is the last thing I can do for you, debt or no debt.'

'Any debt between us will be more than paid, Salim. It already is,' she said. Salim nodded seriously.

'We are agreed. I will take you up, and bring you down again, within a day. I will set you on the path down from here, back to your people. After that, all my efforts must be for the imam.'

'And perhaps we will never see each other again, Salim.'

'We will, if—'

'God wills it,' Joan provided, and Salim smiled.

'You're learning,' he said.

Knowing how early they would have to wake, Joan barely slept. Not even the cockerels were stirring as they left the village by the light of a single smuggler's lamp that Salim carried, constructed so that its light shone down at the ground and not ahead. As the sky began to pale, he shut it off completely. He moved in silence; Joan tried her best to do the same but the route was steep, and soon her breathing was the loudest thing around. The muscles in her legs burned and her heart raced, but she kept up, refusing to slow him down. The rocks were sharp through the soles of her shoes; sometimes she was forced to scramble, using her hands as well. If they were following a path Joan could not discern it, but Salim never hesitated. After a while she forgot about the sweat trickling down her face and back; she found a rhythm to her breathing and her steps, and let it distract her. She counted to a hundred and then started again, and again, and thought of nothing but carrying on. Ahead of her, Salim's shoulders were set straight; he didn't look back or check on her. It rained fitfully for a while but, as the sun rose, the sky dried and turned milk-white, too bright to look at. Hours passed and Joan saw nothing but her own stumbling feet, set down between the rocks, over and over.

At first, she didn't recognise the dead soldier for what he was. The whiteness of his bones, glimpsed through shreds of weathered skin, made puzzling, abstract shapes. She stopped because Salim had, and stared down at the depleted corpse until she saw a face, teeth, toes, a withered ribcage, a ragged patch where his genitals had been. She clamped one hand across her mouth, and Salim looked back at her, his face expressionless.

'One of the Muscat and Oman Field Force, most likely. They almost reached the plateau last year but they over-reached, and were cut off. They were all but wiped out. Some escaped into the rocks to die of thirst.' Joan couldn't speak; Salim's dispassion was as shocking as the desiccated corpse. 'If he'd belonged to the mountain, his people would have come for him.' The dead man had been stripped bare, his boots and weapons were gone. Any soft flesh had been picked off by scavengers and the mountain had blanched the rest; on his scalp were the remains of soft black curls, tugged at by the breeze. 'Come, we mustn't waste time,' said Salim, walking on without a backwards glance. The skin across Joan's shoulders tightened; she felt an echo of the uncontrollable jitter she'd felt inside as a child, during the war; a thinning of the air in her lungs. She stumbled after Salim, reminded, powerfully, that she was walking into danger.

They reached the plateau without her even realising. She'd been waiting for the cliff face, waiting to toil up near-vertical steps; but from the south there was no such obstacle. The approach was heavily guarded as a result, and Salim took out the white flag of the imam and tied it to his rifle, holding it aloft as they went. Daniel had told her of the confusion, early on in the conflict – when the imam's white flag had been mistaken for surrender, and the red flag of those loyal to the sultan as defiance. The ground levelled out; the peaks, some of them ten thousand feet high, stood around like monumental sentries. Barely seeming to have noticed the climb himself, Salim offered Joan water.

'You have arrived, Joan,' he said, smiling guardedly. 'You

have reached a place all of the sultan's military strength could not reach. Not even Maude has been here. Come, this way.' He led her on until they reached a spot on the plateau's edge, above a vertiginous drop, from which it was possible to see the sharp outer ridges marching into the distance, towards the coast. They looked endless, like the waves of some hostile, petrified sea. Joan understood completely why no army had ever managed to storm such a stronghold.

'Are we opposite Muttrah?' she asked.

'More or less, yes.' Salim shrugged. 'You cannot see it from here, though.'

'That doesn't matter,' said Joan. She was at the place she had often gazed up at – against all probability, she was standing looking down at Muttrah, rather than standing at Muttrah, looking up and wishing. She raised both arms and waved, breathless with a kind of mad elation. Daniel was behind her, in Nizwa; she had no idea if Rory would be looking up, looking for her; it didn't matter. They were level with the clouds, and the sun cast a patchwork of light and shadow on the ground far below them. The wind changed the pattern constantly; it dried Joan's skin, and cooled her. There was no sound other than the wind, and Salim stood at her side, looking out. Joan wondered how it felt to belong there in that wild, hard, beautiful place.

'What do you see?' asked Salim.

'Everything and nothing,' she said, with a slight smile. 'I see that . . . very few things are impossible.'

The normal size and shape of time abandoned Joan there; she had no idea how long she stood, looking down at her past self from that far distant place. By the time Salim took her elbow to rouse her, she was cold, but resolute.

'Come, Joan. We must move,' he said.

'So soon? Must we?'

'Yes. Listen.' Joan frowned. At first she heard nothing but the hum of the wind, but then she noticed it – the low, persistent wail of a Venom in flight. She took a sharp breath and searched the sky, squinting, seeing nothing but the clouds.

'Never mind looking for it, just move, and quickly!' said Salim. Startled, Joan followed him. He ran lightly across the uneven ground towards a bulging outcrop of rock, and Joan stumbled to keep up. She didn't understand his plan until he stepped behind one enormous boulder, near the base of the outcrop, and disappeared. She followed him, into the mouth of a cave that burrowed away into the mountainside like a worm hole into an apple. It was cool and black inside; Salim pushed Joan further in, behind him, then crouched by the entrance with his eyes on the sky. Joan felt fear stealing up on her in quick, panicked waves. The noise grew louder as the plane got nearer; she shut her eyes and waited for the moment that the sound would start to fade again – that tipping point when the plane had gone over, and was moving away, and they would be safe. She waited, and longed to hear it. The explosion took her completely by surprise.

It seemed to come up through the ground and straight into her bones rather than into her head through her ears. It cracked through her skull like a physical blow and she shrieked, instinctively putting her arms over her head. She felt Salim's hand grasp her wrist, and the earth shook beneath them. For a second everything went dark and there was a moment of complete, perfect terror: she was back in Bedford, under the kitchen table with her mother, waiting for a German bomb to fall on their house, waiting to die. For a moment the fear had complete control of her, and she was certain she'd be trapped beneath the rocks in darkness for ever. A shower of loose scree hit her head and the air filled with dust, but then the light and stillness returned and the sound of the plane receded, and some of the sickening rush of fear went with it. For a while Joan listened to the ringing in her ears and her own breath soughing in and out, then she opened her eyes. Salim was watching the sky again; after a while he looked back at her and grinned.

'Don't be afraid, the mountain has a thick skin. Now you are truly one of us, Joan – one of the imam's soldiers, dodging the British bombs,' he said cheerfully. Joan thought of Charlie Elliot's blasé, almost joyous attitude to danger, and realised it could be a good way to weather it. She tried to smile, and even the attempt steadied her a little. Her hands were shaking uncontrollably.

'That was ... so close!' she managed to say, between short breaths. Salim tipped his head to one side.

'Not so very close. The shockwave travels fast and hard through the rock.'

'That *wasn't* very close?' Joan was incredulous, but then she gasped. There was the unmistakable sound of movement from behind her, deeper inside the cave. 'Salim!' she said, loud with alarm.

She scrambled back towards the entrance as a match was struck, and a lamp lit, and a figure emerged from the pitch black of the tunnel. Joan's heart gave a strained lurch, but in the next moment she recognised Bilal, the man Salim called cousin. He gave her a crooked smile that didn't quite reach his eyes.

'Welcome to Jebel Akhdar,' he said to her, and after that spoke only to Salim, in Arabic. They followed him deeper into the cave, crouching low until it opened out into a broad chamber about thirty feet across. The lamplight capered up the rippling walls, one of which was slick with water. The other men of Salim's group were crouching or sitting in a loose circle; a coffee pot was keeping warm on the dying embers of a fire that hardly smoked, and the remains of a meal was on a large pewter platter. They had a lot of weapons – two mortars and the disassembled pieces of what Joan guessed to be a pack howitzer, as well as rifles and grenades; a portable radio set, piles of maps and paper. There were rugs, blankets, cushions. Joan could have conceived of the cave being a cosy place to sleep if it hadn't been for the creeping damp chill of the air, and the startling blackness at one end where the tunnel narrowed again, and carried on. Bilal noticed her staring into that abject lack of light.

'The cave goes on for many miles,' he told her. 'Sometimes dry, sometimes wet. Sometimes a man walks, sometimes he crawls like a worm. In a hundred years, a hundred men could not map all the caves of this mountain.' Joan listened, and shivered. Beneath their voices was the soft music of water, chiming invisibly, constantly, somewhere deep in the earth.

Joan accepted a cup of strong, bitter coffee and waited as the men spoke at great length. One of them took the radio outside, and returned a while later with more news. Then, when a decision was reached, the men all stood and shouldered their rifles, and bent over to make their way out. Salim was the last to rise; his expression was troubled.

'What's happening?' Joan asked him.

'We must go. There has been movement of the SAF, which we did not expect. And of the new squadron that has arrived. The specialists.'

'The SAS?'

'They are not far away – not far enough. We cannot go back the way we climbed up. We must go another way. The others will walk with us until it is safe.' He gave her a hard look but it soon softened. 'They are angry with me. I should not have agreed to bring you up here. It was foolish of me.' Joan began to feel afraid.

'I'm glad you did. But . . . we will get down again, won't we?'

'You will. Perhaps you will have to go alone . . . perhaps you will be safer that way. But let us try this way first. Put on your veil.' Joan did as she was told, and followed Salim out of the cave into a steady downpour of rain. It soaked through her robes and the clothes underneath in moments. She felt the first cold touch of it as it found her skin; the slipperiness as it got into her shoes. Her toes began to go numb, but the men walked fast, and she was soon warm again. She wanted to pause; she wanted to look back at the plateau, and fix it for ever in her memory, but there was no time.

The rain hid the distant views they'd had before; it blurred the air, turning it grey, but Salim said it was a blessing because the pilots would see nothing on the mountain, and would return to Nizwa. The rocks grew slippery and Joan turned her ankle more than once, trying to keep up. In the full light of day, and going down rather than up, Joan felt more exposed, and also that her last reason to delay, her last excuse not to return to Muscat, was now behind her.

A kind of steady, grim sadness settled over her, as grey and relentless as the rain. They walked on in silence, veiled in cloud, always downhill, and Joan could no more guess the thoughts of the men she was with than she supposed they could guess hers. They came to a narrow ravine not even an arm span across, zigzagging down, as steep as a ladder, to join a wadi which then ran away down the mountain. A shallow stream of water poured down the ravine. The men halted, and talked in low voices; Joan sat down to rest her tired legs. She was hungry, though the strong coffee had made her empty stomach ache; she was wet through, weighted down with loneliness and a persistent sense of danger.

Salim's face was drawn, guarded. The man who'd used the

radio before did so again; there was a rapid burst of Arabic, distorted with static. Salim listened, and his face grew grimmer still.

'What is it?' Joan asked. Her throat felt tight, as though tears were coming. Any feeling of unreality had gone; everything seemed very, very real.

'There are soldiers in the wadi. A section of the sultan's men. They are trapped a long way down, in good cover – our men have them in range, so they dare not move. And when they break cover we must remain here to stop any survivors climbing higher.' Joan listened with rising unease. Salim gave her a hard look. 'You are not a part of this, Joan. Remember?'

'I know. I know I'm not,' she said, but she no longer sounded sure, even to her own ears. 'Will we have to go down another way?'

'No.' Salim shook his head and looked away. 'You will go this way. Keep your veil on, and follow this ravine down about seven hundred feet. There is a path that runs away to the south – it will be on your right-hand side. Look closely for it. Do not miss it, and do *not* go all the way down into the wadi. Do you understand? This is the best way for you. This way will be safe for you, but not for me. Wear your veil so they know at once you are a woman. You will not be stopped, or shot at. But do not go all the way down to the wadi where the soldiers are.'

'But . . . why would they break cover to come any higher? Won't they just wait for darkness, and go back down?'

'Soon they will have no choice but to move,' said Salim grimly. Joan stared at him uncomprehendingly, and was aware of Bilal watching her closely in turn. 'Soon, the wadi will flood.'

Nervously, Joan licked rainwater from her lips. She stood and took an involuntary step towards the head of the ravine, and then froze. Bilal's eyes followed her; he was no longer smiling. Joan began to understand better than ever the danger she was in, and where it lay. She began to understand that she might not ever be allowed to leave the mountain. She wished Salim's cousin did not speak English.

'Where will the path from the ravine lead me?' she asked, in a voice that shook.

'It goes along the side of the mountain for several miles,' said Salim.

'I think she must remain with us,' said Bilal. 'It is not safe. The men are near.' He was talking to Salim, not to Joan; his tone was chilly, suspicious. There were knots working in the corners of Salim's jaw.

'Joan is not a part of this,' he said stonily. 'She is not safe here – she's no soldier, and fighting is coming. This is the best way. She will not betray us.' As he spoke, Salim looked at Joan with his dark eyes searching, and Joan shook her head anxiously. She was ready then – ready to go on alone. Ready to be free of them.

'I will not betray you,' she said. 'I swear it.'

'You will come to a village called Al Farra'ah,' said Salim. 'I will send word ahead; they will take you in, but you must keep a good pace to reach there before nightfall. From there you can go down, out of the mountains towards Nizwa – they will show you the way.'

Joan nodded, but she hardly heard him. She was thinking of the men trapped in the wadi, caught between the sniper fire of their besiegers and the rising floodwater. She felt mounting panic on their behalf; the sudden, suffocating dread that Daniel could be with them. She stared down the ravine, through the incessant rain, and then walked to the edge of it, a little way away from the others. She hoped Salim would follow her and was relieved when he did. 'I must stay and fight,' he said. 'If these soldiers begin to climb the ravine, we must stop them. And there are more men, more soldiers. Further down the wadi, out of danger. They do not know that the others are trapped – or if they know, they do not seem to wish to help them.'

'Bilal thinks I will go to them and tell them?' Joan asked, and in the pause before Salim nodded, she understood that he thought so too. They looked at one another, and for a long time neither one spoke. There was another burst of static from the radio behind them, and some muttered words. 'Will he let me go at all?'

'If you do not go now, I do not know. The more you see, the more you could reveal. I have told them I trust you; I am not sure it is enough. It's better that you go now. Do you understand?'

'Yes,' she said. A raindrop landed on her eyelid and she blinked it away, letting it run down to her chin.

'I would not have chosen to part this way,' he said.

'No. This is my fault. I made you bring me up here.' She tried to sound resolute, and calm, but the thought of walking alone on the mountain, trying to find a strange village with night coming, filled her with fear.

'You must follow you own path now, Joan. You do not need me as your master. Go, quickly, and be safe. Do not look back. God go with you.'

Feeling the hostile eyes of Bilal and the other men behind her, Joan did as he said. Her legs were shaky; she knew, deep in her gut, that she wouldn't see Salim again. She also knew she had to help the soldiers in the wadi. The fact that Daniel could be one of them was enough – even if she discovered he was not, the possibility would have been enough. She slipped and stumbled down the steep ravine, sitting down and edging herself with her hands in some places, where the drop below

froze her blood and turned her muscles liquid. Water was flow-
ing freely over the rocks; it crested the heels of her shoes, and
filled them. The leather swelled and rubbed; within a few paces
she felt the sting and pain of blisters bursting on her feet. Her
legs slid out from under her at one point; she landed bruisingly
hard, and the nearness of the fall made her queasy.

The veil and robes were a cumbersome weight of sodden
fabric, swinging around her, hampering vision and movement.
After a while she risked a glance behind her, but Salim and his
men were nowhere in sight. The twisting path of the ravine
was difficult to see, and the rain fell into her eyes. She turned
away and carried on down, keeping an eye to her right, and
soon spotted the track Salim had told her to follow. It was
well defined, and climbed gently again, keeping high above
the course of the wadi. From where she was then, Joan could
see a rush of brown and white water already running along
the riverbed below. The rain from the ravine and the cliffs
all around poured down into it, feeding it all the time. The
soldiers must have been aware of the danger they were in; they
must have known that soon they would have to risk being shot,
or else stay and be drowned. Imagining their fear gave Joan a
jittery echo of it, building all the time.

She turned around. Directly opposite the path Salim had
told her to take was another – or rather, the same one – leading
in the other direction, down the wadi, where Salim had told
her there were more soldiers. Soldiers unaware of the danger
their comrades were in. Again, Joan glanced back the way
she had come: grey and brown rocks, running with water;
an endless array of sharp cracks and outcrops, as steep as a
staircase. Could Salim and the others possibly still see her?
Could Bilal possibly have her in his binoculars; could any of
them have her in their rifle sights? She stood there, frozen in
indecision. She had sworn to Salim that she wouldn't betray

them, but was it really a betrayal if she tried to help those soldiers? She need not give away Salim's position at the top of the ravine. She need say nothing about them – their numbers, their equipment, their cave.

She thought and thought, as the rain ran down her back and her legs, and dripped from her fingertips. Its cold touch was steadily chilling her, but she couldn't move. Why had Salim told her about the other soldiers further down? Why had he told her the precise way in which Bilal feared she would help the trapped men, if he had not meant for her to do exactly that? The rain hammered; she thought she heard the crack of a rifle shot somewhere, but couldn't tell. The torrent of water in the wadi had grown visibly in the few minutes she had lingered, wider, deeper, faster. But she thought of Daniel, and in a heartbeat found she was more frightened for the men in the wadi than she was for herself. She took a deep breath and held it. Then, still half expecting to hear a shout or a rifle fire, or even to feel a bullet hitting her, she set off down the track to the left.

She tried to run but her legs were clumsy with fatigue and she could only manage a cautious kind of jog. Going downhill helped, though she slipped and stumbled often. She felt naked, visible, wide open to attack. Her eyes raked the opposite wall of the wadi, trying to find the fighters who had the SAF men trapped; she tried to spot the trapped men themselves but she didn't dare to stop to look properly. Once she thought she saw movement – a dark, darting shape that could have been a booted foot or a rifle butt, pulled quickly out of sight. She searched all around for some landmark, some way to fix the place in her mind and be able to describe it later, noting a massive triangular rock above the spot, jutting out like a nose. She checked the water level every few strides, alarmed by how quickly it was rising; she could hear the roar of it above the rain now – the steady, churning din of white water. It was the colour of milky tea; it twisted like an angry snake. It was growing so quickly that Joan began to think she would be too late anyway – she had no idea how far away the other soldiers were, whether she would reach them in time, or at all; whether they would have time to help the trapped men. Winded, she was forced to stop running; she dug the heel of her hand into the stitch in her side, and sobbed with frustration. She might hear, she realised. She might hear the exact moment the men were forced to break cover, and were shot. The idea made her feel sick.

She was a part of it, now; whatever she had said to Salim. She felt the terror and anguish of having lives in her hands, and a wild disbelief that it should be so. Her eyes searched the hillsides ahead for men from either side of the war until she started to see shapes that weren't there, that vanished when she blinked; she tried running again, lungs aching, the blood thumping in her face. She wondered if she was visible – a moving black mote – or if she was wholly lost in the chaos and jumble of it all. One more shape that would vanish if you blinked. Then a man rose up in front of her, out of nowhere, and with a shriek she ran straight into him. Joan felt his hands close on her arms and struggled wildly; the mask was knocked crooked and she couldn't see.

'Don't touch her, you prat – it's not allowed,' she heard a voice say, in clear English; she stopped struggling and almost sat down in relief. Still gasping for air, she reached up and adjusted the mask over her eyes until she saw the pale, mournful face of the man she'd sat next to at dinner once, at the Residency, a hundred years before. She couldn't remember his real name; only the nickname Charlie had given him.

'Smiler?' she gasped, between breaths. The pale man hesitated, and frowned into her eyes.

'What did you say?' he said.

'It's ... it's ...' She couldn't get enough air into her lungs to speak. She grasped at the man instead, desperate to be heard.

'Is she carrying a message?' said another voice, instantly familiar, and Joan didn't know whether to laugh or cry. Charlie Elliot stepped up beside Smiler, squinting into the rain. A waterproof poncho over the pack on his back gave him a weird, hunched outline; he was unshaven, soaked, had the sodden end of a cigarette tucked behind one ear. He looked entirely at his ease. 'Well?' he said, looking her up and down. 'Do you have some message for us? Where's Ridwan – Ridwan, we need a translator here!'

'Charlie,' Joan managed to say. Charlie froze. Between heaving breaths she managed to speak. 'There're men trapped further up the wadi – our men. They're pinned down by snipers. The river's coming up. They'll have to break cover soon. You ... have to ... help them,' she finished, leaning forwards. Her head spun; dark spots crowded her vision.

'Who the hell is under all that?' said Charlie, but she could tell from the pause and the incredulous tone of his voice that he already knew – he just didn't believe it.

'It's me,' she said, tugging off the mask and veil, feeling the light of day and the splatter of rain on her hot face. 'It's Joan Seabrook.'

Charlie stared. Smiler stared. Behind them, more men appeared, and they stared too. Joan tensed as though a blow was coming; she felt as though one was due. She lifted her chin, braced to feel it, and waited. Then Smiler blinked, and Charlie bent forwards and she didn't understand why until she realised he'd dissolved into laughter. He was helpless to it for a moment, and, unexpectedly, Joan felt herself smile in response. After all the fear and all the doubt and all the strangeness of the past two weeks, Charlie's laugh was the most welcome sound in the world. In that precise moment, she loved him. When he'd got hold of himself he wiped his face with one hand.

'Joan? I can't *wait* to hear how in God's name you got here! They've been looking all over for you – were you trying to find your brother? Nobody thought to look on the mountain.'

'I can explain,' she said, wondering if it was true. 'But right now—'

'Yes. These men. Tell me everything again, more slowly, and in as much detail as you can. Come over here out of the rain. We can deal with how come you know any of it later on.'

'You have to help them right away! The water's rising so quickly . . . they're in terrible danger – as soon as they're forced to move, they'll be shot!'

'All right. Tell me where – can you do that? How many snipers? Where are they?' The two men were serious again at once, and didn't waste time with pointless questions, and Joan felt relief flood through her. As best she could, she described where she thought the trapped soldiers were. Their expressions blackened, and they exchanged a look. Then Smiler nodded and went to talk to the rest of the section, and Charlie stayed with her, chewing his lip. There was something he wasn't saying, and Joan's fear came back in a shuddering rush.

'Is it . . . is it . . .' She had to swallow, and force the question out. 'It's Daniel, isn't it? It's his section that's trapped. I can tell.' She started to cry, the tears lost in the downpour. Charlie nodded, a simple gesture that seemed to crush her. Joan flung out her arm, leaning against the rock to stay on her feet.

With quiet efficiency, the rest of the group, with their local guide and an SAF translator, rose and got ready to move. Joan stared at the guide uneasily, wondering if he was playing both sides, and would send word of her actions back to Salim and Bilal. Charlie checked his weapons, adjusting his pack. He looked past Joan and nodded to Smiler.

'The rebels know we're here, you say?' he said.

'Yes. But they don't know you know about the men further up – that they're in trouble, I mean. They think you're waiting for something – I don't know what.'

'Right. Is there anything else we should know? Anything at all that might be important?' he asked. Joan stared up at him. Her tears had stopped; they'd seemed pointless. She thought of Salim, Bilal and the others at the top of the ravine. But Charlie had said nothing about carrying on up; as far as she knew, neither they nor the SAF even knew about the ravine. She was sure Salim's men weren't relevant to the rescue but still she wavered, knowing that she should disclose everything, also knowing that she'd sworn to Salim that she wouldn't. In the end she shook her head, not prepared to risk harm coming to Salim as a result of her actions.

'No,' she said, praying that the lie would have no consequences. 'No, there's nothing else.'

'Smiler's going to start down with you now.'

'What? No! I . . . I need to know Dan's safe before I go . . . I need to see him!'

'Look, Joan, this isn't a game. Things could get a bit hot here – this is no place for you. You'll be in the way. Whether your brother comes through this or otherwise, you need to get down off this mountain and to a safe place – right now.' She'd never heard Charlie sound so serious; it silenced her for a moment.

'Promise me you'll rescue him,' she said then, like a child, needing to be told kind lies. She took hold of Charlie's arm and stared hard into his face, desperate to see some reassurance there. After a moment Charlie smiled his mocking half-smile, and chucked her chin with his scuffed and dirty knuckles.

'I wouldn't worry, Joan. If he's anything like you, he's probably rescued himself already. Now, get going.' He raised one arm to signal the rest of the men, then turned and set off up the wadi.

Joan watched until he was out of sight around some rocks before she turned. She had the heavy feeling that she might not see him again, either. Smiler was waiting, his rifle in his hands.

'I can't remember your real name, Smiler,' she said brokenly.

'Corporal Walter Cox, miss,' he said. 'Let's go, shall we? Here – put this on.' He handed her a spare poncho, and she wriggled into it, all her muscles stiff with cold and fatigue. 'You look done in. Long day?' The words were laden with irony.

Joan nodded.

'Yes. I think it might turn out to be the longest ever.' The path was narrow so they had to go in single file. Walter went ahead, his eyes everywhere, his finger on the trigger.

'Well, it's not too far to go down. If I say to go for cover, don't hang about to ask why, all right?' he said, quite calmly. Joan nodded. 'With any luck, we'll sneak down without anyone the wiser.'

'Thank you, Corporal Cox,' she said.

'I imagine you must be looking forward to getting back to safety. To Muscat, and your people.' Walter glanced back over his shoulder and she felt appraised, mistrusted. She knew that her reception would be a difficult, volatile affair; now she wondered for the first time if she would actually be punished for her trespass, for her flouting of the rules and her involvement with Salim, if it was discovered. She said nothing. They walked on in silence and she decided that she didn't care as long as Daniel was safe. Daniel and Charlie Elliot too, she realised. But they'd only walked for ten minutes or so when the sudden sound of rifle fire erupted behind them. With a gasp, Joan turned back. Walter took her arm to stop her, his face set, his eyes intent. She pulled against him, gripped by the instinct to run back to her brother. Then, from the direction they had come, a wave of water like a tidal bore came crashing down the wadi, rolling boulders with a sound like thunder – an opaque torrent that no man could have stood against, doubling the width of the flood.

'*Daniel*!' Joan shouted through the rain, seeing nothing, frantic. Walter heaved on her arm, turning her again.

'Move!' he snapped. 'Right now!'

The Empty Quarter, Oman, March 1909

Maude and the Bedouin didn't talk as they waited for Sayyid to return. The impossible dunes towered over them, cowing them into silence. Sayyid had disappeared, muttering to himself, north-westwards along the foot of the massive rise, and been gone for three hours. Maude had spent the time staring up at the dune and seeing, more and more, that it was a wave – that the desert was an ocean of sand, as sculpted by the wind as any large body of water. It moved in just the same way – it rippled, it formed crests and troughs; high winds tore spindrift from its peaks, just as it did with water. Many deserts had once been seas, she knew. She'd seen the ancient cave paintings, and found fossilised shells in some of the most desiccated places on earth. She'd been wondering whether the desert had tides as well – vast, invisible, slow-moving tides – when an exasperated shout from Fatih announced Sayyid's return. The old man's sunken shoulders quashed any hope that he might have found them a route up the dune. Earlier on, Maude had tried to climb, experimentally. The sand was soft, and giving. She'd slithered back, again and again, and was soon exhausted. And she weighed a lot less than a camel. And so they decided to make camp for the night.

The sun was bloated in the western sky. In silence, they moved a short distance to a rocky outcrop, beyond which were a few small devil's thorn bushes, incongruously green. The camels snatched at them hungrily, rumbling and arguing amongst themselves. Maude and Majid pitched the smaller tent, then the boy brewed the last of the black tea and served it to her in a cup with sand crusted around its rim.

'If Haroun were here he'd clip your ear for that,' she told him sadly, but in English because she didn't have the energy to really reprimand him. The tea tasted strongly of goatskin anyway – all their water did. They had enough to delay moving until the following day, but that was all. They all knew this without anybody having to ask, without the need for discussion. It came down to a day here, two days at the outside; that was all the leeway they had left. They had to keep moving, either onwards or back, and there was some peace in that. Maude had already decided – if Sayyid didn't find a way up the dune, then she would. She knew it was mad, she knew she would likely fail, but a steely resolve had grown in her at the thought of having to turn back. *I'll be damned to hell if I'll come all this way and not at least try to get up it*, she wrote, without ink or paper, to Nathaniel. She was glad to have her invisible letter back; glad to have found the will to share her stories with him again. Without that, there had truly been nothing, and no one. She started to write her journal again too, and made sketches of the dune pitched against her. The sunset wind chased up a dust devil, and whirled it near their camp – a small tornado of sand, spinning all alone with a kind of merry anger. Sayyid's lips move in silent prayer as he watched it. Maude's dinner was dry flatbread – she'd starve to death before she'd touch dates again, and they'd run out of other supplies.

The Bedouin were quiet that night, their arguments muted. Maude fell asleep easily; her fatigue was like a strong undertow that she swam against all day long; it was a relief to surrender to it and be dragged under once night fell. She dreamed of Marsh House, and of her mother, and in the dream she had never left and would never leave, and she fought and struggled to wake and see it wasn't so. Then a shout did wake her and she sat up, confused. Her eyes strained in the smudged grey of pre-dawn light, listening, and then there was a rifle shot and a voice she didn't recognise, shouting, and she scrambled out of her blankets to stick her head out of the tent.

'Raiders! God take their eyes!' she heard Sayyid shout. The sand around the fire's embers was a maelstrom of moving figures, kicking up dust. There were shouts, curses, the rumbled complaints of camels, the flash of pale clothing in the near dark; everywhere the blurred flurry of movement, angry and fearful and purposeful, and Maude glanced here and there, her heart lurching.

'Khalid!' she shouted, but couldn't pick him out of the melee. There was another rifle shot, deafeningly close, and the sand by the entrance to Maude's tent exploded into the air.

She fell backwards, blinking, coughing, then the terror of being trapped inside took hold and she scrambled out on her hands and knees, got up and ran for the cover of the rocks. She climbed, bruising her bare feet and shins, panic hauling the air from her lungs. There wasn't enough light; she stared down at the darting figures and at first couldn't tell friend from foe – but gradually she saw. There were four men attempting to steal their camels and supplies, and her men were fighting them, with hands and knives and rifles. One mounted man was already trotting away on his own camel, leading two of theirs, including Midget. 'Oh, *no!*' Maude shouted furiously. If the raiders succeeded, and if they left them alive, then those lives would be short indeed. Her outrage at the thieves was all-consuming.

She thought desperately for some way to help. She saw Fatih running after the mounted man with his rifle in his hands; saw him kneel down and take a shot that missed, and then run on again, not letting the thief get too far ahead. Then there was a gunshot just below her, and she looked down to see one of the raiders in the rocks lower down, taking aim at Fatih again. His first shot had missed, but his second might not. Down below Maude saw Khalid's face looking up as he raced towards the rocks; she saw him see the sniper, and the danger his son was in; his eyes locked with hers for a second and in the next instant Maude jumped. With her hands outstretched, she plummeted the ten feet down and landed square on the man with the rifle. She locked her fingers into his clothes and hair, and struggled to keep hold as they both slammed hard to the ground. Maude had the softer landing; she heard the air whoosh out of the man's lungs with the force of the impact but he twisted at once, with the instinctive speed of a fighter, rolling them so that she was pinned down by his whole weight, and in the next instant his khanjar was at her throat. She grabbed his wrist with both hands as the tip bit into her skin; she felt the warm trickle of her blood and used the mere second she could delay his strike to shout, with all her breath and as loudly as she could, 'Get *off* me, you *bloody* Bedu!'

Whether it was the fact that she was a woman, or the strange language she spoke, Maude neither knew nor cared. The man hesitated, his eyes widening, and she brought her knee up into his groin as hard as she could. He grunted, shuddering, and then Khalid was on him, grabbing him from behind, drawing his khanjar across the man's throat and releasing an arc of blood that splattered onto Maude. The man's gaze locked on hers for a moment – full of incredulous surprise at this sudden end. She was struck by the pristine clarity of the whites of his eyes, and the start contrast of the black irises. He was young to be dying. Then his eyes rolled upwards and he slumped with a wet sigh, and Khalid shoved him off to one side before turning to look out across the sand. There was more daylight with every second that passed. Fatih was walking towards the three camels, including Midget, who were now sauntering aimlessly ahead, leaderless and riderless. The raider lay in a heap on the sand, unmoving.

'Thanks be to God,' said Khalid. He turned to Maude, and defied all convention by offering her his hand to rise. She wiped at her face with her filthy sleeve; the man's blood was in her teeth, in her eyes, sticking in her hair. 'You fell on him like a falcon,' he said. 'You saved Fatih, and it was brave. Not like a woman.' He spoke with a kind of calm recognition, and approval, which gave Maude the strength not to burst into tears. She was shaking uncontrollably, and hoped Khalid wouldn't notice. The dead man's blood was salt and metal on her tongue.

Majid was dead. Two of the raiders would also stay where they lay in the sand, and the other two had given up and made their escape empty-handed. Majid's eyes were relaxed and had a faraway look, no longer afraid; Maude closed them with her filthy hand. He had a single deep stab wound in his chest, and little smear of scarlet on his lower lip. Maude wondered if he had a mother somewhere, waiting for him. She didn't know what to feel about his death; she had the sudden notion that she was becoming as hard and empty and fierce as the desert. Khalid examined the camel of the man Fatih had shot and pronounced her a useful animal, though ugly, underweight and better suited for gravel than dunes. They would bring her as far as she would go, and then butcher her. Fatih and the other young men were jubilant, full of tales of their own role in the victory, each one bragging, shouting his story louder. They kindled the fire to make coffee, and for a while the adrenalin carried them, and all thoughts of the challenge ahead and the danger they were in fell away.

'Even old Sayyid fought them off,' said Fatih. 'He cut the

harness of the long-bearded one's camel so that he had to ride slowly – that's how I could shoot him so easily!'

'Even old Sayyid, you say!' the old man grumbled. 'I'd killed twenty men like these as you still suckled your mother's teat, boy.'

'It is the lady you should thank, Fatih,' said Khalid, pointing the tip of his khanjar at Maude. He'd been using it to scrape dried blood out from under his nails. 'She fell on the man who would have shot you with no hesitation, though she had no weapon. Just empty hands and fury. She swooped down like a peregrine. He never saw it coming.' Maude saw a look of distaste cross Fatih's face as he heard this news; she saw him swallow it, and make the best of it.

'God is merciful, and I thank you, lady. From now on we should call you Shahin, I think,' he said – the Arabic word for peregrine. The others nodded, looking at Maude with more respect, and more warmth.

The camel they had captured was carrying a good water skin, half full. Fatih praised God and let off three *feu de joie* when he found it. They moved away south and east, always close to the foot of the mighty dune. There was no spare water for Maude to wash with. She'd done her best with handfuls of sand and a dry rag torn from her shirt, but the blood was tightening on her scalp as it dried. Her left ear itched and when she scratched it flecks like rusty metal came away beneath her nails. She had a memory of the raider's black and white eyes that was all too vivid; she was sure she would see them again, in dreams. But she wasn't sorry he was dead; she couldn't be. He had brought death with him to their camp; she felt no pity that it had rebounded onto him. *I watched a man die*, she wrote to Nathaniel. *He was young but he would have killed us if he could, one way or another. The Bedouin now call me Shahin.* She couldn't help but be proud of her new name, as much for its romance as because it proved she'd been properly accepted at last. It was a cold, contained kind of pride, a small satisfaction; she could feel no actual happiness that day. Then, late in the morning when the sun was hard and high, Sayyid veered off towards the dune; he peered up it and along it, and then turned to wave them over.

'God be merciful, this is where we must climb,' he said, with obvious relief.

'You are sure?' said Maude. There was a rounded crease in the face of the dune; a diagonal shelf running up it, still frighteningly steep, but not as precipitous.

'As God is my witness, this is the place,' said the old man. They stood shoulder to shoulder for a while, staring up, contemplating what was to come.

'Then we have no reason to wait. Let's begin,' she said, at last. Sayyid looked her up and down for a moment – her small, skinny form, caked in blood and sand. His face betrayed no confidence whatsoever as he nodded.

It was clear that the camels would have no chance of climbing with any excess weight. Maude's tent, cooking equipment and furniture – even her folding chair – were left behind in a sorry heap on the ground. From that moment on she would have a blanket and her small canvas bag of papers and personal items, and would sleep by the fire with the men. She felt no compunction about doing so, and wasn't sorry to see the other things go. She only regretted wasting money and effort on them in the first place, and carrying them as far as they had. Those bulky items belonged to a gentler world, and to a gentler Maude; not to Shahin, and this journey that dwarfed every other she'd ever made. Once stripped to their bare essentials, Khalid allowed each of them a single mouthful of water.

'We will need it,' he said. The mood was sombre again;

even Fatih was quiet. Then Sayyid began to sing quietly, and led his camel forwards.

The pale, finer sand was harder, more densely packed and easier to walk on. The darker, coarser and more yellow sand shifted and gave way, dragging at their feet or pouring into an avalanche that might easily carry a person or a camel back down a slope. Maude learned these things quickly. She hadn't known her heart could beat so fast, or feel so laboured; she hadn't known it was possible to breathe so hard and not faint. Bright spots swirled in front of her eyes, and she couldn't swallow. Her thirst was like claws in her throat.

Sometimes she thought she was still climbing, until shouts of *Shahin! Lady!* roused her, and she found herself sitting in the sand, holding Midget's halter rope, staring at nothing. They climbed on, sinking to their knees, cursing, praying. It was easiest going at the edge of the narrow shelf Sayyid was leading them up, but it was treacherous too. One of the camels went too close and slithered, splay-legged all the way back down to the bottom of the dune. She stood there, head down, sides heaving, defeated, and when Kamal went down to her she wouldn't take a single step back towards the dune, however much he cajoled her. With tears in his eyes the young man took off her harness, threw his blanket and the water skin she'd carried over his shoulder, and began the climb again without her.

It took three hours; the longest three hours Maude had ever known. She teetered over the edge herself at one point, and started to slide. Only Midget saved her, standing rooted with all the stubbornness a camel could muster as Maude dangled from the lead rope. She ended up wrapping her arms around the camel's scarred knees to haul herself to safety. She kissed those knees in gratitude, because if she'd slithered to the bottom she knew she would have stayed there, as beaten as Kamal's camel. Without shame, she groaned with relief when they reached the top and she was finally allowed to lie down. She shut her eyes. Khalid brought the water skin around again, and lifted her head like a father might to give her another mouthful. The sun was pitiless; her lips felt hard and deadened, and they cracked when she moved them. They rested for over an hour. A pair of ravens mocked them, flying with ultimate ease to the crest of the dune that had almost finished them. They picked a few stray hairs from the camels, and strutted insolently along their backs. When Maude was able to sit up, she looked back at the way they had come – flat sands between distant rock walls – and could hardly believe how long ago it seemed, when it was still so close. Then she looked the other way, in the direction they must continue. Below them were a series of low, rolling dunes which ended in another huge dune chain. Then another beyond that, and another. She could see nothing but sand. For the first time, she despaired. It was a feeling of being hollowed out, of being a shell with nothing left inside her. She knew she would die there – probably, they all would.

Then she heard a strange sound. Khalid was singing; Ubaid and Kamal joined in, then Fatih – the tune was teasingly familiar, and the words were sounds and syllables that almost made sense, but somehow fell short. Not Arabic, not quite English either. Then she realised: they were trying to sing 'Jerusalem the Golden'. She shut her eyes for a moment because the tune, and the spirit of the gesture, pulled at something so deep inside her it was almost unbearable. She joined in, her voice thin and whispery, but had to stop to catch her breath.

Khalid smiled as she struggled to her feet, every muscle shaking with the effort.

'Shahin is ready to go on,' he announced to the others. They rose up from the sand, and brushed themselves off.

'That climb was the hardest,' Sayyid told Maude. 'I can find a better route through the other chains, do not fear, Shahin. It is hard, and long, but it is less steep.' He spoke in encouraging tones, and Maude understood then that the old man hadn't expected her to make it as far as she had. She straightened her shoulders as best she could and nodded, not able to speak.

Any relief at going down the gentler, windward side of the dune was spoiled by seeing the climb ahead rising up and up. But Sayyid was as good as his word, and he led them on a twisting route that climbed the ridges, not the slopes themselves. It was exhausting, it seemed to sap everything from them down to the marrow of their bones, but they were over the second high dune chain before the sun began to set, and they made camp at the foot of it, where they happened to stop, too tired to continue. Nearby was a huge crater in the sand, a hundred feet across and sixty deep, its sides all but vertical. Maude couldn't imagine the quirks and vagaries of whatever wind had sculpted it, and the thought of stumbling into it in the dark gave her chills. There would be no climbing out of it; ever. She stayed so close to the fire it scorched her eyelids as she tried to sleep. She turned her face to the sky instead, to the cold touch of the night and the careless glitter of the stars; staring up, letting her mind stray into the far, far heavens. In spite of the thirst and the death, in spite of the danger and the strain, she realised with complete clarity that there was nowhere else she would rather be.

Khalid was strict with their water supply, so strict that Maude didn't know if she could carry on with so little. She thought about ordering him to give her more, but she knew it would get her nowhere. She was no longer their leader – she wondered if she had ever been. Out there in the desert, Khalid was the only thing keeping them together, and keeping Maude safe – as safe as she could be on the mad course she'd plotted.

Halfway through the second day, they found tracks. Sayyid studied them, and Fatih studied Sayyid – he wanted to be as good a tracker as the old man.

'Four men. They are lost, they carry very little. One of their camels is nearly finished, another is growing weak,' he said.

'How do you know they're lost?' said Maude.

'Look, over there.' Sayyid pointed to where the tracks had come over a big dune, and then into the distance where the tracks appeared again, going back. 'They have walked in a circle, trying to find a way through this chain. They have gone back – they must be hoping to retrace their steps to escape.'

'Raiders?'

'No. Travellers. Their camels are from the Batinah coast, that's why they struggle so. They are in a bad way.'

'Should we follow the tracks, and help them?' said Maude. Fatih and Ubaid protested vociferously at once; Maude looked at Khalid, and he shook his head.

'If we see them, we will help. We cannot change course to find them or we will perish ourselves.' They set off again, obliterating the strangers' footprints with their own.

Maude stared out along the tracks, feeling pity and a stab of vicarious dread for the lost men, who would no doubt finish as bones in the sand. She thought of the ravens, and of vulnerable, sightless eyes. She thought how quickly blood dried in the desert sun, and that even if the lost men saw them from afar, they would probably be too thirsty to call out for help.

It took two more days to clear the dunes. Two more days of trudging, struggling, and flailing upwards, slithering downwards, shouting at the camels and driving them on with the switch; too thirsty to sweat, too thirsty to talk. Now and then Maude's heart fluttered strangely in her chest, like a butterfly caught in a glass – a sudden burst of small, erratic beats that left her dizzy. When it happened she had to stop, and sink to her knees until it passed. One time she stayed like that until Khalid came and hauled her up by her armpits. He gave her another mouthful of water, no more, and they laboured on. Maude tried not to think. She tried not to think about how far they'd come, or how far they had to go. She didn't think about home, or where they were heading; she didn't think about her brothers or her father; for a while she didn't even think about Nathaniel. There was room in her head for finding the will to lift each foot in turn, to take each step; there was no room for anything else. Then they halted at the bottom of a shallow slope, in the shade of the dune behind them, and at first Maude didn't realise why.

'Shahin, I have brought you across,' said Sayyid, to prompt her. Maude looked up. Ahead were low, flattish dunes of pale, hard sand; no more great dune chains. The horizon shimmered in the far, far distance. Maude swallowed painfully.

'We're through?' she whispered.

'We're through,' said Khalid.

'Thank you,' she said to Sayyid, and then glanced at the others. 'My thanks to all of you.' Then she sat down.

They slaughtered the raiders' camel that night. She died without a struggle, sagging obediently onto the sand while the other camels shifted against their hobbles a short distance away, smelling her blood. Much of the meat was cut into strips and tied to the drying frame, but Fatih also made a stew with some of their precious water. It was little more than boiled meat and liver with salt, but it tasted like a feast as they dipped their bread into it.

'We are only a day's ride from the well. I could find it with my eyes closed,' Sayyid reassured Khalid, when he questioned the extravagant use of water. With her stomach straining and full, Maude spent the precious moments before sleep updating her map, annotating it with as much detail as she could remember.

'Will other white men use your map, Shahin?' Ubaid asked her. The firelight sank into the hollows beneath the young man's cheekbones and his eyes lifted at their outer corners; he had the face of a feral cat. 'Will they come to the desert and follow it?'

'It isn't likely,' she said, with a smile. 'Most white people have never heard of Oman, let alone made plans to come here. God be praised.'

'Then why do you draw it?'

'So I will never forget. So I can show to the world where I have been, and what I have done.'

'The dunes shift; God's hand moves them. Trees die. Wells run dry. There can be sudden rain that brings up flowers, and paints the sand green.'

'Yes, I understand. This is a picture of a moment – of *this* moment. Do you see?' she said. Ubaid shrugged, and left her to it.

In the morning they crossed the strangers' tracks again. Sayyid frowned down at them.

'They have left one of their number behind in the dunes,' he said. 'They move slowly; thirst has taken their wits. They can no longer keep a straight line.'

'They will soon be dead,' said Fatih, in a matter-of-fact way.

'Are they close?' Maude asked. Sayyid nodded.

'These tracks were made in the night. They did not stop to sleep. They cannot be far.'

'Then, since we are close to the well and have full stomachs,

and a little water to spare now we have cleared the dunes...
can't we go a little way aside and try to find them?' she said.
The men were silent, and she felt their reluctance. 'Put yourself
in their shoes. You know what is right and good.'

'God is merciful,' Khalid agreed. 'Shahin is right. We will
follow them for half a day. If we do not find them in that time
we will continue on our way, and they will go with God.' He
looked at Maude for her agreement, and she nodded. With
an impatient tug of his camel's halter, Fatih set off along the
tracks; the others wheeled and fell in behind him. The sun was
sharp, the sand pale and bright. Maude paused to drag the kohl
wand along her eyelids before following.

A scant hour had passed when they saw the lost travellers
up ahead. Four scrawny camels sat listlessly in the sand, their
riders in the receding shade of a dune. There were three men,
one sitting up and the other two lying down, spent. Their
possessions were scattered around them as though they'd made
a half-hearted attempt to pitch a camp – blankets and a cook
pot, a flaccid water skin, their rifles and ammunition belts.
The seated man didn't notice them approach until they were
almost on top of him, then he reached in front of himself for
a handful of sand and threw it into the air to signal friendly
intent. His movements were sluggish and weak.

'Peace!' Khalid called, as the man attempted to reach his
rifle. 'We bring you help, if you need it.'

'God be merciful! He has brought you to us. We are dying,
we have no water,' the man croaked. His jaw was slack, face
scored with fear; his eyes had a deranged look.

'He is from the north. Be careful,' Khalid said softly, as
they approached. 'Thirst can make men mad.' He went over
with a water skin and gave rationed sips to the seated man.
Sayyid and Ubaid went to one of the fallen men, Fatih and
Kamal went to the other. Maude looked at this last man, who

was much taller than the others. She stared. Her mind turned slowly, taking in details she couldn't believe she was seeing – couldn't possibly be seeing.

She went to Fatih's side and stared down at the man. Her breathing paused. A tall man with a fox-like face, dark hair and whiskers; dressed as an Arab but with the peeling skin and burnished look of a white man scorched. Her legs buckled underneath her as her mind reeled. She grabbed the man's shoulder and shook it frantically, afraid that he was already dead.

'It cannot be,' she whispered. Fatih stared at her in confusion.

'What is it, Shahin?' he asked. Maude kept on shaking until the man turned his head weakly, and opened his eyes, just a fraction; relief convulsed her, and she gasped.

'*Nathaniel?*'

Nizwa and Muscat, December 1958

By the time they reached the bottom of the mountain, Joan couldn't tell how long they'd been walking. Her thoughts were far behind them, in the flooded wadi where three men she cared about were fighting, possibly dying; the one she cared about the most in by far the greatest danger. They emerged from the steep rocks into the shallower foothills to the south, and Walter Cox led her to an askar outpost in an ancient round tower with a radio aerial on top.

There was no rain on the lowlands; the ground was dry, though the sky was iron grey and a restless wind chased the clouds. Joan was dumb with exhaustion; she remembered Salim talking to the askari, and remembered that they were treacherous, but she had no idea what she should say about it, or to whom. She couldn't, without revealing exactly where she'd been, and with whom. They were admitted to the tower by a stocky man with shifty eyes and a short nose bedded deep into his face. He looked Joan up and down with obvious interest, and she realised she'd left the mask and veil up on the mountain. She felt naked without them. The small room inside the tower was stuffy, rank with the smell of unwashed men. There was a trapdoor in the wooden ceiling through which a rope ladder dangled; the sound of movement came from above and a curious face appeared, upside down, to see what was going on.

Communication between Walter and the askari was difficult – they had a few broken words of English, and he a few of

Arabic, but in the end he was allowed to use their radio to call the army base at Nizwa.

'Won't be long,' he told Joan. 'They're sending a jeep from base. About an hour.'

'Thank you, Corporal Cox,' said Joan. 'Thank you for coming down with me. I know you'd probably rather be up with your . . . comrades.' She wasn't sure of the word.

'Yes. I would.'

'I've wasted your time. I'm a nuisance,' she said. Walter gave her a steady look, neither friendly nor otherwise. Then he relented.

'I've no idea how you got up there, or what you thought you were playing at. But if you hadn't come down to tell us about the boys in the wadi then they'd certainly be in a worse fix than they are now. Let's hope the colonel goes easy on you because of that. I wouldn't count on it though, if I were you.'

Walter gave her a nod when they heard the sound of a Land Rover's engine. They stood, and Joan winced at the stiffness in her joints and muscles. She longed to lie down and sleep, and wondered how long it would be before she was able to. She steeled herself as they went out, but of course it wasn't Colonel Singer at the wheel, just an Omani trooper she'd never seen before, wearing rumpled khaki drill and chewing a clove. The smell of it hung around him, and he stared as Joan peeled off the sodden abaya, and bundled it up in her hands. Her trousers and shirt were just as wet. The jeep's floor was covered in sandbags. 'There could be land mines,' said Walter, as Joan tripped over them. 'A lot of the time the sandbags don't help at all, but they're better than nothing.'

'The askari are supposed to prevent mine laying,' said Joan carefully. Walter nodded.

'Yes, they're supposed to. Half of them are in cahoots with

Talib and bin Himyar though,' he said, and Joan nodded, relieved that this was already known. With a roar and a spray of gravel they set off, and the noise and movement of the vehicle seemed reckless after Joan's slow, peaceful time on the mountain. She stared out at the blurred landscape as she was carried further and further from her brother, but soon had to shut her eyes because it made her head ache. She sent out a silent prayer that Charlie had reached Daniel, and saved him, though she didn't know quite who she was sending the prayer to.

The army camp at Nizwa was outside the limits of the old city. Seeing the city's walls, palaces and enormous fortress from the ground, when she had already seen them from the air on another illicit journey, gave Joan a strange feeling of recognition, and guilt. Her desire to explore forbidden places seemed childish now, compared to what Daniel was facing. Compared to what could happen. Any satisfaction she might have felt in her adventures faded away; she no longer felt she had any reason to crow, not even to herself. At Walter's request, the jeep took them straight to Colonel Singer's operations tent. As they climbed out he squinted at Joan. 'It might be better if you wait out here for the moment. Let me . . . explain the situation,' he said. Mutely, Joan nodded. She felt a kind of fatalistic dread about seeing the colonel, and no little embarrassment, but it wasn't quite fear. All her fear was with Daniel on the mountain, and not even the remote but real chance of becoming a resident of Jalali could compare. She stood outside, since there was nowhere to sit; put her hands in her pockets and shifted her weight from one trembling leg to the other.

It was more than half an hour before Walter reappeared, by which time Joan felt light-headed. He took in her pale face and his distracted frown turned apologetic. 'You look done in,' he muttered. 'Sorry. I forgot you aren't used to all this.'

'Is there any news?' she asked. Walter shook his head.

'Go in, Colonel Singer wants a word. I'm going to have some hot tea and food sent in, and see the quartermaster about a tent for you to use.' He was gone before Joan had a chance to answer. She went in, unsteadily, and had a sudden clear memory of being called before the headmaster at school when she'd thrown paint at a girl who'd pulled her hair – of how afraid she had been, how shocked and aghast to have stepped out of line. She'd spent her whole life being afraid to step out of line, when it turned out not to be frightening after all; it turned out to feel like living at last. She blinked in the darkness of the tent and made out the colonel behind a long desk covered in papers. There was a radio set at one end, and an operator sitting in front of it with a headset over his ears; he didn't look up as Joan came in, but Colonel Singer did.

Singer looked at her steadily for a long time. His blue eyes betrayed no emotion; his expression was focused, calm, measuring. His innocuous face was entirely immobile.

'Miss Seabrook,' he said eventually. 'Do sit down. I understand you've had something of a busy time of it.'

'Thank you,' said Joan, sinking gratefully into a canvas chair.

'So. Would you mind telling me how you came to be on Jebel Akhdar, with knowledge of your brother's position? You've been in contact with him somehow, I surmise.'

'Oh no, not at all. I happened upon them by chance.'

'On a vast mountain, held by rebel forces, you happened to find your brother's section by chance?'

'Yes. After all . . . there are only so many navigable paths through the outer escarpments.'

'I see. And what about how you came to be on the mountain

in the first place? Robert Gibson's been going frantic, and I'm sure your fiancé will also be interested to know you've been found.'

'I just . . . I needed to . . . There was some trouble between me and . . . my fiancé. I needed to get away.'

'So, you set off, alone, into enemy territory, when it had been expressly forbidden. When it was utterly stupid.'

'Yes.'

'Rot. I don't believe you, I'm afraid.'

'Have you heard anything about the men on the mountain yet? Did Charlie manage to get my brother's men down? Please – I must know.' A steward in a white apron brought in a tray of bread, fruit and tea, and put it on the desk in front of Joan. She reached for it at once but Singer pulled it towards him, out of her reach.

'Not just yet with that. We're still talking,' he said, and Joan understood her status a little better. She swallowed.

'May I have a glass of water, at least?' she said quietly. The colonel poured her one from a jug beside him, and slid it across to her.

'You've been missing for two and a half weeks. You were picked up coming *down* the mountain, past enemy combatants and your brother's section, dressed as an Arab. Explain.' He stared at Joan.

She took a sip of the water and realised that there was no way she could. There was no story she could concoct that would be in the least bit convincing, and she couldn't tell him the truth. She couldn't admit to knowing Salim without arousing suspicions about how she'd come to know him, and surely, then, the veiled woman who'd visited him in Jalali would be remembered. She stayed silent, until that silence grew taut and strained. 'You struck up quite a friendship with Maude Vickery while you were in Muscat, I understand,' said Colonel Singer.

'I'd thought so. Until...' Joan pulled herself up, thinking of Maude's cold treatment of her after Salim's escape. 'What has Maude got to do with anything?' she said instead.

'We know she supports the imam's claim to sovereignty of the interior; Sultan Said suspected it for a long time. She lived in the mountains for many years before he invited her to Muscat – which he did primarily to keep an eye on her, and to stop her making any more generous donations to Imam Ghalib's coffers.'

'I didn't know that.' Joan paused, remembering the unidentified men she'd seen coming and going from Maude's house, over the weeks – several of them; she thought about the heavy bags and packages they'd often carried. 'I always thought she was on good terms with Sultan Said, and with the sultans before him as well,' she said.

'I dare say she was. Or pretended to be.'

'I still don't understand what Maude Vickery has to do with my being on the mountain.'

'Nor do I. Yet. But I hope the matter might become clearer in time,' said Singer. The silence returned. He leaned forwards on his elbows, and tapped the desk with his thumbs.

'There are rules, Miss Seabrook. This isn't England. You cannot simply go wherever you choose, whenever you choose, and expect there to be no consequences.' Joan felt the weight of his scrutiny, and his suspicion. Her head was aching again, and hunger was making her nauseous.

'I'm very tired, Colonel Singer,' she said, in a small voice. 'Please, won't you tell me if Daniel is safe?' The colonel seemed to think for a moment longer, then he pushed the tea tray towards her.

'I shall get to the bottom of this, Miss Seabrook, be certain of that. We've had no word from the men on the mountain yet. It's a bloody fiasco. However we try to surprise them, the buggers always seem to know we're coming, and which way.'

'The muleteers,' said Joan, before she could stop herself. Singer glared at her.

'Is that so? I had my suspicions. Drink some tea, Miss Seabrook, and then go and rest. And stay put – do I make myself clear? I'll send someone for you if there's any news.'

A young private took Joan to an officer's tent that had been hastily cleared out. There was a pillow and blanket on the bed, but no sheets; a metal-framed canvas chair sat out from the desk, as though only just vacated. Joan sat down with the tray of food and picked at it; as hungry as she was, she was almost too tired, too preoccupied to eat. She wondered if it had been Daniel's tent; she wondered if he would ever be back to claim it. As she lay down, she thought of the kiss she'd seen in his tent at Bait al Falaj; she wondered if Rory, knowing of Daniel's peril, would be as frightened as she was. She wondered if they loved each other as much as she'd loved Rory, as much as she loved Daniel, or if it was a different thing altogether. It was beyond her understanding. Her head was muzzy, thick with thoughts and fears, but when she lay down she was asleep in moments, and didn't dream.

She woke in confusion, because the sunlight outside was bright and she had no idea of the time, or even the day. It was light that had woken her – a sudden flare of it as the tent flap was lifted; it was a moment before she realised that somebody must have come in. She sat up, sleep still dragging at her, then the mattress dipped as someone sat down beside her and Joan caught her breath. It was Daniel, his face filthy and bruised but wearing the hint of a wry smile. Wordlessly, flooded with relief, Joan wrapped her arms around him and held him tight. For a long time she couldn't speak.

'I was so scared, Dan,' she said at last, her voice muffled against his shoulder. '*Why* must you be in the army? You could have chosen any other job in the whole world!'

'I shan't bother to answer that,' said Daniel. 'And you've a nerve, claiming I scared you – how do you think I felt when I heard you'd gone missing? And been up on the mountain? Joan – what on earth were you *doing* there?'

'I . . .' Joan sat back from him; keeping hold of his upper arms with both hands as though he might vanish if she didn't. 'Well, I knew I could do it, so I did it. I can't really explain it. Not yet. I think . . . oh, I think you'd be furious with me if I did.'

'I'm furious with you anyway,' he said, but he smiled again. 'Well, I want to be. But I'm told you sent the rescue party up to us, and we'd have been in serious trouble if you hadn't. So how can I be angry, really?' He took a deep breath. 'Except I am. How could you do something so stupid, Joan? And so reckless? What in heaven's name were you thinking of?'

Joan looked down at her dirty, broken fingernails, knowing that she was heading into unknown territory again, and into danger of a different kind. When she looked up, Daniel was watching her; she saw love in his eyes, and trust, and it made her brave.

'I was running away. I was running away from Rory, and from our engagement. From going home and having every-thing carry on just the same,' she said quietly. At the mention of Rory's name Daniel fell still. Joan looked hard, and saw a veiled wariness in his expression.

'Why?' he said. 'Did you have a row?' The question sounded fake, and hollow, and Joan knew they both heard it.

'I've wondered for a while why our engagement was going on so long. Why I couldn't make him settle on a date for the wedding. I've been worried, for a while, that he didn't really want to marry me at all. And now I . . .' Joan swallowed, her mouth dry with nerves. 'Now I know why.' She paused, but Daniel said nothing. He didn't move a muscle. 'I think . . . you're the reason, Dan. I think Rory loves you, not me. I think he wanted to marry me so that he . . . he would always be close to you. I think . . .' This time she broke off because Daniel stood abruptly and took two quick steps away from the bed. He stood with his back to her, arms clamped across his chest. Joan waited, but he didn't speak. 'I'm not wrong, am I?' she said softly. 'I'm . . . I'm not angry. At least, I don't seem to be. Perhaps I ought to be. That was what you argued about, wasn't it? About the wedding. He didn't really want to marry me. Did he?' There was a long and ringing silence.

'Yes, he did. He wanted to set the date. He'd have married you years ago, if I'd have let him. He does love you – be sure of it. Just as I do. He promised me he'd be a good husband to you, but how . . . how could I let that happen to you? How could I let you go into it so blindly?'

'You let me get engaged to him so blindly! You let me *love* him!' she shouted, a sudden anguish surprising her. She realised she wasn't angry; she was betrayed. The pain of it was terrible. Tears brimmed in her eyes, then fell. 'You let me waste years, loving him.'

'I wanted to tell you. I was going to tell you, I swear it . . . I just . . .' Daniel's chin dropped down to his chest. He turned around but couldn't look at her; his face was full of pain.

'When? When were you going to tell me?'

'Soon! I wouldn't have let you marry him. I wouldn't. Rory said it was the only way – the best way – but it isn't. He said it worked for Mum and Dad, so it could work for us, you see? But he . . . he made you a means to an end, and I couldn't . . . I couldn't stomach that. You've always looked after me, and been so dear, and I do love you—'

'Do you love him?' she asked. It was all a strange, unknow-able tangle, and she had no idea of her place in any of it. Daniel frowned; he twisted as if he wanted to run but was pinned there.

'Yes. I . . . I always have. It's so . . . difficult. It's so hard, for people like us. Do you understand that, Joanie?'

'I don't understand anything,' she said, shaking her head. 'That's the only thing I'm sure of. Do I . . . do I even know you, Dan? Do I know Rory? I don't feel at all certain any more.'

'Of course you know me!' Daniel's head came up; he came back to the bed and sat down again, taking her hands. 'Look at me – am I a different person, now? Aren't I still your brother?' He looked frightened, desperate, and Joan couldn't bear it.

'Of *course* you're still my brother,' she said, the words thickened by her tears. 'Of course you are!'

They held each other for a long time, until Joan's eyes were dry and Daniel had stopped shaking. He let go of her, pulled his cuff down over his hand and used it to wipe her face.

'You look revolting when you cry,' he said, and she laughed.

'How kind of you to say so.'

'We're going to get all this straightened out, Joanie – I promise. Once we're all back together again, in Muscat or wherever, we're going to sort it out, and there'll be no more secrets or pretending. Between us, at least. It's going to be all right – we're going to be all right. Aren't we?' His need for reassurance was obvious, but Joan just didn't know. All she knew was that change was coming, and she had secrets of her own.

'I waved to you from the top of the mountain,' she said instead quietly.

'What? You went up to the plateau?' he said incredulously. Joan nodded.

'When all this is over, I'll be able to tell you about it. But I can't now; I swore to it.'

'Swore to whom?' he said, but Joan only looked at him apologetically. 'Look, if you know something, Joan . . . You have to say. I lost three of my men in that riverbed yesterday; we might all have been picked off if you hadn't sent Elliot up. But not everybody came back down again. The situation is . . . it's still very bad. So please – if you know something else, tell me now.'

'Who didn't come back down? What do you mean, bad?' Daniel looked away, pinching the bridge of his nose between a finger and thumb, obviously unsure how much to tell her.

'After they got the snipers off our backs, Elliot's men found a ravine – a new way up to the summit, which we'd been looking for. He took a handful of men and went up to recce. They . . . there's been no word from them since.'

'What?' Joan went cold.

'When they went overdue, others went up to look in case they'd got into trouble. There was no sign of them. No bodies, nothing, and a couple of snipers firing down warning shots, closing off the ravine. It's very strange and it's . . . it can't be good.'

'Oh, no! Oh, *why* did he go up there? I thought . . . I thought he'd rescue you and come back down! The rain was so awful . . . the flood . . . I thought you'd all come down together!'

'Joan – what do you know?' Daniel grabbed her shoulders and gave her a shake. 'You have to tell me. This is serious.'

'Nothing!' Joan thought desperately. 'If . . . if there was no sign of them in the ravine then I don't know anything that could help. I'm sorry. Oh God, I'm sorry!'

Daniel stood and looked down at her for a long time, his

expression bewildered. From outside came the roar of an engine and the sound of running feet. Daniel glanced out, squinting against the sunlight.

'Is something going on?' Joan asked, going to stand behind him. Daniel let the tent flap drop.

'I don't know, but I ought to go and find out. The colonel's sending you back to Muscat – that was what I was meant to come and tell you. There's a plane on its way down now, and it'll take you back. I don't know what's been going on with you, Joanie.' He shook his head. 'But I've no choice but to believe you if you say you can't help us.'

'You're not . . . you're not going to go back up the mountain, are you?' she said fearfully.

'Probably. Unlike you, I'll go where I'm told to, Joan,' he said, with a mirthless smile. 'That's how it works in the army.'

'We shouldn't even be here – the British, I mean. This isn't our fight.'

'Well, even if that's true, it's hardly relevant. It's not my job to question government policy, and I dare say the government knows a bit more about it than you do. Stay here – if I find out anything else, I'll come and tell you. We'll . . . we'll talk properly when all this is over. We'll sort everything out.' He kissed her cheek and squeezed her arm, then turned to go.

'Wait!' said Joan, grabbing his sleeve. She couldn't bear him going again so soon, and right back into danger. She shut her eyes tightly, trying to sort through the jumble of her thoughts, and in the end had to do whatever she could to make him safer. 'Wait . . . Salim bin Shahin was up there. At the top of the ravine.'

'The man who escaped from Jalali?' said Daniel, and Joan nodded. 'How on earth could you possibly know that?' He frowned down at her, but this time she could only shake her head.

'He was waiting there with a group of six men. Perhaps . . . perhaps they've taken Charlie and the others prisoner?'

'Why would they do that?'

'I don't know. I promise, Dan – I don't know why. I don't know anything else.'

Daniel's expression was so hard, so angry and mistrustful; it hit her like a blow. 'Am I a different person now, Dan? Aren't I still your sister?' she said.

'You're still my sister,' he said quietly. 'But I do think you might be a different person as well.'

For a while Joan waited for Daniel to return, but half an hour became an hour, and she grew restless. She wanted to see him before she quit, and she expected to be summoned by Colonel Singer again, but when she left the tent for the dust and sunshine, there weren't many soldiers around. The camp felt deserted. She went to the mess tent and found a few men eating lunch, and retreated from their curious looks. She saw nobody she recognised, nobody British she could ask for information, and when she arrived back at the tent she'd been loaned, a thin Baluchi trooper was coming out. He grinned, showing an array of pitted teeth.

'Good!' he announced, with a bob of his head. 'You come. Please. To plane now.'

'Wait – where is everybody? I need to talk to the colonel – to Colonel Singer,' said Joan. But the young man only bobbed his head again.

'Plane now,' he repeated, and Joan had no choice but to follow. Her eyes searched everywhere as she was driven out of the camp towards the runway, but she saw no sign of Daniel. She was still searching as she went up the plane's steps, feeling small, irrelevant and discarded. She sat down and buckled her seat belt with the notion that she'd kicked a stone and started an avalanche, and could now only wait to find out how big it would get. The plane lurched into the air and still Joan stared out, as though she might read something on the ground as it fell away. Salim had Charlie Elliot and his men, of that much she was sure. But she had no idea what either man would do. And try as she might, she couldn't imagine how they could both come out of it alive.

Rory was waiting for her at Bait al Falaj. Joan spotted him through clouds of brown dust, standing beside the runway with his hair flapping in the breeze as the plane taxied to a standstill. Her heart clenched horribly, and she wished he'd stayed away. He jerked when he saw her, standing up straighter, waving eagerly but then frowning, and letting his arm fall. Joan smiled. He had no idea how to treat her, or how to react to their reunion; no more than she had.

It explained why he'd come to the army base, and come alone – so that they could have the worst over with without an audience. They hugged briefly, squeezing hard. The familiar smell and shape of him gave her a pang – something slightly sad; a memory of a feeling. She realised that everything had already changed between them, without her having to say a word. There were dark circles under Rory's eyes; he smelled stale, and his face looked heavier, less mobile than before. He kissed her forehead, and took hold of her hand.

'I've been so desperately worried about you, Joan,' he said.

'I'm sorry. That's not what I wanted.'

'I won't ask where you've been. Or . . . who with. The main thing is that you're back safely.'

'I saw Dan. He's safe . . . at least, for the moment he is.'

'Good. Good, I'm glad.' Rory swallowed hard, and Joan waited to feel his betrayal – the pain of it, the outrage. But if she had ever felt that then it seemed to have come and gone as she'd come undone; it had blown away in the breeze on top of the mountain, or washed out in the clear waters of Misfat, or been silenced by the steady rhythm of climbing the ancient rocks of Jebel Akhdar. Rory had had no such release; she couldn't guess his thoughts, but she could see he was suffering. She squeezed his hand.

'It's all going to be all right, Rory,' she said softly. He squinted at her, puzzled, as though seeing something he hadn't expected to.

Joan turned to look at the sleeping bulk of the mountains; distant again, hazy again, insurmountable again. But she could still feel them under her feet; she could still see from the summit into the far, far distance. They walked in silence to the waiting car, and set off along the six miles of gravel road that would take them to Muscat. The sea glittered beside them, jade green and silver. Joan looked down at her engagement ring. There was dirt in the setting, dulling the topaz and the tiny diamond chips. She buffed it against her shirt until it looked a little better, then worked it off her finger and handed it to Rory. It left a pale echo of itself in the tan and grime on her skin. Rory opened his mouth as he took it, as if to speak; but in the end he only sat with the ring clasped in his hand and unshed tears gleaming in his eyes.

'It's going to be all right,' Joan said again.

'*How* is it?' said Rory, taking a long, uneven breath. He shook his head, and looked out of the window; hunched, miserable.

'You'll find a way,' she said. Suddenly a comment Daniel had made, lost in the maelstrom of their conversation, resurfaced. *It worked for Mum and Dad.* Joan felt the shock of realisation as a physical jolt, a small kick in the spine.

*

Back at the Residency Robert hugged her until she was breathless, and then shook his head sadly, incredulously.

'What on earth has been going on, Joan?' he said.

'Never mind that – look at the poor girl!' Marian appeared at her side, taking her arm. 'She needs a bath, some tea and some rest. You can interrogate her later,' she said firmly.

'Thank you,' Joan said quietly, as they went upstairs. Marian pursed her lips.

'You've a fair amount of explaining to do. I rather thought you might need a little time to gather yourself.'

'I suppose I caused a bit of a stir?'

'That's putting it mildly. A word of advice – don't try to make light of it. Robert's not ready to laugh this one off.'

'No. Neither am I.'

Outside the door to her room, Marian took her shoulders and kissed her cheek.

'Were such drastic measures really necessary? A disappearance, I mean? The poor man's performed incredible feats of obfuscation to keep news of your antics in British ears only. He could have got into very hot water.' She sighed, shaking her head. 'Never mind. You're back now; I hope you achieved whatever it was you intended to.'

'I did, Marian,' said Joan, realising how true it was. 'I really did.' Then she thought of Charlie Elliot, and Salim; she remembered Bilal's simmering hostility, and the three dead men in the wadi, and was no longer sure what she was responsible for, and what she was not. The possibility of Charlie never coming back from that ravine lurked ahead of her like a chasm she might stumble into, witlessly, and be lost.

Joan took a long bath. The warm water brought on irresistible waves of fatigue, and she dozed. It seemed a lifetime since she'd walked out to find Salim in the darkness beyond the gates of Muscat; it felt as though years had passed, not mere weeks. When she got out of the bath she found a tea tray in her room, the tea gone lukewarm and stewed. She drank it anyway, and ate three slices of the honey cake that was with it. Once she was dressed, she went to find Robert in his office. He looked up and frowned as she sat down in front of him, but she didn't see anger in his face. She saw disappointment, relief, a deep weariness. He still looked like a lion, too big for his chair, too big for the desk. The pen in his hand looked too small, and he sat hunched, uncomfortable, out of proportion with the world.

'I'm so sorry I've caused you such trouble, Uncle Bobby,' she said sincerely.

'I believe that, Joan.' He took a slow breath. 'I've managed to hide your vanishing act from Governor Shahab, thank goodness. I just don't understand why you ran away in the first place – why on earth did you? And where on earth have you been?'

'I went up the mountain.'

'Up the mountain? You can't mean . . . Jebel Akhdar?'

'Yes. I went to the summit. For a while I stayed in a village called Misfat al Abreen . . .' Joan trailed off, thinking. She'd decided to answer his every question as fully and honestly as she could. She had no fear of him; she trusted him completely. 'At first it was wonderful. Restful.'

'Restful?' Robert echoed incredulously. 'If it was restful you wanted, couldn't you have run away to Wales?' He stood up and went to the window, linking his hands behind his back. Joan waited for whatever he would ask next. 'Perhaps,' he said softly. 'Perhaps there are some things it would better I didn't ask; things I would be better off not knowing.' He gave her a shrewd look over his shoulder. 'You're not wearing your engagement ring.'

'No. The engagement is . . . off.'

'A pity. But I can't say I'm surprised.'

Robert was silent for a long time. Joan wanted to say something about Charlie Elliot; she wanted to ask for news, though
she had no idea if Robert would get word if there were any.
She bit the question back, and waited impatiently as Robert
continued to stare out of the window with his back to her.
'Your father ran away once, you know,' he said eventually.

'When? I didn't know.'

'When we were eleven. We made a plot to run away from
school at midnight. It was David's idea – he was being bullied,
you see. He was always so tidy, so lively; so full of mirth.
People like that will always attract the attention of the less
happy, the less kind, you see. Human beings are such envious
creatures. I'd no idea where we were going – David said he
had it all worked out. We sneaked into the kitchens the night
before and stole some biscuits and two oranges. David hid
them in his pillowcase.' Robert turned, smiling into the past;
he came to stand beside her.

'What happened?'

'I refused to get up. I was sound asleep when he came to
wake me on the night of the escape. The dorm was cold, and
it was raining – I could hear it hitting the window. I didn't
want to go. I was warm, and comfortable, and I refused to
budge, even though I knew I was letting him down badly. Your
father went anyway. Alone. They found him the next morning,
soggy, shivering, sitting on a bench at the station – his tuck
money hadn't been enough for a ticket.'

Robert smiled again. 'But by God, he'd made a good stab
at it, however warm and comfortable his own bed had been.
And he forgave me instantly for letting him down. *Next time*,

he said to me, when the headmaster had finished with him and he could hardly sit down; *next time I'll take the bus.*'

Joan thought for a moment, seeing her father on that bench, seeing him undefeated. She welcomed any new stories about him.

'I thought Dad's school days were happy,' she said. 'He always said they were – and he saved up all that money to send Dan there, when they couldn't really afford it.' She realised that when she pictured her father as a boy she pictured Daniel – the same bony strip of a body, the same irrepressible sense of adventure. 'Dan's like that too, you know,' she said. 'He was always off, doing what he shouldn't have. Having adventures.'

'I told you that story because it's *you* who reminds me of him, Joan,' said Robert. 'If he were here, he'd want to hear about everything you'd seen and done. But it's a serious matter.' He shook his head. 'You put yourself in great danger; and you caused people who love you a great deal of worry – and your government potentially a great deal of embarrassment. Thank the Lord we've managed to keep it quiet. Singer's taking a soft line, for once, since your intervention did help save the men in the wadi. Your father could never hold a grudge, and I don't think I can either; not when it comes to you and your brother.' He patted her shoulder with his heavy paw, smiled down at her and then returned to his chair. 'But you'll have to go home. You and Rory; as soon as it can be arranged. You understand.'

'Yes,' said Joan, and her throat tightened around the word. 'Yes, I see.'

'Whatever's happened between you young people, you'll sort it out for the best. I have every confidence in you, my dear girl; but running away is rarely the answer. It buys you time, nothing more.'

'Yes. It was time that I needed, you see; time to see that I could be different. Not the same old Joan. I needed some proof of that.' She looked at Robert, searching desperately for a sign that he understood her. He smiled again, and shook his head slightly.

'Poor girl. Listen to me – there was nothing whatsoever wrong with the old Joan, and you're still her. But perhaps you know yourself a little better now, and that's all to the good.'

'Thank you, Uncle Bobby.'

'You will remain here in Muscat for the remainder of your stay. Please. If you want to go beyond the city gates, I must insist that you let me know.'

'Yes. I promise.'

'Then go and get some rest, and we'll say no more about it.'

Joan thought about going to find Rory, but couldn't think what she wanted to say to him. He obviously didn't need her to spell out the reasons for their broken engagement; he obviously didn't want to ask how she'd found out the truth. The thumb of her left hand kept returning to the gap where his grandmother's ring had sat for the past two years, fascinated by the softness of the newly exposed skin. Experimentally, she thought about home: about her mother, and how empty the house she'd grown up in felt without Daniel or her father. She thought about the job she'd wanted at the Bedford Museum, and how small it seemed now.

She tried to keep an open mind, but it all brought on a lifeless feeling, a weariness coming from within her that she'd never felt before. Realising that she had no idea of the date, she went into one of the empty offices and found a calendar. It was the twenty-second of December. One way or another, Olive Seabrook would be spending Christmas without Joan and Rory. Joan went to her room to lie down, but there was too much in her head; too much fear and doubt about Daniel, and Charlie, and Salim. She was restless and awake for a long time, and only managed to drift off in the small hours of the morning.

'We tried to wake you, but we didn't try very hard,' said Rory, as she sat down late to breakfast. 'It seemed better to let you rest, after all you've been through.'

'Thank you. I do feel better,' said Joan, thinking that Rory could have no idea what she'd been through. She noticed the slump in his shoulders, and the way he couldn't quite look her in the eye, and realised that the inverse was also true. The potted oleanders bobbed their pink flowers in the breeze. 'Have you been in touch with Mum while I've been . . . away?' she asked. Rory nodded.

'We didn't tell her you'd gone off. We thought we'd wait until we had definite news, so she didn't worry too much.'

'Oh, good, well done. Thank goodness. I'm glad.' Joan exhaled. She realised she'd been clenching her fists, and stretched out her fingers.

'You did spare her a thought at some point, then?' he asked unkindly. Joan stared hard at him.

'Rory, please don't—'

'Joan, would you be a dear and pass the butter, please?' Marian interrupted her. Joan swallowed her angry remark. 'Thank you,' said Marian. She buttered a piece of toast and slid it towards Joan. 'Here, do eat. You've got horribly thin during your time away. The two of you clearly have a lot to talk about, so I'll leave you to it. But as my old nanny used to say, least said, soonest mended.' Marian got up, wrapping the arms of a white sweater across her chest. There was a new coolness in the morning air, a new pallor to the sky.

When she'd gone, Joan ate the toast in silence and Rory stared down at the tabletop with his jaw clenched.

'We've both got things we could be very angry with each

other about, if we let ourselves be,' she said carefully. 'Perhaps I've behaved badly lately, and without much consideration for others. But ... if you think about it, I'm sure you'll find ways to reprimand yourself as well. So perhaps it would be better to ... not to fight. About any of it. Don't you agree? Rory?' She waited; he didn't reply at once. The breeze lifted the edges of the tablecloth, and brushed Rory's curls across his forehead.

'She wrote a letter, your mum. It arrived a little after you'd gone off. You didn't get the job at the museum.'

'Oh,' said Joan. 'What else did she say? Is she well?'

Rory looked up at her. 'Aren't you upset? I thought that job was the be all and end all?'

'It was, before. I suppose it was.' She thought about it. 'It doesn't seem quite as important any more.'

'You'll have to make a living somehow, without a husband to support you,' he said coldly. 'Or are you planning to stop at home with Olive for ever?'

'Oh, please stop it, Rory. You're acting like a child.'

'And you – you're acting like ... like ...' He stood up abruptly, scraping his chair across the tiles. 'Like somebody I don't even *know*.' He stalked away, and Joan watched him, marvelling at her calm.

She stared across at Jalali, and thought about what would have happened if she hadn't done as Maude asked, and had never visited Salim. He would never have escaped, and she would never have gone into the mountains; Charlie Elliot would not now be lost, his fate unknown, and perhaps Daniel would have drowned in the wadi. Many things had happened, good and bad, since she'd made that decision; try as she might, Joan could not regret it. But as she sat on the terrace by herself, she felt a long way from Salim, a long way from Charlie, a long way from Daniel, and from Rory. She couldn't remember ever having felt so alone, and though it wasn't necessarily bad, and it wasn't frightening, she knew she wouldn't be able to stand it in the long term. For the first time since her return, she thought about Maude. Salim could never return to Muscat now; there was every chance Maude would never see him again. Joan pictured the tiny old woman, upstairs in her grubby house with only Abdullah for company. What then, for Maude Vickery? Joan thought about the care with which she'd organised Salim's escape, and her coldness towards Joan once her mission had been accomplished; she thought of the things she'd noticed about Salim during their time together on Jebel Akhdar, and with her mind now lucid and clear, she knew at once what it was she'd realised. She thought about how quickly and easily news and messages were passed on the mountain. She thought about Charlie, held captive by Salim, and her heart sped up. She stood, left word for Robert that she was going to visit Maude, and set off directly.

Abdullah smiled as he let her in. 'You have returned, sahib,' he said. 'The lady wondered if you would stay on the mountain, and marry Salim.'

'No,' said Joan, also smiling, but cautiously. 'Although perhaps it wouldn't have been a bad life, if I had. If the war were to end.'

'We did not expect to see you here again,' he said, as Joan headed for the stairs, and she couldn't tell exactly what he meant. Maude's chair was set near her desk, she was writing, leaning forwards over the page. The pewter ring with the blue stone, which had only ever sat untouched in the pencil tray before, was now on the paper near her hand.

'Hello, Miss Vickery,' said Joan, walking over to her slowly. The salukis snored.

Maude pursed her lips, and finished her sentence before

laying down her pen and looking up. She blinked a few times, adjusting her eyesight.

'Joan! And back in Muscat? I'd rather thought you'd vanish into the mountains or the desert, and never come back. God knows, I would if I could.'

'I did think about it.'

'Where did he take you? Tanuf? Al Farra'ah?'

'Misfat al Abreen.'

'Ah!' Maude sat back in her chair, lacing her hands in her lap. 'Lucky girl. Isn't it the most beautiful place you've ever been? And you still came back?' She shook her head, as if disappointed. Joan stared hard at her.

'Events transpired,' she said, and in the pause that followed, she understood that there was little going on up the mountain that Maude didn't get to hear about. Maude gave a dismissive grunt.

'Yes, well. You should never have been up there – you had no place in any of it. I was very upset with Salim when I found out what he'd done.' Joan took a long breath to steady herself.

'Salim . . . Salim is your son, isn't he, Miss Vickery?' As he'd washed in the falaj at Tanuf she'd noticed the fairness of the skin on his back, and had realised that the swarthiness she'd thought was inherent had only been caused by the sun – it had begun where his clothing ended. 'He told me that the people of Tanuf take their mother's name as their surname. Shahin was the name the Bedouin gave you when you crossed the desert. Isn't it? Salim bin Shahin is your son.'

Maude stared at Joan without blinking. If she felt anything about Joan making this connection, she didn't betray it.

'What of it?' she said, at last.

'Why didn't you just tell me? Why lie, and obfuscate?' she asked, but Maude didn't answer her. 'I suppose . . . I suppose you wouldn't have been allowed to remain in Muscat, if your relationship to such a man were known? The salukis . . . when we first met you told me they were a gift from bin Himyar. Suleiman bin Himyar, the Lord of The Green Mountain. One of the men now leading the fight against Sultan Said. Tanuf was his home village.'

'What of it, Miss Seabrook?'

'You led me to believe that you were a good friend of the sultan – and those that went before him – but all the while you've been supporting the rebels. Sending them money. And your son is one of their key lieutenants.'

'I have no control over what you believe, Joan. Especially about things that are none of your business.'

'But it is my business now, Miss Vickery. I choose to make it my business, when Salim has taken men hostage – men I inadvertently sent into his path.'

'Did you, indeed?' Maude leaned forwards; her chair creaked. 'He didn't mention that. No wonder you look so het up. Well, you're out of it now. Put it out of your mind, why don't you? You've a wedding to plan, and a life to get back to.'

In a flash, Joan was so angry she couldn't find a single word to say. She stood mute as Abdullah brought in the tea tray. It was something Joan had seen him do ten or fifteen times before, but this time he set it down and then remained, staring down at Maude.

'This one is not our enemy,' he said quietly. Maude glared at him, and he turned to go.

Without waiting to be invited, and to show that she wouldn't just leave, Joan sat down in the chair nearest the old woman.

'That man has gone soft in his old age,' Maude muttered.

'Perhaps he remembers that I visited his son in Jalali, and helped him escape,' said Joan.

'His son? You think Abdullah is Salim's father? No, child.

He is my slave; perhaps he is my friend, but he has never been anything more.'

'Oh. I thought . . .'

'I know what you thought. Pour the tea, why don't you. I expect the others will be here soon.'

'Which others might those be, Miss Vickery?'

'You'll soon see, since you appear to be staying. And since you appear to be staying,' she said, resting back in her chair with a distant smile. 'Tell me everything you saw. I shan't be able to go back and see it myself. Tell me how it was.'

'Miss Vickery, please . . . If there's any way you could help Captain Elliot and the others, won't you do it? Won't you ask for his release?'

'Ask for his release? Don't be absurd. I have that young fool exactly where I want him.'

'Where you want him for what, Miss Vickery?' Joan's heart thumped anxiously. She perched on the edge of the chair, caught by an emotion she couldn't quite name. The tiny old woman waited, tapping her thumbs together.

'Tea, and the chance to tell me about your travels. That's all I can offer you for the time being, Joan.'

Joan sipped her tea in outraged silence for a while, and then began to talk, stiffly; an outline of where she'd been. But talking about it awoke the wonder of it, and her descriptions grew. Everything she could remember; everything she had seen and done, everyone she'd met; the women she'd lived and worked alongside in Misfat al Abreen, and how quiet the village had been with all the young men away, fighting; the bomb that dropped near them on the plateau, the cave, and the endless view that had crowned it all. 'So, you went to the summit. Up onto the plateau,' said Maude, after a long pause. Joan nodded.

'I was the first,' she said, feeling an unusual thrill of profound satisfaction. 'The first westerner ever to see it.' Maude studied her for a moment.

'Indeed. And yet you came back down, and will doubtless have to keep quiet about it, unless you want to land yourself in very hot water.'

'When we first met you told me I had to be the first to do something, or it meant nothing.'

'Hm. Well, sometimes it means nothing either way.'

'How can you say that? I don't believe you – and it will always mean something to me, even if nobody else ever hears about it. I came back down because . . .' Joan broke off, and ran her thumb around her empty ring finger. She shook her head. 'I'm not like you, as it turns out.'

'Well, I could have told you that. But in what way do you mean?'

'I'm not . . . an explorer. I'm not intrepid. I found it lonely. It didn't help that I couldn't speak to anybody, of course, but it was more than that. I found that I . . . didn't want to cut all my ties with home, and with my family. I was homesick, I suppose you'd say.' Joan smiled a bit sadly. 'I couldn't face staying there for ever, and trying to build a new life. Such a strange and different life. So, not much of a trailblazer after all.' Maude stared at her with a peculiar expression.

'You think being homesick means you're not a traveller?' she said quietly. There was a pause and then Maude looked away. 'You've taken off your ring. No wedding to plan after all, then?'

'No. That particular adventure is over with.'

'Well and good, I would venture.' Maude sighed a little, and leaned back in her chair.

'Yes,' said Joan sadly. 'You already told me that marriage is fetters.'

'Indeed. Marriage to the wrong man, in any case.'

'Perhaps it doesn't have to be one thing or the other. Life, I mean – perhaps it doesn't have to be marriage and feeling trapped, or cutting all ties with everything you know and love. Perhaps there's a middle ground.'

'Perhaps you've found it. Or you will,' said Maude abruptly, and Joan nodded. 'I never did. Did you see Tanuf?'

'Yes,' said Joan. As she described the ghostly ruins of bin Himyar's village, Maude's eyes swam with tears. 'Another home I once had, to which I can never return. I was happy there, when Salim was just a boy,' she whispered. 'For a while, I was happy. Salim means whole, you know; it means flawless. And he was. And he is, in spite of everything. My son.' She shook her head sadly.

'He treated me with respect, and kindness. He is a good man, and a . . . fair one,' said Joan carefully.

'I don't need you to tell me that,' said Maude, but not unkindly.

'Don't you think he would welcome the chance to show mercy? To act kindly, and fairly? Those men, Charlie's men—' She was cut off by a loud knocking on the door below. Maude's head snapped up, her eyes gleamed. 'What is it?' said Joan.

'The time has come. Finally,' said Maude. Her fingers curled and uncurled over the arms of her chair, she shifted her weight, gripped either by excitement or trepidation.

'Time for what? Who's come?' said Joan.

She stood up as footsteps sounded loudly on the stairs, and stared, astonished, as Colonel Singer, Robert Gibson and Lieutenant Colonel Burke-Bromley, the SAS commander, filed into the room. For a bewildered moment she thought they'd come for her; she took a step backwards, fighting the urge to run.

'Gentlemen,' said Maude, her voice taut with emotion.

'You're here ever so slightly sooner than I expected you, but never mind. May I offer you some tea?'

'Miss Vickery, this is no time to be flippant,' said Singer severely.

'No tea, then?' she said innocently, and Joan realised that the old woman was enjoying herself. Behind the men, Abdullah appeared in the doorway; tall, glowering, implacable.

'I shall get to the bottom of all this, mark my words,' Singer went on. 'But it would appear that for the moment, time is of the essence. Men's lives are at stake.'

'Oh, they are. They are indeed. One man's in particular,' said Maude.

'Miss Vickery, what's going on? What have you done?' said Joan. The three men seemed to notice her for the first time, and she flinched from their scrutiny. Robert frowned, folded his arms, and wouldn't look straight at her.

'And Miss Seabrook. Fancy finding *you* here,' said the colonel acidly.

'I'd pipe down if I were you, Joan; these chaps look rather tense. You wouldn't want them finding out just how their men came to be taken hostage, now, would you?' said Maude, and Joan felt the blood rush to her head, flushing hotly across her skin.

'I've no idea exactly what has gone on, but these appear to be the facts. Captain Elliot and seven men of his section have been taken hostage by insurgents at the summit of Jebel Akhdar. One of those insurgents being Salim bin Shahin, newly escaped from Jalali.

'Bin Shahin sent down a messenger informing us that the men will be executed at sunset tomorrow, starting with Elliot, unless he hears that we've agreed to *your* demands. What your link to him is, and what the hell is happening here, I've no time to fathom just now. I have no option but to hear you out. So, Miss Vickery, out with it.'

Silence fell in the room; even the dogs, awake and staring in wonderment at so many intruders, had stopped snoring. Joan looked from Colonel Singer to Maude and back again; her thoughts trying to keep up. She was baffled, but she thought back to the dinner at the Residency, when Maude had met Charlie – the hostility she'd shown. She thought of all the vitriolic things she'd ever said to Joan about Nathaniel Elliot, and a terrible fear began to grow in her. They all watched Maude; they all waited for her to speak. Slowly, shakily, she pulled herself to the edge of her wheelchair and then stood up at her diminutive tallest, fighting for balance. Instinctively, Joan went and took her arm to steady her.

'I want Nathaniel Elliot brought here to face me,' said Maude, in a high, imperious voice.

'You want *what?*' said Robert.

'Nathaniel Elliot. I assume you've all heard of him? Charles Elliot's famous father. I want him flown out here and brought into this very room to face me. That is what I want, and that's the price of those young men's release. I know you can make it happen; I know you army lot could have him here in twenty-four hours if you put your minds to it. Joan tells me you need this campaign to go smoothly, and quickly, and with the minimum of casualties and embarrassment,' she said, and Joan's face burned anew. 'Well, if you want there to be any chance of that happening, I suggest you get to it. And as you yourself said, Mr Elliot's son's life depends on it.'

The Empty Quarter, Oman,
April 1909

It was a while before Maude really believed he was there. Nathaniel Elliot was there, at the foot of the Uruq al Shaiba dunes, and she had found him. She thought she was mad, delusional from thirst and exhaustion; she thought she was dreaming him. She sat next to him for a long time, and administered him sips of water, thinking how close they'd been to abandoning these men to their fate. She thanked God she'd persuaded the Bedouin to deviate.

She held Nathaniel's hand as he slept, with the water seeping slowly into his dying body, bringing him back; she tried to think how on earth he could have got there. He was supposed to be in Berbera, in British Somaliland, hundreds of miles away across the Gulf of Aden; that was where she'd planned to send the letter she'd been writing to him. She stared into his face, impatient for him to wake up and explain things to her. There was sand and dirt in the creases around his eyes; the skin across the bridge of his nose had cracked and peeled, showing raw and pink underneath. Maude used some of their precious water to wet a rag and, as gently as she could, cleaned his face. He was wearing the remains of a linen shirt with a crisp collar and a narrow grey pinstripe; Maude recognised it – she'd seen him wear it before, in England. It was like he'd been picked up from there and dropped down here by some mighty, all-powerful hand. No wonder he'd got lost.

He slept for a long time and then, as the sun was setting, sat up shakily and asked, in flawed Arabic, for more water.

Quietly, with a smile, Maude corrected his pronunciation, and he looked at her. It was some moments before any recognition showed in his expression.

'Maude? It can't be!' he said. His voice was hoarse, stretched thin.

'What do you mean, it can't be? I'm *supposed* to be here!' she said. 'But you . . . Nathan, how are you here?' She took his hand again, but he didn't answer; he hadn't recovered from the shock of seeing her yet. He put up his hand and cupped it around her jaw, turning her face this way and that.

'I can't believe it,' he murmured. 'I can't believe it. You look like a Bedouin. Your eyes . . . your clothes. You look like a Bedouin lad! But it is you . . . it is you . . .'

'It's me. You're safe now; we're close to the well and we know the way. And we have water to share, and camel meat.' Nathaniel clenched his eyes shut; a single tear beaded on his black lashes.

'I thought we were dead. I thought I was dead. When I felt the water in my mouth I thought I was imagining it – I'd imagined so many other things that might have saved us, and each time they proved false, and my hopes were dashed. Oh, it was unbearable! Don't disappear, Maude; don't be a hallucination. Be *real*, Maude . . .'

He fell asleep still murmuring her name. She held his hand tightly, close to her face, and wept silently for a while, so that her own tears were salty on his knuckles when she kissed them. She saw Khalid nearby, watching; his son and Ubaid were building a cook fire and propping up blankets for shade. With a wrench, she left Nathaniel sleeping and went over to Khalid.

The Bedouin tipped his chin at the men they had rescued. 'Those two are Bani Kitab. They are pirates; I do not trust them. The white man hired them in Buraimi; they are three weeks out from there. He hired them to lead him across the desert to Salalah. But you know him, Shahin? How is this so? Who is he?'

'Yes, I know him. It's . . . incredibly strange. I've known him since we were children. He is . . . he is a traveller, like me. But I had no idea he was coming here. He never told me . . .'

Maude frowned. For the first time, she realised how odd it was that she'd had no word of his plans.

'So, he is your brother, your cousin?'

'We are not related, no.' She realised how inappropriate it would seem to them that she had sat and held his hand. 'We are like family though.' Khalid nodded as she said this, his eyes on Nathaniel's limp body. 'What should we do?' Maude asked.

'Let them rest until tomorrow. Let them eat and drink a little. Then we will ride on to the well; God willing, we will reach it by sunset. It is a good place to wait a while. There are some trees, a pool. But we cannot wait for too long, if we want our food to last out the journey.'

'I understand. Perhaps there'll be some others at the well who can trade or sell us something?'

'God willing,' Khalid agreed, with a shrug of his brows. 'The way ahead is still far, and dangerous. We must stay true to our course if we are to cover it.' He gave her a steady look to reinforce his point, and then went to crouch by the fire where Kamal was brewing coffee. Maude sensed his unease; he didn't like the burden of the extra men, or the delay. She guessed that he didn't like Maude's ill-defined relationship to Nathaniel, either. She watched the Bedouin for a while before returning to Nathaniel's side to take some rest herself. She didn't really care how the Bedouin felt, or what they thought; she was too awash with relief, and too full of wonder – at having Nathaniel there, and having made him safe.

*

When the cool of the night woke them, the three men drank more water and ate the flatbreads and dates they were offered. The bread was singed and full of sand, and the dates had gone stiff and dry, but the men ate as though they hadn't in a year. Maude tried not to question Nathaniel too doggedly, but she couldn't help herself.

'Technically, I'm supposed to be looking for locusts . . . the board finally decided I should look here for the breeding sites of the great African swarms. I could hardly believe my luck – I knew straight away that I'd come to the Empty Quarter, and try to make a crossing. I didn't know exactly where you were, or when you were planning your crossing, or by which route. I knew you were starting in the south . . . the odds of our meeting up were so tiny, Maude.' He shook his head, wearing a haunted expression. 'If you had not found me, I would have died. I would be dead.'

'Hush, now. I did find you, and you're not dead,' said Maude, pleasure colouring her face. She thought for a moment. 'I hadn't known you . . . you wanted to cross the Rub el Khali. I thought that was my dream,' she said.

'Come along, Maude – what explorer wouldn't want to try it? But look, see – if it wasn't for you, I'd be one more failed attempt. One more valiant fool who died trying.' He sounded despairing, bitter and self-mocking. The firelight fluttered over his gaunt face and shone in his eyes. Maude smiled fondly at him.

'Better a dead hero than a live worm, as Father would say.'

'But I'm the worm, Maude. Don't you see? I'm not a dead hero, am I? So I must be the worm.'

She noticed the thinness of his body and the acrid, unwashed smell of him; one front tooth was chipped across a corner, and his lips were pale and cracked. She suddenly wondered about her own appearance – Nathaniel had said she looked like a

Bedouin boy. Her eyes were still smudged with kohl, her hair was filthy and flat to her head. Her clothes were almost in rags, and she smelled no better than he did. She was used to being plain; now she realised she must have lost all femininity entirely. From old habit, she pressed her lips together to encourage a little colour into them, but they were too dry, and felt as though they'd split if she persisted. She tried to put it out of her mind. Nathaniel had made it quite clear that he didn't think of her in that way, anyway – as a woman. It made no difference if she no longer looked like one. They sat in silence for a while, as the Bedouin swapped news and stories with the men from Buraimi.

'We were five when we set out. Raiders killed one man, and stole half of our water skins. We lost another in the dunes. Those infernal dunes! No man could cross them! But . . . you have, of course. You have, haven't you, Maude?' said Nathaniel hopelessly.

'Yes,' she said, with a spark of pride. 'Yes, I have. But it was dashed hard; one of the hardest things I have ever done, but Sayyid led us safely through them. We lost one camel, that was all.' Nathaniel nodded slowly, staring into the fire.

Then, because she didn't want him to think her own journey had been without mishap, Maude told Nathaniel how she'd lost Haroun; about the sicknesses she had endured, and Majid's death at the hands of the raiders. She told him about the man she had pounced on, and how he had died. 'Khalid mentioned a pool at this well we're going to. It sounds like a substantial oasis,' she said, after a pause.

'A pool? So close at hand?'

'Yes; and I do hope it's true. I long to wash . . . I do so *long* to wash. I have that man's blood on me, still.' She shuddered. Nathaniel looked at her wonderingly.

'You are incredible, Maude. I mean, I knew you were

already, I just didn't realise . . . to what extent. Few men could have done what you have. Few men, and no women.'

'Few men? As I understand it none have, as yet. None from Europe, in any case.'

'Yes. You're the first.' He sounded despairing again, so Maude smiled.

'I have to get to Muscat yet. I've come a long way but . . . it doesn't do to count one's chickens.'

'But you've done the hardest part. You are a wonder, Maude Villette Vickery. A wonder.' He raised his coffee cup to her. 'What is it your men keep calling you?'

'Shahin,' she told him awkwardly. 'It means falcon. Peregrine, to be exact. Because of the way I jumped on that fellow, you see.'

Nathaniel nodded and, for the first time, he smiled. 'It suits you perfectly, Maude.'

That night Maude was awake for a long time. She lay a discreet distance from Nathaniel, on her back, staring up into the stars. Her face was cold, damp with the dew. She thought, and thought, and realised she had never been happier in her whole life than she was just then, with the movement of Nathaniel's chest in the corner of her eye, rising and falling as he breathed. She felt the heat leech steadily from the embers of the fire, and slept with the faint tang of smoke on every breath.

By morning, the three rescued men were stronger, and they set off at dawn, sharing out the extra load between the southern camels, since it was touch and go whether Nathaniel's Batinah camels would make it as far as the well. It was a long day's ride; Maude watched Nathaniel as surreptitiously as she could, but he stayed on his camel, and only once swayed as though he might faint. Sayyid nodded in satisfaction as they came over a low dune, late in the day, and saw a smear of green on the horizon.

'Another hour should see us there,' said Maude encouragingly. Nathaniel nodded, his eyes fixed on that dream of water, coming ever closer.

'Looks like you might get your bath, Maude,' he said. The Bedouin had been unusually quiet that day; nobody had sung or argued much, or spun any tall stories. But then a breeze wafted over them, light and playful, and it carried the unmistakable scent of green, living things. They all tasted it, just for a single breath, and Fatih laughed, and started to sing a long, winding song that accompanied them all the way to the well.

Maude got her bath. The oasis was no paradise, but after the relentless aridity of the desert it seemed nothing short of miraculous. Water swelled from the ground into a shallow green pool about thirty feet across, flowed out through a narrow channel and then vanished into a patch of cracked mud. There were date palms around it in a ring, and smaller acacia trees and devil's thorn bushes further back. The camels drank noisily and then disappeared into this sudden feast of hard, prickly foliage, to graze with silent intensity. Khalid drank a little then began to fill all the water skins; Ubaid, Fatih and Kamal flicked water at each other, and splashed their bare feet through the shallows. Maude, fully clothed, submerged herself. She felt the tepid water close over her face; it rustled and tickled in her ears. She lay below the surface for as long as she could hold her breath, suspended in oblivion, trying to remember when she had last swum. Water had become so scarce and strange an element, it had slipped almost entirely out of mind.

She scrubbed the sand and blood from her hair, skin and clothes as best she could, then climbed out smiling, her stomach swollen with water, and told the men about the sea off the southern coast of England, and about the River Thames, and Welsh waterfalls and the Lake District, and the rain that fell and fell, all year round. They listened and laughed, and she could tell they didn't believe her. The men from Buraimi seemed well recovered from their hardship, their near disaster. Nathaniel drank a great deal and then slept for several hours before Maude woke him with dinner. An extended Bedouin family were camped at one end of the oasis – several generations of veiled women and children, and a toothless old man, living beneath blankets and skins tented between the acacia trees. Sayyid and Khalid sat and spoke to them for a long time, and they took some of Maude's silver Maria Teresa dollars in return for flour, salt, and milk from their goat.

Nathaniel ate well; his return to full strength would take a little longer, but already his eyes were brighter and his movements more sure. He questioned Maude about her route, and her planning, and how she had come as far as she had with only the food they'd carried from Salalah. Maude showed him her map and journal, and told him about the oryx and gazelle they'd seen, the hares they'd occasionally shot or snared, the camel they'd slaughtered. She quizzed him in return about his route, and how he'd planned to reach Salalah. He had begun a map of his own, but it was wayward and stopped far short of where they'd finally collapsed, as thirst, hunger and panic had confused him. He shook his head as he reviewed it.

'Pathetic. We were hopelessly lost, you see – we'd been chasing our tails for days.' He sighed. 'Terrifying, how quickly it can all go to pot. One mishap . . . one bad decision, one raid, and that's it. We deserve to be dead. We were meant to die here.'

'I don't think that can be so,' said Maude.

'Why ever not?'

'I don't know I . . . I'm not particularly devout, as you know, and perhaps our God simply hasn't made it out here. The Bedouin talk of djinn, and spirits; they believe in them every bit as much as they believe in God. And we each have a qareen, they say; a djinni who goes everywhere with us, from birth. Khalid would say that your qareen came to find mine, and they conspired to lead me to you. I'm not saying I believe it, but . . . I suppose I am saying that the very unlikelihood of us finding you would indicate to me that you *weren't* meant to die here. Quite the opposite. Do you see?'

'Oh, Maude,' he said, wrapping his arms around his knees and resting his chin on them, just as he'd done as a boy. The posture caused Maude a stab of unbearable love. 'Perhaps you *did* know I was near. You're remarkable in so many ways; why not in that way too?' Maude said nothing, looking away bashfully. She thought then that perhaps it was love that had led her to him, but she didn't dare say so.

They stayed for two whole days and three nights. The camels revived themselves with the grazing and the water and the rest; another Bedouin family arrived with a small herd of goats. They were willing to sell one, and Ubaid roasted it on a spit over the fire. The smell of it cooking held Maude and Nathaniel in thrall. They talked of home, and of family; Nathaniel talked about Faye, and the children she'd miscarried during their short marriage. His eyes filled with tears as he spoke, but he was calm; sad, but not still grieving. Maude noticed this, and tried not to hope. It was difficult, though; they were both still young, and now both single again. She reminded herself of the circumstances, and of her appearance, and resolutely quashed any such thoughts. Sayyid portioned out the goat meat, and they each took their turn to claim a portion – the smallest, as custom dictated. They ate in silence, with grease on their chins and the fire hot on their faces. Afterwards, Maude and Nathaniel walked a little way apart, to the water's edge, and sat with their backs against the ridged trunk of a date palm.

'Are you ever tempted to grab out of turn, and for the biggest portion, just to see what they'd say?' Nathaniel asked, smiling.

'Yes. Every single time,' said Maude, and they laughed.

The night was deeply black, and stars glimmered on the surface of the pool; in their borrowed light Maude could just make out Nathaniel's outline by her side. He smelled of the green water they'd washed in, heavy with minerals. It had made their hair dry stiff. Maude had tied hers back into a snarl at the nape of her neck; Nathaniel's stood up from his head in wild tufts. Still laughing, Maude attempted to pat it down.

'You do look a yahoo, old thing,' she said.

'And you look like you truly belong here, Mo.' She could hear the smile in his words. She stopped patting his hair and let her hand slide down, resting on his cheek for a moment. The silence between them changed shape, and grew deeper, stranger, and she dropped her hand, embarrassed. They didn't speak for a long time; she couldn't guess his thoughts. She hoped this unwanted reminder of her feelings would be allowed to pass. 'Perhaps you do,' he said in the end. 'Belong here, I mean. I can't imagine you returning to a life of respectable dinners and drawing rooms.'

'Well, I suppose I must, at some point; to see Father if nothing else. But, no; a life like that doesn't interest me in the slightest.'

'You always did say so, and you've stuck true to your word, Maude. So few people do. Most people let the world shape their lives, but you've shaped your own.'

'So have you. You could have stayed in England and got any

old dull job – like John and Frank. But you wanted to explore, and so you have. You wanted to wed, and you did...'

She trailed off, wishing she hadn't mentioned it.

'Yes. And again, you always said you wouldn't wed and let yourself be tied down by a family, and you haven't. You're remarkable, Maude. You're so strong, and so sure.'

Maude felt a little breathless. She couldn't believe she would really say what she was about to say, and half expected the words to refuse to come out. But something about the darkness and the wildness and the distant stars told her that this was the last time, the absolute last time she might try.

'There... there is one man I would marry,' she said quietly, and then couldn't breathe. Nathaniel reached for her hand in the darkness, squeezing it when he found it.

'Yes. I had... I had wondered if that was still the case. But you do love me, don't you Maude?'

'I always have,' she managed to say.

'I think you love me better than any person alive, in fact.'

'Yes.'

'And why shouldn't we marry? What couple could know each other better? I know there isn't a woman anywhere in the world braver, cleverer, or more decent than you, Maude.' He squeezed her hand so tightly it almost hurt, and she welcomed the discomfort. 'I owe you my life, so really I ought to give it to you. My life, I mean.' He turned towards her, but their features were hidden in the darkness. Maude wanted to speak but found she couldn't. Like Nathaniel before they'd rescued him, she thought she was dreaming her salvation – she thought she was hallucinating.

'Well, what do you say, Maude? Don't keep a chap waiting. Won't you marry me?'

He took her hand to his lips, kissed it soundly.

'Of course I will.' Astonishment rocked her, making the words wobble.

Maude scrambled to her knees, reaching for him, finding his mouth to kiss. Their travel-wrought bodies were hard, pressed against each other. Nathaniel wrapped his long hands around Maude's waist and his fingertips touched together.

'You're like a little bird, Mo,' he whispered wonderingly. 'How can a body so small be so strong?' He kissed her with a steady conviction, and laid her down, and Maude gave herself up to him completely, stormed by his touch and the taste of him; the feel of him, warm against her skin, knotted together with her. She didn't believe it was actually happening; as they made love she decided that if it was a dream it was a delicious one, and she didn't want to wake from it. She didn't care a jot for decency, for convention or waiting for marriage. She'd been his for so many years that their union seemed long overdue, and right – utterly right. She ran the tip of her tongue over his broken front tooth, felt the sting of it and tasted blood; his whiskers were rough on her fragile lips, and seem to burn; there was a stab and a strange ache as he lowered himself between her legs. She welcomed every sensation.

Maude woke at dawn, wrapped in a blanket by the water's edge. Nathaniel was nowhere around her; she sat up, wincing at the stiffness in her spine. For a second everything was as it had always been, and then she remembered, and was filled with fear and tentative joy. She looked around with the sinking feeling that she had dreamed it all, in spite of her sore mouth and the smell of him on her skin. Then she saw him, coming over from one of the Bedouin camps. He smiled when he saw she was awake, and dropped to his knees beside her.

'I hope you don't mind, but you've advanced me a small

loan. I took a dollar from your bag. It was an awful thing to do, but my motives were good.' He took her hand.

'Of course. Whatever you need,' said Maude. She blushed to see him, though he seemed at ease. She wondered if he realised that last night had been her first time with any man.

'It wouldn't do, I thought, for an engaged woman to go about with no ring. So here – it's not quite a diamond, but it'll have to do for now.' He slid a heavy pewter ring onto her finger. It was simply made, the kind of jewellery the Bedouin women wore; with a twisted band and a rough square chunk of blue lapis in a solid setting.

'It's perfect,' she said.

'I'll pay you back the dollar as soon as we reach civilisation.' Nathaniel stood, and pulled her up behind him. 'Come on. Come and have some coffee.'

Maude told a white lie to Khalid and the others – that in England a betrothal was as good as a wedding. That way, they caused less scandal when they touched, and when they smiled at one another. She wasn't sure that Khalid believed her entirely; he watched Nathaniel neutrally – not hostile but not entirely friendly either. Maude puzzled it over for a while, and wondered if Khalid had come to think of her as family, and in need of protection. She loved the idea. Fatih and Ubaid grinned, clapped Nathaniel on the shoulder, and sang a song for a bridegroom as they set off with the first glimpse of the sun. Maude looked back at the oasis from time to time as they left it behind; she was loath to leave it. It was a safe place, and a place she wanted to remember for ever. All too soon it was a blur on the horizon; a shimmer that could have been make-believe. The camels moved with long, rhythmic strides; they rode in single file, and Maude's jubilation soon settled back into the seriousness of travel, into the need for endurance. But she looked down at her left hand regularly, where she felt the unfamiliar heft of the lapis ring, and smiled every time she did. Once Nathaniel turned and caught her doing it. He'd wound a kaffia around his head and draped it over the bridge of his nose to keep the sun off his damaged skin, but she thought she could see him smiling, in his eyes.

They spoke little during the day. Maude had always known they would travel well together. Nathaniel expected no favours to be done for him; expected no special treatment for being British. At night they sat close together, not touching, and didn't make love again. Without the trees and the pool and the other Bedouin to hide them, they agreed it would be impossible without causing offence. They made plans – where they might wed, and when, and where they would travel to afterwards.

'You needn't work another day, if you don't want,' Maude pointed out, when Nathaniel wondered out loud where his job would send him next. He stopped, thinking for a moment.

'I'd quite forgotten that,' he said, with a slight smile. 'How clever I've been, to pick such a wealthy bride.'

'You might have picked her long ago, if only you'd had a mind to.'

'Some things must be arrived at in their own due course, though; mustn't they?'

'Yes. Yes, I suppose that's true.' She took his hand and was happy, and forgot that she was plain, weathered and filthy.

They were three days out from the well when Maude looked across the cook fire and saw Nathaniel staring through it, lost in thought. His face was heavy, careworn, almost desolate. He squinted into the restless breeze, against the grains of sand it flung at him; he looked far away, lost to her. She waited until they'd finished eating to ask him what was wrong.

'It's nothing, really. No more than I deserve,' he said sourly.

'Tell me, please – what is it?'

'I'm just . . . I'm so angry with myself. And I shall be a laughing stock when we get to Muscat. Do you see? I haven't your reputation as a scholar, Maude, but I was starting to make a name for myself as a traveller. And here I am, on my first real attempt to cross the desert, and I'd be dead if I hadn't been rescued by a w—'

'By a woman?' said Maude, wincing at the remark.

'No ordinary woman, by any stretch; but . . .' He shook his head wretchedly. 'But still a woman.'

'By your fiancée, in fact. Who better to save you?' she said staunchly, in a tone she hoped was cheering. But Nathaniel didn't smile. 'Nathan . . . we will have so many other journeys. *You* will – I needn't always go along with you, if that's not what you want. I do . . . I do understand the need to be alone, and to make one's own way. I do understand about that. And besides, nobody need know what's happened this time.' She thought about it for a moment. 'We'll just say we met up in Muscat. You were only supposed to be looking for locusts, after all,' she said, but Nathaniel shook his head.

'I wrote to the Royal Geographical Society, and to the *Fortnightly Review*, and a couple of other magazines. I told them I was crossing the Empty Quarter.' He smiled nastily. 'I thought if I did that, I'd *have* to make it, you see. I wouldn't be able to let myself fail.'

'Oh, *Nathan*!' Maude took his arm; held it tightly. 'But it doesn't *matter*! It really doesn't. You'll do it another time, in another way.'

'That's easy for you to say – you've already done it, haven't you? The great Maude Vickery triumphs again – or the great Shahin, I ought rather say.'

Maude recoiled, stung, and let go of his arm.

Nathan shook his head again. 'I'm sorry! Forgive me,

Maude. It's myself I'm angry with, not you. It's myself I can't stand.'

'Isn't it about being here, Nathan? Isn't it about the wonder of this place . . . the wildness of it? Coming here and . . . knowing yourself? Must it only ever be about being first?'

'It's about being where no one has been before. You know that — you can't deny it.'

'That's a part of it. I know that's part of it — must it be the whole of it?'

'I'd just thought . . . I thought my moment had come. That's all, Maude. Instead, this has been the biggest disaster of my life. Well. I must face the consequences of that; and if I am derided then I deserve to be.' They sat in silence for a long time, with the desert wind pulling at the fire with a tearing sound. Maude stared at Nathaniel's face in profile, lit by the flames. He seemed very far away from her, and she couldn't bear it. She thought of all the times when they were growing up that her brothers had schemed and pulled rank, and pushed Maude and Nathaniel into third and fourth place; she thought of the struggle Nathaniel had had to pick himself back up after every visit to his mother; of the years of work he'd been patient through after university, always just waiting for the chance to travel when Maude had already started, with the Vickery money, and never stopped. She thought back to her mother's decline, and the torture of having to wait even that short while, tethered to her. She thought of all the many, many times she'd wished Nathaniel was by her side, to share everything with her.

'We'll share it, Nathan,' she said, at last.

Nathaniel glanced at her without comprehension. She couldn't stand the look of defeat on his face.

'Share what, Mo?'

'This.' She waved a hand at the jewelled sky and the endless dark all around. 'When we get to Muscat, we'll say we made the journey across together. Who's to contradict us?'

'Well, the Bedouin may,' he said, frowning.

'Nonsense. Nobody will ask them, and, anyway, they'd agree with whatever they were asked to, for the right number of rifles and coins. I love them dearly, but only a fool would claim that they cannot be bought.' She paused. The more she thought about it, the easier and simpler it seemed. 'You can tell the journals that you changed your plans; that we communicated beforehand, and you sailed south to cross northwards with me, instead. Did you meet with anyone official in the north before you set off? Anybody who could spoil things?'

'No.' He thought about it. 'No; only local officials with no English, and no interest in me once they'd seen my papers.'

'Well then. It's ours for the creating, this little fiction.'

'I don't like it, Maude.'

'I know. But do you like the alternative any better? You'll come back, and you'll make the crossing another way – a different way; a way nobody has taken before. You'll do it, Nathan; I know you will. All this does is buy time, save face, and keep your spirits up.' She could see he wasn't quite convinced, though he wanted to be.

'Besides,' she began again, more softly. She took his arm again, made him look at her. 'Besides, Nathan; you *were* with me. I thought about you every step of the way. I . . . I might have given up without the thought of you to keep me going. So, you see, you were there. You *did* cross the desert with me.'

Nathaniel laid his hand over hers on his arm, and gripped it hard. Some vast emotion ruined his face for a moment, and brought tears to his eyes.

'You amaze me, Maude,' he whispered tightly. 'You are so much better than I am. I don't think there was ever a more generous spirit.'

'There's *nothing* I have that I would not share with you, Nathan,' she said, meaning every word. He moved towards her, resting his forehead against hers, and Maude smiled. Her heart squeezed itself tight in her chest; the air in her lungs seemed to swell. His happiness, she realised then, was of far greater importance than her own.

That night, the wind dropped and it wasn't too cold – the temperature rose with each day nearer to summer that passed. The only sounds were Sayyid's soft snoring, and the occasional sighing of the camels, and Maude slept deeply. She felt so peaceful that she didn't dream, and woke up refreshed, with the feeling that they were on the homeward stretch. It was a bittersweet thought – she wanted to finish the journey and never finish it, to go home and never go home. But she had Nathaniel by her side now. When she went home to see her father, it would be with a fiancé on her arm that she knew he would approve of, once he'd got over the surprise of it. Nathaniel was still subdued and thoughtful as they set off, but his spirits seemed to improve as they went. Maude rode towards the rear of the string and saw him chatting awkwardly to Sayyid and Ubaid during the day – there were a lot of smiles and hand gestures and nods, and Maude guessed that Arabic still didn't come altogether fluently to him. She was pleased to see him trying to get to know the men, though; to see him animated again.

They made good progress, and camped at the end of the day in a wide hollow surrounded by rocky outcrops, scattered with boulders and stunted trees. They were coming out of the sand sea at last, and onto harder ground, ground which would lead them to the foothills of the high mountains, and beyond them, Muscat. 'What's the name of this place,

Sayyid?' Maude asked, with her pencil in her hand and her map on her knees.

'That mountain on the horizon is Jebel Fahud, Shahin,' the old man told her. 'We will have no more dunes to climb. Only rocks.' They ate the last of the dried camel meat for dinner, with the standard sandy flatbreads, and Maude and Nathaniel indulged themselves with dreams of the food they would eat once they were back in England.

'Roast chicken,' said Nathaniel. 'Juicy, white meat with crisp, golden skin; potatoes dauphinoise, and gravy with a little Madeira wine in it.'

'I long for pea soup. Of all the things I could have in all the world – fresh pea soup with mint, made only an hour after everything's been picked from the garden. That *greenness* – can you imagine it? I can't remember the taste, exactly, but I *yearn* for it.'

'Those devilled kidneys we ate in Oxford before your viva exam. That peppery cream sauce, and the fresh parsley – do you remember?' They stopped when their stomach began to cramp with hunger.

Maude woke at dawn and thought at first that everything was fine. Then she felt a light movement on her chest and lifted her head to look. There was a camel spider sitting on her ribcage. It had turned towards the movement of her head and was watching her, eye to eye. A low, strangled groan of horror was the only sound she could make. The spider was huge, pale and bristled. Its clustered black eyes were wholly empty. Despite always checking her boots and her bedding, Maude hadn't encountered one before. Now she couldn't move. She wondered how long it had been there; wondered if it had eaten a hole into her with its monstrous jaws that she couldn't yet feel. Her skin shuddered in abject, helpless revulsion. It seemed a terrible omen of some kind, to awake face to face with such a soulless thing.

'Nathan!' she managed to call out, in a strangled whisper. She'd gone to sleep not five feet from him, but now she couldn't sense him nearby; she assumed he'd got up already, perhaps gone hunting or to see to his camel. She lay, immobilised, until she realised that everything was far too quiet, the campsite far too empty. Minutes ticked past and a terrible fear began to grow in her – that all was not well. Something was very wrong. There was too much space around her, and too few sounds. She couldn't take her eyes off the spider, and it was a long time before she could make her muscles obey her. They, with a cry, she rolled violently to one side, throwing the creature off, and scrambled to her feet, clawing frantically at her clothing in case she was bitten, in case there were more.

When she could stop, and look around, she didn't believe what she saw. Khalid and Fatih lay at opposite ends of the campsite, and neither one was awake. All but three camels were gone – only the weaker three from the Batinah remained, hobbled. Nathaniel and the other men, the camels and the gear were nowhere in sight. There were some strange, pale shapes on the ground to one side. Maude went over to investigate and couldn't fathom it – the shapes were water skins, one bulging and three that had been emptied out – the ground around them was still damp. Bewildered, frightened, she went over to Khalid. He was lying down as though still asleep, with a bruise spreading across his left eyebrow. *Raiders*, Maude thought, at a loss as to how she could have slept through it. She fell to her knees and shook him urgently till he woke, wincing, groggy.

'Khalid, forgive me. You *must* wake up!' she said.

'What has happened?' He ran his fingers over his brow, flinching.

'I don't know. I don't know,' Maude couldn't get the air

to stay in her lungs. 'It must have been raiders. But I don't understand . . . I don't understand.'

They went together to rouse Fatih, who had also been battered. Maude climbed the nearest rocks and searched the horizon, but there was no sign of the other Bedouin, or of Nathaniel and their camels. She was gripped by a wild, lurching fear for him; for all of them. She shook from head to foot. 'I don't understand,' she said again, when she came back down. Khalid's expression was bleak; Fatih was searching the ground to the east of the camp.

'They have left us enough water to go back to the well. Four days' ride. They have left us enough to get there, and fill the other skins before continuing. They have left us enough food to get there, if we are careful; but no more,' said Khalid, his voice tight with anger.

'What are you talking about?' said Maude. 'Who has left us? We can't go back to the well! Where are the others?'

'God curse them! They left in the dark of the night, like the thieves that they are! They have poured water into the sand! It is forbidden!' said Fatih, back from his search. 'God blacken their faces! If I ever see old Sayyid again, I will slit his throat!'

'Sayyid would not have gone willingly. They must have forced him,' said Khalid.

'What's happening?' said Maude breathlessly, but a terrible dawning was creeping through her. All of the men's possessions had gone with them; the patch of sand where Nathaniel had bedded down was empty, flattened and scuffed by his blanket.

'See the tracks. They carried everything to the far side of these rocks. They led the camels and then loaded them there, so we wouldn't hear them. They crept like devils! They vanished like devils!' Fatih was so outraged he could hardly articulate; spit flew from his lips. Khalid stood rigid and stared into the east with a hungry look.

'We will have to go back to the well. I do not know where we will next find water; only Sayyid knows. We cannot go after them, simply hoping; it's difficult to track on this hard ground. Sayyid knew this. They gave us enough water to go back to the well and fill the other skins because they knew we would have no choice but to do so,' he said quietly.

'But why? Why?' said Maude desperately. Khalid gave her a hard look.

'That man has betrayed you, Shahin,' he said. 'I saw a great hunger in him that I did not understand. Now, too late, I understand it.'

'No! No, you're wrong. Raiders must have come . . . they've been driven off, somehow!' Khalid stared at her, and said nothing, and his implacability made Maude see the truth. She ran to her own bag of possessions, and saw that it was open. Scrabbling inside it, she found that her map, compass and journal had gone. Then she curled forwards, unable to breathe for a while. Her head pounded with blood.

Finally, when she could get up, Maude set about searching for Nathaniel. Stupidly, pointlessly; hanging onto a hope that was just a mirage. After a while, when she accepted that he'd gone, and realised what he'd done, she suffered a seizure of sorts. She stopped calling his name, stopped looking – all that frantic optimism, as though he might only be hiding from her. She collapsed to the ground and didn't notice the stones digging in, or the dust getting into her hair.

Muscat, December 1958

For twenty-four hours, Joan could only wait. Colonel Singer had Robert put her under something like house arrest at the Residency, though she overheard Robert insisting to Singer that he was convinced Joan had been a pawn in it all, knew nothing useful and hadn't wilfully got involved in Maude's scheme; this after a conversation with Joan in which she'd sworn to all of that.

'Never mind – that young lady has had more than enough adventure for the time being. Keep her here, and keep a close eye on her, Mr Gibson,' the colonel had said severely. Joan thought of the bewildered, rain-soaked moment beside the wadi in which she could have told Charlie about Salim and hadn't, and knew she was at least partly a liar. She blamed herself, and though there was much Salim had not told her, he personally had not endangered her. She didn't see how enraging the colonel any further by mentioning her acquaintance with him would help. She continued to eavesdrop, and heard that an attempt to rescue the hostages had been made, and had been an abject failure. There'd been no sign of them, and the ravine had been closed off by snipers. The army felt they had little option but to comply with Maude's demands, or risk the embarrassment of losing an entire section of highly trained men.

'So, you're officially forbidden to wander,' said Rory, coming to find her on the terrace. He stood above her chair, eyes hidden behind sunglasses, not quite smiling. 'I wonder if that will stop you? After all, it was forbidden the first time.'

His tone had a kind of studied lightness that she took to be an olive branch.

'It'll stop me,' she said. 'Besides, I've nowhere I need to go right now. Won't you sit down, Rory? There's something I'd like to ask you.'

Rory drew a chair around to face her and sat down. He was wearing a freshly pressed shirt; he'd shaved, and when he took off his sunglasses it looked as though he'd slept well – his eyes were far less pink and puffy. The sky was flat white, a ceiling of solid high cloud; the air was soft and mild.

'I still don't quite know why you needed to go,' he said.

'You mean how I found out about you and Dan?' she asked, and saw him flinch. 'I saw you, in his tent when we went for dinner that time. I saw you . . . kissing.' Rory looked away, staring into the featureless rocks behind her as if he wished he could disappear into them. The air seemed to leave his chest, and all the righteousness went with it. He deflated, his face crumpling.

'I . . . I wouldn't have wanted you to find out that way,' he said.

'I gather you wouldn't have wanted me to find out at all. Otherwise you might have told me, at any point in the past five years.'

'You must . . . you must hate us. And me especially, I suppose.' He sounded abject. Joan paused, letting him suffer for a little while longer.

'It was . . . an adjustment. But I'd far rather know. I'm better off knowing. And there's no point wishing things were different than they are, is there?'

'I've wished it, sometimes,' Rory said quietly. He shook his head. 'But no. It does no good.' He held tight to the arms of his chair, just as Maude sometimes did. Joan looked at the familiar shape of his hands and remembered how safe holding them had always made her feel. She felt the same sadness she'd felt before, like when he'd hugged her as she got off the plane; the same stinging feeling of being cut adrift. Rory took a deep breath. 'I . . . I don't know what life will look like, once we're home,' he said. Joan nodded, and saw how frightened he was.

'I'm not going to tell everyone, if that's what you think. And I don't know what life will be like either, other than different. For me it will be, anyway. I think perhaps we oughtn't to see each other for a while. It might make it easier. You know – rip the—'

'Rip the plaster off quickly? I hardly think it's the same thing.'

Joan waited for a minute, until Rory's hands unclenched and he relaxed back in his chair.

'I imagine Dan tells you everything,' she said. Rory shrugged. 'The fight he had with Mum before he left home last time, after Dad died . . . was it about . . . this? Was it about you and him?'

'Not exactly. Not me, specifically.'

'But the fact that Dan . . .' Joan realised that she didn't know what word to use – what was right, and not derogatory. 'The fact that Dan's queer?' she tried, in a rush. 'Did he tell her, I mean?' Rory looked at her with an unfamiliar expression, one she hadn't seen before.

But he nodded, so Joan took a breath and pushed on. 'Rory . . . was my dad the same way?' She could feel her pulse in her throat, a rapid flutter. She had no idea why the answer was so important. Rory nodded again. 'Did Mum know?' she asked. She wanted to know it all, and quickly. She wanted to rip the plaster off.

'Yes – well, he said it was never spoken about, but he believed she knew. Your father believed she knew.' Rory looked at her intently. 'Does it matter? Would you have loved him any less if you'd known? Do you love him any less now?'

'Of course not! It's only a . . . a very strange feeling, real-ising that you never knew something so important about a person you adored . . . It's strange that I never realised. And the same goes for Dan. The most important people in my life, and I never realised. I feel stupid – blind.' She thought for a moment. 'Was that why Dad was disinherited by his family?'

'I don't know, Joan.'

'I wonder if Dad married Mum because he was afraid of doing something illegal . . .'

'Being . . . like us isn't illegal,' said Rory. 'And it's as old as the hills.'

'Making love to another man is, though.'

'You think I don't know that? Why do you think we have to hide, and lie, and—'

'Marry unsuspecting women?' At this, Rory frowned unhappily, and looked away.

'Wasn't your dad a good husband? Couldn't I have been?' he asked softly.

'He was a wonderful father. The best. But I've no idea whether he was a good husband or not.'

'Your mum told Dan he was no longer her son. She said he was dead to her. It was brutal. I think he thought . . . I think he thought that because she'd known about your dad, she'd understand. But she didn't.'

'Poor Dan,' said Joan. 'I wish . . . Most of all, I wish he'd told me. I wish he'd told me a long time ago.'

The feeling of waiting got stronger as the day drew to a close. Joan stayed out on the terrace with her patience fraying, watching the light fail. She wrote a letter to Daniel, and then one to her mother that she had no intention of posting – she'd have beaten it home if she had. She just wanted to get her thoughts straight. When her hand began to cramp and her eyes were straining to see the paper she stopped, looking down at the tan leather sandals that had seemed so gauche when she'd arrived in Muscat. Now they were scuffed and ruined; they had carried her up the mountain, and into Jalali; down the drenched ravine to her brother, and back to Muscat again. It seemed a long time since she'd come racing down the wadi, and sent Charlie Elliot ahead to rescue Daniel. And all that time, Charlie had been on top of the mountain with Salim and the others. Was he frightened? He had to be, he wasn't stupid; but she struggled to imagine it. Or at least, to imagine him letting on. *Dear Charlie*, she started another letter she would never send. *I hate that you're in danger. I never meant harm to come to you, or to anyone. I tried to do what was best, but perhaps I have no idea about what's best and should keep out of it all.* She thought of Charlie's laughter when she'd taken off the mask and veil on the mountain that day; thought of the way his first impulse was always to smile at life. *Your father is on his way. You'll be down soon, and safe,* she wrote, pausing for a moment. *I keep thinking of the time you kissed me – I remember it very clearly. I think, perhaps, that it was my first real kiss, and I'm glad it was from you.* She stopped writing and tore the sheet from the pad, screwing it up tightly in her fist.

Joan was awake the instant she heard Robert's knock on her door, early in the morning. It was Christmas Eve. She thought briefly of her mother, and of home; of Daniel as a boy, lying on his front, staring into the nativity scene underneath the tree; but it all seemed too far away and out of her reach. She snatched the door open, not caring if Robert saw her in her pyjamas. His face was grave; he was dressed and freshly shaven.

'What's happened? Is there news?'

'Nathaniel Elliot's plane just landed at Bait al Falaj. He's on his way to Maude Vickery's house now. She's asked for you and me to go along. She wants witnesses, she says. To what, exactly, we still have no idea, but we're to do as she asks.'

'I think I have an idea. Let me dress,' said Joan, shutting the door again. She pulled on the same wrinkled slacks and blouse she'd worn the day before, ran her fingers through her kinked hair and splashed some water on her face. She caught sight of herself in the mirror – thinner, browner, older than when she'd arrived. She'd never dreamed she'd meet Nathaniel Elliot; she could never have imagined the circumstances in which it was about to happen. She had a tumult of nerves in her gut, and as she went out to meet Robert for the short drive through Muscat, she made a silent, fervent wish for things to end well, though she didn't see how they possibly could. Not for everybody.

They reached Maude's house before Nathaniel Elliot, and Abdullah admitted them in silence. The old man's face was troubled – Joan knew him well enough by then to see it. He wasn't Salim's biological father, but he had raised him as his son. Joan took his hand as she passed, and gripped it hard, and Abdullah gave her a single nod before they carried on up the stairs. Maude had positioned her chair in front of her desk, and looked smart. All of her clothing was dated and worn, but it was clean; a blouse with a lace collar tucked neatly into a long felt skirt; a small green metal brooch pinned to one side of her chest. Her hair was combed back into a perfect bun at the nape of her neck. Her eyes were clear and sharp; if she'd lost any sleep in anticipation of this meeting, it didn't show. The only thing that betrayed any tension was her very stillness, her composure, which looked carefully constructed and held with an iron will. Her hands were crossed in her lap, and the ring with the blue stone, which had always been on her desk, was now on her ring finger. Joan noticed that the thumb of her left hand returned to it repeatedly, to fiddle with the unfamiliar object, and she finally had an idea what the ring might mean.

Maude cleared her throat when she saw them.

'Good. Come and sit down. I want as many people as possible to hear what's about to be said here,' she said. Her voice was hard, steady. Joan watched her closely, thinking of her involuntary reaction to Charlie Elliot and wondering what would happen when his father walked in.

'Tell me again how long it's been? Since you saw him, I mean,' she asked.

'Forty-nine years, eight months and twenty-one days,' said Maude. She glanced over her shoulder at the carriage clock on her desk, and for the first time, her composure fractured a little. A look of anguish passed over her face, quick as a shadow, and then vanished.

'You don't have to go through with this, you know,' Joan said carefully. 'Whatever you have planned . . . you could send word now that the men should be released, and that'd be the end of it.'

'Oh, do be quiet, Joan,' said Maude absently. 'I've waited a very long time for this moment.' Robert patted Joan's hand, as if to console her after this slight; she took hold of his hand and kept it. He was quiet, and Joan could sense his confusion, and how out of his depth he felt; the situation was unique and deeply unsettling. Then came the sound of a car's engine outside and, without thinking, they both stood up, turning anxiously towards the door.

Nathaniel Elliot made slow but steady progress on the stairs.

'Up here?' they heard him say, in a voice that was firm but thinned by age, and Joan sensed Maude stiffen in her chair. Her own pulse was speeding; she felt electrified, she could hardly sit still. Nathaniel came in ahead of Singer and Burke-Bromley, with a walking cane in his right hand on which he rested heavily; Joan recognised him at once from the photo Charlie had shown her. Beside her, she sensed Maude stop breathing. Nathaniel's height was disguised by the stoop in his shoulders and spine; his leanness had become the bony fragility of old age. The hand not holding his cane had a visible tremor; gnarled fingers, mottled skin.

He crossed to stand in front of Maude, and for a long time the two of them stared at each other in silence. The quiet was loaded, the moment obviously so significant, so long in coming, that even Colonel Singer, who was clearly tense and impatient, didn't dare interrupt it. Maude's ribs rose and fell quickly, shallowly, but she didn't blink, and Joan could not guess at her feelings. Finally, Nathaniel cleared his throat slightly. 'Hello, Mo,' he said, in a voice that shook.

'Nathan,' said Maude. 'It's been a while.'

The silence returned and Nathaniel seemed to wilt beneath the weight of it. He swayed on his feet, his cane swivelling against the floor, so Joan went and took his arm.

'Come and sit down, Mr Elliot,' she said. Nathaniel nodded and let her help him to the sofa, where he sat down stiffly. Maude didn't break off her gaze for a second; her eyes were wide and bright.

'You've got *old*, Nathan,' she said, sounding surprised.

'It happens; though you look just the same as you ever did, Maude. Apart from that, I suppose,' he said, indicating the wheelchair. 'Did you have an accident?'

'No. I just got old as well.' Joan studied Maude and tried to decipher her expression. It was odd, keen, almost desperate. It looked more like hunger than anything else. Nathaniel shrank from that gaze as if it repelled him.

'What's this all about, Maude?' he asked curtly.

'I want you to tell them.' Maude's stare hardened to stone, and even Joan was afraid of it.

'What difference can it—'

'What difference can it make? Perhaps none to you, other than to decide whether one of your sons lives or dies. But to me? A great deal. It will make a great deal of difference. I want you to say it in front of all these people, so it can't be refuted later, or taken back. I want you to say it, and I want them to tell the rest of the world.'

'The rest of the world?' he echoed. 'Maude . . . nobody *cares*. It's ancient history!'

'*I* care!' Maude's sudden shout shattered the fragile calm. For a while after it, her mouth worked on silently, as though she had words that were too huge to say. 'You . . . you took *everything* from me, Nathaniel.' The words came out on a shudder that went right through her, like a convulsion; it could have been a sob that she refused to allow.

Nathaniel nodded. He ran his tongue over his dry lips and swallowed laboriously.

'I know,' he whispered. 'I know I did.'

'So, tell them.' Maude gripped the arms of her chair, her hands like the talons of some little hawk. 'Tell them, or I'll make a fratricide of your son.'

'What? You'll do what?' He shook his head, confused, but Joan felt something slide into place.

'Salim is Mr Elliot's son, isn't he, Maude? He's Charlie's brother,' she said urgently.

'Yes. I had a son by you, Nathan. After you left me in the desert to die.'

'I didn't . . . No – that can't be so,' he said adamantly.

'Can't it?' Maude leaned forwards, pinning him. 'Look me in the eye and tell me it's not possible.' She was wrought with emotion. Nathaniel stayed silent; he looked down at the floor, curling into himself.

'Miss Vickery,' said Joan quietly, cautiously. 'Does Salim know it's his own brother he's holding hostage? Does he know?'

'Of course not,' the old woman snapped. 'I never told him about you, Nathaniel. I told him I had a husband who died. You are *nothing* to our son.'

'Oh, but you must tell him! It's wicked not to . . . wicked!' said Joan.

'You're here to watch and listen, and that's *all* you're here for, Joan,' Maude told her, still never taking her eyes off Nathaniel. Joan turned to Colonel Singer.

'Somebody has to tell him! Salim would never harm his own brother – I'm sure of it! You have to send a messenger up to him – I'll go myself! I could get up safely, I only need a veil. Please, you have to—'

'Enough, Joan! He doesn't need to know,' said Maude.

'I'd as soon walk up there dressed in my pyjamas as send you back up, Miss Seabrook,' said Colonel Singer indignantly. 'Nobody's going anywhere for the time being.'

'I have another son?' Nathaniel whispered brokenly. There were tears in his eyes, but the sight of them only made Maude harder.

'He'll soon be your only one, if you don't do as I say.'

'What do you want me to say?'

'The truth. I want you to tell the truth. I want you to tell them who the first person to cross the Rub el Khali was, in 1909.'

There was another long silence. Joan and Robert exchanged a look of mutual helplessness; Colonel Singer folded his arms, staring hard at Nathaniel Elliot. Burke-Bromley, Charlie's commander, betrayed his impatience with the scene by drumming his fingers against his forearms. Nathaniel Elliot cleared his throat again, and looked up. His cheeks were flushed, his eyes calm.

'Very well. It doesn't matter so very much, I suppose. Not compared to Charlie's safety. You were first, Maude. You made the crossing first. I . . . I cheated.' Maude shut her eyes, and squeezed them tightly. She drew in a long, slow breath.

'Don't you dare say it doesn't matter when you ruined my life, Nathaniel; when you let your lie stand for all these years – when you published my notes and map as your own. When you discredited me, and lied to me, and left me to die . . . don't you *dare* say it doesn't matter.'

'I didn't leave you to die! I was adamant about that – we left you the means to continue safely, once you'd been back to the well—'

'You took our guide and tracker with you. Sayyid. What if we hadn't found the well again? What then? Did you give it a thought?'

'Yes, I did. Of course I did!'

'And yet you did it anyway,' Maude said sadly. She swallowed, her eyes gleaming, then looked down and worked the blue ring off her finger. She tossed it over to him; it hit his leg, then landed on the floor by his feet. 'I release you from our engagement, Nathan,' she said softly. The old man stared at the ring as if she'd thrown a spider at him. He shook, and tears finally ran from his eyes. 'Now – talk. Carry on. Tell them everything.'

So Nathaniel Elliot spoke. He told them how one of his guides had come up with the idea while they were recovering at the well – a plan for Nathaniel to still be the first across the desert, to still claim that accolade, by stealing Maude's maps and getting the head start they needed; how Maude's Bedouin had been bought, one by one, and young Ubaid had warned them not to approach Khalid, who would be loyal to

Shahin until death, and his son Fatih by extension. How, once he was in Muscat, it was easy to send a telegram announcing his success, and easy thereafter to write about it with Maude's journal and map to help him. How nobody ever questioned him.

'I kept expecting you to come after me, Maude. I kept expecting you to stand up and denounce me. But you never did ... you never did.' He shook his head incredulously. 'It was a mad, desperate, vile thing to do, and I don't think I ever truly expected to get away with it. Why didn't you speak up, Maude?' he said, staring across at her. The past was like the shadow of something frightening, hovering behind him, making him cower.

'Was it so important, Nathan?' she asked, instead of answering him. 'Was it so important to save face, and to win, that you could throw me aside so easily? Me, who loved you better than anyone else ever could?'

'It ... it seemed it at the time,' he said sadly. 'Young men are foolish creatures, though they think they're wise. I should never have proposed to you, Maude. I wanted your love to be enough for both of us, but it wasn't. When you said you would share your victory with me, I knew it could never work. I ... I would not have done the same for you, Maude. I knew then that I was an unworthy creature, and I suppose I fell into a despair of some kind. It seemed more important than anything else that I should win.' He shook his head slightly, not wiping his wet face. 'Foolish,' he said again quietly. 'I should never have asked you to marry me.'

Joan saw Maude recoil from this remark; she saw how it hurt her, and that Maude was still in love with him after all the years that had passed. Joan could only guess at how angry that might make her, and how much pain he had caused her.

'I didn't speak out because I knew I wouldn't be believed.

I had a taste of it here in Muscat – a taste of how I would be received; a mere woman, half-mad from the desert, trying to claim a victory that wasn't hers. And then I realised I was . . . carrying your child, and still unwed. I couldn't go home . . .' She shook her head, breathing hard. 'I never saw my father again, you know. I didn't even go back for his funeral. Did you go?'

'Yes. Of course I did. And I . . . I named one of my sons Elias, in his memory.'

'That took some nerve, after what you'd done to me.' She looked up at him, her face weary now. 'And you never did pay me back the dollar for the ring.'

'Maude—' Nathaniel began to say, but she cut him off with a wave of her hand.

'Look at me, Nathaniel,' she said, and he did as he was told. 'You ruined everything for me. Do you understand? You took *everything*.'

'Yes. I understand.' He spoke in hollow tones, teetering on the edge of despair.

'I've written down the truth – I've written my journey down, as best I can remember it.' Maude pointed to the pile of papers on her desk, and looked around at her assembled witnesses. 'One of you can publish it for me. Perhaps you, Joan. You need a job, after all. Do you still have my original map, Nathan? My journal?'

'No. No, I burned them,' Nathaniel admitted. 'I couldn't risk anybody finding them. And I . . . I couldn't stand to see your writing, Maude. The guilt . . .'

'I do *not* want to hear how you've suffered!' Maude shouted again, smacking her hand down on the arm of her chair. 'But you *will* suffer! You'll suffer. As I did.'

'What do you mean?' Colonel Singer interrupted, as

Nathaniel's face drooped into disbelieving fear. His eyes widened like a child's.

'You can't mean to . . . Not Charlie,' he whispered. 'You said if I confessed he'd be safe! You said so!'

'You're not the only one who can break a promise,' she said coldly.

'Not my Charlie . . . I can't lose him too,' said Nathaniel, shaking his head. 'Please, Maude. Please – not my Charlie.'

'Send somebody up to Salim! Send me,' Joan said to the colonel and Burke-Bromley, leaping to her feet, desperate. 'Tell Salim that Charlie is his brother!'

'It's too late,' said Maude. They all turned to her. Joan felt as though she might be sick; her throat tightened horribly, chokingly. 'It'd be too late. He's probably already dead.'

Muscat, Nizwa and Tanuf,
Oman, April 1909

In the aftermath of Nathaniel's betrayal, Maude lay in her stupor for a long time. When the sun set, Khalid lit a fire of pale, starving flames, two feet high, and Maude felt the heat of it on her face. Her body had gone cold and stiff; her soul had retreated from the shock, and it felt as though something dark and foreign had crept in to take its place.

'We must go after them!' she heard Fatih say, over and over. 'God fetch a plague to them! They will die for this. We've waited too long already.'

'We cannot go,' Khalid told him, over and over. He brought Maude a plate of meat and bread, and put it near her. 'Shahin, you must eat your share. I know you are listening. You must rise. This is not the way,' he said, but Maude could not reply. Her thoughts wouldn't connect to her body, to her bones or her blood. She had no will to speak, no will to move. Only when they branded her did she find her way back.

The sun was setting on the second day and the wind rose as the light failed, rushing cold across the dunes. Khalid spoke lines from the Quran, and walked around her in circles as the iron heated in the fire; his words were whipped away from them, carried off into the sky. Above their heads was a riot of stars, and one streaked across the blackness, beautiful as it died. Maude watched it, but she had no wishes. She knew what Khalid was about to do, but she had no opinion on it, no fear of it. Fatih lifted her into a sitting position and tipped her head forwards; Khalid wrapped his hand in a cloth, lifted the glowing iron from the coals and pressed it against the back of her neck.

The pain was bright and incredible. It was a sudden white light, obliterating the night, impossible to ignore; Maude had no choice but to scream. Sand blew into her mouth and got caught in her teeth; she twisted in their grip and smelled her own hair burning, her own skin. She screamed and screamed, even when the iron was removed, and perhaps the men understood that she was screaming out more than the pain of the branding – that she needed to scream, and by doing so would begin to heal. It was the sound of a greater pain than that of burned skin – a greater outrage. It was the sound of the dark thing inside her. Her heart was broken and she was stunned by her fury, and as she stared into the black and silver sky she felt as cold as the stars, and just as lonely. She wondered if she would ever feel anything else, from that moment on.

They set off the next day, heading back towards the well. Maude was still silent but she was awake, and could ride; the wound on her neck hurt unremittingly. She let Khalid lead her, and lost track of time, paying no attention to the route; not worrying about their dwindling water; making no decisions for herself. They reached Muscat about a month later, and at the city gates the guards eyed them suspiciously: three ragged Bedouin, one just a lad, with the pale, cracked lips of a near-lethal thirst, riding Batinah camels at the point of collapse. Maude was half-delirious; she was so bewildered by the sight of the city and the big, square gates that for a second she thought she'd ridden all the way to London. She looked around half expecting there to be some celebration of her arrival; a welcoming party, or bunting in the colours of the British flag. There was nothing, of course; just ancient stone and mud brick, seething in the sun.

The guards made them leave their camels at the gate; they

scowled, but they gave each of the travellers a cup of water. Maude's tasted like blood and she spat the first mouthful out, bewildered by the trick. She wiped her hand across her mouth and expected it to come away red. The three of them walked slowly down through the city to the harbour, where the glitter of the sea was blinding and unreal, and stared in torment at so much water that could not be drunk. Then, wobbling on her feet, Maude went to the door of the British Residency and knocked.

She forgot the wazir's name as soon as he told her it, which bothered her because she knew she'd known it once – before she'd even set off from Salalah. He was a tall man with cadaverous eye sockets, and as he spoke Maude found her attention wandering. There was a portrait of King Edward VII on the wall, and sunlight from the sea danced across the ceiling. The scabs on the back of her neck where Khalid had branded her itched furiously. She gulped at the tea she was given, and burned her throat.

'Here,' said the wazir, and she looked up, surprised to find him at her shoulder, handing her a handkerchief. 'Rotten luck to be pipped at the post, as it were. But take heart – soon you'll be at home, returned to the bosom of your family; a far more suitable place for a lady.' He patted her shoulder uncomfortably and Maude realised that she was crying – noisily and messily. She didn't remember starting to.

'But *I* have crossed the Rub el Khali – not Nathaniel. Do you understand? He didn't cross at all . . . he was lost. We found him and he . . . he . . .'

'Now, Miss Vickery, that's enough. Mr Elliot is already on his way back to England. I myself saw his map of the crossing. He arrived with a large group of tribal men who'd crossed with him, and confirmed his success—'

'But half of those men crossed with *me*! He's bought them,

that's all . . .' She fell silent because she saw it was hopeless. The wazir's discomforted pity had turned sour, and hardened off. She was a nuisance, nothing more; he couldn't wait to pack her off. As if to confirm this, the wazir sat back down and cleared his throat, steepling his hands in front of his face and saying, 'There's a cargo ship leaving the day after tomorrow, as luck would have it. I'm sure we can arrange you a spot on board. It might not be quite what you're used to, but you can make better arrangements onwards from Salalah, or Aden.'

Maude stared at him, wondering, given her appearance, what exactly he thought she was used to. She sat in silence for a while, with the fine, washed fabric of his handkerchief impossibly soft in her hand. It was such a conventional thing, such a deeply British thing. She looked down and saw that somebody had stitched his initials into the corner of it for him. On the third finger of her hand was the lapis engagement ring Nathaniel had given her, just weeks before. Maude started to cry again, and hated herself because it was the fact that there was nobody to stitch her initials onto a handkerchief for her that had set her off. She had an ache inside her like the cold of midwinter; she wasn't sure if she could stand it.

The cadaverous British official offered her a room in the Residency until the boat departed, but Maude declined, getting to her feet unsteadily. 'You have somewhere to stay here in Muscat?' he sounded doubtful, but perfunctory. She knew he wouldn't check.

'Yes. I have friends here,' she told him. He nodded encouragingly.

'Rest is what you need, Miss Vickery. You've clearly had rather more adventure than was entirely prudent. Off you go then. I'll speak to the ship's captain, and let's have no more foolish talk of desert and double-crossings, yes?' Maude said nothing. She looked at him a final time, and felt a different religion, a different race, a different species to him. But she was too weak to contradict him, or deride him, or fight. Nathaniel had taken everything; when she looked inside herself there was nothing left.

Khalid led her to a barren room in Muttrah, on the top floor of a house down a narrow street that stank of goat hides. She lay down on a woven mat, beneath a palm-thatch ceiling that fidgeted with vermin, and slept for a long time. Several days passed like that – Khalid woke her from time to time to give her bread and water, and stayed to watch her consume them. Occasionally she woke to the sound of voices outside, or because the heat in the room was such that the sweat was itching in her eyes. Once or twice she woke up and tried to rise but the room rushed around her sickeningly and she fell back, her mouth filling with saliva, certain she was going to throw up. Flies zigzagged above her face. She thought of nothing.

One day Fatih strode into the room with an air of purpose, but then he merely stared down at her, arms folded, his resolve waning from him. He left again without a word, but she knew what he wanted to say. She knew Khalid would not abandon her there, feeble as she was. She knew that they wanted to leave; they had no business in Muscat, and were wasting money on the lodgings. She knew she had become a burden to them. She knew she had to get up. The thought exhausted her.

Summer was snapping at spring's heels; the heat built every day. Maude shuddered at the thought of being in the desert under that ferocious sun. Weathered as she was, she felt her skin burning beneath its glare as she swam, fully clothed, off the beach at Muttrah. Her wobbly legs had carried her that far, driven by the need to be rid of the stink of herself. The damp sand beneath her feet made her think of England; her mind cowered when Nathaniel wandered into it, aged eleven, inspecting some shells she'd collected – naming the species, choosing a best and a second best. Nathaniel *was* home, and she couldn't return to either.

The water was awakening, and soothing, and oblivious. Maude floated, paddling slightly, and stared up at the dark massif of Jebel Akhdar. The hazy mountain seemed to beckon to her; it seemed to offer a place to hide. She floated, and drifted, and thought about Nathaniel, even though it wasn't safe to. She couldn't tell if she still loved him, or loathed him. The thought of him made something inside her whine in pain. She tried to picture him in England, celebrating his success, his momentous achievement. She imagined letting him keep it; letting him have his fiction. She tried to imagine him visiting Elias Vickery – being congratulated by him, being asked where Maude was, whether he had heard anything of her while he'd been in Arabia. Did they think she was dead? Was Nathaniel letting them think that? Anger flared, burning hot, and died again as quickly. She simply hadn't the energy, and she realised then that she couldn't go back yet; either to let Nathaniel keep what he'd stolen, or to try to wrest it back from him. She simply couldn't. She would write to her father so he would know she was alive, but that was all. Alive, but not well.

Khalid offered to marry her when she realised she was pregnant. She was so thin, so sparse, that when her abdomen began to round out in spite of her continued sickness, she realised at once, with a kind of incredulous horror, what it meant. By then she'd made up her mind not to cry any more, but she couldn't help herself. Khalid found her sobbing and she told him without thinking.

'In your country this is a disgrace?' he asked softly, seriously.

'Oh, yes,' she said, distraught. 'Perhaps if I tell him, he'll go through with the wedding? Perhaps if I tell Nathaniel?' she said, thinking aloud, panicked, wildly hopeful.

'You would still want such a man?' said Khalid, his expression darkening. Maude didn't dare to tell him that she would, and the more she thought about it the more she realised it wasn't true. She wanted the Nathaniel she thought she'd known; she wanted herself back, as she'd been before. She didn't want either of them as they were now – not him, and not herself. She shook her head. 'Would you take another, then? I would be honoured,' he said, and the kindness and dignity of his offer brought more tears.

'And would you take an infidel?' she asked him. She realised she had no faith in God left at all, Christian or otherwise. It had burned out in the desert, somewhere, and she hadn't noticed when. Perhaps ousted by the dark thing that had crawled into her when Nathaniel left.

'You would need only pledge your faith to God, and live as a good Muslim . . .' said Khalid, trailing off. She saw a heavy resignation settle onto him.

'It would be a lie,' she said quietly. 'You deserve better.'

They were at Nizwa. Maude had presented herself to the sultan's representative, the wali, and been invited back for a ceremonial dinner with the local sheiks. Heaps of rice with greasy goat meat on top, then piles of honeyed pastries. They made her think of Haroun, with his box of sweet treats that he'd guarded so fiercely as they'd left Salalah. It seemed an impossibly long time ago. The wali seemed to approve of her utter joylessness, and the peculiar gravity of her demeanour, and gave her leave to remain. Khalid and Fatih itched to set off south, back to familiar lands and their family; Maude sensed Fatih's growing impatience to leave before high summer made it impossible, but Khalid was still reluctant to abandon her to her fate.

'Shahin, what will you do?' he asked, on a daily basis, with the kind of patience that told her he would wait until she knew, for as long as it took.

'You should leave,' she told him, every time. 'You owe me nothing. You have been the best and most faithful companion I could ever have wished for.'

'Friends owe each other nothing, that is true,' he said. 'But I cannot go until I know what you will do.' She paid him for staying, for their time. Khalid took the coins reluctantly and used them to buy her provisions, clothing, lodging. In the end she realised that he was telling the truth – her indecision could keep them there indefinitely.

They were staying in a house in the labyrinthine streets around the souk, where the blood, soot, sweat and rot stink of the marketplace was almost unbearable. Nizwa was flies and garbage and feral dogs that ran at you, snarling. It was the wail of muezzin from mosques, and the panicked shrieks of goats strung up to have their throats cut. Maude longed for the clean, empty silence of the desert; but again, she longed for it from *before*. She longed to be again the person she'd been before, and began to see that she couldn't have either thing back again – the desert, or the peace she'd felt there. Again and again, her eyes turned to the mountain instead; stark and huge and wild. Distant. She wanted to be distant. She could imagine finding peace there, and silence; she could imagine the stony coolness of the air, empty of human stink. Khalid frowned when she told him her decision. 'I know nothing of the mountain, or its people,' he said uneasily.

'Nor do I,' said Maude. 'But I will find out. There are villages up there, I have heard tell; and gardens full of fruit and flowers. It sounds a good place to live. I insist you and Fatih set off for your home.'

'Won't you do the same? Won't you go *home*, Shahin?'

'I don't have one any more.' Maude ran her hands across her bump in what was already becoming an unconscious gesture. 'I need to find a new one.'

'You might not be welcome. You should not go alone,' he said stubbornly.

'I'll hire a guide,' she assured him. 'And I'll travel as a boy. I'll be fine, Khalid. Please go home.'

Fatih shook her hand and wished her well, and couldn't hide his delight to be off. She gave him gifts – a new shirt, an ammunition belt, a tooled leather satchel – which he took cheerfully, with no excess of gratitude. Khalid was different, quieter; removed from her as though they'd already parted. He clasped her hand, which he could do in public when she was dressed as a young man. He held it for a long time, his eyes searching her face as if looking for something he'd lost. Or was about to lose.

'I hope you will come to find me once your baby is born,' he said, and they both knew that they would never see each other again.

'Perhaps I will, one day. I'd like to go back to the desert. One day,' said Maude, and had to stop because she didn't trust herself to continue.

'If God wills it,' he said softly. Maude turned and hurried away before they'd even mounted their camels, unable to watch them riding away.

In the scrubby foothills below the mountain, Maude and her guide came across a cave full of men; a wide, shallow inlet in the rock, echoing with voices and shuffling feet. Money was changing hands, as greasy as the aroma of so many unshaven, unwashed faces. The whole thing had the calculated air of the marketplace, and something else, something darker. A taint of ingrained, callous disregard; sideway glances, greedy, gloating. A slave auction, Maude's guide told her; women were not permitted. Maude disliked her guide, who was haughty for a man of such limited mind. She ignored him and went in for a closer look.

She walked past slaves who stood tall and resolute, with their arms folded and expressions of disdain on their faces; she walked past others who swayed woozily, their faces cut, their ankles hobbled. There was laughter around one tall, thin man, who was hopping on one foot, fighting for balance. Maude eavesdropped for a while, and heard that he had been born into slavery but had run away, so his owner had condemned him to the indignity of the marketplace. He'd been lashed, and he was hopping because he had a deep, suppurating wound in the calf of his right leg, and couldn't set it down.

'Fool. Perhaps now you see you should have shown more gratitude?' The man selling him was young and handsome, but his expression was malicious. 'No one will buy a lame slave. You'll die in this cave like a dog, for I shan't bring you back from it.' He gave the slave a kick that knocked him onto his backside in the dust. The man, who Maude guessed was already past thirty, gazed up at his owner with such a dignified mixture of defiance and resignation that Maude liked him immediately.

'How much for this man?' she demanded of his owner.

They made slow progress while Abdullah recovered. She treated him as a servant, but not as a slave; very soon, she began to treat him as a friend. He was intelligent and industrious and had a welcome aura of calm. When they arrived at the village of Tanuf, they stopped to let his leg finish healing, and also because the village had spreading tamarind trees for shade, and an open falaj where the children squealed and played, and Maude had the compelling feeling that she had found a place where she could rest. Tanuf's houses nestled into a massive, precipitous slab of the mountainside, like a child nestling close to its mother. There was a forest of date palms that clattered their leathery leaves in the breeze. The women covered their faces but laughed often. Maude doffed her boy's clothes, put on a veil and begged an audience with the sheik, bin Himyar, who called himself the Lord of The Green Mountain, during which she spun him a story about her husband, murdered by thieves outside of Nizwa, and begged to remain in safety until her child was born. A good number of Maria Teresa dollars helped him to believe her. Already, before that time came to pass, she and Abdullah had been woven into the fabric of the village, and weren't asked to move on.

When her son was born, Maude named him Salim because he was perfect, and whole, and for the first time since she'd left the desert she began to feel whole again herself. She searched his face for signs of Nathaniel, but saw none – the darkness of his eyes and hair could have come from Elias, after all. Later in the year she went to Muscat to make arrangements with the British Bank there, and to send a telegram home, and that way learned of her father's death, and her inheritance. So she stayed in Tanuf, and watched Salim grow.

She walked on the hills and slopes around the village, and occasionally went along one of the ravines that climbed to the central massif, and stared up at the plateau. But she never attempted to climb any further. The ticking of the clock had finally stopped. Like so much else, it had not survived the desert. Maude could sense the high peaks, the summit and the onward road like a small movement in the corner of her eye that always made her look; but the urge to follow those roads, and to conquer, belonged to a person she no longer knew.

She went out in the dark and watched the stars, alone, and she did not fight against this new order of things, or the new person she had become. The dark thing was still inside her – if she looked for it, she found it easily. But she hated it – she feared the thoughts that welled up from it; the sensation of raging, shattering, and flying apart. The feeling of being poisoned. So she let herself love Salim and never spoke of his father; she tried not to think of him at all but it was difficult. She watched the stars wheel slowly over the mountain, marching their ageless routes, and for years refused to ask herself what she was waiting for. She slept deeply, and dreamed of the desert. Night after night, she dreamed of the desert.

Muscat, December 1958 and
January 1959

There was a navy frigate anchored outside the harbour, too big
to come any closer. Half the crew had come ashore on landers
and dispersed into the city; to drink coffee and buy souvenirs
and remember not to smoke in public. Joan kept catching sight
of the ship in the corner of her eye – sleek, pale grey metal, its
upper decks a mess of funnels, guns and antennae. It looked
out of place against the foreground of little boats, brown rocks
and stone buildings – far too big and clean and modern; and it
was a constant reminder of the world she was soon to rejoin.
Whenever she passed an open window, Joan paused and stared
out at it, and then at Jalali, Merani with its canons, and the
huge graffiti on the harbour walls – the names of ships from
all over the world that had called at Muscat over the centuries.
She understood better, now, why so many seamen had made
the perilous climb to undertake such a thankless task. The
place gave you an impulse to prove you'd been there, to prove
you had discovered, and seen, and survived. It was something
to do with the way it hid from the rest of the world; it made
you feel as though you'd stumbled upon treasure, and there
was something magical about that. Joan wanted to write her
own name on those harbour walls; after all, she felt as though
Oman had written its name on her. Perhaps, she decided, that
was enough.

Christmas Day was the oddest and quietest Joan had ever
known. She went out in the morning to send a telegraph to

her mother, promising to see her soon; the decorations that the servants had put up looked wan and out of place; there were no presents, except for the modest gifts the Gibsons exchanged, and the envelopes they gave to the staff. Marian tried her best to jolly them along, playing records and starting the aperitifs very early, but the lack of news about Charlie hung so heavily on Joan that she couldn't raise a smile. The Residency kitchens produced an approximation of a traditional Christmas lunch, with guinea fowl, thin gravy and limp vegetables. Joan and Rory sat down to it with Robert and Marian, and a few men from the oil company and the British Bank who hadn't got leave to go home, and said very little. Joan's tongue felt wooden and her stomach uneasy. She wished she had Daniel with her, even though she knew he'd have difficult questions for her. At least she knew he was safe – having Christmas lunch with his unit down at Nizwa. She thought back to Christmases past, in Bedford – the simple joy of them – and realised that finally, well into her adult years, she had lost the magic of it.

There was no way she could explain to anyone why the thought of Salim harming Charlie was so particularly horrific to her. She couldn't tell anyone how well she knew Salim, or what had happened between her and Charlie, or that it was her silence that had sent Charlie and his men into their captors' hands. There was no way to explain that she felt responsible, and was terrified. The pressure of it built until her head was throbbing and she felt the world around her receding.

Then, on Boxing Day, Robert was called away from the breakfast table to a phone call. Joan watched him go, sick with dread that the bodies of the SAS men had been found. She dropped her fork with a clatter and gripped a fistful of the tablecloth, and Marian reached out to squeeze her arm.

'We don't know yet,' she said soothingly. 'Just hang on.'

When she heard Robert's footsteps returning along the corridor, Joan stopped breathing. She almost wanted to run, but he was smiling as he came in. Relief jarred through her, blurring the room, making her dizzy.

'They're all right, they're back at base,' said Robert.

'All of them?' said Joan.

'To a man. Apparently, they just appeared at the Nizwa camp on foot – thirsty and exhausted, but fine. They've walked two days' straight without food or water. They must have been released as soon as Nathaniel Elliot arrived – the rebels must have got word of it somehow. Perhaps they saw his plane land. Anyway, the old girl was bluffing!'

'Oh, thank God,' said Joan, tears burning in her eyes.

'There – you see? I said it'd all come out in the wash, didn't I?' said Marian, but Joan was too overcome to reply. She sat in silence for a long time as the others talked, and Robert went upstairs to let Nathaniel know his son was safe. There was one last thing worrying her, and when Robert returned she took him to one side.

'The men were released, you say? They were let go – there was no battle to free them? No ... violence?'

'None at all. Goodness only knows where bin Shahin and his motley crew are now,' he said. Joan shut her eyes for a moment, and let it sink in. They were, at that moment, all three of them safe: Daniel, Charlie, and Salim. The release of pressure left her weak. 'I expect young Charles will come over here to see his father before long. After a few days of rest, of course,' said Robert.

Nathaniel Elliot had been staying with them at the Residency ever since his arrival, recovering from his impromptu journey and the sudden shock of Maude's scheme. He kept to his room most of the time, and took his meals in private, on a tray.

'I expect he's embarrassed, poor dear,' said Marian. 'Really, I wish there was some way to convince him that nobody *minds* what went on all those years ago.'

'I'm not sure that's strictly true, Marian,' Robert remarked. He'd been shaken by what Maude had done, and what she'd revealed. He didn't seem to know how to behave towards a person who'd been so wronged, nor towards her disarming wrongdoer; but he was taking the matter very seriously. Only his most strenuous interventions with Sultan Said and Governor Shahab had meant that Maude was allowed to stay at home until she was deported with the rest of them, rather than being moved directly to Jalali. She wouldn't be entirely safe from the sultan's retribution until she was out of Omani jurisdiction. The army men had washed their hands of the whole business and returned to Nizwa. Maude had fallen silent once she'd wrested the confession from Nathaniel that she'd waited so long for; she was refusing all callers, and didn't seem to care what punishment might come from either the Omani or British governments. When Joan asked Robert what charges could be brought against her, he merely shrugged.

'I doubt Her Majesty's government will have much appetite for retribution, once the full circumstances are known,' he said uncertainly. 'The army doesn't seem to, now that the men are safe.'

Maude's ban on visitors included Joan, which tormented her. She'd been struck dumb as everything she'd read about Maude and Nathaniel at that time was revealed to be lies; she'd sat stupidly, stunned, and said nothing, and now she itched to tell Maude that she understood just a fraction of the injustice that had been done to her, and was staggered by it.

She had no idea what she would say – she suspected nothing could be adequate – but she still longed to be able to say *something*. She went up to visit Nathaniel a few times, knocking shyly on his door, feeling apprehensive. Nathaniel let her in and was polite enough, but he wouldn't discuss what had happened in the desert all those years ago. He, too, stared out at the sea and the boats a great deal, with the sunlight bright in his eyes.

'I never thought I'd come back to Muscat,' he said distantly. 'I never wanted to.' Joan wanted to be angry with him but it was impossible. She wanted to be outraged on Maude's behalf, and glad that she'd finally brought the truth to light – and she was, when she shut her eyes and thought about it; when she imagined herself there – imagined Maude's long, lonely life and all the things she'd lost, or had never had. But any such feelings slipped away when she was face to face with Nathaniel. Life had taken just as much from him, she realised. There was no malice in the man, and certainly no glory. 'It was the shame of it, you see,' he said one afternoon, out of nowhere, as they sat either side of a game of backgammon. 'The shame of admitting what I'd done. I was too much the coward. And it only got more shameful the more years that passed.'

'My dad always used to say there was no pride in winning if you'd cheated,' said Joan. Nathaniel smiled sadly.

'I taught my children the same thing, because it's wholly true.'

Eventually, late in the afternoon on New Year's Eve, Joan persuaded a troubled Abdullah to let her in, even as Maude shouted down from upstairs.

'I said no visitors!' She sounded querulous, elderly.

'Hard cheese,' Joan called back, as she made her way upstairs. She found Maude out of her chair, sitting propped on a pile of cushions in one of the low windows, so that she could look out into the east. Her eyes were narrowed against the light, and her face shone wetly. Joan went to sit down beside her, shoulder to shoulder. She crossed her legs and waited a while. There was something deeply unsettling about seeing Maude cry, though the cause of the tears was no mystery. 'What will you do once we're back?' Joan asked eventually.

'England,' said Maude, sniffing. 'I haven't seen the place since 1909. I should imagine it's changed somewhat.'

'Yes, rather,' said Joan. 'Are you frightened?'

'Wouldn't you be?'

'Of course I would,' said Joan, with a smile. 'But you've never been afraid of things that frighten you, have you, Miss Vickery?'

'I don't know,' said Maude. 'I can't remember. I can't... I can't quite remember who I am. And I don't remember England – what it's like to be there, I mean. The smell of it... the people.' She shook her head. 'I don't belong there. I'm not sure I belonged there all those years ago; and now...'

They sat in silence for a while, as the sun slunk towards the rocks and a gang of seagulls wheeled and bickered across the sky. There was so much Joan wanted to ask, so much she wanted to say, and however loath she was to upset Maude any further, she couldn't keep quiet.

'Captain Elliot is safe. And his men. They're on their way here from Nizwa – it seems they were already on their way down the mountain when Nathaniel came to see you. But I suppose you knew that already.'

'Of course,' said Maude. 'I would never have actually *harmed* the boy. In fact, if I hadn't interfered they'd most likely have been shot as they went up the ravine in the first place. I just... I wanted to frighten Nathaniel. You understand? I wanted to make him feel even a *fraction* of what he made me feel...'

'I can't believe what he did to you, Miss Vickery. I can't believe he betrayed you like he did,' she said.

Maude tutted, and took a breath. 'Neither could I, at the time. But . . . I understand people a little better now. Some, when you help them – when you save them – cannot bear to be beholden. It breeds a fury in them, a kind of madness, until they hate you for it. It makes them capable of anything.'

'But . . . you let him win, Miss Vickery,' said Joan. 'Back then, when it happened and in the first few years afterwards, when you might still have changed things . . . you *let* him win. I don't understand why you did that.'

Maude took a deep breath, and shook her head. 'They wouldn't have believed me. He redrew my map, rewrote my journal in his own hand. And he was a *man*. Back then, people didn't have the first clue what a woman was capable of.'

'They might have listened, if you'd caused enough of a stink. You'd have had your reputation and your family name behind you . . .'

'And an illegitimate child in my womb. Perhaps that sort of thing passes without a murmur in the 1950s, but back then it was a calamity.'

'No,' Joan admitted. 'There'd still be murmurs now. But . . . that's not the only way you let him win. I thought you'd chosen to make this your home. But you didn't choose it, did you? You went into exile. You let Nathaniel exile you from your own life. Even if you'd had to wait until Salim was old enough to be looked after by friends or a nanny – or by Abdullah – you could have carried on travelling then, and exploring, writing. You could have carried on with your life. But you let him *win*, Maude – in every way imaginable.' She shook her head. Maude turned to look at her with eyes that were tired, full of pain.

'Yes,' she said quietly. 'Yes. He took the heart right out of me.' She wiped her face, and blew her nose. 'At least people will know now. You'll make sure people know, won't you, Joan?'

'Yes, I will, I promise. But . . .' She broke off, struggling for words. She'd been about to say, just as Nathaniel had, that it hardly mattered now. They sat in silence for a while and then she took Maude's hand, squeezing it. 'This wild plan you hatched, to bring Nathaniel out here to face you . . . why wait until now, when it's too late? Why wait until you can no longer travel, until a lifetime has passed and people have forgotten all about you?'

'Because,' said Maude, turning to stare out at the softening horizon, 'because for the first time, I saw the chance to. My first chance – and my only chance. You came out here and found me, Joan, and gave me that chance. And you didn't even realise it, dear girl.'

When Maude began to doze, Joan helped Abdullah lift her over to the bed.

'You'll come with her? To England, I mean?' Joan whispered to the old man, as they left her there. Abdullah nodded.

'Wherever the lady goes, I will be at her side.'

'And I'll be there too, of course. To begin with, at least. I'll help however I can.'

Abdullah nodded again, wearing an enigmatic expression that was almost a smile as he shut the door behind her.

Joan went down to the seafront and sat on the wall in front of the customs buildings, where bales of dried fish, dates and firewood were waiting to be shipped. The shoreline had a fish and seaweed smell, seething from the warmth of the day; she watched the little crabs running here and there, and a stray dog rolling in the sand. She thought about Maude Vickery; she thought about it and realised that in bringing Nathaniel out here, in finally bringing the truth to light, she had lost everything again – the place that had become her home, and any chance of seeing her son again. Try as she might, Joan couldn't decide if the truth was worth that, or if, unwittingly, Maude had just let Nathaniel ruin her life one last time. She felt a vast, ill-defined sorrow and, after a while, traced the cause of it – she could change none of it, mitigate none of it. The course of Maude Vickery's life was already mapped; what was left to her was to follow that path. She could be a pioneer no more.

Nathaniel came down from his room when his son arrived at the Residency, on New Year's Day. Joan's heart gave a peculiar squeeze when Charlie walked in, wearing a clean, tidy, tropical uniform; freshly shaven, with his sun-kissed hair combed back more neatly than she'd ever seen it before. Spruced up to see his father, she realised, smiling. A cut on his forehead had been closed with three small black stitches, and the bruise surrounding it had spread down to his left eye. Other than that, he was unscathed after his sojourn on the mountain. Joan's blood kept on thumping, even though she felt calm, and she was glad nobody could see or hear it; she decided it was relief as much as anything else. Relief that he was back safely, and that her lie hadn't done him or the other men harm. She didn't like to think what life would have been like if things hadn't gone so well after his capture – if Maude had followed through on her threat, and left Joan with blood on her hands for the rest of her life. Joan realised then how easy it was to make the wrong decision in a moment; to make a mistake, and for life to change for ever as a result. She may have only tried to do what was best, but still she felt she'd had a lucky escape.

Nathaniel wept without shame as he hugged his son.

'Nasty scrape,' he said, and Joan couldn't tell if he meant

the cut on Charlie's head or the whole affair. 'I am sorry, my boy. I seem to have got you into a bit of a fix.'

'Nonsense!' Charlie grinned. 'Got myself into it – walked right into their hands. No harm done.'

'I'm not so sure,' said Nathaniel, shaking his head. Charlie started to say something else but stopped, his smile fading slightly.

'Come onto the terrace, all of you,' said Marian, before the silence could grow strained. 'There's iced coffee, or something stronger if you need it. I think I do.' Charlie and his father spoke privately for a long time, their heads close together. Joan noted all the similarities between them, from their posture and gestures to the width of their foreheads and the shape of their eyes. She wondered if there was much of his mother in Charlie at all, beyond his fair hair. And as she looked, she saw little traces of Salim as well, there all along but not marked: the angle in the turn of the jawbone, the narrowness of the bridge of the nose, the square shape of the shoulders. Joan hadn't dared ask anyone for news of Salim; she longed to ask Charlie, and she knew that Nathaniel had appealed to Singer and Burke-Bromley to somehow get a message up the mountain to the man they'd been fighting – his son.

She saw her chance once Nathaniel, exhausted, had gone to his room to rest before dinner, and cornered Charlie out on the terrace.

'Happy New Year, Joan.'

'Happy New Year to you, Charlie,' she said. 'It's good to see you – safe and sound, I mean. I hope . . . I suppose you've heard about what happened with Maude and your father all those years ago?' Charlie's face fell, and he nodded. 'I've been visiting him,' she said. 'I thought he'd be very . . . grand. But then, perhaps this isn't the time for grandness.'

'No, he's always been like that. Understated,' Charlie demurred. 'He did a terrible thing, back then, but God knows he's sorry for it. I've never seen him so unhappy, but there's something else too ... I think he's almost *relieved* to have been found out at last. Like it's taken a load off him, you see? Thinking back, he's always been a ... sombre man. Always reluctant to celebrate his past glories.' Joan said nothing for a while, and Charlie frowned. 'You can't imagine I'd think any less of him for it?'

'No! No, I—'

'Because would you? Would you love your father any less if you found out he'd had secrets, or had done things he wasn't proud of?' He stared at her intently, and Joan swallowed.

'No,' she said, entirely truthfully. 'No, I wouldn't.'

Charlie blinked and took a swig of his drink.

'Well then,' he said. He thought for a moment, then shook his head. 'I hate secrets, but ... I'm just not sure how much of this to tell my mother. She's rather frail ... I'd hate to upset her.'

'I suppose it will shock her to learn that your father was engaged elsewhere before he married her. And that he has a son with that woman.'

'And that he almost killed that woman. It'll certainly shock her. Wouldn't it shock you?'

'It's devastating, yes; but ... it was an awfully long time ago. Your parents have had their whole lives together since then.'

'Salim bin Shahin is not a long time ago. He's right now.'

'Yes. I suppose he is,' said Joan. 'But then, isn't it up to your father how much he tells your mother – and when? These are *his* secrets, after all.'

'That's true, yes,' said Charlie.

'Your eldest brother was called Elias, wasn't he? Did you

know he was named after Maude's father, Elias Vickery? I heard your father say so. He must have thought about the Vickerys – and about Maude – all his life.'

'Yes,' said Charlie quietly. 'Yes, I believe he did.'

For a moment they were silent, and Joan's head crowded with everything she wanted to say. 'Anyway,' said Charlie, interrupting her thoughts. 'You owe me a long and detailed story of your time on the mountain, Joan. Singer's washed his hands of you. He tells me you're keeping schtum.'

'I think it's best that I do,' said Joan. 'I don't know anything useful, and now you're down safely . . .' She trailed off. 'I hope he doesn't take it out on Dan. And . . . I'm sorry.'

'Said with feeling.' Charlie frowned thoughtfully again. 'I wonder what you have to be sorry about? Unless . . . I did wonder about the ease with which we were picked up by that motley crew. It was almost as if they knew we'd be coming up that ravine, and who we were. And they were very careful not to shoot us. I wonder if the muleteers aren't the only ones who've been playing both sides.' He looked at her closely, and Joan felt her face flush.

'It wasn't . . . intentional. I didn't say anything about who you were,' she said. 'But then . . . I'm afraid I did tell Maude about the SAS, and you being in it. I didn't realise what she might do with the information. And I did rather suspect Salim knew I'd send you up to help Dan. And then, I suppose he guessed you'd spot the ravine. But I just thought you'd all come straight back down, you see.'

'Who were you protecting? Him or us?'

'Both of you. All of you.'

'Interesting. I simply . . . *can't* get to grips with the idea that he's my brother.'

'I know. I worked it out too late, though . . . too late to let Salim know.'

'You think it would have made a difference?'

'Definitely. He'd never harm his own flesh and blood, I'm sure of it.'

'Perhaps you're right, but I'm not so sure – he's a consummate soldier. But a decent type. Resolute, steady, obviously bright.' Charlie paused, and grinned. 'Actually, I rather liked him, which is quite something, given the circumstances.'

'Yes,' said Joan. 'I like him too. What happened up there? When they caught you?'

'Not a lot. They're like cats when they want to be, the Arabs. We had no idea they were even there until we were surrounded. They marched us to a cave and kept us there under constant guard. We could hear the planes going over, but there was no way we could signal to them. They didn't tell us what was going on, but I assumed we'd be for the chop, sooner or later.' He shrugged, but for a second the shadow of that fear crossed his face. 'But they fed us, and they didn't manhandle us more than was necessary . . .'

'So how did you get that cut on your head?'

'That was my brother.' Charlie smiled. 'Knocked me out cold – I'd managed to get loose and was making a run for it. Never had a headache like it when I woke up, but at least he didn't shoot me – and he made sure none of the others did either.' He took a deep breath. 'Then they let us go. Just like that, no word as to why – they just pointed us towards Nizwa and told us to start walking. I thought they might be about to shoot us in the back . . .' He shrugged. 'But here I am, alive and kicking after my first and possibly only visit with my big brother, Salim. My *brother*. I didn't believe it when the colonel told me. I've got used to having no brothers left.'

'Yes,' said Joan gently. 'It must be . . . very strange.'

'Quite some way beyond strange, I would say. I'd like to get to know him, but I can't see how that will be possible.'

'Maybe it could be . . . after the war.' Even as she said it, Joan knew how unlikely it was. She could tell from Charlie's sad smile that he knew it too.

'Still,' he said, with a shrug. 'At least I made it up onto the plateau, eh?'

'Yes, but I beat you to it,' Joan pointed out, smiling.

She wished she might see Salim again as well. There was hope, but it was slim. She knew the army planned to win the hearts and minds of the men of the interior once the imam had been defeated – the SAF's Pioneers had dropped more conciliatory leaflets than bombs – but whether that clemency would extend to the leaders and lieutenants was another matter. But Salim wasn't just any lieutenant, after all. He was British by birth, though he didn't know it yet, and she hoped that strings could be pulled for him, somehow. Most likely he would disappear if the war was lost, and she didn't mind that idea too much. What she couldn't bear was the thought of him ever returning to Jalali.

'One day,' said Charlie, breaking into her thoughts. 'One day in the not-too-distant future you and I are going to sit down with a bottle of wine between us, and you are going to tell me the *whole* story. I insist.' He tried to sound severe, but intrigue lit his eyes.

'All right,' said Joan. 'One day I will.' She realised that she wanted to, that she was looking forward to it. There weren't many people she would ever be able to tell the whole story to, and she didn't want this most momentous time in her life to pass into obscurity; she didn't want it kept secret, to fade into old age with her, as Maude's achievement had been.

They went in for dinner, and Rory seated himself as far from Charlie Elliot as he could when there were only eight of them – the commander and first officer of the navy frigate had joined them.

'I don't think your fiancé likes me very much,' Charlie said quietly to Joan.

'He doesn't like me very much at the moment, either,' she said. 'And he's not my fiancé any more.' She rested the bare fingers of her left hand on the table, and saw Charlie glance down at them. 'Ah,' he said. 'And you've told him it's because you're wildly in love with me? Then no wonder he's cross.' He bumped her shoulder and smiled, and the way he looked at her stole the rebuttal from her lips. So she simply smiled back at him, and rolled her eyes discreetly.

After that, Charlie fell into conversation with his father, who'd returned, and Joan left them to their reunion. She tried to catch Rory's eye but he kept his gaze on his plate and only looked up as often as was necessary to be acceptably polite to Marian, sitting opposite him. He'd made almost no comment on the revelations about Maude and Nathaniel; almost no comment about Joan's part in it all. He avoided her, generally, and looked at her as though he hardly knew her. Joan had the nagging feeling that they had a great deal to talk about, but then, when she really thought about it, they didn't. Perhaps they needed to agree on a reason to give for their break-up, but that was all, and they could do that on the plane; he and Daniel had far more to discuss, though opportunities for them to do so would be hard to find. She wondered if her urge to talk to him was more the force of habit than anything else, but that wasn't quite right. He'd been her best friend for years, and the new distance between them felt like a yawning chasm. She was no longer afraid to be without him, but she wanted to tell him that she didn't want him to vanish from her life altogether. Perhaps time would show that, anyway; and perhaps it wasn't only up to her.

Joan stayed up with the men after the meal, not caring a jot for the put-out look of the navy commander, or the fact that Rory slunk off to bed with a barely audible *goodnight*.

Marian stayed with them as well.

'Quite right, Joan,' she said. 'I enjoy a brandy as much as the next man.' Robert came to sit beside her, put his arm around her shoulders and squeezed her until her she creaked.

'I shall miss you terribly, little Joan,' he said. His face was flushed from the wine, shining with sincerity. 'It'll go back to being very quiet and . . . businesslike around here, without your company.'

'I'll miss you, too,' she said. 'And I think Bedford will seem even quieter. Quite humdrum, in fact.' The thought of leaving panicked her a little. Daniel, Charlie, Salim, the desert and the mountains. She was ready to go back, in some ways – to see her mother, and to find out what her new life would be like – but in other ways didn't ever want to. At least she knew life *would* be different. She could never have gone back if it had been to walk the same blinkered path she'd walked before.

'Rather a big adjustment to be made, I should imagine,' Robert said kindly.

'At least I'll have Maude's papers to work on.' They were tucked away in her satchel upstairs, safe. 'I need to find a publisher for them – though it shouldn't be difficult. I imagine Maude Vickery is about to become a great deal better known. Rory told you I didn't get the job at the museum?'

'Yes, he did say. I'm terribly sorry, Joan.'

'No, it's all right. It doesn't seem quite right for me any more, anyway. I'm . . . I'm looking forward to seeing Mum,' she said.

She was nervous about it as well. The conversation she foresaw them having was not like any they'd ever had before. But when she thought of the dismissive way Maude had spoken about her own mother, and how detached from her she'd become by the time of Antoinette's death, Joan felt determined to work things through. Perhaps both she and Maude had looked up to their fathers more, but Joan loved her mother and refused to allow resentment to take root, or distance to grow between them. 'It feels like years since I saw her,' she said.

'I wonder if she'll recognise you?' said Robert, giving her a shrewd look. Joan paused, startled, wondering how much he saw. 'With you so tanned and slim,' he said, sipping his brandy. 'You look so very grown-up. I shall have to stop calling you little Joan.'

'No you won't, Uncle Bobby.' Joan smiled. 'Not ever.'

'You've enjoyed your time in Arabia, then?'

'It's been the best time of my whole life,' she said frankly.

'Well, you have a lot of catching up to do at home, of course. But, after that, write to me, or telephone. I've just heard about a job at the consulate in Aden. I wondered if you might be interested in applying for it.' He watched her closely, and smiled at her incredulous expression.

'*Really?*'

'Now, don't get too excited. It's third junior girl to an assistant of an attaché, or something like that. There'll be an awful lot of tea to make, and buff files to move about from place to place. But who knows – it might lead you somewhere.'

'I want it!' Joan said at once. Excitement shot through her like an electric charge. 'That is, I'd very much like to apply,' she amended politely, and Robert laughed.

On the last morning, Joan went to see if Maude needed any help before they were all rounded up and driven to Bait al Falaj, where an army plane would fly them to Aden to pick up their flights to Cairo, and onwards with BOAC to London. In the cool of the early morning, she knocked on the acacia wood door, then, after a while she knocked again, harder. She tried not to think about leaving; she tried not to look around, or take last glances. It was too much. She needed to take things one step at a time, though she couldn't help but think about the job in Aden, and the possibility it offered – like a fork in the road. She felt the thrill of it every time, undiminished.

'Abdullah?' she called, putting her ear to the door, hearing silence inside. She knocked again, frustrated, and then tried the handle. The door opened, swinging wide with her push. 'Miss Vickery – Maude? Abdullah?' she called into the shade within. Joan's stomach flipped as she stepped inside; she took a deep breath of the old smoke and ammonia smell of the place and then went upstairs, knowing what she would find but not quite believing it. The house had the unmistakable, indefinable feel of abandonment.

No Maude, no gazelle, no Abdullah with his tea tray. Only the salukis remained; they stood up and stretched as she entered, as if making ready to depart. Maude's bed was neatly made, her books and journals stacked away on the shelves. Her wheelchair was by the desk, discarded, and on the desk was a piece of paper and the blue lapis ring that had been left on the carpet after Maude's meeting with Nathaniel. The paper was a note for Joan:

Thank you for your help, Joan – unwitting though it was, in part. Make good use of my papers, and please find a home for the dogs, they're too old to travel. Do what you like with the ring. Warm regards, and on you go, MVV.

Tears blurred Joan's eyes, and she couldn't tell whether they were happy or sad. They were probably both; and somehow, she wasn't surprised. She hadn't been able to imagine Maude in England, or Abdullah. *Wherever the lady goes, I will be at her side*, he had said, when she last saw him. She remembered his mysterious smile, and realised they'd never had any intention of leaving Oman.

Well, where the bloody hell has she gone? She could already hear Singer's voice, his exasperated tone. Maude had left no clues to her destination, but Joan had hopes. She might have gone onto the mountain, to join Salim; to don a veil and mask and hide amongst the people she'd lived with before. But perhaps – and Joan shut her eyes and wished, fervently – perhaps she would somehow make her way back to the desert, and disappear into its vast, mesmerising calm, as she had longed to. In a moment of panic, Joan thought she had no real evidence that she had actually even met Maude Vickery, and been her friend. Then she remembered the photo of them Abdullah had taken, surreptitiously, down at the seafront. The film was safe in its canister, waiting to be developed. She stood a while in the empty room, listening to the buzzing flies and the push of the wind through the window. It was bright and sunny outside; the light was fierce and dazzling. Just like Maude. Joan was quite sure that she would never see her again. After a while she whistled to the dogs, and found their leashes, and they followed at her heels as she left.

'Well, she shouldn't be too hard to find,' said Robert hotly, when she told him. 'She can barely walk. And that slave of hers is a good foot taller than most men around here. No, they oughtn't be too hard to find.' He shook his head and ran his hands through his hair, and Joan said nothing, knowing in her gut that Maude would never be found unless she wanted to be.

'Oh, aren't they *handsome*?' Marian exclaimed when she saw the salukis. 'How could she bear to leave them?'

'They need a home,' said Joan smiling, and handed their leads to Marian.

'Oh!' she said, startled. She frowned for a moment, but then she smiled. 'Jolly good.'

'Colonel Singer will hit the roof. As will the governor. And the sultan. Hell and damnation! Confound the woman,' said Robert.

'Nonsense,' Marian told him blithely. 'They love nothing more than an excuse to bristle and wave their arms. If they were that determined to keep her, they ought to have posted guards at her door.'

'I suppose they didn't imagine a tiny old lady in a wheelchair was much of a flight risk.'

'Well,' said Marian pointedly, crouching down to ruffle the salukis' ears. 'There you all go, underestimating a woman, as is your wont.'

Joan had hoped against hope that Daniel would appear at the airstrip at Bait al Falaj to see them off, but of course he couldn't; he was down at Nizwa, still on active duty. Singer was there, with a face like thunder, to make sure none of the rest of them absconded before they were safely airborne. He'd refused to tell her whether they were searching for Maude or not, or how hard. Joan hugged Robert and Marian; the latter had long, blonde saluki hairs stuck to her pristine white jacket, and didn't seem to mind one bit. Joan looked around at the dusty, deserted field; the thought that everything would go on without her was strangely painful.

She was just steeling herself to ask the colonel to deliver a letter to Daniel for her when she was rescued by the sight of a tall, loose-limbed figure walking across from the barracks. Of course he would come to say goodbye to his father; still, Joan couldn't help smiling.

'Really?' said Rory sourly, squinting as he followed her gaze. 'He's such an insufferable toff.' Joan looked at him, surprised, guilty at first and then unsure how to feel, or what to say.

'He's not so bad. Not that I know him particularly well,' she said guardedly. Rory climbed onto the plane before Charlie reached them. Nathaniel hugged his son tightly; they exchanged a few quiet words as Charlie helped his father up the steps of the plane, then Charlie came back down to speak to Joan.

'Well, cheerio, I suppose,' he said.

'Cheerio,' said Joan. 'I wonder if you'd do me a small favour? Would you please give this to Daniel when you next see him? I was going to ask Colonel Singer, but he looks like he'd rather clip my ear than oblige me.'

'Yes, I can do that.' Charlie took the folded envelope and frowned down at it for a moment. 'It's a shame you've got to go off,' he said lightly. 'There's precious little entertainment around here.' He smiled, but there was something serious behind the words.

'I'm hoping to take a job in Aden, actually. So I could well be back in this neck of the woods in a few weeks' time, on a more permanent basis.'

'Really?' He looked around at the barren landscape and the glowering mountain. 'Have you gone completely daffy?' Joan smiled up at him for a moment. 'Well, you do still owe me a drink and a story. Perhaps I'll come down and find you there,' he said.

'All right then. It was nice to meet you, Charlie.' She looked past him at Colonel Singer, who was scowling. 'I'd better get on board before Singer comes over and bundles me on himself.'

'It was nice to meet you, too.' Charlie put out his hand; when she took it to shake, he pulled her closer and kissed her cheek soundly. It made the blood hum beneath her skin;

unsettling, not at all unpleasant. 'Perhaps you might find the time to write me the odd letter? Otherwise I only hear from my mother, and she mostly just tells me to wear clean socks.'

'All right,' said Joan, liking the idea at once. 'All right, I will. But I warn you – the news from Bedford might not be all that thrilling.'

'But the thrill will come from knowing you wrote it,' he said disarmingly. Then he grinned and released her. 'Bon voyage, Joan Seabrook. Write to me with your plans, so we can make a date for that drink.' He stepped back to allow her to board and, for a second, Joan felt the urge to step forwards, and stay close to him.

Charlie went to stand with Robert and Marian as the plane's engines stuttered into life, and they taxied slowly towards the head of the runway.

Nathaniel Elliot tipped his head back against his seat and closed his eyes; he looked exhausted. Before he went to sleep, Joan touched his arm gently. She held out the lapis ring in the palm of her hand.

'Maude left this. It's yours really, I suppose.' Nathaniel stared at the object with a look of ineffable sadness. He shook his head.

'I don't want it. Do what you like with it, Miss Seabrook. Keep it, if you want.' He shut his eyes again. Experimentally, Joan slid the ring onto the little finger of her right hand. It fit perfectly. She didn't know if she ought to wear it, or if she wanted to; she left it there for the time being, craning in her seat to wave to Robert, Marian and Charlie. She saw Charlie slip her letter to Daniel into his shirt pocket, and was glad to know her brother would get it.

In it, she'd written of her intention to move out of the family home, whether she got the job in Aden or not. She'd written that she knew what had gone on between Daniel and their mother – that Rory had told her what had been said. She'd written that if their mother didn't change her mind, then she'd lose Joan as well as Daniel. It was dramatic, and in fact she would probably never say or do anything so hard on Olive; but the sentiment was the same. They were still a family, the only one any of them had, and if Joan couldn't reunite them by persuasion then she felt quite prepared to do it by force. Mostly, she'd wanted to tell Daniel that nothing had changed between them, as far as she was concerned. She hoped it was true as far as he was concerned, given all that had happened – given her outrageous incursion into his professional life. *When you get to the top of Jebel Akhdar*, she'd written, *don't forget to wave to me*. She tried not to dwell on what that moment might mean for Salim.

By the time they were airborne, the people on the ground had been obliterated by dust. Only the sea, the sky and the mountains were visible, and Joan stared at each one in turn, fixing them in her mind. She had the bulky weight of her satchel on her knees, with Maude's papers inside it. She thought that when she came to collate them, she might write her own part in as an afterword – how the truth had been brought to light; how Maude had vanished like a djinni once she'd made it happen. Only once the war was over, Joan realised. Only then could she write about it fully, and even then there were things she ought never set down in print – about Jalali, and Salim. But she would not allow the truth to be lost, as Maude had done. She remembered what Maude had said about Joan giving her the chance to change things, and realised Maude had done exactly the same for her. If she hadn't persuaded her to go into Jalali – if she hadn't broken Joan's habit of a lifetime, of letting her fears dictate to her – then she would doubtless have been at home already – still engaged to Rory, still stuck silently in her ruts. Joan wished she'd thought to thank the old lady for that. She stared longest at the mountain, as it receded into the haze behind them. Jebel Akhdar, The Green Mountain; a formidable obstacle that she, first of the westerners in Oman, had scaled. It slumbered on, oblivious, and when she finally turned her back on it, to face the front and the onward journey, it was because she was ready to. *On you go*, she thought.

Author's Note

This novel is not intended to be a full account of the Jebel War of 1958–59, or of the men or battles thereof. However, the true events of that campaign are the essential backdrop to the book, and as such I hope that the story remains faithful to the time, the place, and the mission. All characters with speaking roles are entirely fictitious, with the exception of Sultan Faisal bin Turki. My character Colonel Singer was inspired by Colonel David Smiley, the sultan's chief of staff at the time. It is highly unlikely that the officers of the SAS would have had the time or inclination to dine at the British Residency, or to take trips out to the oil camp – but you never know. Though many of the details and situations described are historically accurate, all inaccuracies, improbabilities and flights of fancy are entirely my own.

On 9th January 1959, A Squadron, SAS, arrived in Oman to join D Squadron. After a few weeks of reconnaissance and planning, the final assault of the combined SAS and Colonel Smiley's SAF was planned for the night of 25th January, by the light of a full moon.

Imam Ghalib, his brother Talib, Suleiman bin Himyar and their fighters were successfully misdirected by the feeding of false information to loose-lipped local guides and muleteers, so that the final assault – a brutal nine-hour climb along a route previously thought to be impassable – met with almost no resistance. As dawn broke, RAF Venoms began to drop supplies and weapons to the SAS who'd reached the plateau, and it's thought that these parachuted supplies were mistaken for a full-scale aerial invasion. For whatever reason, Talib, bin

Himyar and their men simply melted away from the mountain. The coffee pots in their abandoned caves were still warm. Most were never caught or seen again, or went back to their village lives under the sultan's rule. The SAS lost two men, troopers Carter and Bembridge, when a stray bullet happened to hit and detonate a grenade in another man's pack. They were the only casualties of the final storming of Jebel Akhdar. Earlier, in November 1958, Corporal D 'Duke' Swindells had been shot and killed by a sniper as he climbed along a ridge soon after D Squadron, SAS, arrived in Oman. It was his death which led to operations taking place by night rather than by day. British forces, including the SAS, were out of Oman in time for the UN summit on the Middle East in April 1959, but returned to Oman in the early 1970s to help the sultan suppress another uprising, this one in the southern region of Dhofar.

In letting Maude and Nathaniel be the first and most famous travellers to cross the Empty Quarter of Oman, I have expunged a few heroes of exploration from the history books, all of whom made inroads into this previously unexplored wilderness – James Welsted in the 1830s; Bertram Sidney Thomas, who was the first to cross the Rub el Khali inland from Salalah in 1930; Harry St John Philby, who penetrated southwards from Saudi Arabia in 1932; and, of course, Wilfred Thesiger, known as the last of the great explorers, who crossed the Empty Quarter twice – in 1947 and 1948. Fort Jabrin was actually 'discovered' and explored by Major R. E. Cheesman in the 1920s; he wrote about his travels there in *Unknown Arabia* (Macmillan, 1926). I have borrowed some details from Wilfred Thesiger's career – for example his job with the Political Service in the Sudan, and his work tracking locust movements – for Nathaniel Elliot's life; similarly, Maude Vickery's education and early travels are based loosely on some of Gertrude Bell's.

I highly recommend that anyone interested in learning more about the Jebel War and the history of Oman read Colonel David Smiley's wonderful account of his time as the sultan's chief of staff, *Arabian Assignment* (Leo Cooper, 1975). It was invaluable to me in the researching of this novel, as was a book by another British officer in the SAF, P. S. Alfree's *Warlords of Oman* (A. S. Barnes and Co., 1968); and also *Sultan in Oman*, by Jan Morris (Faber & Faber, 1957), who accompanied Sultan Said bin Taimur on his triumphant crossing of the desert by motor cavalcade in 1955. The article on Muscat from the *Fortnightly Review*, which Maude reads as a child, was 'Under British Protection' by J. Theodore Bent, and was actually published a little later, in 1893.

Oil was discovered at Fahud, as well as at other exploratory sites in Oman, in 1963. The first export of Omani oil took place in July 1967, and in July 1970, His Majesty Sultan Qaboos took over from his father, Sultan Said bin Taimur, as ruler of Oman. A thoroughly modern man, educated at Sandhurst, Sultan Qaboos soon began to use his new oil income to bring his country into the twenty-first century. He remains in power at the time of writing, and is much loved by his people. Oman today is a prosperous, stable country, fascinating to visit. The Empty Quarter of the Arabian desert, while less empty than it once was, is still an astonishing place.

The following books were also valuable to me as I researched this novel, and I would recommend them to anybody who wants to find out more:

Old Oman by W. D. Peyton (Stacey International, 1983) – full of wonderful old photographs
Who Dares Wins: The Story of the SAS 1950–1980 by Tony Geraghty (Fontana, 1981)
Arabian Sands by Wilfred Thesiger (Longmans, Green, 1959)

The Selected Letters of Gertrude Bell (Penguin, 1953)

The Southern Gates of Arabia by Freya Stark (Penguin, 1936)

Adventures in Arabia by W. B. Seabrook (George G. Harrup & Co. Ltd, 1928)

Arabia Felix by Bertram Thomas (Readers' Union/Jonathan Cape, 1938)

Desert Queen: The Extraordinary Life of Gertrude Bell: Adventurer, Adviser to Kings, Ally of Lawrence of Arabia by Janet Wallach (Weidenfeld & Nicolson, 1996)

Acknowledgements

My thanks, as ever, go to all the wonderful people at Orion, for all their hard work, enthusiasm and expertise; especially to Susan Lamb, Juliet Ewers and Laura Gerrard; and, of course, to my editor, Genevieve Pegg, for her insightful, sympathetic treatment of the manuscript, and for being such a joy to work with. Huge thanks to Nicola Barr, agent extraordinaire, for being wise, brilliant and endlessly supportive. A shout-out to Dee, Chuck, Chris, Libby, Jackie, and Peki; and thanks to Ahmed al Zadjali and Khalid Alsinawi for their expert guidance in Oman, and for folk tales around the camp fire.